Airfoil: Origins

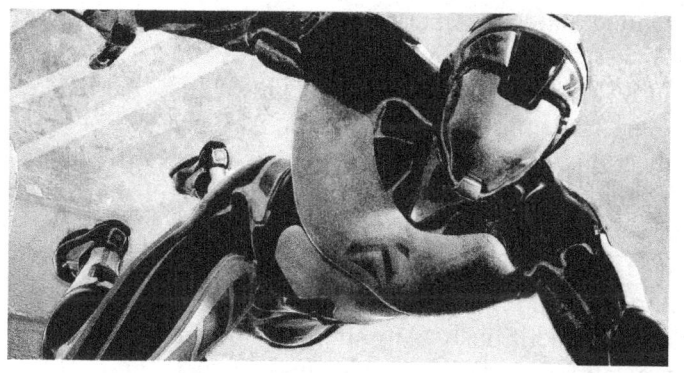

Steve Rzasa

Airfol: Origins by Steve Rzasa
www.steverzasa.com

This book, or parts thereof, may not be reproduced or transmitted in any form or by any means—electronic, mechanical, photocopy, recording or otherwise—without prior written permission from the author, except as provided by United States of America copyright law.

INTERSTICE BOOKS and the INTERSTICE BOOKS logo are trademarks of Steve Rzasa. Absence of TM in connection with marks of Interstice or other parties does not indicate an absence of trademark protection of those marks.

This is a work of fiction. Names, characters, places, and incidents are products of the author's imagination or are used fictitiously. Any similarity to actual people, organizations, and/or events is purely coincidental.

Cover illustration and design: Kirk DouPonce

Copyright © 2021 by Steve Rzasa
All rights reserved

International Standard Book Number: 9781736741115

Books

The Interstice Universe
- *The Echo Watch*
- *Mercury On Guard*
- *Airfoil: Origins*
  - *Airfoil: Drake City*
- *Mercury For Hire*
- *Mercury At Risk*
  - *Mercury Is Hot*
  - *Mercury Out Cold*
  - *Mercury Off Course*
- *Mercury With Style*

Space Opera
- *The Word Reclaimed: The Face of the Deep 1.0*
- *The Word Unleashed: The Face of the Deep 2.0*
- *Broken Sight: The Face of the Deep 2.5*
- *The Word Endangered: The Face of the Deep 3.0*
- *Severed Signals*
- *Cryptic Commands*
- *Failed Frequencies*
- *Mixed Messages*
- *Empire's Rift: A Takamo Universe Novel*
- *Strife's Cost: A Takamo Universe Novel*

Science-Fiction
- *For Us Humans*
- *Man Behind the Wheel*
- *Multiverse*

Fantasy
- *The Bloodheart*
- *The Lightningfall*
- *Just Dumb Enough* (contributor & editor)

Steampunk
- *Crosswind: The First Sark Brothers Tale*
- *Sandstorm: The Second Sark Brothers Tale*

airfoil

noun
air·foil | \ ˈer-ˌfȯi(-ə)l \

Definition of airfoil:
A body (such as an airplane wing or propeller blade) designed to provide a desired reaction force when in motion relative to the surrounding air.

Prologue

Officially, it's called "localized gravitational distortion and manipulation." That's the pseudo-scientific term for the phenomenon that lets me pick up this Chevy Impala with my left hand.

I hurl it across the street, wind rushing around me, right at the guy in the dark cape and mask. My aim's dead on. How can it not be? It's a *car*.

He's fast. Puts both his arms together and without making any contact that the eye can see, the car tears in half from bumper to bumper, spraying its guts out in twin clouds of glass shards, fiberglass fragments, and upholstery shreds. The engine block, though, grinds to a halt in midair, floating in front of him like a dandelion caught in the breeze.

He flings the engine back at me with double the force, a cloud of debris trailing behind.

There's just enough time for me to lift up my arm and disperse the detritus with a focused blast. Everything scatters to either side of the street, shattering the few intact windows left on the storefronts. The engine block's tougher. Giving something momentum is one thing. Stopping or redirecting someone else's shot at you, well, that's another. I have just enough focus left to send the motor careening to the ground at my feet, ripping a long gouge in the asphalt. The impact sends me sprawling.

Just like that, my energy evaporates. My chest throbs in icy agony where the burnished metal touches skin. My throat is raw, my body's bruised and cut, my lungs are begging for air, and my muscles are burning. There're wrecked cars strewn about us. Small fires crackle around the pickup that exploded. Sirens wail in the distance. Glass is everywhere, covering the ground thicker than autumn leaves after a strong wind.

Lord grant me strength.

My opponent raises both arms, a conductor ready for his final symphony, complete with all black outfit and cloak the color of smoke. The ground trembles, rumbles, shakes itself apart behind him. A subway train surfaces from the newborn canyon. Two of its cars, still connected, their roofs crumpling and their windows popping, rattle into the air. He pulls them apart with a horrendous squeal of metal and a hot spray of sparks. They dangle there, thirty feet up, swinging slowly on nothing.

"You should've taken me up on my offer!" he shouts. "You've no idea the forces you're meddling with!"

Meddling? Do people really talk like that?

He yells. Loudly. And hurls the subway cars.

Great.

All I can think in that second as I scramble my last-ditch defenses is, *I could be shelving books right now.*

Airfoil: Origins

Part One

Spring

Chapter One

My name's Brandon Tusk. I live in Drake City, on the west side of town, in a middle- class neighborhood called Nine Square. It's one of the quieter corners of the city, bound by Tenth and Thirteenth Streets on the north and south, with the brownstones of Gunnison State College bordering to the west and the brick stores of Vine Avenue on the east. The blocks are wide, with alleyways crisscrossing the neighborhood between houses and apartments. Lots of oak trees with skinny trunks that are only a couple decades old.

It's seven fifteen in the morning. My son, Sean, is always up before me. He's 13, and that means—well, it means he's 13. He's left me a note on the kitchen table. He used to leave me crayon scribbles on scraps of paper–puppies, robots, and UFOs signed, "For Daddy."

This masterpiece is tucked under my mug. "Pay bills."

Sneakers squeak on linoleum. Sean's by the front door, at the edge of the kitchen, with a black DK backpack slung over one shoulder. A pair of pins cling to the straps—the Batman emblem and the Avengers logo. He's tall now, up to my chin. His hair is dark brown, thick and curly like his mom's. But his eyes are the same hazel I saw in the mirror last night. I can't believe thirteen years ago I brought him home from the hospital in a car seat smaller than the backpack he's sporting. He's got on a rumpled blue shirt, a short-sleeve flannel in blacks and whites unbuttoned over top, and blue jeans fading from constant use.

"You get the reminder?" he says.

"I did, thanks."

"I'm going to the mall with Tucker after school. We'll be out late."

"Right. Make sure you have your homework done."

He rolls his eyes. Reaches for the doorknob.

"Sean? I mean it. If you'd read the notes from your teachers—"

"Yeah, yeah, I get it." He bangs the door shut.

I crumple the note and fling it to the trash can. Dawns on me that this is why people own dogs instead of having kids.

Takes me a while to plow through the bills, which I do while managing not to burn a Pop Tart. A banana and cup of tea later, I can finally enjoy a shower. Some people wake themselves up with coffee. Ten minutes of steaming spray and all's well.

Clock's ticking. I gear up for the morning commute with a gray Columbia pack stuffed with the essentials for the day—ID badge for Hull Branch library, leftover lasagna cooked by yours truly, apple, sketchpad, and pencils. On my way out the door, I pause by the picture of my wife and rub my finger along the frame. It's the eyes, powder blue like the sea's horizon, and gorgeous grin, that bid me farewell every morning. Makes the day better.

I wrestle my metallic blue Diamondback Edgewood hybrid bike down the steps, one wheel popped up. It's a plain, red brick four-story complex dating to the 1890s, fronting on Twelfth Street. Supposedly, a ship captain from a large, prominent family—the Bonythons or the Gales, can't remember which—built it with insurance money he collected from a cutter he shipwrecked off Cape Cod. Still haven't found the whole record at the Drake City Free Library in Center, but I'm looking.

The sun's out, with temperatures in the 60s. There's enough

of a chill breeze coming off Sculpin Bay that I slip on my favorite brown fleece and zip it to my chin. It takes me ten minutes to get to the Hull Branch Library of the DCFL system. Twelve blocks, dodging Hyundais and Subarus and Hondas, with the odd pickup and the occasional lumbering bus. Don't get me started on the fearless pedestrians who step out in front of me, in full-on smartphone coma. I whoosh by one with six inches to spare.

The city in mid-April smells of damp everything—damp garbage stink, damp oak tree bark, even damp people, the whiffs of whom I get are, thankfully, fleeting. The further I go from the apartment the stronger the sea salt from the bay gets. There's the squawk of seagulls as they wheel overhead, loud enough to cut through the rumble of the traffic.

Hull Branch is a squat, single story building of ugly brownish, concrete and dark bronze glass at the corner of Ninth Street and Hull Avenue. Little Warsaw's a block over, starting on Tenth and stretching south six blocks. The deli across the street smells of sweet, baked pastry temptations. I've spent way too much money at Halverson's over the years. A coffee shop, the Shattered Mug, competes diagonally from the library with the aroma of imported beans and the promise of caffeine. A florist, SpringIn, resides on the fourth corner. Still closed, but I catch glimpses of riotous colors of their blooms under glass, behind the metal grating.

I veer my bike into the parking lot behind the building. There're no cars yet. I'm always the first one in on a Monday.

A police car goes wailing by, a black and white blur of a Dodge Charger with emergency lights flashing on top. It's followed by another, both with their engines growling. Serves as a reminder that this isn't a safe part of town. That makes me snort. What is? I lock the bike to the rack and let myself in the steel door reserved for library staff.

Inside it's completely silent, and dark as night. There's little light back here at the end of the narrow hall that has doors to storage on the left, and another door to the staff break room and restroom on the right. Ahead, the silhouettes of the bookshelves and the u-shaped front desk are stark against the gray light coming through the front windows. I toss my coat and helmet onto the break room's one and only comfortable piece of furniture, a couch upholstered in a hideous olive green. Besides that, there's just a small fridge with faux wood paneling—where my lasagna goes for lunch—a pair of wooden chairs, and a card table.

First thing's first. I head up to one of the two seats at the front desk, the one on the left. My bag goes under the counter. The lights are still off in the children's corner off to the left, and the manager's glassed-in office to the right. Yeah, definitely here first, as per the schedule.

Check my watch. Ten minutes to eight. The keys are in the top left-hand drawer of my counter. I snag them and spin them around, jingling them as loudly as I can as I walk to the front door. Morning wake-up call.

Shelves are packed with books on all sides, framing a wide-open avenue that gives the front desk a clear view of the public two-thirds of the library. Someone didn't clean up the sci-fi rack Saturday night—there's a slew of Bradburys shelved with Asimovs. It'll wait.

Drip. Drip. Drip. Ten steps from the front desk is a silver bucket half full of water. Duct tape holds a rusted handle in place. I squint up at the ceiling. Leak's getting worse. The tile's the same color as earwax. There's a yellow "Wet Floor" sign in front of the bucket. I'll need to empty it before the patrons show up,

I head through the double doors, just past the men's and women's restrooms on either side, that lead into a small vestibule for the library's front entrance. Without looking, I jab the keys into the door of the book drop. Could do it blind, too. Habits develop after seven years working in the same place. Inside is a big clunky wooden cart, with spring-loaded shelf and a very squeaky wheel. The top is laden with a dozen books and another dozen DVDs. "Slow morning," I mutter.

My knee bumps the side as I reach for the books, the cart slides backwards with ease. I expect the problem wheel to start squealing. Nothing. I crouch to see if the janitor finally greased up the noisy wheel or replaced it.

There's three inches' clearance between the wheel and the floor. Tilting? No, the top's level. The distance is between *all four wheels* and the floor.

BANG!

The cart hits the floor hard enough to bounce the springs, rattling the plastic DVD cases inside. Sounds like a gunshot. The whole thing shudders. I scramble back, flat onto my butt.

It's quiet again.

I get up, smooth out the front of my shirt with a tug on both sides, in true Captain Picard style. That was strange. I give the cart a shove. It rolls against the inside wall of the book drop. The wheel squeaks reliably.

The cart must have been stuck on something I couldn't see. Like the seam where the floor meets the wall. Or been lodged under the metal lip of the book drop's chute. I give my head a thorough shake, as if I can rattle my brains back into position.

From the back of the library, a door slams open. Muffled voices echo through the building. Pushing aside all thoughts of the cart weirdness, I scoop up the books and balance the DVDs on top. My stack has all the stability of the Leaning Tower of Pisa.

As soon as I shoulder my way back through the main doors and into the building, a male voice cuts across, strident and in mid-argument. "—entirely awful! He's the worst superhero. Ever. And by worst, I mean *lamest*. How can you even like him?"

"I always thought he was cute." The reply is softer, much more feminine, and I know for a fact it goes with a far prettier face. It's also not so subtly teasing. "Those curly blonde locks. That orange scaly shirt stretched over those muscles. And the way he swims!"

"You'd better be talking about Jason Momoa and not the original. Which doesn't make him better, by the way." The male voice groans in such misery you'd think someone stepped on his childhood dog. Soon enough he bursts from the back hallway, in a hurry, red winter coat flapping behind him. He's as tall as me, about 6 feet, skinny, and with straw blond hair slicked to one side. Reed Andreen: the blue-eyed, rarely shaven, always loud, branch manager. He grins when he sees me slap down my tottering stack of books on the counter. "Brando! Lift with your knees. I don't want to file any workers' comp claims."

"Whatever you say, Commander. Your slaves live to obey your will." I smile back and bow deeply at the waist.

He laughs. Flips on the light to his office and hangs up his coat as neatly as my wife used to make the bed. That warm memory alone is enough to stifle my humor.

"What were you yelling about back there?" I fire up both computers.

"Your co-pilot. She's telling me Aquaman is her favorite superhero of all time. I'm telling her she's in need of extra vacation. To Arkham Asylum."

Kelly makes a face. "Not that again. It's a terrible idea—the whole concept, I mean. Why put all the supervillains in one place? That is why they break out together all the time, right?"

"Can't fault that logic, Reed." I log in and start zapping the books through the scanner to discharge them. "Hmm. Aquaman. The fish guy, right?"

Reed mutters something I can't hear that's surely profane, directed either at me or his computer. Then he continues the argument. "Fish guy. Really? What have I ever done to offend you that you have to say hurtful things? Of course, Aquaman's powers are fish related. Hence the 'aqua' with the man!"

"Not everyone's as obsessed with handsome men in tight clothing as you are Reed," I say. "You sure Caroline knows about that?"

"My wife supports my habit. She doesn't whine about it as much as you guys."

I chuckle, zap the next book. Rather, I try to. But it doesn't have a barcode in the usual place. It doesn't have one at all, because it's not a DCFL item. Well, that's what I get for not paying attention. *A Tale of Two Cities*, illustrated edition, leather-bound, good condition, no tears or stains or mold. My brain's already chasing down two of the most likely options: Do we need a replacement copy? Or, how much is it worth on eBay? I flip through—

A flash of metal. Something *clinks* onto the counter.

I stand there, book spread open in my hands, staring at it. The object is only a couple inches wide, twice as long, and slim as a couple credit cards pressed together. It looks very old, old enough that whatever shapes and patterns are etched into the surface are worn so smooth they're barely visible. The upper right corner is broken. I say upper because there's a worn-down metal loop inset on one end, like it's meant to be hung from something. It's silvery, but so tarnished with age it shines green and purple in places. Some of the surface has broken off, revealing a brass color underneath, inlaid with tiny black lines and dots.

I touch it, and it's surprisingly cold. As in, just came out of the freezer cold. I rub frost between my fingers. When I turn it over, the only other detail I notice is the crude shape of a coiled rattlesnake carved into the surface. Tiny fangs and all.

The image has a hypnotic effect. Like it's moving.

"Hey."

For a reason I can't explain, I slide the object away, concealed under my hand. Kelly Quirke sets her water bottle onto the counter. "Thanks for starting up the computers. I got behind checking in on my grandpa."

"No problem." Without breaking stride, I pocket the object

while checking in more books. It's still frigid. "How's he doing?"

Kelly shrugs. She has hair the color of raven feathers, cascading just past the tips of her shoulders, and brown eyes that are wide and—well, just lovely. Today she's wearing a purple blouse and a khaki skirt. Not that I notice those things. Like I notice the tip of her nose, the slope of her eyelids and cheekbones, and her scattered freckles. There's a hint of Asian ancestry, though from how far back I've never asked. "Better than yesterday. When I stopped by after church, he seemed badly confused. I read to him, and we talked. It was nice."

"Good to hear it."

"Anything interesting?"

I freeze, midway through putting the discharged books on the little cart behind me. "What?"

She points, smirks. "The book."

"Oh." *A Tale of Two Cities* still sits on the counter in front of me. Meanwhile, the metal in my pocket is threatening to give me frostbite. "Yeah. Pretty interesting."

The next few hours are a blur of greeting people, checking out books, finding missing books, and helping people using our public access computers. Training new users is like speaking English in a foreign land. When the guy asks you if you can scrimmage through the page using the mouse, it takes me a dozen blinks and thirty seconds to realize he means *scroll*.

By eleven-thirty my brain is fried. I tackle the task that's been bothering me all morning: the metallic object. There aren't any names or other identifiers in the book it came in, though there is an impression left where it was stuck between two back pages. Atop that particular spread of *A Tale of Two Cities* is Sidney Carton's picture as he climbs to the guillotine.

This problem I've handled before. The DCFL items in the book drop belonged to only three people. Process of elimination should own the metal object. I round up the phone numbers of those patrons and call them, using the phone we have in the break room.

The first one, a mom of six, tells me loudly but cheerfully over the gleeful sounds of her children playing that the book isn't hers.

The second, a bus driver who's a regular movie buff, is less accommodating.

"Hello?"

"Mr. Beletsky?"

"*Da*. Who is this?"

"Brandon Tusk, Hull Branch Library. I have book and was wondering if it's yours."

"Book? You have book of mine?" A horn blares in the background, filling the cell phone call with static. He lets loose a torrent of Russian profanity. I don't know any. "No. Is not my book."

"It was found in the drop with DVDs you returned—"

"I said no book! Is not mine. Only movies. Hang up now."

Click.

Should have known better. Beletsky is one of our regulars, though not a favorite by any stretch. I cross him off my list. "Two for two."

"What's up?" Kelly sticks her head in the door. She's got several rolls of red and green paper tucked under her right arm, and dangling scissors from her hand.

"Nobody wants this thing, apparently." I show her the object. Doesn't feel quite as frigid, but still stings my fingertips. It made sense before to conceal it, but this is Kelly we're talking about.

"Wow. What is that? It reminds me of antique jewelry." She frowns thoughtfully. "Is that something you could take to the museum? Or do you get to keep it now?"

"I do if no one claims it. 'Lost and found items will be dated and stored in the Lost and Found box at the Front Desk for a period of one week. After this one-week period, all unclaimed items become property of the City of Drake City at which time the Library staff will decide the appropriate method of disposal.'"

"Not all of us have the policies memorized verbatim, oh great nerd."

I chuckle. She's already gone before I can get in a witty response. But she's right. I do know them. And if no one comes for this thing by next Monday, it's tossed.

That gives me a thought. I head for Reed's office. It's quiet in the library right now: no one but us drones. "Reed?"

"Enter, Number One." He's got a sheaf of papers in one hand and Excel spreadsheets on his screen. Budget work.

"Found this thing in a book out in the drop. *A Tale of Two Cities*. I'm gonna take it home tonight and research it a bit. Maybe take it to the main library later."

I show him. His eyebrows rise. "Very cool. No owner?"

"Not yet."

"Bummer for them. Sure, go ahead. Just bring it back tomorrow. You know the policy on—wait, who am I kidding. You have it memorized. Which, yeah, it's great we all know them by heart, but word-for-word Brando?"

"Thanks, and shut up."

"Hey. Come by for dinner tomorrow night, will you?" He grins. "Caroline's making lasagna. Even a Polack like you can't pass that up."

"As long as you're not cooking, I'll leave the stomach pump at home."

"Ha-ha. Dismissed."

I'm out at 5. There're nothing but bills in the mail, which I toss aside. Sean's texted me: "getting dinner with friends, the DiAnnuzzis, at the West Gate Mall." They're a good family. He'll get a ride home with them. Sean's a teenager—he wouldn't listen even if I told him no.

I stand there at the counter in our kitchen, staring across the little living room out the window onto Twelfth Street. Our apartment's small, but nice. Three bedrooms: one large, two small. One's our home library-slash-computer room-slash-art studio. One full bathroom, a small dining area between the kitchen and front door. There's seating for four there and for four in the living room, at the sofa and two chairs.

Samantha insisted we hang my art on the walls. Her favorite was the sweeping landscape scene of Drake City's harbor, between Rittenhouse Island and the Old City, with Romanoski Bridge stretching in its huge arc across the water. It's still above the TV. And she's gone.

Her image smiles at me from the cluster of family photos hanging over the counter. I smile back at her. "Doing the best I can with him, babe. But he argues with *everything* I say. Even when I'm right. We start sniping. Fighting. Yelling. Then nothing. You got any words of wisdom for me?"

I already know what she'd say.

Most days are like this. Not sorrow, but—aimlessness. Drifting. Work and home and out at night. Back to the start again. In the studio, my paint brushes gather dust on a shelf along with my Bible and photo albums. I stand at the doorway, looking in at the shelves and the blank canvas, considering my options for the evening. There is painting. God knows I could get lost in it. Sometimes I've prayed that I'd fall right in, permanently framed off from the world.

No matter how many times I stop in front of those shelves, I can't muster the sense of purpose it takes.

The rest of the night's a burger at Hungry Sam's, then a blur of drinking at two bars I've never tried. Run into a couple of guys with whom I'd entered a bike tour this summer and have some good laughs. At the next place, a martini lounge, I meet a hot blonde who flirts relentlessly, hands everywhere they shouldn't be. She vomits all over the floor. Leave the last of my cash for the bartender and hit the sidewalk after that. She's not getting my number.

Can't remember the last time I had a serious relationship.

I stand in front of the ATM, staring at the screen. Wondering how it got like this. My life, that is.

Rain drizzles between me and the buttons. Enter your PIN. English or French? My reflection gazes back. Dark copper red hair rumpled as my shirt, hazel eyes that border more on green and usually sharp as arrows but significantly dulled now. Haggard is the word. Need a shave to get rid of the orange and silver bristles on my face. Has it been two days already? Good thing Reed isn't that worried about my personal appearance.

There's music playing somewhere down the street. Bluegrass. Drake City's lit with soft yellow and bright white, adding a ghostly glow to the building cornices and sidewalk curbs that aren't hidden in shadow.

Samantha always loved spring. We'd walk for a couple of hours on Friday evenings, people-watching the boisterous crowds of people dining outside restaurants in sidewalk seating, Samantha's wedding ring rubbing against my hand as her fingers curled around mine. When Sean was little, I'd carry him. He'd babble and point.

My arms and hands are empty now.

I punch in my PIN. Fifteen seconds later, the ATM spits out my $50. I slip the debit card and the cash back into my wallet. So what now? On to another bar? Or home? I should get home. Sean's wondering where I am, no doubt. Time got away from me again. I shove the wallet back into its pocket.

My fingers touch something hard and cold. Not my car keys. They're on the right side. Always. No, it's that metal square I found in the book drop. I retrieve it and let the city lights turn it amber.

Laughter cuts the air. A pair of teenage girls slip-step across the intersection, boots kicking up water. The white image of the walking man is blinking. The light's green, and there's not a car in sight, except for the ones hunkered in their metered parking spots under the watchful eyes of the apartment buildings and offices lining the street.

The screech of tires cuts through the quiet. Headlights swerve drunkenly down Thirty-First, flashing across the storefront windows. A big SUV, engine revving and wheels splashing through puddles. It barrels down on the intersection, where the girls are still laughing.

I can't get there fast enough. I'm half a block away. But I start running anyway. "Hey! Look out! Get out of the way!"

The headlights illuminate scared faces. Who knows if they heard me or not? But they see the car. It's less than a hundred feet away, flying down the street, and there's no way they can move in time. Doesn't help that they freeze with apparent fear.

My shoes pound the sidewalk now. My ankles are soaked. I can't help those girls. Won't get there fast enough. By reflex I reach out with my left hand. The right one's still clutching the metal rectangle.

The SUV lurches left, across the opposite lane. It bangs up over the curb, its wheels still spinning, but its body moving distinctly the wrong direction. With a loud crunch of metal on masonry, it hits the nearest building, a law office with a double-glass door at the entry level and no windows. Glass explodes in a shower of glittering fragments. The partners of Tomlinson D'Onofrio & Burgess won't be pleased when they get the bill for their ruined signage.

I skid to a halt at the opposite curb.

Sounds fade. The SUV's engine is still running, a low rumble. The girls snap out of their paralysis. To their credit, both run to the truck and pound on the passenger-side window. Can't see the driver's side. One of them has a phone. Her face lights up blue from the screen as she dials, starts hollering into the receiver.

An elderly man comes walking swiftly down the sidewalk, same side as the SUV. He's pulling on a thick, brown Carhartt jacket over stooped shoulders. A middle-aged couple, wearing dark trench coats, starts across from the opposite side of the street. By now, the girls have wrenched the passenger door open. A short, balding man in his mid-40s slides out. He wobbles, braces himself against the open door of the vehicle. He's not wearing a jacket. Just khakis, loafers, a white shirt unbuttoned at the collar, and a tie—red with blue stripes—dangling around his neck. Looks like he's gone longer than me without a shave. The girl with the phone makes a face, nose wrinkled up, and waves her hand.

The other girl pulls a pair of beer bottles from the seat. Two more fall to the pavement, clinking loudly.

I stare as the middle-aged couple keeps the girls, both now understandably irate, away from the guy. The elderly man gives him what I assume to be a stern talking-to, jabbing with his finger and peppering his tirade with words like "could have been killed" and "sober up", and "revoke your license."

A police car pulls up, patrol lights a garish, eye-watering red and blue. I watch as the officers question the driver. An ambulance comes too, disgorging EMTs in their dark blue jumpsuits. Within moments, the whole intersection is a commotion.

I'm walking back the way I came, sticking to shadows. I don't want to talk to anyone.

The whole way home, it replays in my head:

The girls cross.

I yell.

Gesture with my hand.

The SUV goes 90 degrees off course from where it was headed.

Right then.

The girls are alive.

The SUV is smashed into a building.

Have to shake the thoughts from my head long enough to concentrate on finding my keys, once I get back to my building. I've had too much to drink. That's it. Imagining things. Has to be the booze.

Otherwise, I can't explain why I felt the touch of the SUV's cold metal on my free hand from half a block away.

Chapter Two

The next morning Sean has his breakfast cooked and devoured by the time I roll out of bed. And I do mean roll. My head feels like two trucks have slammed into it, one on either side.

He doesn't look up from his tablet. There's a paper next to it, crumpled, like it used to be compressed into a ball. He's scribbling words down. His left hand crams the last of his toast into his mouth. Kitchen smells of eggs and butter.

"'Morning." My mouth is arid, lips cracked. Give the kettle on the stove a shake. There's still water in it. I set it back to boil.

"You were out late."

I have the object hanging around my neck. Paranoia made me want to keep it where I knew it wouldn't get lost. Last night, I rummaged through the old junk drawer in my bedroom, came up with a steel chain. Gives it more the appearance of a broken, battered medal, which in turn assigns it a better name than "object" or something else nondescript. "I told you I'd be home after ten."

"Yeah, it was like one, Dad."

"Why were you still up?" Not worrying about his homework, obviously.

Sean rolls his eyes. "Whatever. Where were you?"

The memories crash back. The girls. The SUV. The near miss. The strange sensation of metal on my hand. I flex my fingers. That happened, didn't it? Not a drunken memory malfunction? "Sorry. I should have called."

"Shoulda woulda coulda." He wipes his mouth with the back of his sleeve and sucks down the dregs of a cup of orange juice. The paper gets shoved into his backpack, which sits at his feet like an obedient dog. The tablet goes right in after it. I hear paper tear. He stands, flings the bag over his shoulder. "I gotta roll or I'll be late."

"Right. Make sure you stop by the Darrows' when you get home. Check in with them."

"Seriously? Dad, c'mon. They're ancient and I'm old enough—"

"No arguments. Do it."

He clamps his mouth shut. "Fine."

"And you might want to take better care of your homework. I had another email from Mrs. Ripley."

"Again?"

"We just had this conversation yesterday."

"No duh."

The kettle's whistling. "She said your grades would be better, except you never bother to turn in your homework."

"It's lame busy work. Who cares?"

"I care. You need to make sure it's done." I find a mug in the sink. The Snoopy one that my parents gave me for a birthday a decade ago. Needs a rinse.

"Wow. That's great. Lectures from Captain Responsibility. The guy who leaves his kid home all night by himself while he trolls the bars." He stalks to the front door. With one swipe, he removes the stack of envelopes there and waves them at me. "I'm dropping the bills off. So you don't forget. Again."

"I paid them."

"Thanks to my note. I'll text when I'm coming back."

"Sean—"

The door slams. The apartment's suddenly quiet. Except for the insistent tea kettle. I slap the knob, turn it off. The steam dies off in a mournful whistle.

I'm still watching the spot where he was at the door. "Have a good day."

The events of last night and the repeat run-in with Sean make focusing on anything productive at work difficult. I zombie my way through the routine tasks, grunting acknowledgments to Reed and Kelly as needed.

An elderly couple asks me how my family is doing. I smile politely, with a civil servant's placid mask that hides the irritation of someone who's trying not to snarl. "My son's a brat, and my wife's dead. How's yours?" What I actually say is the rote "Fine" and check out the six Fern Michaels novels. Her reading, not his.

He plunks a couple of Louis L'Amours down on the counter, slim books clad in brown leather with stocky, gold lettering. They ask me to give my family their best and depart, he's supporting her arm as she wheels her walker to the door.

"Is it safe now?" Kelly is at her computer, with a stack of picture books and a sheet of barcode labels. She's wanding them in, linking to new records, and inputting call numbers without so much as a pause as she talks. "After you bit the hand that fed you the library card…"

"I didn't bite Mr. or Mrs. Schultz's hand." There's a pile of DVDs to be checked in. Each one gets inspected—disc inside, if so, flip over to see if it needs repair. If it's empty, look up the patron's record and grab a phone number for a reminder call. "I was polite."

"Uh-huh."

"I was."

"Not your usual charming, witty self." The scanner beeps. She grins and sets one of the books to her left.

She's fishing. Speaking of bite... "I decided it was a bad idea to have a couple of our oldest regulars run screaming out the front door with bleeding stumps, so I restrained my appetite for human flesh. Just this once."

She laughs. I can't help but grin at that. Also, can't help noticing that it's fairly empty in here—Susan Firetski is in the children's corner with her three dark-haired, rocket-propelled boys, each one busy tearing apart a puzzle as she checks our card catalog computer. Probably looking for the newest Nicholas Sparks. We don't have it yet.

I finish up with the DVDs. All of them are present and accounted for; *Jurassic Park*, however, has a big enough crack it needs to get withdrawn. A moment later, after a couple insistent beeps of her scanner, I glance at Kelly. She's frowning at her screen. "What's up?"

"That's what I was trying to find out from you," she says. "Well, plus there's no good record for this one."

"You try OCLC?"

"Yes. The only available one has barely three lines of data with nothing under subject and an unauthorized title field." She sighs. "But don't change the subject."

"You're bad at subtlety."

"Yes."

She's not going to let this go. Fine then. "Sean. It was a rough morning."

"I was wondering. You seem tired."

Tired? Yeah, having a hangover and trying to decide if I magically shoved an SUV across an intersection makes sleeping difficult. "Sean's a handful."

"That's what kids are." She says the last word like it's an encyclopedia.

"That's not very helpful to me. I've never had a teenager

before."

"True, but you were one."

"Yeah, I was."

"How's it different, then? You guys must have some common ground you can fall back on. He is your son, Brandon."

People without kids always talk to you like they can solve any conflict with the quotes page of *Reader's Digest*. "Yeah, he is, and with a dead Mom, he can be far more challenging than I was at that age."

Her smile fades. In its place is a pair of lips pressed tightly together. She turns away to inspect the next book in her title and rips a barcode off the nearby sheet.

I shake my head and reach for the rubbing alcohol. The DVDs might be without scratches, but they've got more fingerprints than the handle of a bathroom stall. I start wiping them down.

Kelly's scanner beeps a couple more times. Other than that, it's silent, save the shouts from Mrs. Firetski's triplets, who've decided to use three empty puzzle boards as shields and bash into each other. Somehow, she manages to end the fracas with a few sharp looks.

"Sorry about that," I say.

Kelly raises an eyebrow. "For what?"

"Don't play that way. For me being a jerk when you were trying to be friendly—albeit in very nosy fashion."

That gets a flicker of a smile.

"Much better. So yes, Sean's hard to deal with, and yes again, we do have common ground. Somewhere. On something."

"I don't get the impression you two spend much time together."

"Somehow, I doubt he'd like to join me at the bar or the pub."

"Oh. Is that where you were last night?"

Where else? "Yep. Until my date decided to throw up and nearly ruin my shoes."

"She sounds classy. Really special."

"So, do you have any words of wisdom or just sarcasm?"

"For sarcasm, I go to you." She wands in another book. "But I've got experience with a seventeen-year-old sister. That means I do know what I'm talking about, sort of." She looks right at me. "It might be hard, Brandon, but I really think you should try talking to him about what's hurting him."

"Who said he's hurting?"

She gives me one of those raised eyebrow expressions. "Are you kidding?"

"Yeah, actually." I put the DVDs on the cart, cleaned up and ready to go.

"You're both hurting each other, and—people worry about you."

There's plenty here to go shelve. I scoop up the thick stack of magazines. "People."

She shrugs. Those cheeks have reddened again. "If you need someone to talk to…"

I smile back. "Thanks. Always nice to have the option."

Then I head for the magazine racks, wondering why you don't meet a girl like her every day. Too bad she's got a boyfriend.

By lunch, I'm starving, but it's more than hunger that pushes me to wolf down the cold cut sandwich and guzzle soda in ten minutes, all while reading *The Economist*. a One minute later, I'm wiping mustard off the corner of my mouth and throwing on my helmet. "Reed, I'm going to head out for a ride. Be back in a few."

Reed pokes his head from his office. "Carry on, Number One. Hey, I've got a meeting at Center at three. Be gone the rest of the day. Budget." He gags so realistically I'm convinced he's going to vomit. "Still coming by my place tonight for dinner?"

"Sure. Seven?"

"Yep. Bring something. Also, be there or be fired."

"Aye, Captain." I flip him the bird and bang the back door on my way out.

I head over to a used bookstore on East Second, right at the boundary between Center and Old City. Once I get north of Fourth, everything is towering complexes of glass and steel, some black and forbidding, some silver and white, still others blue and gray with the sky reflected in their fully windowed sides.

Veering off onto East Second, heading toward the waterfront, I drive back in time. The buildings here are gorgeous brownstones and brick structures. I glide by the Ram's Hoof Tavern— once the stomping grounds of the city's shipping kings, and two hundred years later, a very respectable bed and breakfast. The Bent Bookmark is two buildings up the street, in a gray stone building. I recognize it instantly as I lock up my bike—the old Masonic Temple, constructed in 1798 and abandoned in the mid-1960s. Looks like it's four stories of offices now: two lawyers, one real estate broker, and the bookstore. There's a pretzel stand set up across the street. You can smell the mustard. The stand's owner is having a boisterous conversation with a couple of men in suits. He sells what can only be described as cold bricks of dough avalanched with salt.

Inside, a handful of people peruse shelves of books so crammed together the titles smear into bizarre poems. Paperbacks are stacked floor to ceiling, wall to wall, with infrequent gaps for heating vents.

Then there's the smell. Musty paper. Age. History.

"Can I help you?" The man behind the bookstore desk is new—mid-twenties, black, short hair the color of coal. He's got on glasses that could have belonged to Elliot Ness, though I'll bet they're replicas. Tall, slim guy with ropy muscles bulging against a T-shirt worn under an Oxford.

"Yeah, your classics. Has anybody bought a copy of *A Tale of Two Cities* lately?"

"Dickens? Nah. That shelf's been dusty for months."

"You sure?" I hand him one I found.

"Nice." He turns it over in his hands, as gently as if it were a dead, dried leaf. "Binding's tight. Cover's dinged, but not too bad—probably one owner. You got a family copy, right?"

"No, not mine. I found it and was hoping to locate the owner."

"Hmm. Doesn't have an inscription." He fans through the pages. "Few tears, dog ears. Well-read, but handled with care. I dunno. Could be somebody wanted it to find a home with you, right?"

"I work at the library, so it's a possibility."

"Center?"

"Hull Branch."

"My town." He shakes his head. "Only if the mobs don't rip it open. Sorry, man—this isn't from our collection. I'd know it. There're no spaces on the Dickens rack, and I don't get ones this nice. Mine got a lot more dust and way more beatings than a bike tossed down Mount Stafford."

I chuckle at that. "Thanks anyway."

So, no joy. Outside, I put the book away and examine the medal closely. The broken edges, where the metal seems to have worn or chipped away, displays an odd sheen, like mica—multicolored, semi-transparent. The medal stings my hand, it's so cold. Funny it would do so, since it's been riding in my pocket and should have absorbed my body temperature. There doesn't seem to be a pattern to its temperature. One moment, chilled as an icicle. The next, like a lukewarm glass of water.

I loop its chain around my neck. Library policy says I can claim it after a week.

Guess it's in my safekeeping for now.

Airfoil: Origins

It's dark after seven at night in May. Not pitch black, what with all the streetlights in Hull bathing everything in amber glow, but the shadows are deep enough I'm wary. A guy was shot and killed a block over from here two weeks ago. They took his wallet and cell phone, left him bleeding out of four holes into the gutter.

I'm late to Reed's. I stopped by for a drink at Passarella's, a little Italian place not far from Hull Branch. Then I remembered I was supposed to bring something to dinner. The raviolis in my backpack were probably getting mashed out of their normal shape, but knowing Passarella's, they'd be fantastic regardless of their form.

When I pull up to the red light at Tremont, I relax a little. A handful of cars go by, tires swishing. No one's in my lane. It's quiet out. I put a foot to the curb to steady my bike.

"Hey. How's it going?"

The voice could have been a gunshot to my right. The guy must have been hiding on one of the building stoops. There's no porch lights on in this part of town. Not a big surprise considering every third home is vacant.

He's short, thick with muscle, wearing a gray sweatshirt and baggy black track pants with white stripes down the side. The sneakers are blazing green, hideous footwear that likely cost more than my ride. A red knit cap is pulled tight over his head, down to the top of dark eyes. Latino features, a hungry grin, and dark moustache.

I have a four-inch foldable blade in my pocket. With my eyes on this guy, I let my right hand drop lazily toward the knife.

There're footsteps behind me, on the curb. I glance back. A white guy, taller than me, skinny, in a Drake City Dragons hockey cap—black with a green bill. He's got on a blue Adidas coat and jeans. The glare of a passing car's headlights briefly illuminates a gun tucked into his waistband.

My heart rate accelerates. A knife won't do me any good

now. Without moving from the bike, I look at Red Hat again. Now he has a knife.

Two things cross my mind: What'll happen to Sean if I die, and the fact that I won't get to see Reed and Kelly at work tomorrow.

"Get off the bike. Let's go for a walk," Red Hat says.

Gun Guy is right behind me. His voice is high pitched and scratchy, not smooth and confident like Red Hat. "Luis, get his bike."

I dismount like they requested and put my bike against a tree. Luis in the red hat grabs onto a handlebar and wheels it ahead of me. Gun Guy waves the weapon in Luis's direction. No one else is out walking in our vicinity. The way we're walking, with Luis in front and Gun guy ambling at my side, we look like old pals.

Luis leads us to the nearest building, an apartment with four windows lit up and the rest dark. Half the panes are broken. The brick is crumbling, and graffiti festoons the porch. Trash rots by the entrance to an alley.

My instincts kick in. Don't go in there. You do, and you'll never come out. I back up.

Something rock hard jabs into my side. "Keep walking." Gun Guy's breath is hot as car exhaust on my neck.

"Whatever you've got in mind, do it right here, because I'm not stupid enough to go in that alley with you clowns."

Luis sets the bike against the far wall, gingerly, as if it's a rare flower. He turns and puts the knife up to my throat. "Wallet. Phone. Anything thing else expensive you got."

The streetlights are out for a half block. We're right in front. None of the cars driving by show any signs of noticing a mugging in progress. It seems they're not stopping at all in this block. I curse myself for wanting a shortcut to Reed's house. Next time, I'd rather be late. "Okay, be calm. No one has to get hurt. I'll get my wallet."

Slowly I reach into my pocket with my right hand, keeping the left loose from my body.

"Give it over." Luis rifles through my wallet. I'm prepared to let him take the whole thing, until he pulls out a worn glossy photo from a sleeve behind the driver's license. "Hey. Nice *chica*. She yours?"

My fear switches to anger faster than I can change gears on my bike. It's the photo of Samantha and Sean. She gave it to me for a Father's Day gift, five years ago. "Take all the money, and the credit cards. Here, here's my phone." I wave it in front of him, not caring if Gun Guy might think it's a weapon. "Hand back the photo."

"No way." Luis grins. "She's pretty."

The medal stabs what feels like a spear of ice into my chest.

Gun Guy jerks on my backpack. "Luis, forget the picture, man. Dude, give me your bag."

I shrug out of it. They burrow into the bottom, dogs sniffing for scraps. My phone, my MP3 player—they want it all, obviously. Why bother cataloging it? Doesn't matter. I just want the photo back.

The weight of the knife in my pocket's still with me. Against the two of them, though, I'd be better off not making myself a danger in their eyes. But really want to wield it.

Gun Guy glances up. "Good stuff. C'mon, let's jet."

"Nope. He's got more," Luis says. "What's on the chain?"

Chain. The medal. I shift my neck, trying to obscure whatever glimmer of silver they've seen. "Nothing. Give me the picture back and we can all go home."

"Go home?" Luis is on me again, pulling me forward by my coat. The knife's back to the base of my neck, a cold, sharp edge scraping whiskers. "This ain't for spreading butter, *comprende*? We take everything you got or we put you down, and then take it."

"Luis, back off, man, let's go!" Gun Guy's whining is getting worse.

"Franco, what'd I just say?" Luis turns to him.

I ram into Luis with my shoulder, bringing my knife up in my right hand. But he's fast. Pivots away, pulling back from my knife's trajectory. He shoves me down into the alley. My knife's gone, plopping into a dark puddle somewhere. I scrabble for the photo, irrationally grasping for it despite the threat of probable death.

Luis growls, kicks me onto my side. "Franco, get this dead man up!"

Franco pulls me upright. His gun hand quavers.

It would worry me more but I'm just furious now, with an aching side to boot. "I'm not going to say it again. Give me the photo."

Those pins and needles worsen. All I can see is the picture of my family.

Franco raises the gun higher, aiming for my face, no more than four feet away.

No one sees, or if they do, no one cares.

Luis laughs, like a hyena. "Just for that..."

He tears the picture in half.

"Stop!" I put up both my hands, palms up. There's a blast of air. Franco hurtles backward, his legs kicking up from underneath. His body flips feet up and head down, and he soars ten feet into the side of the nearest building. Flesh and bone collide in a sickening crunch with brick. The gun spins off into the inky blackness of the alley. Loose change clinks, landing with a plop in the puddles, just seconds before his face does likewise.

Luis stares at me, frozen in place. He mutters something in Spanish that I don't understand. I stare at my hands, his fuzzy image framed between them. What on Earth?

"You—you're *loco*. I shoulda slit you straight off." Luis's voice is fierce, but it shakes worse than Franco's gun did. His knife is poised to stab.

Whatever trepidation I had earlier is gone. Only certainty

remains. He won't hurt me.

He *won't*.

Luis takes a swipe, diving faster than I anticipated. I jump back but he still catches the edge of my coat. The slashing is surprisingly loud.

My fists clench. I push out with both hands, just like I did to Franco, only this is a deliberate strike. The only thing in my mind is the desire to stop him cold.

Luis flies.

He flings straight up off the ground, three stories. For a second, he hangs there, the silhouette of his head swiveling to and fro, shouting in terror.

I stare in awe.

Something flashes. Is that a car stopped across the street?

My mistake. Whatever I did, taking time to appreciate the insanity of my handiwork or getting distracted by the sudden interest of a passer-by in my predicament, shuts it off. Luis drops like a stone.

"No!" Thug or not, would-be killer or not, I can't let a man splat on the pavement. My hands reach up, moving in every position I can think of. Come on, come on, *stop him*!

Luis is only a story up when he suddenly jerks sideways, to my left—right out onto the street. He slaps into the side of a parked car, breaking the driver's side window. Glass explodes. A car alarm blares into the night. My luck—it's a Lexus with temporary tags, brand spanking new.

Cars are definitely slowing now. Luis's red hat looks like a smear of blood against the black and amber.

Is he okay? Should I check on him? Do I care? Behind me, Franco groans. He didn't drown in the puddle, so that's a plus. For the first time in those tight seconds, I breathe deeply.

Someone yells from a car. Yes, there was a car stopped across the street. A minivan. People are getting out.

I can't stay here. The police will arrive. There will be questions, handcuffs.

The medal's prickles in my chest die off. Yet it's still there, and in the back of my mind, there's a single prodding urge.

Go.

My backpack. I shove everything I can find into it: phone, wallet, money. The photograph is on the ground, thankfully not getting soaking wet. But Luis did successfully tear it in half. Right through Samantha's arm. Her disembodied hand cradles Sean's shoulder in the other half of the image. His face is smudged with dirt or garbage or something else foul.

What have I done?

I sling my bag onto my shoulders, and bounce off the curb on my bike, diving into traffic. Headlights and brake lights blaze around me. Shouts follow me as I weave through the cars, not caring which lane I'm in and not looking back at the havoc by the side of the street.

What is happening to me? What is this thing?

I have to find out.

And I have to tell Reed.

Airfoil: Origins

Chapter Three

R eed stares at me. "You're insane. What do you want, wellness day for mental health tomorrow or something? Don't mess around about something like that."

"I'm not."

He waves a beer bottle at me. Sam Adams doesn't seem perplexed, judging by his visage on the label. "You're one hundred percent making that up."

I get a good whiff of beer and can't wait to crack into one myself. Coupled with the aroma of homemade lasagna wafting from underneath the door of Reed's apartment, the smell invites me to relax.

I can't. Not now.

We're in the hall outside, standing ten feet from the welcome mat. A muddle of sounds trickles out—classical jazz, giggles, a deeper voice, then more giggles. Caroline has her sound system set for dinner company, and Sean is entertaining Reed's kids, the twin girls and their older brother.

Sean's presence is near miraculous, until one remembers this is Reed's home, not his own.

"You threw those guys." Reed doesn't sound the least thrilled by it. He swigs beer. "Just—up?"

"Yeah." This was not a drunken dream. Which cements the

suspicion that the first time, with the runaway SUV, was also real.

"Nope. No way." Reed chuckles, but it's not a happy sound. "Man. This is worse than pretending you don't know who Aquaman is. Just quit."

"This isn't a game, Reed, it's serious."

"Oh yeah? Serious? You tell your pal—who's a complete comic book stalker—that you used that ugly piece of metal you found in a book to fight crime, and that's serious?"

"Absolutely!"

Reed shakes his head. "Not funny. Come up with a better joke."

I can see his perspective, but at the same time, it's frustrating that someone who's been at my side since high school won't see things clearly in a moment when I need clarity most. Right. "Put your wallet on the floor."

"You want my money for your bad joke?"

I roll my eyes. "No, idiot. Just do it."

"Fine." Reed digs a brown leather wallet from his back pocket, but hesitates. I swear the man's cuddling with it.

"You won't lose any cash, Reed, put it down."

Reed scowls and tosses it onto the tile. He spreads his arms wide enough the beer bottle clinks against one wall. "Wow me."

I reach for the wallet, fingers outstretched. Nothing. I clench my teeth, picturing the wallet flying off the floor into my hand. Move. Go up. Fly. I even stick an imaginary spring underneath it, for heaven's sake.

Again, nothing.

Reed chuckles. "This is exciting, man. Really awesome."

"Shut up." Think. I moved a car. I moved two people. What was the problem with a wallet? Maybe…both previous times were reflexive. Reactive. There was an element of the unexpected. "Forget the wallet."

"Easy for you to say. It's not yours."

"Do something different."

"Say what?"

"Something unexpected. Throw something at me. But don't tell me what. Or when."

He shakes his head. "You're out of your mind, you know that? You're not supposed to go drinking before dinner at your boss's home, Brando."

"Reed, come on, listen to—"

There's a flash of light. He's flung his keys at me.

Without thinking, I put up my right palm. There's only the mental image of a strong wind blowing across the hall, in a narrow, concentrated jet. The medal stabs the center of my chest with a cold blade.

Two feet from my hand, the keys bank 90 degrees to the right. They hit the wall and drop to the floor, a raucous clatter of metal.

Reed's expression is completely opposite his sour disbelief of a second ago. He stares, whites of his eyes ringing the pale blues. Then he grins, broad, manic. "No way!"

"Reed?" Caroline's voice sounds from behind the door. "Dinner's almost ready. If you boys are done playing, would you please offer our guests drinks?"

"Sure, yeah, babe." Reed downs the remainder of his beer, staring at me over the bottle. "Be right there."

I hand him the wallet. "Money's still there."

"You...wow. The keys flew...wow." He gets his keys back into his pocket, a mean feat considering he's still staring. "You sure it's that—the metal thing?"

"It has to be. There's this cold sensation from it, like it's coated with ice, every time this happens. Well, the three times it's happened."

"Ever tried it without the thing? It could be you, man."

"No, I don't think so."

"We'd better check it out."

"All right." I take the medal off, set it on the floor.

"Ready?"

"Don't tell me, Reed."

He pulls the keys back out and tosses them—higher, and to my left. I try to block them the same way as before. They fly right over my head and land a couple of feet behind me. Metal scraps on tile.

"No go." Reed scratches at his whiskers. "Definitely the thing."

"Like I said." I hurriedly put the medal back on.

"How does it work?"

"No idea. It's way too small to have a power plant that can produce that much energy."

"Isn't any watch battery, that's for sure. Was it doing weird stuff from the get go? I mean, did you notice anything odd around the book drop?"

"I wasn't sure, at first. It seemed as though the book cart was—well, hovering a few inches off the floor."

He gapes. "That wasn't a clue?"

"It was only for a second. You'd have thought you were seeing things, too."

"Yeah, maybe. Anything else?"

"Ah...yeah. Last night. I was walking home from a bar—"

"Solo or duo?"

"Solo."

"But you met somebody hot. Right? You got that look."

"She was hot. The vomit cooled her off."

"Nasty. Not a keeper."

"Anyway, an SUV ran a red light and there were two girls in the crosswalk."

His body tenses at the mention of two girls. "That's bad."

"It would have been, if the truck hadn't slid and hit a building instead."

"Slid. You mean, swerved."

"I mean *slid*. As in, tires screeching because it slid left without changing its orientation."

He points beyond me. "Like the keys."

"Exactly."

He goes for another swig of beer, grimaces when his lips touch the empty bottle. "You didn't say anything yesterday, man."

"I thought I was hallucinating. You know, drunken stupor."

"Way to keep the captain out of the loop."

"Whatever. You're in on it now, Mr. Fantastic. So now I need your help finding out what this thing is and what it can do."

He grins at the mention of his nickname. "Now you're talking."

Footsteps behind the door.

"After dinner."

Reed chuckles. "Oh, definitely."

The door opens. Caroline peeks around, smiling at us. Her hair's tied up in a ponytail, jet black and curly. She's got olive skin and deep brown eyes, a thin nose and full lips. "What are you two doing? Andrea said she heard someone throwing keys."

"Where're my manners? I owe you a drink, Brando." He thumps me on the shoulder. "Did you want a glass of wine, babe?"

Caroline smiles slyly at him. "Yes. The kids need milk. Dinner's ready."

"On our way."

Caroline slips back inside the apartment. Reed deflates like a balloon.

"Nice job not answering her question."

"Oh, don't worry, she'll nail me on it sooner instead of later. So—drink?"

"The stronger, the better."

Caroline's fixed us a veritable feast: salad of greens, carrots and tomatoes; basket of steaming rolls; heaping bowl of peas; and the centerpiece, the huge pan of lasagna–a landscape of mozzarella-covered perfection.

We crowd around the dining room table, which is meant for six, but since the twin girls Andrea and Marielle are 4, we can all fit. Reed takes the head of the table and me, the opposite end. Caroline sits to his right, with Andrea between them. Marielle sits between Caroline and me.

Sean takes a place right next to Reed, and Reed's 8-year-old, Thomas, is nudged up next to Sean's elbow. He barely pays heed to his mother's commands to eat, so enthralled is he in every sulky word out of Sean's mouth. Marielle needs help buttering her roll; I oblige, and am amazed how fast she crams it down. Andrea, though, mimics Caroline's mannerisms perfectly. Every bit of food is cut and eaten the same way. Every stern look directed at Marielle is copied.

Most of what Reed says to Sean about comics and superhero movies is lost to me. My mind is several city blocks away. The medal presses against my chest, cold and tingling. I expect to see a puddle under my shirt, it feels so much like ice.

Whatever this medal is, it has powers. That's obvious. As dangerous as it was going toe-to-toe with those hoods, I won't lie—it felt great to give them theirs. Not saying I like injuring people, but some people need to get hit.

The TV is on, a glaring screen to my left. The Andreen dining room is a small rectangle wedged between the kitchen and the living room. The living area opens onto a balcony, with the lights of Drake's Center glittering in tall stacks. Behind me, a hallway stretches the other two-thirds of the apartment, with a small bathroom and the twins' bedroom to the right. Reed and Caroline's room is to the left, and Thomas's is opposite the twins.

"Spacedock to Brando. Over."

"Hmm?" I've got a mouthful of lasagna. Reed is chuckling at the head of the table, with Sean—can't believe it—He's smiling too.

I finish chewing and wipe the corner of my mouth. "Sorry. Mind was elsewhere."

"No kidding. Caroline asked you about work."

"Oh. Yeah, it's going well. Though I'm sure you know that from your husband."

"He's only interested in him." She winks at Reed. "Surely you have more interesting stories."

"Definitely." I smile. "None of mine involve budget meetings."

"Well, regale us."

I shrug. Part of one story won't hurt. "There's this book left in the drop the other day, *A Tale of Two Cities*. Not one of the library's. No one claimed it. I tried a mom, a surly Russian bus driver. Even spent part of my break to bike up to Center to try and dig around the Bent Bookmark."

"That sounds like a hassle. Any luck?"

"I wouldn't call it luck. No such thing."

The rest of dinner's a pleasant blur. All the dishes make it to the dishwasher. The adults clean up and the kids separate—girls to the living room to read, the boys to Thomas's computer in his bedroom.

Reed, Caroline, and I enjoy a relaxing chat on the sofa and recliners. Relaxing, more so for them. I can't get the burning building out of my mind. Finally, Caroline ushers the little girls to bed. Reed dispenses kisses, and I give hugs. Marielle clings to me much longer than her sister.

"I'll tuck them in so you boys can finish shop talk." Caroline kisses Reed.

He gives her a squeeze around the waist with one arm. "Thanks, babe. Books and budgets and all that."

She takes the girls to the back, Andrea skipping alongside her mother, with Marielle dragging behind. Reed reaches under the end table and comes up with a tablet. "Okay then. Back to work."

I drag the recliner closer to the sofa, taking care not to spill any beer on the white upholstery. "Shop talk, eh?"

Reed shrugs. "The budget meeting at the main branch wasn't anything new. Economy's treading water, sales taxes are up—slightly—mayor's holding the line on new expenses."

"No cuts?"

"Nope. Everybody gets to keep their jobs next year."

"Nice."

"I know, right?"

"But no repairs, either."

"Nope." The tablet screen lights up Reed's face, a pale blue. "So, we better dig up all the buckets we can from storage to keep the roof leaks from staining the carpet."

"I take it that's my assignment."

"Yep." Reed smirks. "See? Shop talk done."

"Kelly needs a new computer."

"We *all* need new computers."

"Yeah, but hers is painfully slow. We're talking Windows 95 slow."

He's logging in to his account. "She hasn't said a word."

"When does she complain about anything?"

"Right." Reed brings up a search window and taps in 'medal'. "So is this your request or hers?"

"Mine." I point. "You're going to have to be more specific if you want to avoid getting tens of millions of results."

"No kidding." He adds a few more words, one at a time: flying, moving, magic. Each time he gets a different batch of answers, but none are what we're looking for. Mostly, I see advertisements for online games, miniatures, collectible card games, the like. A few fantasy novel series. Cosplay websites.

"This is a whole lot of big fat nothing," Reed mutters.

"Try 'telekinesis' with 'medal.'"

"Alrighty."

That doesn't help. More of the same results, this time with the addition of references to Uri Geller and other supposed psychics.

We keep at it for the next fifteen minutes, stumbling down link after link, six or seven windows open at once. Some promising leads turn into dead-ends in an instant, dumping us into chatrooms about dressing up as elves and mages. Theories turn into nothing. Big fat nothing, as Reed puts it. Fortunately, Caroline does not emerge from the girls' room in that span; she must have elected to sit with them until one or both has fallen asleep.

Thomas's laughter rolls down the hall. Whatever Sean's up to, it's keeping his pint-sized fan entertained. While I'm glad to hear him laughing along with Reed's son, there's a cold lump in the pit of my stomach. Where's the sly, joking Sean when I get home from work? Where's the sociable Sean from tonight's dinner when I prepare a meal?

The accusation boomerangs on me: Where's the Dad who had fun with Sean? Who took care of him? Face it. We don't connect. Bottom line, he needs to shape up.

"Brando." Reed nudges me. "Searching Google isn't getting us anywhere. It feels like all I'm doing is making a shopping list for the next batch of Magic the Gathering cards."

"Yeah, I know." I lean back, swirling the contents of the half-full bottle. "We're going about this the wrong way."

"Okay…"

I pull the medal from my shirt, dangle it off the ends of my fingers. "This is old. Looks old, feels old. It has to have historical significance to someone or some institution. We should look at contemporary sources. First-hand accounts. Things that, apparently, haven't been scanned and put online, or otherwise input."

"Check." Reed sets the tablet aside. "Old school research."

"You said it."

"How do you know it's local, though? 'Cause I'm assuming you want to rifle through main branch's archives, and the maritime museum logs, so on and so forth."

"Well, if the Internet's not helping, it'd be best to start here in Drake City and expand our search outward." The etched rattlesnake on the back of the medal is rough to the touch. I turn it over and gaze at its form. An image search didn't turn up an exact match, but I've got a hunch. "We could start with any mentions of this carving."

Reed peers at it. "Rattlesnake. I assume you're not thinking zoo fanatic."

"No. Think Revolutionary War."

He shakes his head.

"Oh, come on. Gadsden?"

Another shake. "I was a math dork."

I sigh heavily and reach for the tablet. A couple of links later, I spin it toward him. "Get it now?"

A yellow flag with a black coiled rattlesnake and the words "Don't Tread On Me" glare at him.

"Original Tea Party! Got it. That's when that flag dates to."

"Exactly. This carving is worn down enough it could come from that era. I'll need to take it to someone who can say for certain. Like you said, the maritime museum's a good place to start."

"See? Told you I'd solve your mystery." He grins.

"Jerk."

"Dad! Dad! Uncle Brandon!" Thomas sprints down the hall. His little feet thump on the carpet, and his cheeks are flush. "Come see what Sean found! Come on!"

"Okay, Tom, relax." Reed massages his temples. "Last time it was animated dinosaurs playing in a rock band. Earth-shattering stuff."

I chuckle, trailing behind Reed as we head for the bedroom. Thomas is already back there, whispering urgently. Who knows what kids find on the Internet that catches their eye. For months, Sean was obsessed with a website that featured animated shorts of hilarious—his words—revised endings to movies.

Whatever it is they're watching tonight, however, isn't

amusing. They're both seated cross-legged on the bed in the center of Thomas's room, with a monstrous black HP laptop clutched between them. His bedspread is a starry field speckled with colorful planets, and there's a glow-in-the dark mobile of the solar system hanging over his pillow. Thomas made it out of Styrofoam balls, string, and spray paint. There's Star Trek memorabilia crowded on his dresser. It's much cleaner than Sean's room; I can step on islands of carpet without breaking toys.

"Uncle Reed." Sean's waving frantically with one hand. His eyes never leave the screen. "You've gotta see this."

"See what? It'd better not be that 'What Does the Fox Say?' song, or I swear I'll freak out."

"No, no, this guy put this thing up on YouTube while we were having dinner." Sean grins, big and broad. I haven't seen him this excited since…I can't remember. "It's awesome."

He turns the laptop to face us and clicks the play button.

At first, I can't make sense of what I'm seeing. There are shadowy figures, blurred outlines, and lines of windows. The fronts of dilapidated apartments are bathed in the amber light of streetlamps. There's fast motion. Looks like someone is getting attacked. With the cars occasionally flitting by and obscuring the picture, all I get is a sense of interrupted action. As if I were watching the crowd at a nightclub dancing under strobe lights.

Then I read the title of the post: "Superpowers vs. Muggers! Drake City."

Oh boy.

"That's—amazing." Reed sounds excited, but he makes sidelong eye contact with me. "Hey, run that back, Sean, let me see it from the beginning."

Sean drags back the play bar. I watch more closely this time. Definitely the right place. I recognize the buildings at the intersection with Tremont. The confrontation in progress—a shadow grasping at another, the outline of a gun waving. One shadow goes flying away, disappearing from view. That would be the one I knocked to the ground.

The other shadow pivots. You can clearly see my hands push out. The remaining mugger is tossed suddenly up. Even I'm astonished at the swiftness with which he moves.

Whomever has a hold of the phone recording this video follows the mugger, suspended in midair, with minimal shaking. The mugger snaps back down to the ground. I lunge to stop his fall, though from this angle, it looks like I'm trying to slap him.

The video cuts out.

"Wow," Reed mutters.

"I know, right?" Sean's happier now than he is on Christmas morning. "A real one."

I'm still stunned that my self-defense exploit is streaming through YouTube. "A real what?"

He scowls at me. "Superhero, Dad. A real superhero. Not one of those costumed dorks that run around in Seattle or Los Angeles. You know."

"No, I don't."

"Relax, Brando. Sean's right. They're a bunch of self-proclaimed vigilantes who dress up à la Batman, then go out and do their best to stop crime." Reed grins. "Mostly, they get their beat up. Which is funny."

"This video could be a fake." Sean has it playing on a loop.

"Look at all the comments coming in," he says. "Two thousand in the last hour. Dad, he looked like he was getting mugged, whoever he was. And he just tossed those guys around like trash bags!"

"If he is real, then he's dangerous." It's a pat parent answer. Meanwhile, my pulse accelerates just watching the video for a second time. The thrill of disabling my attackers returns. I won't soon forget how the initial fear was banished.

"Of course you'd say that," Sean mutters. "Someone finally stands up and fights, and you're all, 'he's gotta be bad.'"

"The city's police are the ones responsible for handling this,"

I say. "This isn't like your comic books."

"Whatever. Uncle Reed gets it."

I spear Reed with a look that says, *Interfere and I'll slug you.* He smirks. "You better go with your old man on this one, kid."

"You're taking his side? Figures. Old people." Sean immerses himself in the video again. We've been dismissed. Thomas leans over his shoulder, eyes wide, pointing at the screen.

Reed nudges me and we return to the hall. I dig for my wallet. The photo of me, Samantha, and Sean needs taping back together.

"You've got trouble, man."

I straighten out the crumpled images as best I can. If only fixing things with my kid was as easy. "Don't I know it. Sean's actually on his better behavior tonight, if you don't count his snotty attitude..."

"Not him, idiot, the medal." He prods it beneath my shirt. "You're lucky that video isn't clear, or the cops would blow it up life-sized and track you down."

"Yeah, I'd thought of that."

"What're you going to do?"

"Get rid of the thing."

"Are you crazy? You know what it can do! You can't just turn something like that over to the cops."

What I don't want to do is keep lashing out and breaking things—vehicles or people. Best case scenario, I get sued by someone who claims they got whiplash. Worst case...

I see the wreckage of Samantha's car.

"What're you thinking? I know that face. Brando's patented super-serious mask."

"The medal. The powers that it's shown..." I gesticulate but can't find what I want to say.

"Don't say it's a God thing."

"That'd be the first thing out of Samantha's mouth." The doubts since her death nag me, but I haven't had—or maybe made—time to deal with them.

"It's crazy."

I snort. "Crazier than a hunk of metal that let me throw muggers like balls of paper?"

Reed shrugs. "Let's skip theories for now. What's the plan?"

"Find out as much about this medal as we can, and if there are rightful owners—there have to be—get it back to them. As much as you and Sean would like it, I'm not making a habit of taking on muggers."

"Not yet, anyway."

"What does that mean?"

Reed grins. "You shouldn't. Not until you get yourself a full-on costume, Brando."

Me? Putting on tights and pummeling bad guys? I don't think so.

Chapter Four

The next day, I'm sorting through a bag full of returned materials that smell as if they need to cut back to a pack of cigarettes a day. My phone buzzes. I pluck it from my back pocket.

<How about this?> There's a picture of Iron Man attached.

Reed. I glance over my shoulder. He's in his office, talking on the desk phone with someone. Looks as serious as a branch manager should. No sign of his hands or his cell phone. Impressive that he can text me and shovel bull with another person at the same time.

<Nope.> I send it, check the DVDs in the bag. Open up *Patriot Games*, and the former disc spills out in six identical shards, like a cut pizza.

The phone buzzes again. <This one.> Superman. Blue tights. I scowl. <No. Also, some of us have to work.>

Buzz. <You can't go around in your bike helmet thwacking bad guys. Pick something!>

I don't answer that. Instead, I look up the patron record for the person who had the DVDs checked out and dial up their number on the desk phone. As it rings, I scan to see if everything's under control. An older couple are reading newspapers in a pair of chairs near the window. A middle-aged woman is in the romance stacks, her arms laden with seven novels. Three older teens in flashy clothes stand outside the front door, way too close together, hands in pockets and eyes scanning every car that goes by. Another drug deal?

Kelly is discussing a preschool booklist with the Latino woman who runs the daycare a couple of blocks over. "Why don't you bring the kids next time, Mrs. Ruiz? They could pick out their favorites."

Mrs. Ruiz shakes her head. "No, no, I won't have them walk up here. There are too many foul men around, like those boys in front. They should be in school. Young men like that took my purse last spring, and the last time I walked the children up here, there were gunshots. In the middle of day! The city is not safe anymore."

"I'm sorry. We do miss having them."

It makes me think of Sean. He always goes to school on his own. Then again, it's only three blocks from our apartment. And he's a teenager, more adept at not drawing attention to himself. Still, it's disheartening to know kids can't use the library because things have gotten so bad.

Someone finally picks up the phone. The voice is thick and slurs the reply. "Hullo?"

"Hi, this is Brandon Tusk at the Hull Branch Library."

"'Kay."

"You had a couple of DVDs checked out. One of them came back broken."

"Oh, yeah."

I pause. This is usually where the offender pleads innocence. "Ah, we're going to have to charge you for the replacement."

"'Kay. Make sure you guys buy a different movie."

"A what?" Mrs. Ruiz is heading out the front door. The teens are waiting, watching her.

"Different movie. That one sucked. So I broke it."

He hangs up. I stare at the phone for three seconds while

my brain misfires. Okay, fine. He'll be getting a bill for twenty bucks next week.

The gang interrogates Mrs. Ruiz. She tries to shoulder past them, but she's a head shorter, very petite. These kids are skinnier, but they're all muscle. You can tell because they're in long, baggy shorts and T-shirts, showing off their limbs.

They're also right in Mrs. Ruiz's face. One of them, a tall white kid with tattoos slapped on the side of his neck, grabs her arm.

I barge past the older couple, en route with newspapers in hand to the front counter, remembering a cursory "Scusemesirmaam." I slam the first door open, then the second. The medal's tingling at the center of my chest.

I know. Last night, I probably could have thrown it away. But it occurred to me the consequences of doing so could be worse than hanging on to it. What if men like those muggers found the medal? What if someone with criminal tendencies figured out how to use it? Better to keep it close, as unsettling as it is.

First thing I hear is, "—told you about your payments. You're late. Boss doesn't like it when his people are late."

"I'm not his people," Mrs. Ruiz snaps. "You let go and get away! You should be in school."

They laugh at her. "Pay up. You know the fee for walking these streets."

"Hey." I get next to her. "You coming in to check out books?"

Tattoo Kid stares at me a moment, dumbfounded. Not sure which word confuses him in that sentence, but I'm guessing it's "books." "Huh?"

I jerk my thumb at the door. "This is a library. So, unless you're needing a book to read, I suggest you get out of here."

No laughter this time. "What, you gonna call the cops on us?" he says. "You know who we work for?"

I could really use my knife about now, but it's doubtless been swiped from the alley where I fought the muggers last night. "Don't really care. You leave her alone and get lost, or my boss in there's on the phone to the police."

The medal's cold deepens. It stabs like a thousand needles. All I need to do is one big shove, like last night. One push and these punks are in the street—or better yet, across it.

But in broad daylight? With everyone watching? Reed's warning about anonymity sticks with me.

The kid reaches for his shorts pocket. There's a metal clip at the edge. He's got a knife in there. "You're messing with the wrong crew. The *wilki* own Little Warsaw and Hull."

He says the word veal-key. Great. Of all the brats I have to deal with, I get the Polish mob's junior league. I stand firm, waiting for his move, or sirens, whichever comes first.

An idea blinks on in my head.

None of the others make for a weapon, but they've got their hands in their pockets, too. The tattooed leader pulls his knife hand free.

I grab his wrist and bend it back. With every thought I can muster, I will him to get down onto the sidewalk.

It works. He stumbles, falling face first. Has to brace his impact with his left hand. The right hand drops the knife. Suddenly he's panting, gasping. I've let him go.

"Hey, man, you okay? What'd he do to you?" His buddies don't make a move at him, or me. Their hands slowly withdraw from their pockets.

"Couldn't—breathe. Felt like I was gonna suffocate." He takes a few more gasps, gets shakily to his feet. He glowers at me. "You're lucky I almost passed out, or I'd—"

"Just shut up and get out of here." My heart's pounding. I could have disarmed him without the medal, yes, but the other two would have definitely gotten me—and Mrs. Ruiz. It's an advantage I'm willing to have over them.

Right then, a black car pulls up. Brand new Lexus IS, tinted windows, sun gleaming off the immaculate obsidian body. Like watching a bikini model climb out of a pool. The boys see it too, and, for a moment, all our faces are reflected on its hood. Abruptly, the trio saunters off down the sidewalk without further threats. They're talking and joking, like the entire confrontation never happened.

Mrs. Ruiz spits. Misses my shoe by six inches.

"Do you have someone to take you back to your business, Mrs. Ruiz?"

She nods. "I will phone my brother. He works nearby. Thank you."

"You're welcome."

Reed comes out the front door. "You okay, Brando?"

"Yeah. Just some local flavor." Mrs. Ruiz is on her phone. I'm not going anywhere until I'm sure she's safe. "Said they were *wilki*."

He frowns. "Polack kids again. I called the cops two weeks ago, told 'em they'd started pushing for protection money around here. Apparently, they and the Irish mob are elbowing against each other's territories, and we're on the border."

"Great." It's my turn to frown. "And you the library manager know this because…?"

"Dennis."

"Ah." He says the name like some people would say "taxes" or "government." I'm surprised he doesn't spit, too.

"He keeps me up to speed on criminal activity in the neighborhood." Reed snorts. "Like I'm not busy enough as it is, without him emailing me uniform crime reports."

I just nod. Nothing will calm Reed down from harping on his brother-in-law.

The car door opens, and Reed's posture abruptly stiffens. He puts on his firmest smile—not his ballsy grin, but a smile. He's polite and cheerful. "Mr. Vanchev, good to see you."

No wonder Reed is on his best behavior. Mark Vanchev is

the director of the Drake City Free Library System, the one man in charge of the main building and its six branches, including Hull. He's tall, broad-shouldered but slim, filling out the lines of a tailored, charcoal gray suit perfectly. His black shoes shine more than the car. His tie is blood red and his shirt brilliant white. The face is one easily recognized—not only from our website, but from local TV news and magazines. No one else has that combination of confident smile, tanned skin, glittering pale blue eyes, and blond moustache accompanied by goatee. His hair's blond, too, though with more gray streaked through.

"Reed Andreen, a pleasure." Vanchev's voice is smooth, a mellow baritone, and doesn't carry the superciliousness of the TV anchor from last night's news. "Glad to be able to finally visit your branch."

If by 'visit' he means 'unannounced inspection'. I glance at Reed. Can't remember when if ever the director has swung by for a chat.

"Yes, sir," Reed says. "We're glad to have you here."

Vanchev faces me. "And your colleague?"

"Brandon Tusk, Mr. Vanchev." I shake hands with him. The grip's as strong as suspected, testing mine. "Technical services, circulation, general maintenance, eight more assorted titles."

He chuckles. Reed winces like I've stabbed a puppy. "Yes, I remember those days working in a small building such as this. You tend to wear a plethora of hats. Speaking of which, I trust you aren't needing law enforcement to assist with the fracas of a few minutes earlier."

"No, I think they got the message." I wonder how much of the encounter he saw.

"You wouldn't be the first of our branches to have to deal with the rampant crime and corruption in this city." Vanchev shakes his head. "Mr. Andreen, why don't we take this conversation inside."

"Yes, sir. This way."

I look back to see if Mrs. Ruiz has gotten her ride. She's climbing into a blue and white van emblazoned with the signage for *Plomería y Caños*: Plumbing and Pipes. The man behind the wheel is stocky, scowling at me, but the expression softens as she rattles something off to him in staccato Spanish. He still watches me warily as they pull from the curb.

Reed holds the door for Vanchev, who seems to be analyzing everything about the branch building and its state of affairs. His gaze lingers on the taped-up crack in the window and the chipped tile. Can't wait to see what he does when he sees the bucket catching the last of the leaks.

I'm fighting back laughter at my buddy, the conscientious doorman. "You hoping to hold his crown and scepter too?"

"Shut up," Reed mutters. "This isn't funny."

"No, it is very funny."

"This has to be about budget stuff. Nothing else. We just talked about the system finances yesterday, up to and including the branch bottom lines. You think this visit is a coincidence?" He lets the door swing shut at me.

"Reed, relax. He's here for an inspection, I get that. So what? You said the city was holding things and not making cuts."

"That doesn't mean *he* won't. Vanchev never leaves his fortress of solitude on top of the main branch."

"Okay, he's not a vampire, Reed. Get on with the tour."

"I am," he hisses. "And Fortress of Solitude is Superman, you Philistine."

Inside, Vanchev is no less critical of his surroundings. He stands a foot from the front desk and does a slow turn, not unlike a security camera. Kelly's back at her station, eyes wide at the sight of this guy who, incidentally, cuts a much more impressive figure than myself or Reed.

"This facility hasn't had much care put in to it, has it," Vanchev says firmly.

"No, sir, it hasn't," Reed says.

"Mr. Vanchev, we've done pretty well without special capital improvement funds for a couple of years now." *Reed the toady isn't sticking up for us like he should. Isn't he the one who always gripes about not getting enough cash from the city for repairs?* "Some things have to go without fixing, if we can get by."

"Hence the bucket, Mr. Tusk?"

"Yes, the bucket."

Vanchev smiles. "I admire your perseverance. And do you agree, Miss—?"

"Kelly. Kelly Quirke." She blushes. "I'm the children's staff."

"So you are."

"I do agree that we don't get the funding we should. Not always. I mean, it's not always fair." She says it fast and in a soft murmur.

"Never said I didn't agree." Vanchev leans against the counter, a more casual pose than I'd have expected from him. But none of his aura of being the man in command fades. "It's a regular struggle I have with the board of trustees. Unfortunately, it's a struggle that has real losses."

Reed clears his throat. "We're not receiving supplemental repair funds this year, sir?"

"No, Mr. Andreen. The Hull Branch is being closed."

For a moment, the four of us stand there in utter silence. Only the crinkle of the elderly couple turning newspaper pages breaks the stillness.

Reed clears his throat. "I'm sorry, sir, but at the budget meeting the other day—"

"I understand, Mr. Andreen, but the city council and the mayor don't see eye to eye. There's a strong contingent that wants taxes to decrease this year."

"Can't say I blame them," I say, "But I take it holding the line isn't good enough."

"No. Three of the nine councilors are from Rittenhouse, and they know their taxes are going to rise even with a stagnant budget, because property values are up. The mayor's angling to put the extra into reserve accounts, but they want cuts to reduce the overall tax burden. With circulation on the decline, our library system is the perfect sacrificial lamb. They've rallied with the two councilors from Cape Ashwin to call for cuts in our service."

"And we're the target?" I ask.

"Yes, you are." Vanchev ticks off points on his fingers. "As I said, declining circulation, plus deterioration of facilities, increasing complaints to police—"

"The crime in Hull isn't something we control," I interject and ignore Reed's pained expression at my less than obsequious tone. I could care less. Rittenhouse Island has the Coast Guard base and University of Drake City to keep its businesses in the black, plus a heap of luxury homes filled with both year-rounders and summer renters to pay the taxes. The island floats on money. "What do they think we can do about it? Hand out bookmarks to punks with guns and knives? Our branch would look better if they'd give us the cash to fix it."

"I am well aware of that, Mr. Tusk, and I pushed precisely those points." Vanchev's response is even-keeled. He doesn't look irritated—certainly not as much as Reed does. "But this little alliance is powerful. They're targeting Hull because it's poor and because it's dangerous. It also helps that it's not in their backyard. They can save money by cutting it out, and they don't feel the impact in the slightest."

We lapse into silence again. Reed is stone still, staring straight ahead. Kelly has her head down, as if she could force an answer from the computer keyboard.

This isn't right. I don't care what some McMansion owner in Rittenhouse thinks our branch is worth. "So tell us what we can do. There has to be something."

"I've got my hands full meeting with the council and urging them to reconsider," Vanchev says. "My staff and I are hoping the mayor will scrape the bottom of reserves as a last resort if this bloc does indeed cut funding. I don't like this any better than you do, Mr. Tusk, and I'll use whatever clout I can to stop it."

"What we could use is good PR. Sir." Reed scratches at his chin. "I have a buddy at the *Harbor Messenger*. We could lean on her for a couple of human-interest stories."

"That would help tremendously. Get your patrons' pictures out there." Vanchev smiles. "I have a feeling certain highly placed library officials will leak the news of the impending cuts."

I smile back. "That'll tick off the council."

"Oh, that's what I'm hoping it will do." He claps a hand on my shoulder. The medal stabs the center of my chest with ice. Never felt that before.

Vanchev's smile flickers. Did he see the discomfort cross my face? Well, if he did, I can't very well explain it. Instead of inquiring, he says, "I hate to be the bearer of ill tidings, folks, but I wanted you to hear it directly from me. There's nothing more vexing that hearing news from outside our organization before it comes through official channels."

"Thanks for that." We shake hands again. Reed escorts him out, not scraping and bowing as much as he had at first but still trailing in the master's wake.

"Okay." I glance at Kelly. "So. Fun news, right?"

She's not smiling. "It's terrible. They can't close us down. What about the people who still use the library? Like Mrs. Ruiz, and the Schultzes, and the Firetski family."

"My guess, they'll have to travel farther. All of our materials will get either absorbed by the other branches or sold."

"What about us?"

Us. The library staff, she means. Not what I envision, by a long shot. "We'll get absorbed, too, if there are any openings."

She buries herself in her record-keeping again, face stony.

"Hey." I pat the top of her hand. "It'll be okay. Trust me."

One corner of her lips quirks up again. "Thanks. But you

can't chase off every gang kid in these blocks."
"Maybe not."
Reed's words come back to me. *Not yet.*

The plan's fully formulated by the time I reach home for lunch. Feels good to be out of the building for a while. The others are moping since Vanchev's visit. Doesn't matter. This can work. It has to work.

Reed is right. I can't go smacking thugs around wearing my bike helmet. The thought crosses my mind as I unclip said item from my chin. I need a disguise. A uniform. Not a costume. That makes it sound like a kid at Halloween.

If the crime rate dips in Hull, it could be enough to convince the foundation to back off. Coupled with the PR blitz Reed suggested, that Vanchev liked—it should do the trick.

I'm grinning broadly and probably look like an idiot to anyone who notices as I stroll through my apartment building door, front bicycle wheel kicked high.

The woman leaning on the wall by my door smiles back.

I freeze. Never seen her in the building before. No way I would have forgotten, not with those tight black pants, form-fitting gray blouse and blue jacket. Her lips are blood red, her skin porcelain, and her hair—as jet black as the night sky—cascades down her back and either side of her face. She has dazzling blue eyes. Their intensity makes me wonder if they can stare right through me.

"Can I help you?" I ask.
"Brandon Tusk?"
"That's me." I lean the bicycle against the wall.
"You've got something my employer wants."
No small talk, then. My heart skips a beat. I'm immediately cognizant of the icy medal pressing into my skin. "Not sure what you mean."

"You found it, and he wants it. He's prepared to pay. A lot."

"That's tempting. How much?"

"That can be negotiated later. Please come with me. I have a car waiting."

Her voice is very quiet, very bland, and that smile—sultry doesn't do it justice. The way she stares, unblinking, sets off alarms that counteract whatever hypnotic effect her speech has.

"Sorry. I'm on my break and have to get back to work soon. I didn't catch your name."

"Not important. Please. This will be easier if you bring the jewelry with you and he gets what he wants."

That cuts it. She knows about the medal.

I move for my apartment's door. There's barely a whisper of cloth as she draws the gun. The abnormally long barrel befuddles me for an instant until I realize it's a suppressor. There's no one home this afternoon, not at this hour. The building's empty. She let herself in, with a weapon that will make less sound than a normal gunshot, at a time of day when there's heavy cross traffic on Twelfth from Gunnison State.

"You need to get in the car."

"No, I need to the call the cops." And I shove her into the nearest wall with the medal. But this isn't a mugger trying to scare me in the dark. This is a trained killer. Odds of her putting a bullet in my gut before I can muster the medal's power are great.

"Sir, I don't need to kill you. It's better for both of us if I don't. You're not worth it." She shakes her head, as if my performance thus far disappoints her. "Turn around. Walk out the door. Get in the passenger side of the blue Taurus."

"All right, just take it easy. Relax." I turn around, heart pounding. Even without the medal, I've never disarmed anyone of their handgun before.

"I am relaxed. Walk."

I get to the door, push it slowly open. I'll let go, let it swing back at her and use the medal to slam it back harder than she'd expect, assuming I can figure out how to do that—

A car engine roars down the street. Tires screech to a halt. It's a gorgeous ride: silver Camaro Z28, 1973. Kudos to Dad for all those years of car magazines left on the dining room table. He'd love to see this one, all shiny with a black stripe on the hood and down the roof. The wheels gleam with chrome. Windows and windshield are tinted opaque. The engine growls, and the whole car shakes as it sits there, brakes applied, straining to be unleashed.

The driver's side window rolls down and I spot an older guy—buzz cut gray hair and full beard, all trimmed neatly—in the seconds before he points a silver handgun our way.

I duck on the steps. Four shots boom out. Glass crashes behind me, and I hear my escort's shoes squeak on the linoleum.

"Get in!" The man in the car flings open the passenger side door.

I look back. The woman with the gun—I'm amassing too many of these contacts lately—is getting back to her feet from a deep crouch. She aims, for me or the car, I can't tell.

So I run for the open door.

More gunshots. These sound dull by comparison. They'll kill me just as well. Air rushes by my head. Bullets careen off the body of the Camaro. I scramble around the back, keeping my body low. The driver revs the engine. I'm coming!

"Get in!" he bellows.

I dive through the passenger door, hitting my head on the gearshift in the process. There's barely time to register the sharp pain when my rescuer throws the car into third gear and peels out from the curb. He fires off two more shots. Someone somewhere yells.

My feet dangle out the door. The angle I'm at, I can plainly see pavement rolling by underneath them. I yank my legs in and grapple for the door handle.

Finally, I get it shut. Gasping, I untangle my limbs and sit upright.

The driver's face is stony, his eyes glued forward. I was right about the gray beard and hair—up this close they're speckled with silver. His eyes are dark, fierce brown. He's tanned, and fit, but not overloaded with muscle. Blue jeans, brown shoes, a pale green dress shirt with the sleeves rolled up; casual Friday wear. It's only the huge, nickel-plated semi-automatic pistol that clashes with the image.

"Frank Belasco. Stay put and put your seatbelt on." He dons a pair of aviator shades. "Safety first."

I look up.

There's a car heading right for us.

Chapter Five

Frank swerves sharply right. I holler a warning, too late. The other car flashes by to our left. It's a miracle we don't hit any vehicles in the other lane.

Other lane? I crane my neck. "You're driving the wrong way!"

"You noticed." He cranks the wheel and we go flying around the corner onto Vine. My window comes so close to a delivery van I'm sure the astonished driver can reach out and adjust my rearview mirror. "Genius."

"What the—? Who are you? What's going on?"

"Don't know what word you're looking for after 'what the' but I've lots of beauties. Second question: already answered that. Frank. Belasco. B-E-L-A-S-C-O. Third question: I'm keeping you out of trouble."

We're in the correct lane, mercifully. That doesn't stop Frank from veering around a lumbering city bus into the opposite line of traffic. He doesn't blink. Jaw set, he jerks the wheel right once more and we slip into a narrow gap just in front of the bus and just prior to a head-on collision with a Dodge Ram.

"If you're trying to keep me safe you should pull over and let the woman take me to her boss! I'd be less dead!"

"Shut up. She was going to kill you. Whether on your doorstep or later at her boss's office, she was going to put a bullet in your face, or some other part of your skull."

"I—wait. How'd you know about that?"

"Because that's what she does. And she's not going to kill you until after she has the medallion safely in her possession. That's why her boss was after you."

That shuts me up. It stuns any commentary from me, even as we go blasting through the stoplight at 9th Street. "Medallion."

"Yes. Medallion."

"It's not actually a circle, you know."

"Used to be, long before your great-great grandparents could walk." He smirks. "The thing you're wearing around your neck."

I zip my jacket.

He chuckles. "Nice concealment. I already saw the shape under your shirt."

"I don't know what you're talking about."

"You're a pain already, you know that?" He sneers. "Wait 'til the Garrison gets a load of you."

"I don't—"

"You're too visible already. Showing up on YouTube. Do you know how often that's happened to a medallion holder?" He starts ticking off numbers on his fingers, then suddenly slaps the wheel. "Never! You're the first idiot to get yourself forty thousand views in a single evening!"

Forty thousand. I can't help a smile.

Gunshots ring out behind us, nearly drowned by the roaring engine. There's a car following us, weaving around traffic like Frank's shadow. A blue Taurus, half a block away. Something flashes on its driver's side. Glass breaks into a spider web around the impact on the rear window of Frank's car.

"Just paid to get her detailed and now this." He glowers sidelong at me. "You'd better be worth the trouble."

"How about we forget that, and you back up to the part where you explain why I'm getting shot at."

"Hold that thought." He cranks down his window. Wind rushes in. "Gun."

The pistol's tucked in a holster shoved between his seat and the gearshift. I draw it and carefully hand it over to him, stock first.

"Thanks." He brandishes it, muzzle up, as we tear pell-mell into the next intersection.

Oh no.

The light's red on our end. Green for the crossing lanes. There's a white Prius coming from the left and a green Mercury sedan from the right. Frank arrows us right toward their center.

A silver Suburban comes racing up behind the Prius. I brace my hands on the dash. and get a glimpse of a man with dark sunglasses leaning out his passenger side window. There's something black in his hands. My librarian's brain classifies it as an Uzi.

Frank barrels through the cars, tires screeching. Horns explode on all sides of us. The Uzi chatters, cutting over the sounds of drivers yelling and vehicles swerving. Frank glances sideways, long enough to fire two shots from his gun.

The windshield of the Suburban explodes. It sideswipes the front end of the Mercury, barely missing our bumper as we streak through the mess. Can't see what happens to the Prius.

We're through. I breathe again.

Sirens start blaring in the distance. Finally. I sag into the seat, thankful law enforcement or fire or someone official is on the way. Frank hands me the gun, its slide back, without speaking. I tuck it back in its holster.

"No, idiot, reload first," he snaps. "We're going to need it soon enough."

I take it out, eject the empty magazine.

"Back seat."

There's a duffle bag, straining at its zipper. I reach around, open it. Rummage through several changes of clothing.

I come up with ten magazines, all identical. "You're, ah,

prepared."

"And you can see why. Reload and put one in the chamber."

I follow his instructions, noting with some concern there's a car behind. Our buddy in the blue Taurus, and he's picked up a follower in a second white Suburban. I say second, because it's not bashed on the front end like the one we encountered back a block.

Our surroundings fly by so fast that I anticipate a severe case of vertigo. North on Vine, just passing the fire station on Eighth. The sirens I'd hoped would intervene in this mess sound no closer than when I first heard them. So, count them out for immediate assistance. Though judging from the past five minutes, this Frank guy didn't need any help from law enforcement.

"Hold on." Frank takes a right onto Seventh at the red light like he's taken all turns and red lights—at high speed, his foot only tapping the brake, ignoring the traffic signals and the traffic itself.

"You are going to get us killed!" I snap. "That guy won't have to shoot me or bribe me into handing over that thing if you wrap us around a truck!"

"You don't usually whine this much," Frank muses. "Why don't you concentrate on activating the medallion to keep us from getting cornered. Like here."

Up ahead is the busy four-way intersection with State Highway Three—Broad Street in this part of town, three lanes in both directions. I don't know what Frank's talking about until the black Lincoln Town Car barrels out from an alley, a block in front of us, and parks at the intersection. Two men step out, one from either side of the car. They have dark sunglasses, too, and hold Uzis close to their bodies.

"I'm sensing a pattern," I mutter.

"Shut up and give them a push."

"What?"

"Focus. Push them. Shove them aside. I don't care what you think it's called, just get rid of them."

I freeze up, eyes glued to the two gunmen. They've got their weapons leveled at us. I can't marshal the same will. No matter how much I strain, no matter how much I demand that something happen, the medallion stays cold and inert against my chest. Not a single spike of energy.

"Brandon, get it in gear!"

"I can't! I'm trying!" Doesn't even occur to ask him how he knows my name. Though given a trained hit-woman knows my name and address too, I'm not surprised.

"That figures." He's got the window down again and his gun ready. "There's a .357 under the seat. Open the window. Shoot them."

"What?"

"Do it or we're dead!"

I fumble under the seat. The floorboards vibrate from the strain of the engine. Somewhere over my head, the twin chatter of the Uzis opens up. My fingers yank the .357 Magnum from a holster strapped under the seat. "I'm behind on my target practice, by several years."

"You don't have to hit anything, but it would be preferable. Shoot!"

I rolled the window down, hold the gun in a two-handed grip, and fire until it's empty. The sound smacks me around the head. My ears ring, pain lancing through them. Can't tell if any of the bullets hit anything. It looks like a trash can takes the brunt of the impact. My poorly aimed, haphazard fire does encourage one gunman to duck for cover behind the open door of the Town Car.

The man standing to the left ignores my futile attack and blazes away with the Uzi. Cracks spider-web across the windshield, but it doesn't break, just like the rear window stayed intact.

Frank's gun explodes with four shots. Two dark red holes punch into the gunman's chest. His torso and upper body whiplash against the car door, and he falls over.

Frank changes course enough to avoid the body but also rip the left door off. We're past them, plunging into the midst of Fourth and Broad Street.

Here we go again.

The Camaro flies so close to a Toyota Corolla that I'm sure we're going to tear its side off. It swerves by a minivan, and I turn in time to see our pursuers slam on their brakes.

Blue and red lights flash in front of us. Two DCPD squad cars are coming at us, cutting across the intersection at Fifth Street. Frank doesn't even blink, and definitely doesn't slow down. He puts up the tinted windows and races past them.

"That doesn't help," he snarls.

"Maybe you should have thought of that before we got into a high-speed pursuit," I snap back.

We barrel down Broad Street, skipping through lights, ignoring oncoming traffic, and managing somehow to neither bash into other motorists nor vehicles. Frank's mood improves from sullen to taciturn.

We're rounding the bend by Diamond Park when there's a blare of car horns behind us. The blue Taurus and its silver companion are back. Frank swears and stomps on the gas. The Camaro thunders down the road.

I reach for the window, gun ready.

"Nope," Frank says. "It's a clean shot from here to the on-ramp for the interstate. We'll get on there, and then I know a place—oh, great."

Ahead, a semi is halted across the highway, its huge container blocking the entire set of left lanes. The driver is running away, hands over his head, toward the other curb. A man is in the passenger's seat, door flung open, aiming an Uzi at us. A white SUV jerks to a stop, bumper to bumper with the semi.

Airfoil: Origins

"Your turn," Frank says.

"What? No. I tried that already. I can't"

"Yes, you can. Move them out of the way."

"No."

"You did it with the muggers—"

"That was an involuntary reaction! I was caught by surprise and did it just on instinct."

"Yes, that works, but that's not what spurs the medallion. It's all in your mind, Brandon. Use it."

"I can't."

"Do it, or we're going to have a very painful collision."

Gunfire erupts behind us. The two cars are closing in. The semi and SUV ahead of us loom. Soon, their occupants will add their weapon fire to the onslaught. I grit my teeth. "I tried!"

"You move those trucks right now or we're both screwed! Picture it, and do it!"

"Shut up!" The image pops into my mind: Two hands, pressed knuckles to knuckles, sandwiched between the trucks. I shove them open.

A surge of cold stabs out from my chest, up my arms, through my fingers. At first, I think I'm having a coronary—but then the trucks fling apart from each other. The semi slides back so fast it buckles at its connectors, bashing two light poles on the opposite curb in the process. The SUV's front end tips up, and its rear rolls the opposite direction. When the front slams down, the men inside flail around against doors and windows.

Frank blasts us through the gap. No bullets follow. The pursuing cars slam on their brakes, and I watch the driver of the lead car—the woman who tried to abduct me—get out and remove her sunglasses.

I grin.

Frank grins, too. "Nicely done, rookie."

Our car races up the ramp and we explode onto the wide lines of the interstate north. Frank weaves a path between a fuel truck and a coach bus, before settling into the traffic streaming past Mount Stafford.

I finally relax into the leather seat. With shaking fingers, I pull the medallion from around my neck. And I say to Frank, "What is this thing?"

Frank doesn't blink. "Your new life."

He pulls off the road fifteen miles later, at a rest stop full of six fast food restaurants, two gas stations, and a two-story visitors' center made of glass and stone. Off to one side is an old, singled family diner called Oscar's. Frank's car, freshly scarred, looks as beat up as the rest, though he has the accessory of bullet holes.

The waitress is gray haired and brown skinned, with more wrinkles on her face than my hands after swimming. She brings Frank a requested cup of coffee. I don't order anything. My appetite is gone. I want answers.

Frank dumps in a creamer and half a sugar packet. He's terribly meticulous for someone with big, wiry hands. "We call it the medallion. No one's come up with anything fancier, and that makes it easier for us to talk about among others."

I turn it over in my hands. "It's old."

"Very. Our best guess is a thousand years."

The answer stuns me. I'd thought a couple centuries.

"It resists all forms of spectroscopy and metallurgy. There's nothing like it on the planet. We don't know what metal it's made of, or how much damage it can sustain. What we know is that there's many of them, and they are very, very powerful."

So I'd seen. "You can use it to move things."

"Not that simple." Frank sips his coffee. "It manipulates the Earth's gravitational field in select areas. You can lessen the pull or increase it. You can even shape it. Whatever you want."

"Gravity. That explains a lot. So, those trucks I moved—"

"Your reflex was to create a field of localized gravitational distortion between the trucks that expanded outward, simultaneously decreasing the pull of gravity in twin points under their front wheels. The result was them pummeled." Frank grins. "Very few people can do that without prior training."

"And the guys in the alley—I tossed them up in the air."

"Same thing. Sudden shifts in gravity can cause severe damage. Acceleration g-forces. Think of fighter pilots who have to guard against blacking out when they pull combat maneuvers."

The medallion looked so small in my hands. A piece of tarnished silver metal, with worn and broken edges, sitting in my palm. It gave no inclination of tremendous power. Freezing, but warmth seeps in. Suddenly, I'm very much aware how vulnerable we are to anyone walking by, spying what's on our table. I loop it back over my neck and tuck it beneath my shirt.

"It was no accident, you finding that medallion," Frank says, pointing. "This is how it is."

"We always find odd things in there. Money, used Kleenex, bacon. That's the not foul list."

"This isn't a joke, Brandon."

"Isn't it? Isn't this some kind of gag? Answer this: why don't you take this thing and get rid of it?"

"Now you're talking stupid." Frank scowls. "The medallion was meant to come to you. Do you believe in destiny?"

I stare at him. Destiny. An impersonal force throwing me from one event to the next for some universal purpose with no thought or care to what happens to me. It fits with what my life has been like for the past couple of years. "I don't know anything about fate. The things I used to believe..."

"Doubts. You've got them. You think you're the only one?" He continues on, watching me keenly. "That's what's at play, Brandon. These medallions, there's no lottery to give them out to whomever happens to have the right number. There is a reason she left it for you to discover."

"She. The mom I called? She's got a bunch of kids, not a

mystical medallion."

"Wrong she." Frank dipped his fingertips into his jacket pocket. "I was talking about your wife."

"What does my wife have to—" The rest of the words evaporate as Frank sets a piece of white paper on the table, creased in the middle. One edge is dog-eared. Ink smudges a corner.

"Open it."

A photo, worn at the sides, slips out. It's Samantha, though the picture must have been taken at least ten years ago, when she used to wear her hair in one long braid to the right side. Later, before her death, she had it tied up in the back for her nursing shifts. She's gorgeous.

The paper is a handwritten note. Seems it was written a long time ago. I recognize her handwriting in an instant, so neat and tidy:

Brandon,
I'm so sorry I couldn't tell you this in person. Because I've gone, the medallion is yours. No one can keep it safer than you. It's the gifts you've been blessed with that will allow you to hold it and use it for good: your bravery, your kind heart, your creative soul.

God has granted me a great mission, greater than any I could have imagined. Use the medallion in the way it's been passed down for centuries, from generation to generation. You have a sacred duty to uphold, in service of the Garrison.

Know that I always love you, no matter what. And tell Sean, my little boy, tell him I love him, too.
Samantha

My eyes brim with tears. The kind of certainty she showed, the words and deeds free of any doubt, only sink me deeper. There's been nothing like it filling my days. That phrase—bravery, heart, soul—she said it to me many times. It's her way of telling me why she loves me. This is a treasure. "Thank you."

Frank shrugs.

But after a moment, questions bubble up from beneath my nostalgia. "Where did you find this?"

"She gave it to me. Wanted you to have it, when you were ready to take on the medallion and all it entails. When her time was up."

The impact of his first sentence takes a while to soak in. "She gave it—you knew Samantha?"

Frank nods. He rubs at his chin, looks away out the diner window. When he speaks again, his tone is softer. "I trained her. She was good. One of my best. Her death—I stayed away from the Garrison for a while. That is, until they told me her medallion had turned up. We thought it was destroyed in the accident. Next thing I know, I'm pushing a book through your book drop."

"You put it there?"

"As per my orders."

I rub at my forehead. "This doesn't make sense. None of it makes sense. My wife was a nurse. She was dedicated to her work, loved her patients and worked difficult hours. But she would never hide anything from me."

"Really."." Frank snorts. "You're telling me you know every detail of every late shift, every back to back 24 hours she worked, and where she was at every instant."

"No, I'm not." His coy questions-within-answers are grating on my nerves. "Those hours were all part of her job."

"Those hours were part of her cover. Anything that gave her time to fulfill her duties to the Garrison was part of her cover. She knew the risks, and she knew the rules. No one outside the Garrison could know she possessed a medallion."

This was not a good moment to mention my test run of the medallion at Reed's last night. "You're telling me you helped hide that part of her life from me."

"That's the job of every trainer: to make certain a medallion holder is called and prepared."

"This doesn't make sense. Called to do what?"

"To serve the Garrison. To keep the medallions safe, to keep them secret, and, when the call arises, to use them to oppose the Ashen."

"The Ashen?"

"The ones who, like us, swore an oath, centuries ago, to hide the medallions from the nations at large. They, however, opted to use their medallions to influence world events for their own avaricious ends. Our job is to get in their way, keep them from exerting the wrong power. It started in Europe, and we followed them here in the late Sixteenth Century."

He's kidding. Has to be. "There's no evidence of a secret war."

"Listen to yourself. 'Evidence of a secret war.' What evidence? We time our actions perfectly. We kept it hidden under the chaos of the Revolution, and the Civil War. Our first conflict was a disaster. Google Roanoke."

This whole thing is ludicrous. But the mugging, the woman with the gun at my apartment, and the wild car chase that ended with me flinging two carloads of killers apart like wet cardboard. All of it because of the cold metal under my shirt.

"You don't believe me," Frank says.

"I'm not inclined to, rationally. But everything else I've seen pushes me in the other direction. You show up at my home, force me into...whatever this is, and tell me my wife was involved with it. With this medallion. That she was some kind of vigilante."

"Don't kid yourself into thinking you knew everything about her. Samantha understood how serious this is. She valued her oath and recognized the greater good the Garrison did. It required sacrifice, so she kept silence. She did love you, too, even though she could never let you inside this part of her life."

"We were married for fourteen years."

Frank takes a swig of coffee but shares no comment.

I stare at her photo for a long time. The conversations ebb and flow around us. Traffic shoots by on the interstate, the steady rush of air broken periodically by the thunder of a fully-loaded semi.

"It's a lot to process." Frank swirls the dregs of his coffee in the mug. "I understand. Not everyone who's called has an easy time of it. You know, when you sign on, they tell you about Nathan Hale's first assignment and… well, I'm getting ahead of myself."

"His what?"

"Later. It's a story they share with all newbies. I heard it, too, and rolled my eyes. Such was my attitude about things historical at the time."

"You had a medallion?"

"Oh, yeah. I was twenty-one, fresh out of college. Dropping out, I should say. Didn't have a dime on me or an ounce of brains in my head. But my old man died—lung cancer. All those years I thought he was a traveling businessman, out on the road, ignoring me and Ma. Smoked a pack of Marlboros every day for as long as I could remember. The old house in Cape May still smells like cigarettes. I always thought he loved the those things more than us." Frank smirks. "Guess what showed up in the backseat of my Seventy-One AMC Hornet the next day. A manila envelope with his medallion in it and an eight-track explaining why."

"Your Garrison has a penchant for leaving these medallions of amazing power lying about for any Joe Blow to find them," I say. "Seems dangerous."

"Hardly. We monitor the potentially called very closely. My trainer was watching me for weeks—because he knew Dad was adamant that his son follow in his footsteps. As for you, well, *A Tale of Two Cities* has always been one of my favorite books. The point is, we know precisely when the called will get a medallion. It's not left up to chance."

"This is crazy. What do you expect me to do with this thing?"

"The same thing you just did three times."

"I can't."

Frank rolls his eyes. "I just saw you do it. And forty thousand people on YouTube saw you disable those muggers."

"No. Look—I have a son, and a job. I have responsibilities."

"You're right about that. The medallion is the greatest responsibility of all. You've been tasked to guard it, keep it safe, and use it when we need you to."

I raked a hand through my hair. This is insane. *He's* insane. "I'm not going to give up my life for some crusade."

"Why not? You have your nights free." Frank's smirk returns. "Unless you prefer blondes who puke on your shoes."

Whatever preconceptions I have about my personal life being private are completely deleted.

"Brandon, don't ask me any more stupid questions." He digs out his wallet, slaps bills on the table. It's far more money than needed to cover our order. "Let's go."

"No. I told you—"

"Shut up and listen. How are you going to explain everything to the police? They're going to be at your apartment by now. Gunfire tends to attract them. So do bullets and broken glass. You need my help, and more importantly, you need my training. You also need my ability to injure large numbers of our enemies without getting caught by law enforcement."

"None of it would be necessary if your Garrison hadn't thrown this thing my way." I follow him out of the diner.

"Careful. Samantha was part of the Garrison. You can't dump on us without disparaging her."

In the parking lot, he digs out his guns, stuffs them in the bag. He also removes the registration from the glove box. With the help of a massive, red Swiss Army knife he unscrews the license plates. He removes a different set of plates from the bag and installs them.

"Ah, are we planning to walk back to Drake City?"

"Only if you need the exercise." There's a dark green Subaru Outback wagon parked at the end of the lot. Frank unlocks it and tosses the bag and the Camaro's old plates into the back. "No, the police won't find the Camaro. Don't worry, someone will be by to pick it up in five minutes. They have the transponder."

"You're thorough, I'll give you that."

"Get in." He starts the engine, a considerably demurer sound than that the Camaro's primal thunder. "Or have a nice walk."

I put on my seat belt. "I haven't agreed to anything."

"Sure you haven't." He's smirking again.

We head back down the Interstate to Drake City. Soon, I see the skyscrapers poking their heads over the slopes of Mount Stafford. With all stories of secret conflicts and powerful medallions and the questions about Samantha's involvement, my curiosity about something Frank said cuts through the fog like Braddock Island Light. "Wait. Frank. You said the medallion can alter gravitational pull to move things."

"Yeah."

"Can it move me?"

He glances at me and grins.

Chapter Six

Drake City Police Lieutenant Dennis Marchand scuffed a shoe at the shell casing on the sidewalk. Forty-five caliber. He'd seen plenty of them working first homicide, then the gang unit. What surprised him was not the fact he was standing in a cluster of the shell casings, but the location of the cluster: Nine Square. Come on. White Collar Haven, stuck between the college full of kids from around the country, and a burgeoning ghetto of European immigrants. Shootouts were rare.

Especially at this address.

The front door was ajar. Only a few shards of ragged glass remained in the frame. What was once the window was blown all over the floor. Blown inward. Hall was empty, with the exception of a bicycle propped against an apartment door. There was a helmet discarded just inside the door.

"Shooter One was outside," he said. "Exchanged fire with Shooter Two over here, fired from the curb to the hall."

Officer Dillard frowned. He was tall, lanky, early twenties, and had less hair on his head than Marchand—shaven cleaner than a cue ball. He took notes on a huge smartphone that beeped with every tap. "Sir, how can you tell?"

Marchand muttered under his breath. He'd rather be a balding, paunchy detective with gray at his temples and silver streaked through a thick black moustache than an Academy clone. Of course, he was exactly that, and had been one of those clones decades ago. Dillard had on the DCPD blues, carbon copied from every person in Patrol, except that Dillard had issues with using an iron. Marchand preferred well-pressed, gray pants, a light gray jacket, and a white shirt with forest green tie. There wasn't a stray thread within a city block of him. His shoes shined until he could see food stuck in his teeth. Which he didn't have. "They don't teach you kids anything useful. Look at the impacts. I got a .45 caliber shell casing there, in the street by the curb and on the sidewalk. There's a .40 caliber in the hall. The glass is blown inward. Fragments all over the tile, hardly any on the porch. Means the exterior shots were the ones that broke it."

Dillard chewed on the end of his styles. "So, the outside shooter shot first."

"Can't tell. You can only assume that if you also assume the door was shut when everything went down. If it were open, Shooter Two could have shot first. But..." Marchand turned back to the curb. He knelt, exposing bright blue socks. Waited for Dillard to comment on them but heard only a clearing of the throat, like someone holding back a laugh. Good. Last newbie who joked about Marchand's preference for garish footwear wound up transferred to Parking Enforcement.

Instead, Dillard craned his neck like a giraffe, angling over Marchand's shoulder. "A .40 cal."

"Bingo." Marchand got his Swiss Army knife from his jacket pocket and pried out the flattened slug embedded in the asphalt. Didn't touch it, just let it roll. CSIs would gut him if he grubbed up things with prints.

"I don't get it," Dillard said.

"That's because Google's rotted your brains," Marchand snapped. "Both shooters were good. The .40 cal shots are precisely grouped. Aimed toward the curb, one location. And those tire skid marks there? Means there was a car here. I'd put money on it being the same vehicle that went tearing up Vine and down Broad Street. The .45 cal shooter was in the Camaro, shooting into the hall. When the boys finish cleaning up the messes between here and the interstate, they'll find more .45 cal there, you can be sure."

"But there's no blood."

"No, Dillard, no blood. What's that say?"

Dillard frowned at his notes. "Ah, that … no, wait, you said they were aimed well. Then neither guy wanted to kill the other."

"Also bingo. Whatever went on, it was a warning on both sides. Restrained."

"That's weird."

"You think? Gang hits, there's always a body. No, something else happened…" Marchand tugged at his moustache.

Dillard nodded eagerly, his phone beeping away as he took more notes.

"What reports do we have from witnesses?"

"Ah…" Dillard scrolled through screens. "Nothing on the driver. Windows were too dark. Only thing we have is that it was the same silver Camaro, like you said."

"Well, there's already an APB, so that's taken care of. I want to know the second it comes back."

"Yes, sir."

"Plates?"

Dillard shook his head.

"Okay, what else."

"Ah, one resident across the street is working with forensics on a sketch of the gal she says was the shooter inside. But she's eighty, has cataracts."

A lady hitman? Hit-woman? None sprang to mind.

"Oh, apparently there was also a third individual at the scene, a man the lady says lives here. Said she saw him ride up on his bike, part of a normal routine."

And here we go. Marchand could always tell when a case

was going to be obnoxious. As soon as he'd seen this address, he'd known what form it would take. "Go for it."

"Brandon Tusk, age 35, no criminal record. Well, a couple of tickets for improperly parking a bicycle. Works at—"

"Hull Branch Library, Ninth and Hull." Marchand sighed. "Yeah. Know him."

"Oh."

"Works with my sister's husband."

"Ooooh." Dillard's eyes went wide and he stopped talking. Didn't even tap on his phone.

Marchand stared off at the buildings across the street. Great. Just great. If that idiot Reed's buddy was involved with this case, there'd be some pressure to hand it off to someone else in the department. There usually was.

Marchand knew how to get around those roadblocks. Captain Urquhart owed him. He'd been paying for a while. Any pressure he applied to Marchand would be for show. Unless he wanted certain images to make it to the *Messenger*. The ones involving prostitutes

"Lieutenant." Officer Sutton waved from the barricade a couple parking spots away. He was a foot taller, Marchand swore, dark-skinned, eyes blue as the sky, with a beard and moustache trimmed with immaculate care. Now there was an officer who knew how to look the part. He and the other patrolmen had taped off the four spots along the curb, and restricted traffic to one lane. "Got a couple of civilians waiting. One of 'em says he lives here."

Perfect. He'd been waiting for Tusk to show up. One phone call to the library had confirmed that he was on break until noon. "Let them by."

So, who was the other person in Sutton's "couple" description?

A nice shiny Subaru Outback, gleaming green the same shade as Marchand's tie and bearing Massachusetts plates, pulled up. Tusk got out of the passenger side. He looked dazed, pale. Marchand assessed the rest of his appearance. He'd put on some more muscle since they'd last met. Hair, brick red and uncombed. Eyes, hazel with dark circles underneath. Stubble on his chin and face. Blue jeans, gray polo shirt. Tattered watchband. Pair of brown Keens, sufficient for work dress but sturdy. Had a backpack slung over one shoulder.

Tusk spotted him a second later. His features tightened. "Dennis."

"Brandon." Marchand kept his tone as civil as possible. Tusk was only an enemy by association. In and of himself, he was an okay guy. Seemed to have his head screwed on tight. Widower, which Marchand supposed should make him sad. As for him, he'd be happy as a kid on Christmas morning if ex ran her Mazda into the side of a fuel tanker. Considering her propensity for DUI, it wouldn't surprise him if that was the way she ended up. "How are you?"

"Doing all right." Tusk's gaze flickered to the apartment. "I heard there was a shooting."

Marchand's eyes narrowed. "Yeah. Your bike's inside, I see. No hits. Helmet's okay, too."

"Can I get them back?" Tusk checked his watch. "My break's up."

"Sorry, no, got to hold on to them as part of the crime scene." Plus, stuff got lost in impound occasionally. Especially when Marchand found one of his regulars who was willing to sell it and give him 30 percent of the take. "I'm going to need your statement."

"About...?"

"Whatever you saw. Where you were when the shooting started. Who was the woman in the hall of your building? Take your pick, but I need answers on all of the above." Marchand dug a notebook from his pocket, the pages guarded half-heartedly by a worn red cover. Its sheets were spiked with a rainbow assortment of sticky notes. Screw computers. "Witnesses saw you enter the building. Later, the shooting started."

"I didn't see anything that could be helpful," Tusk said.

Marchand nodded. Truthfully, no one had seen anything of the actual shooting, except for Tusk arriving home and the Camaro peeling out when the bullets were done flying. Gunshots have a tendency to make the few people home this hour of the day hide instead of gawk. "Here's what I got.: two guys, one in a silver hotrod and one in your hall start shooting at each other. I've got shell casings and bullets from two weapons all over the place, plus your helmet and bike smack in the middle. No one knows where you were. Care to fill me in?"

Tusk opened his mouth, but a deeper, older voice interjected, "He was with me, Lieutenant."

The driver of the Subaru got out and joined them on the curb. He was average height, trim, dressed casually in jeans and a nice, long-sleeved shirt. The man exuded confidence. Everything about his bearing suggested service. Haircut and beard lent more credence: Marchand had seen sloppier grooming on Academy grads, Dillard included. "Your name, sir?"

"Frank Belasco. An old family friend." Belasco smiled easy, offered a handshake.

Marchand ignored it, kept right on pressing. "What variety of friend?"

"The variety that doesn't visit nearly often enough," Belasco said. "Brandon's late wife, Samantha, was an old friend. When I heard she'd died—well, I wanted to come back then but the grief was too much. I didn't manage it until now."

"I'll need to see your ID."

Belasco plucked a black leather wallet from his back pocket, handed over his driver's license. Massachusetts Class B. Holo looked good. However— "Dillard! Run this."

"Yes, sir." Dillard took the license and trotted down the street to their car.

Marchand considered Belasco again. "How long have you been in town?"

"Oh, a few weeks."

Tusk glanced sideways, a brief flicker. One Marchand noted. "Okay. So you stopped by here, to pick up Brandon."

"That's right. He met me at the end of the block." Belasco gestured west. "I wanted to drive through Gunnison, see the campus. Samantha went there."

Marchand would have Dillard run the details. "Brandon, you met up with Mr. Belasco here and you guys went—where."

"Just out for a drive. Onto the interstate."

"Stop anywhere?"

"Got lunch at Oscar's."

Marchand nodded. He knew of it, quiet place with a rep for decent grub and good chatter. There were a couple guys on State Police who ate late dinners there. He'd get the name of a lunch shift waitress from them. "You dropped your helmet."

"What? Oh, yeah." Tusk shrugged. "Must've fallen off my bike."

"My arrival was a surprise," Belasco said.

"Surprise enough to make you drop your helmet." Marchand smiled.

Tusk's face was still pale, but he managed to return the expression. Something didn't fit. But he couldn't keep Tusk on vague suspicion alone. He'd work with the sketch, and get Belasco run through the system. See what Dillard could dig up on him. "Okay, gentlemen. You're good to go. Brandon, we'll leave your bicycle with one of your neighbors if that's all right. Assuming we don't have to impound it for evidence."

"All right. You'll let me know if you find out anything."

"You bet." Marchand took the license back from Dillard and returned it to its owner. "Mr. Belasco, good to meet you."

"Likewise." Belasco didn't offer a handshake.

Once they'd left, Dillard said, "License checks out, sir. Frank

Belasco's registered in Massachusetts DMV. No restrictions. Record's clean except for the occasional parking ticket and one speeding violation in '12."

"Hmm. Okay." Marchand tucked his notepad away.

"Everything okay, sir?"

"No, Dillard, there's something off."

Dillard cleared his throat. "You know the Tusk guy?"

He sounded like he was asking whether Marchand had terminal cancer. "Yeah. Met him several years back, at dinner at Caroline's apartment."

Dillard winced. "That dinner? The one you told me about when I started?"

"Yeah. Caroline's husband Reed busted my lip."

"You broke his nose."

Marchand glared at Dillard, and the kid shut up. "Fair enough. Anyway, Tusk wasn't good with a napkin. His place at the table had the biggest pile of crumbs. Not a neat eater."

"You noticed that?" Dillard frowned. "In the middle of a fight?"

"No, before the fight. Just like I noticed Reed smirking at my comments, and Caroline's smile every time he touched her," Marchand snapped. "They're called details, kid, and I did it without my phone."

"Yes, sir."

"Point is, Tusk said he and this Belasco had lunch. Well, there wasn't a single crumb on Tusk's shirt, or pants, when he'd gotten out of the car. And he sure didn't smell like he'd eaten anything.

"Ah." Dillard nodded.

Marchand dug for his car keys. "Come on. You've got some Googling to do."

"What about the semi and the truck, sir? The ones that got mauled out by the interstate."

"What about them?"

"Well—" Dillard chewed his stylus. "Sutton says they got pushed apart. Not rammed."

"He's an idiot."

"But he thought it was like that guy on YouTube, the one with the muggers."

Marchand chuckled. "You guys still on about that? It's a hoax, Dillard. There were no muggers. No one ever came forward to report a mugging, and no muggers came by to say they got thrown around an alley by… by what, the Force?"

Dillard's face went red, and he clammed up.

Marchand shook his head and went for the car. Flying muggers. Invisibly smacked cars. Mysterious gunfights.

He needed to lean on his informants.

Consolata Acciai stood just inside the doorway of the room, still as a statue. Her employer was in the middle of an important meeting. He had a lot of those. Normally Acciai could count on making her report and leaving before the boring minutiae started piling up. Meetings were lifeless wastes of time. She preferred her work done out in the streets, in the cars, in the corridors. Whether or not blood was shed, it was always invigorating, and she felt refreshed at the end of each assignment.

Except for this one. This one was a failure.

Her employer didn't take failure well.

The room was in a chained and locked warehouse in one of the foreclosed factories in Newport, on Drake City's east side. Like everything in Newport, it was streaked with rust, dirty, and poorly lit. Which worked well for illegal extracurricular activities. This room, an old foreman's office, was dark, owing to there being only one small window barely big enough for Acciai to fit her head out.

The square of light framed a short, stocky man in khakis, dark blue jacket and pale blue, pinstriped shirt. His face was red, either from exertion or drink, Acciai thought. The little hair he had was snow white and cut short. There was a glittering Rolex on his left wrist and a pair of gold rings on his right hand. His name was Danny Sheehan, and he ruled the Irish mob in Drake City with force that had blooded those rings many times.

"You know the terms of the deal," he said in a lilting accent that made him sound like he should be cheerful, when instead his face broadcast to the room that he'd like to kill someone. "I give you the shares, you give me my forward base of operations."

Sheehan drummed the fingers of his left hand on a manila folder.

"And I am, if nothing else, a man of my word," said Acciai's employer, his tones muddled by a voice modulator. All she could see was a shadowy figure, seated as far from the light as could be permitted. "Once I am satisfied the transfer of shares is complete, I will be able to move forward on the closing of the property."

"Yeah, you see, I'll be needing a wee bit more collateral than that." Sheehan grinned. "You said fifty grand."

"That I did." A briefcase slid across the floor, likely shoved by his employer's shoe. "Count it, if you like."

"No need for that." Sheehan picked it up. Inside was a mouth-watering pile of cash, nice green Benjamin Franklins. "You've never cheated me. That's why we do business well together."

"Indeed. And the papers?"

Sheehan snapped his fingers. "Lass. Take your master his part of the deal."

Lass? She'd killed thirty-seven people. Acciai took the folder off the desk and restrained her urge to put a .40 caliber slug through Sheehan's brain to make him thirty-eight. Who'd the fat Irish pig think he was? True, he controlled crime in most of Hull and Westerville. And there were two young blond men standing outside the door with automatic pistols under their coats. Acciai knew she'd be dead before she could savor the smell of his spilled blood.

She snatched the folder from Sheehan. He started. A thread of blood appeared on his finger. Acciai smiled. A hint of blood would have to do, for now.

She handed her employer the folder. A hand gloved in gray reached from the shadows and took it. Papers rustled. "Very good. You fulfilled your end of the bargain, or so it seems."

Sheehan clapped the briefcase shut. "It doesn't make any more sense to me, though. Mining's never been profitable in Drake City. Every wonder why there's so many abandoned holes in the ground beyond those cliffs? It wasn't lads at the beach digging with plastic shovels. Gold, silver, copper, even uranium—everyone's gone digging for something. And found nothing."

"I understand that Otte-Vaughn Corporation has sound reports about the availability of tungsten in several of the closed mines in the vicinity. Hence their interest in reopening exploration and exploitation."

Sheehan shrugged. "Whatever you say. All I know, I don't want those shares hanging 'round my neck anymore. You're welcome to them. Enjoy your six percent of the company."

"Thank you."

"Now. Your further part of our arrangement. Can't you move things along quicker?"

"No. The budget cycle ends June 30. Any action sooner than that on the part of the council will only arouse suspicions."

"What? Even if there were an accident?" Sheehan grinned. "I'm sure there's electrical problems in a building as run down as that."

"And you're that impatient? Arson will only draw unnecessary suspicion." Acciai's employer sounded like a teacher explaining arithmetic to a slow student for the third time, with no results. "Wait until after July 1. The new budget will be in place, the closing will happen, and you will have your foothold."

"You're right I will. Bloody Polacks, think they can step

across onto my neighborhood. Hull belongs to me." Sheehan pushed out his chair, the legs screeching. "If you've got nothing more…"

"No, I daresay I don't. Make certain of one thing. Do not cross me, Sheehan. If these documents are forged, I will find out." The voice, disguised as it was, brooked no argument.

Sheehan chuckled, a deep belly laugh. But Acciai thought it was too high-pitched, too boisterous to be a hundred percent mirth. "Don't you worry about that. We have a deal. We'll keep our end."

He left, slamming the door behind him. Acciai exhaled.

"Do not relax just yet, my loyal axe," her employer said. "We have your failures to discuss."

"I understand." Acciai stood firm. As much as this man frightened her, her ire overshadowed her anxiety. "But to be clear: you said this would be a simple escort. An escort, and possibly an execution. Instead, I get a maniac in a car who evades a half dozen of our interception—whom I'm assuming the Poles provided—and nearly run headlong into our own barricade."

"Which your target managed to avoid."

"Yeah, he did. You want to let me in on that trick?"

"I haven't the faintest idea what you mean."

Acciai chuckled. "I'm no fool. Not like that beer for brains Sheehan. The barricade was perfect. The semi was nose-to-nose with the other truck. That car got right up on them, and they parted like the Red Sea."

Her employer was quiet.

"You getting what I'm saying? Something made them move. Both drivers swear to their saints they didn't back off. And the way the one truck flipped up—" Acciai shook her head.

"None of that is your concern. I'm paying you well enough that you can ignore any irregularities. What I, however, cannot ignore is that the target is not standing here before me."

"He was stubborn. Wouldn't give up the jewelry."

"It is incredibly valuable."

"I got that. I also got that you didn't want the target dead yet

"I very much would like him to enter my employ, hence my desire to see him here, face-to-face."

The man stepped forward into the light. He wore a jacket and pants the color of smoke, boots a shade darker, and gloves. His face was obscured by a thick gray mesh, a mask that hid every inch of his flesh and hair. He must have been able to see through, but Acciai couldn't discern any features. It reminded her of a fencer's mask, only darker, dull instead of shiny. Weird, yes, that he shadowed his face and his hands. But stranger than previous clients? No. Few had engaged her interest for this long.

"Tell me about the man who shot at you, and this time, don't tell me how you failed at something."

Acciai felt a twinge in her chest. It passed quickly, so quickly she thought she'd imagined it. Angina? Impossible. "My height, older—50s, possibly 60. A good shot. He missed me on purpose, no doubt about it. Every squeeze of the trigger was tightly controlled. Amazing driver. Very Steve McQueen. Wish I'd had one like him on that pursuit."

"Did you find out his name?"

"Nothing. Guy's a ghost."

Her employer produced a phone, tapped a few keys, and held up a glowing image.

Acciai's mouth went dry. That was him. The image was blurry, taken from a distance, and the beard seemed thicker, darker. But the same guy. "How'd you get that?"

"His name is Frank Belasco. Watch him."

"I don't get paid to babysit. You want me to retrieve a necklace or whatever, fine. You want me to snatch someone, fine. But this just got way more expensive. It'd be a lot simpler if you'd let me put bullets in them." She relished the thought. "Two bullets each. Close up. Close enough to smell."

"I do not want the target dead. I cannot employ his talents if he is a corpse."

"You're assuming he'll work for you."

"You do."

Acciai snorted. This was getting ridiculous. "You owe me twenty grand more for this mess. You gave that much to Sheehan for stock in some defunct company with a crazy get-rich scheme in mind. You know, better make it thirty."

The employer sighed. "So disappointing. No vision in this generation."

Suddenly the twinge in Acciai's chest was back, this time as a full-on squeeze. She couldn't breathe. Her vision swam. When her legs buckled, she grabbed at the wall with her left hand for support. With the right, she drew her Springfield XD 40 with extended magazine and suppressor.

The throbbing increased. She could feel her heart struggling beneath her ribs, laboring to get blood to her brain and the rest of her body. Her lungs were starved for air. She had no grip left. The gun dropped.

"I very literally have your life in my hands, Consolata. An interesting name, by the way. Does it give you consolation now, as I squeeze your heart from the inside?" The employer stepped forward. "I purchased those six percent shares because they give me 53 percent, and thus majority control over the company. With that control, anything that comes out of those mines belongs to me. The same way the Polish criminal organization and the Irish mob are now both in my employ, without each other's knowledge. What I truly desire is for Brandon Tusk to make my acquaintance—and to bring the object which I sent you to retrieve with him."

Acciai couldn't see through the black splotches If she could just get to her gun—

"Enough discipline."

The pressure lifted. Acciai gasped, slumped back against the wall. Even as her vision cleared and her heart beat furiously, she scooped up her gun and fired. Ten shots.

The bullets all missed.

Not possible. She was only seven feet from her employer. There was no way she could have missed.

Yet, there were ten distinct glimmers in the floor, right in front of the man's shoes, grouped in a crater in the concrete. Dust motes sparkled.

"Don't be so stupid. You didn't need to threaten me. Or try to threaten. I will gladly pay you an extra five thousand, and it will be adequate. Won't it?"

Acciai nodded. She holstered her gun. The reasons for him staying in shadows and hiding his identity were suddenly abundantly clear. He had powers not to be trifled with. This was no mere *malocchio*—the evil eye—like her great-grandmother had warned about. *Bisnonna* terrified her with bedtime tales of dark magic and evil beings who ruled from the shade.

Acciai would tread carefully around this one. She had a feeling the next time she smelled blood in her employer's presence, it would be her own.

Chapter Seven

Everyone else was more upset by the shooting than I was. Sean especially. He didn't say much that afternoon or night, but he didn't go out. We stayed in, with me keeping a close watch on the guys the building owner sent over to replace the door pane.

Frank's gone off somewhere. I have no idea where he's staying. But there's a new phone in my pocket now, a nondescript cell phone that doesn't merit a "smart" prefix. "Call the preprogrammed number," he said. "There's only one on it. I'll catch up with you on Saturday."

The next morning, Sean is waiting awkwardly by the front door. He's got a note in his hand. "Here."

I read it. It's from his advisor, Mrs. Tanachion. Permission to stay home from school. Something about reducing mental strain and improving academics. I frown. "This is legitimate."

Sean rolls his eyes. "If we're walking, we're gonna be late."

"You—want to come to work with me."

He shrugs. "Mrs. T says I can do community work for Civics. It'll be good for my grades."

Since when does he care about those? I bite off that retort. "Okay. Sounds good."

First thing I do when we get to the library is give him the

task of pulling out any children's book that needs its spine label replaced. As soon as he starts yanking copies from the shelf, I call Mrs. Tanachion at school to double-check on his homework status.

"He spent both his study breaks and time after school in my classroom, getting caught up on his assignments," his teacher says. "Not sure what spurred this streak of responsibility in your son, Mr. Tusk, but keep it up."

I watch him thumb through a worn-out copy of Eric Carle's *The Very Hungry Caterpillar*. There's a smile lurking at the corners of his mouth. Wonder if he remembers when I read that to him, last time at age four.

The back door creaks open and bangs shut. "Brando! You're not dead. That's awesome." Reed's shaking his head, looking thoroughly disgusted with me as he storms down the hall.

Kelly brushes by him and hugs me, both arms around my chest. "You're not hurt!"

"Hey, yeah, I'm okay." I pat her on the back. This is not how I imagined touching her but it'll do nicely. Reed winks at me from behind and I give a thumbs-up.

"That's great to know, considering I had to find out my best friend's place had got shot up on the news this morning," Reed says. "You're lucky Caroline missed it. She'd have your head on the dinner table next."

"I'll bet." I look at Kelly. "I'm all right, really. Wasn't even there. Some gang fight that was in the wrong place, I guess."

"It doesn't mean I can't worry. How's Sean handling it?"

"See for yourself. I've got him on dirty book patrol."

Kelly smirks. "Dirty books? That's the wrong section."

"You know what I mean. Go check out your new intern."

She heads for Sean, who manages to unplug his earbuds from his head long enough to give a disinterested nod. Man. The kid is either totally in a funk or doing an excellent acting job pretending a hot girl isn't smiling at him.

"Hey. Brando." Reed's leaning against the desk. "I saw the news reports. The whole thing. You know, with the car chase that happened around the same time—and some funny business with a barricade that onlookers said moved apart. By itself."

"That's interesting."

"Uh-huh. Spill it."

I summarize the events as rapidly and in sotto voce. By the time I get to the diner, narratively speaking, his eyes are bulging. "Yikes."

"Yeah."

"Gal tried to kill you."

"Actually, she was trying to abduct me."

"For the medallion."

"Yep."

"And the guy. He knew about it?"

"Right."

"And said Samantha was—"

I glare at him and put a finger in front of my mouth. Kelley's chatting amiably with Sean, who's doing his best impression of a cathedral gargoyle. "Not a word. To anyone."

"Oh, no sweat, I got it." He grins. "Can't believe you moved those trucks.

"It was pretty great."

The front door opens. Vanchev, again? He's dressed more casually this time, that is, without a jacket and with his sleeves rolled up. The shirt's the same crisp white and the tie's striped red and blue, his pants coal black. He's smiling like he's won the lottery. "Good morning, folks. I have some tidings of good cheer."

"Mr. Vanchev, sir. A pleasure to see you again. I didn't know you were coming." Reed rapid-fires his words with the subtlety of an Uzi.

"You should have guessed, Mr. Andreen. I'm here to let you all know the *Harbor Messenger's* Suzanne DiStefano will run a feature on Hull Branch next week. Courtesy of Mr. Andreen's contact."

"That's great!" Reed blurts. He goes red in the neck, as if he remembers he should carry himself with greater decorum around the library system director. "I hadn't heard anything back from Suze."

"Apparently her editor was mulling the idea over. It took a call from a city official to convince him the merits of the story," Vanchev says. "That coupled with the article I provided on the proposed cuts. Which helped him scoop the other media in town, of course."

"We'll make sure everything goes smoothly," I say. "Don't worry about it."

"Oh, I'm not. I requested additional police presence in our neighborhood, for what seems like the umpteenth time, but to no avail." Vanchev shakes his head. "The police are stretched too thin and there's too many lining their pockets."

I glance at Reed, expecting a cutting comment about Dennis, but none is forthcoming. I'm also wondering the cost of getting my bike back from impound. There'll be some fee, legal or otherwise.

"Too bad we can't hire the man who tossed the muggers to clean things up," Reed says. "The Poles wouldn't know what hit them."

I glare at Reed. His expression is impassive, but I know him well enough to glimpse the mischief behind those eyes.

"It sounds like a con artist to me," Vanchev says. "There's better ways to improve our communities than relying on a supposed vigilante—and again, I think that video is nothing but a convincing forgery." His cell phone beeps. "Sorry, I must be going. I'm on my way to a meeting with the library foundation. If you gentlemen have other ideas, we can use to bolster my position, don't hesitate to contact me."

He's out the door, talking in hushed tones into his phone.

Reed shakes his head.

"What?"

"I've got to prepare for the interview. Suze is detail-oriented."

"At least you like to talk." I scowl. "Though sometimes you say too much."

"Couldn't help it. That is your plan, right? To put the smack on crime?"

"If I can." Frank's commentary about the Garrison and the Ashen, about secret societies warring for control, Samantha's role, swirls inside my head. "I've got to get better at this first."

Saturday dawns overcast and cool. Rain's in the forecast, 30 percent chance. Sean and I say nothing to each other over breakfast. His mouth is full of waffle and his face glued to his phone. I'm likewise enamored with Friday's *Messenger*. There's a brief mention of the YouTube video, with the police chief calling it a hoax. Shocker. But it's a relief.

Don't need anyone nosing around, especially after the shooting.

"Hey Dad. Check this out." Sean's voice is full of eagerness. He's got the phone in my face. "Dad. Look."

"Hmm?" I look up, and freeze staring at the playback of the semi and SUV flying apart. It's grainy, but it's daylight. No mistaking what I'm seeing.

"He was there again! I know it!" Sean's beaming. "That guy who stopped the muggers!"

"Where was that?"

"Out on Broad Street. Some shoot out, probably gangs. That's what the cops said. There's a story on the *Messenger's* site. Someone dropped the video on their Twitter feed." He grins. Looks a lot like mine. "But you should see it. The comments, everyone's calling this guy superhero."

"It was probably a malfunction in the brakes or the gas, Sean. The person wasn't even in those shots."

Sean rolls his eyes. "No way. He's out there. He has to be."

I've got nothing else to add besides blurting *It was me!* so I keep my mouth shut.

The door buzzer sounds. Sean gets the intercom. "Yo."

"Hey, it's Frank. Is Brandon there?"

Sean gives me a look that says, *Who's Frank?*

"One of Mom's cousins," I say. "Old friend of mine."

He ambles back to his seat without another word.

I meet Frank at the new front door. Still has the manufacturer's stickers in the corner. "What are you doing here?"

"We're starting your training this morning." He's wearing jeans and a black coat, zipped up. The Subaru's parked out by the curb, in the proper direction.

"Right now."

"Yep. Good thing you're showered and dressed. Less to explain to your son if it looks like you had this planned all along."

"Look, I was going to—"

"No, you weren't. Throw on something warm. You have three minutes."

I go back up, yank off my T-shirt and pull over an Under Armour long sleeve instead. On my way by the kitchen, I grab my dark blue fleece off the chair. "Sean, Frank and I are heading out. Going to take a drive, show him around the city."

"Whatever. I'm going to Tucker's and the comic book store."

Well, that means he'll be within a four-block radius of home, on the nicer side of town. Then again, I thought here was the nicer side of town and I was shot at yesterday. "When will you be back?"

"When will *you* be back?"

"Never mind. Call me if you need anything. I'll be back by lunch."

"Have a fun date," he mutters.

Airfoil: Origins

"Sean."

He looks over his shoulder at me.

"Let's go for a bike ride sometime, you and me, out by the boardwalk."

He shrugs, turns back to the solace of his phone. "Maybe."

I'll take maybe.

Frank drives us up into the Vista neighborhood, curving along the east slopes of Mount Stafford. About halfway up he turns onto a poorly marked fire road. The ritzy homes get left behind, and thick forests of pine replace them. The only sounds are the hum of the Subaru's engine and the crunch of the tires on dirt and gravel.

"Made the Internet again," I say.

Frank grumbles something unintelligible.

"Hey, that was your fault, remember?"

"That's irrelevant. The point is you're supposed to conduct low profile missions for us. If the Ashen hadn't intervened in your calling, there wouldn't have been a need for it."

The fire road is unmarked and more overgrown with ferns the higher up we drive. Lush green branches form barricades to either side; a strip of milky gray sky is the illumination. I shift in my seat. I'm far too hot in this weather but Frank insisted on warmer clothing and boots. I wasn't about to argue.

After ten minutes, the ferns, having grown thicker, suddenly drop off. I stare at a rusty chain stretched across the road. And I do mean road. There's asphalt stretching up a quarter mile, disappearing under a canopy of broad oaks. It looks old, pale, but not crumbling.

"Hold on." Frank puts the car in park. He gets out, unhooks the chain. A pitted metal signs says, "PRIVATE PROPERTY— NO TRESPASSING." He gets back in. We roll forward, and Frank stops again so he can put the chain back in place before we head off.

The tires hiss softly on the pavement. The canopy shades us for a while. I glance about. "What is this place?"

Frank doesn't answer. He just points ahead.

The Subaru rounds a bend, back into the daylight. The road widens out into a rough, paved area, stretching out a half mile beyond and quarter mile wide. There are six rusted buildings hiding amongst the overgrowth at the edge of the forest. Ugly orange streaks of rust drip down flaking gray paint. The tallest building s only a skeleton of girders. Two more are squat cubes, each two stories tall, their windows shattered and vacant. Most striking are three octagonal towers, three stories tall, with rickety metal staircases winding up the bases. The tops are flat, as if the rest of the structure was shorn off.

Frank kills the engine. "Welcome to your training base."

I'm already getting out of the car, tripping over my feet, gawking at the silent spectacle around me. The chill mountain air feathers my breath. "I know this. I've read about it. The U.S. Air Force built a radar installation on the northwest side of Mount Stafford, in the mid-1950s. It was barely up and running for a decade."

Frank chuckles. "You're one of a handful who know that. The old lady I bought the property from had the whole history."

"It's fascinating." I'm walking slowly, picking my way over discarded corrugated metal siding, taking care to avoid jagged, rusty edges as common as the weeds cracking through the concrete. Behind me, the trunk of the car opens and then slams shut a moment later. "You know, I picked up a book at the main library a while back and they had just a paragraph's worth of information…" My babble trails off. "Wait. You bought this?"

"Every last square foot." Frank passes me his smartphone. Glowing text informs me—courtesy of the Drake City Records Office—that one F.L. Brickwell purchased the property from the Cyr estate. The date imprinted in one corner was November.

"How did you know?"

"I believe in planning ahead. Thus far, the Garrison agrees with me." Frank's got a duffel bag, navy blue. He nudges it with his knee. "Come on."

We hike to the nearest tower. I hesitate, eyeing the rusted metal steps.

Frank gestures. "Don't worry. They're fine. Installed them myself as soon as the snow melted. Painted 'em, too." He clambers up.

I'm right behind him. He's not kidding. They're as sturdy as the stone front porch of my apartment building. At the top, I see the tower's roof—or the floor of the huge, white radar dome that used to cover it—has long since collapsed. Deep shadows fill the space below. It's thick with structural debris. A trio of doves springs into flight, their coos echoing.

All along the edge of the tower is a six-foot-wide walkway. There's a lot of bounce to the metal grating. But the vantage from up here distracts me—thick carpet of green forest and gray rock spreading out to the north and northwest. A white ribbon of interstate slices through off to the west, barely a thread in the distance. A few scattered homes and subdivisions break up Nature with sharp lines. It's cloudy and gray above, thick clouds scudding along from the coast. Behind us, the peak of Mount Stafford blocks the view to the south and east.

"All right. Put this on." Frank drops the duffel bag on the walkway with a resonant bang and unzips it. He hands me a black object.

"A mask."

"For paintball. I've modified it appropriately." He helps me fit it, pulling it down and strapping something thick around my throat. There's a cap attached to the top that pulls down over the ears. The whole contraption stays snug all over my head, face, and chin. Something rubs under my chin and another object presses to the side of my skull over my left ear.

"How's the visibility?"

"Decent." The lenses are smoky brown, tinted. "What's the lump under my chin?"

"Two things. There's a tiny pressurized oxygen supply—in case you have to go really high. Wouldn't recommend it, because you'll freeze your balls off first. The other is a throat microphone. Laryngophone, technically, because it translates the vibrations from you yakking through a transducer into sound. There's a speaker pressed to your noggin, too."

"Yeah, I feel that."

"Test it." He walks a dozen paces, then talks into his phone. "One, two."

The words buzz right into my head, like he's speaking next to me. "Perfect. Okay, then?"

Frank nods. He gets something else out of the duffle bag, a very rugged tablet. The thing's fourteen inches across and locked in a thick plastic casing studded with rubber. "Let me check your GPS transmitter and bring up the local radar."

"Radar?"

"Sure. I've got to keep track of aircraft somehow when you're out of visual range. You don't want to fly into a turbine intake. Sennebec County International Airport has an excellent array."

"Okay." I cinch up the collar of my fleece. The Under Armour is still too warm, even in the cool morning air.

"All right. Stand by." He puts a Bluetooth over his right ear. "Volume check."

"Sounds good. Where's the on/off switch?"

"Over your left ear."

I touch the mask. This is one fancy piece of gear. A laugh escapes me.

"What's so funny?"

"This get-up. Do you really carry it around hoping the next medallion holder's going to say yes? What would you have done with it if I'd said no?"

"Brandon, no one ever says no."

That shuts me up.

"Step to the edge."

I plant my boots at the rim of the walkway. It's a 20 foot drop to the concrete. Another thirty feet away is a steep cliff to the forest below.

"You good?"

"Yeah."

"Not afraid of heights?"

"No different than standing on the front step."

"Okay. So, here's the deal: the field. You know what you need to do to form one. You know how to exert the field to manipulate objects."

"Got it."

"This is no different. You're manipulating yourself, though, so it requires more finesse, because you don't want to smack yourself around."

The field. I can see it in my mind's eye. A vague, shimmering bubble, indistinct and flowing. Like a soap bubble that's being squeezed without popping.

"Visualizing the field? Good. You're an artist. You paint your own stuff. Do the same here. You see the field around you, and you will it to do what you want. Some people see wings. Others, rockets. It's up to you."

Right. Imagine. I can feel the field forming around me, even as I cast about for a picture. The medallion grows colder, and heavier, burning frost against my chest. I could see it in my head, when I'd moved things before: a huge fist or shoving hands. That's how I hit the trucks and the muggers. I blow out a breath. Wings. Rockets. Doable.

My mind keeps drifting to superheroes, thanks to Reed's influence. Lots of them fly. Who're his favorites? The guy in the robot suit. Iron Man. He has rocket boosters on his hands and feet. We watched that movie with Robert Downey Jr., great actor. That's as good an image as any.

Okay. Let's do this.

Force slams me upward. My stomach lurches. I'm fifty feet straight up in an instant. My arms flail and legs kick awkwardly. Those imaginary rockets whip me around, throwing me onto my side.

Shut them off!

I plummet.

"Catcher's mitt! Pillow!" Frank's voice hammers inside my head.

Pillow. Big one. I slam into a field of gravity reduced to a tenth of normal. Pound into nothing visible, just four feet from the walkway. My body sinks slowly the last inches, and my butt bangs against the metal grating.

Frank's laughing, a full-on belly-shaker. There're tears at the corners of his eyes.

"Yeah, hysterical," I mutter, brushing off my pants.

"Brandon, the first time always goes like this. That was by far one of the best—and by best, I mean most ridiculous looking. You were spinning around like a top."

I snort. "I got off the ground, didn't I?"

"Sure did. That's why I'm not reaming you out for being an idiot. Hey, you didn't scream like a toddler. That happens."

"Controlling the medallion is not just about your mind—it's your body. The whole thing works together. Whatever strength you have is amplified. The stronger your body and mind together, the more formidable." Frank waves his hand as if brushing away a fly. "Go again."

I roll out a kink in my neck. Rockets again, this time throttled back. I burst from the ground, but keep myself locked in place 20 feet up, wobbling. My hands stretch out to either side, acting as stabilizers, as I conform the field to match the image of thrusters streaming from each palm. It works—no shooting off out of control, no falling to the ground.

"Getting better," Frank says.

My heart's pounding with sheer exhilaration.

"Not going to puke, are you?"

My stomach's churning, but I ignore it easily. "Nope."

"Good. Quit floating around and put on some speed."

"Okay." Increasing thrust. The sudden leap jolts my bones. Higher, faster. Wind rushes by in a roar but doesn't buffet my body. The field's handiwork, I assume. The tops of trees compress into a flawless sea of green with gray islands.

"That's it. Keep it steady. Good." Frank could be reading the financial pages of the *Harbor Messenger* newspaper as calm as he sounds. "If you're done going in one direction, angle your trajectory into something more horizontal."

"Copy that."

"Don't say 'copy,' Brandon. You sound like an idiot."

I scowl. Angle my trajectory, without falling on my face from—how high up am I anyway? The radar buildings are cardboard boxes, Frank an action figure discarded atop them.

Carefully, I spread my arms wider, keeping my legs clamped together. I bend my feet back, slowly, picturing the imaginary rocket thrust tipping upward. Simultaneously, I cup my hands away from my body. The force propels me in an arc that drops me like an invisible roller coaster. I rotate my hands back and adjust my feet. From below, my flight path resembles that of a drunk navigating Hull Avenue, but I am going forward now, curving upward.

"That did it. Sloppy, but you made it happen."

He has to have done this before. As I level out my flight, I wonder, is this how he dealt with Samantha? Was he nicer to her because she was a woman? Or harder on her?

Now, I clip along among the lowest clouds, marveling that they're so close, and I wish Samantha was here with me. My gloved fingers brush through the nearest patch of white. They come away damp.

I'm flying. It sounds childish. I've been on airplanes. But this is far different. This is my body soaring through the sky, with nothing but the warping of the planet's gravitational pull holding me aloft. A grin accompanies the realization.

There's hardly any buffeting by the wind, even this high up, and when I bounce suddenly over what feels like a pothole in the air I realize why. "Frank?"

"How're you doing up there?"

"The field keeps me shielded from the wind, doesn't it? I feel turbulence, not bad, but I'm not nearly as tossed about as I figured—not as cold, either."

"Bingo. The airflow around you doesn't adhere to your body. It's the shape of the field that interacts with the wind. Like an airplane's wing, an airfoil shape that provides lift." It's strange having his voice as clear in my head, as if we were still talking in the diner. "Funny thing is the field molds itself to your body on the inside of that shape. Helps insulate you, cuts down on vibration and impacts. Not sure why."

"Someone has to know."

"Did you think about protecting yourself inside the field?"

"No."

"No one else does either. It's something the medallion does itself. For as long as we've had these things, very little research has unlocked their secrets. But we've figured out enough over the years to make them more than serviceable. Now if you're done worrying about your pleasure cruising, bank up into the clouds."

The mass of cottony white nimbus over my head looks impenetrable. They're low-hanging, with dark gray bottoms heavy with imminent rain. "How's my flight path? Clear of aircraft?"

Frank snorts, creating a burst of static. "No, there's an inbound 737 from Chicago to SCIA that I'm directing your thick head toward so you can splat on its bottom like a bug on my windshield. Yes, it's clear. Get up there."

"Roger that."

He grumbles again. I keep my chuckle quiet.

One deep breath later, I twist my hands and feet, arch my back, and shoot up like a champagne cork into the bottom of the cloud bank.

Everything goes white. I could be a kid again, under a bed sheet at home, playing hide and seek with my brother. The field keeps me somewhat warm, but water beads along the edges of my fleece. The air's cold, damp—I can feel it just beyond the fringes of the field, which aren't solid like I expected, but hazy. Comfort envelopes me, and I'm thankful I can see the inside of a place no man has seen outside of an aircraft.

How long have I been in here? I don't dare look at my watch. Shifting my wrist will spin me in circles, and with zero visibility, that would be dangerous. Frank says there are no planes near, but he also didn't define "near." "Frank, what's my speed?"

"A hair more than 120 mph. Not too shabby."

A hundred and twenty miles per hour. I smile. Let's top that. I feed more thrust into my hands and feet. The cloud's curves blur past faster.

The white gets brighter. My childhood rushes back. Daniel's found me. He turns on the light in our bedroom.

I break through the upper layer of the clouds into brilliant blue sky. Huge towers of cloud surround me, great burly white sentinels. I can't catch my breath. This is beautiful. This is how I've always dreamed the throne of God will appear.

When my words come back, I whisper, "You'd think this was amazing, Samantha. I hope you can see it."

"Everything okay up there? Thought you said something."

"No, ah, I'm good." I slow my imaginary thrusters until I'm hovering steady among the titanic clouds. Nothing up here but me and the angels—no planes, no birds. The rumble of wind and the rush of my breath are the only sounds.

"It's one of a kind, Brandon," Frank murmurs. "You never forget it."

"I take it you miss it. You've been up."

"Of course I miss it. When I flew—well, forget it. Past is past. I'm not going back up." He's silent for such a long time I think the radio's failed, until he says, "Your altitude is three thousand eighty feet."

A wave of vertigo washes over me. Deep breaths. I look down. The clouds are close below my feet, drifting slowly along. The dizziness passes. The sensation that I can walk on the clouds is an illusion, but it's comforting nonetheless.

"Anytime you're done sightseeing, I want you to take a spin south. Come down below the cloud cover but stay near it. Get your bearings there."

My hands angle, putting me into a slow rotation. What a view. "Fancy helmet and no compass, Frank?"

"There's room for modifications. Let's move. Don't dawdle at 120 this time."

"No problem." I shift my imaginary rockets and, with a drop that's accompanied by a spike of adrenaline, dive down into the clouds. "I want to see how fast I can go."

# **Chapter Eight**

My speed tops three hundred.
That's the best I can manage before I get distracted by the increased buffeting of wind currents and almost lose control. One rollover and another spell of dizziness later, I'm gasping. *Slow up. Take it steady.*

Soaring east, I watch Drake City sprawl beneath me, a grid of silver and gray latched onto the coast. Suburbs stretch across the interstate to the west, jagged teeth of loading docks jut into Sculpin Bay. Neighborhoods cling to the edge of the Great Stone River, stuck between the cliffs below Mount Stafford and the blue ribbon of water. Newport, Drake City's industrial offspring, looks grungier and darker than its parent even from up here. Tiny wisps of steam and smoke ripple from factories on the east side of the river. The neighborhood ends abruptly at Van Buren Cliffs and Burnt Clearing State Forest, an unbroken stretch of wilderness hemming in Drake City.

I've seen it before, while returning from vacation, but never like this. Never at my own leisure, without an airplane's fuselage between me and the sky.

Frank guides me away from air traffic, and I cruise into the fog closer to the waterfront. Fortunately, there's not much about today in the way of aircraft. It's also becoming easier to adjust my course and vary my speed. In just a half hour, Frank puts me through various maneuvers, stalls and bursts of acceleration.

Hopefully SCIA radar doesn't spot me—or if it does, considers me nothing more extraordinary than a large vulture.

"You're getting the hang of this," Frank says. "Take a loop out over the cape, and let's call it good for today."

"Okay." Turning north, I spot a smattering of boats. The tops of the long container vessels are a patchwork of tiny, colorful rectangles. The solitary white arrowhead of the ferry from Rittenhouse Island and gaggles of sailboats cluster here and there, from Braddock Island Light all the way around the Cape, stretching for several miles. One of the sailboats has a red hull with a white stripe that arcs across the keel—

Wait a minute. The keel is at the very bottom of the hull. There's no way I should be able to see it. Unless it's capsized.

There's a tiny white splash, a constant flurry of motion in the water about a quarter mile away from the sailboat. It's difficult to tell from this distance, but it looks like someone's gone overboard.

"Brandon, keep an eye toward the sun. It'll burn off the fog soon enough, and you'll be out in the open."

"Got it. Frank, there's a capsized sailboat off Cape Ashwin, about two miles from Ashwin Light."

"Coast Guard will get it. Come on back to the barn."

I start to turn, but only get halfway around. USCG Base, Rittenhouse Island, is several miles away. They should be able to rescue the sailor. But the water has to be frigid; April or not, it's still steeped with cold from the winter ice. And what if the person's injured? Or unable to swim.

What if it's a kid?

Instantly, I see Sean flailing in the water, swallowing a lung full of ocean as he gasps for air.

I barrel roll back onto my original heading and do it without losing speed or bearing. A thrill races through my chest. "There won't be time. I'm going help them."

"No. You return, right now, Brandon. The Garrison requires specific and controlled missions for its medallion holders. I'm not training you to be a lifeguard. Return to the barn, immediately."

"Tough luck, Frank." The wind's roaring by my helmet as I plummet. My heart hammers, and a small corner of my brain, way in the back, cautions me against doing anything rash. But there's not a chance I'm slowing down.

"Turn around this second or—!"

I slap the side of the helmet, killing the radio signal. The inside of my head lapses into wonderful silence.

The waves grow nearer, larger, white caps flickering. The person in distress is still a way off, but details emerge. Blond hair, pale arms, red clothing. There's a tiny orange circle. A life preserver. It looks too far away from the person to be any use.

The person is caught in the current sweeping up the coast. The *Messenger's* always running stories about hapless swimmers getting swept away when they misjudge the ocean's pull.

Speaking of misjudging, I need to slow down. I visualize flaps on an airplane's wings, morphing into a generic, broad surface acting as air brakes, and reduce the imaginary thrust from my hands and feet. My momentum slows. Good.

Now to get them out of the water.

It is a woman. I can see a small face now, mouth wide open. A faint scream reaches my ears. Without getting distracted, I focus on making a controlled descent. How to do this? If I stop to hover, like I did in the clouds, I'll have to use my hands to pick her up, unless she grabs onto my legs. But that will make landing again awkward.

Maybe I can extend the field around her, away from myself. Let's see—make it like a bubble being pinched in half, so that it stays connected by—

It's a bad idea. Instantly my flight turns into a dead drop.

There are rocks that fall more gracefully. I force my head to stay calm, not panic. Just reform the field, light those rockets.

That's better. I level out for a couple seconds, satisfying myself that the field is intact, then arc downward again.

The water's near. I give my trajectory a bend so that it brings me within ten feet of the sloshing waves. It's close enough to launch twin sprays to my side.

The woman's only a few hundred yards off. Her screaming's louder now. Any shouts I could give to reassure her would be pointless with the mask muzzling me. Every few seconds, I see her blonde head, hair slicked to her scalp, bob through the trough of a wave.

Too many variables. Don't know how fast I have to be going to stay aloft. Don't know my exact speed—if I grab her arms doing a three hundred, I'll kill her. Probably myself, also. I find myself wishing I'd had more training.

Frank's protests pop up again in my memory. That quashes any doubt. No. He'd have left her here, likely to drown. I can't. I *won't*.

I'm so near the water now my clothes are getting damp. Her eyes are wide as she spots me from a hundred yards away. Can't imagine what she's thinking. Likely, *Don't let me drown!* Or even, *Is that guy flying? Am I seeing things?*

I slow as much as I dare. Sure enough, I start bumping along. Barely staying in flight. Come on, come on. My hands skim the water, cutting channels with the field, then dip in. That really ratchets up the jouncing around, shutting off my imaginary hand rockets. Only the feet keeping me going now. But I'm dead set on that picture of an airplane wing. An airfoil, Frank said.

Fifty feet away.

The field maintains its form. I make sure to fix the thought firmly in my mind: Can't be solid. Have to reach through the field and carry her.

Almost there...

Her hands shoot up suddenly from the deep dark of the bay water.

"Hold on!" No time to tell if she's heard me. I'm right on top of her.

I grab for her arms and pray for us both. Flick the field off, pull!

My hands connect with skin, and I grasp with all my strength. She latches on, with a good grip, but her fingers are slick and soaked.

Flick the field on—less than a second off. I stutter in the air, stagger on my boosters, and pull up. Our ascent is achingly slow. I grimace and drag her up toward my chest, closer into my body—

And just like that, she weighs less than Sean did when he was five. She slaps against me with a sodden *whump*, surprising us both. Her arms loop around my neck and she buries her head in my shoulders, shaking with sobs.

The field. It must be enveloping both of us, reducing gravity's pull on her just as much as it's reduced on me. No sweat.

Stop talking and start flying.

I soar up and over toward land, making sure the mental image of the field encircling us both is still in place while simultaneously keeping the wings out and the rockets going. It'd be a much more stable flight with both hands, though. So, I make sure her grip is tight around me before letting go and "igniting" those hand thrusters.

Perfect. Much smoother.

She starts screaming.

Vibrates right through my helmet and makes concentrating arduous.

But I'm still grinning behind the mask.

That's when I see Ashwin Light growing huge ahead. I can't be a quarter mile from the white tower with its triple band of black stripes.

I'm coming up on it far too fast. In all the excitement of pulling the woman from the water and carrying her off, I must have increased my speed—well, by a lot.

With only two hundred yards to spare before the green grass and black stone rises up to meet us, I hurriedly instruct the field to slow us. It reacts, with more efficiency than I intended. In my momentary panic, the image of a sudden stop gets through my thoughts.

We tumble toward the rocky ledges between the lighthouse and the coast.

The woman's screaming gets worse. She flails at me, in full terror. I forget the hand rockets, grab her arms and fold them in against me. "We're almost there! Hang on!" I roll us over, reform the field as an even bigger wing, and try for that pillow again.

Not enough time. My back hits dirt, blowing the air from my lungs, and I see a balloon popping instead of a pillow cushioning our fall. So that's what the field does. I'm up again, flying ever so briefly, before slamming down again, and we both go tumbling over the field. Blueberry bushes rake at our clothing.

Finally, we skid to a stop a foot from a looming gray rock, four feet tall and as big around as a Toyota. She stops screaming, but she's breathing fast and hard. Her breasts press into my chest as she heaves. All I need now is for her to hyperventilate and pass out.

She stares into my helmet visor. Her eyes are a hypnotic, pale blue with pupils rimmed in bright green. Stars within skies. "You... you can let me...up, please," she stammers.

Right. She's laying atop me, an entirely comfortable position as far as I'm concerned. My back doesn't even hurt, though it will later. I release my grip, uncurling my fingers from their death hold on her body. She backs off, staggers a few steps, and sinks to her knees.

I roll over onto my side. Inventory: no major injuries, mercifully. The pain starts working its way up from my lower back.

My shoulders are scraped, and there's blood visible through tears at either seam. The backs of my legs burn. But the mask's in place, helmet's undented, and I'm otherwise unscathed. Miracle, considering the brown gouge in the grass we left for sixty feet stretching out toward the ledge.

We're near a picket fence that looks like it's lost its paint to the frequent storms and sea spray. The ledge drops off two hundred feet to ocean waves that slap and slosh at its base. Seagulls wheel overhead, black arcs on a slate sky. One big gull alights on the nearest fence post as easy as a man walks down the street, and starts up that familiar, grating cackle.

Show off.

"You... you saved m-me." I finally get a good look at the woman, besides the close up of her eyes. She has long blonde hair, soaked dark and dripping all over, hanging in streams over her face and shoulders. She's wearing a long-sleeved red shirt and khaki shorts, both of which cling to her like plastic wrap. Thin, but not waif skinny. Stunning curves.

I instantly get to my feet and straighten my posture. "I had to help. You were in trouble."

She's shivering so bad her legs shake. I unzip my fleece, revealing the Under Armour shirt beneath, and wrap it around her shoulders. "Here. You need to get warm."

Next thing I know, she kisses me, a brief peck on the face, then laughs. "Why don't you move the mask out of the way?"

"That's a problem I can fix." I reach for the bottom of my helmet and pull up.

Suddenly, there're voices behind us. A handful of people run over from beyond the fence. I spot emergency lights flashing in the gaps between the trees, coming from the parking lot. Police, fire, or ambulance. Likely all three. That was fast response time—probably were en route when they first got word of the capsized boat.

I have to get back. Frank's probably freaked out of his mind by now. I jerk the mask back down and turn.

"Wait!" She grabs my arm. "My name is Alicia."

"Ma'am, I have to go." I step up onto the big rock right by us. Time to turn the field back on.

"But who are you?"

"Just a guy who serves others," I say, and nod to her. With a visualized boost of invisible rockets, I leap off the rock and soar off in a rising arc.

Really? That's my line? I shake my head.

Within seconds she's a red spot on a green blanket, with more figures in dark clothing joining her. There's a pair of police cars, a fire engine, and an ambulance in the parking lot of the lighthouse site. Farther off, a bright white Coast Guard boat, its twin orange stripes visible even a mile off, races toward Cape Ashwin with a huge trail of spray following.

My heart's swollen enough to burst through my ribs. A successful rescue. No one hurt. Most excellent.

Too bad I didn't get Alicia's number.

Frank's still at the abandoned base. I spot his car from the air, then come in low over the treetops. He's standing atop the same radar post.

Okay, Frank. Watch this.

I roll over twice and come down quickly onto the walkway. The thrust cuts out a second before I touch down, my boots banging onto the metal framework.

I pull the helmet off. My arms are cold, my head's sweaty, and I'm grinning. "Pretty good, right?"

Frank scowls and uncrosses his arms to poke me hard in the chest. "You screwed up, Brandon. Don't let it happen again."

He stomps over to his bag, starts rooting through it like a dog angry it can't find the bone it buried.

I stare after him, holding my helmet, considering if I can

bean him with it before he fights back. "Are you serious? I just rescued a woman from drowning."

"Bet she was hot."

"Well, yeah, she was. Look, are you mad because I cut off the radio? I didn't want to get dragged into an argument, not with her in danger."

"Oh, no, that was fine," Frank says, increasing the ferocity of his rummaging. "I like it when my trainees cut off contact in the midst of a daylight appearance that I didn't authorize in front of potentially dozens of witnesses."

"You wanted me to fly. I did that. Don't you guys have protocols in place?"

"For covert flight, yes, not public rescues! That's not your role."

"She needed my help."

"Not your problem." Frank waves his hands skyward. "What am I supposed to do with you if choppers start flooding the air, looking for a flying man? You're lucky the emergency frequencies are treating it like a joke."

"Look, I'm sorry I broke your rules, but seeing as how you're training me to handle this immense power, maybe we can skip the panic and reinforce what else I'm supposed to know."

Frank glowers at me until I'm almost certain he's going to take a swing, but instead he resumes digging in his bag. "Training. Fine. Let's deal with what happens if someone does decide to come after you."

He finally comes up with another weapon. There's a magazine in the other hand; he locks it in, and the thing's long enough it has to hold at least 30 rounds. "Steyer TMP automatic pistol." Without another word he sets it on the walkway, safety engaged. Then he unzips his jacket and removes a second gun. "We need to teach you a necessary defense mechanism."

I'm staring at the pistol. The gun he used in the pursuit. Except this time, it's aimed at me. "Ah, Frank...?"

"You can deflect bullets. The field created by the medallion manipulates gravity, right?"

"Right. Wait. If I deflect bullets, they'll ricochet all over the place. Hit a whole lot more people."

"If it were as simple as holding up a shield in front of your face, then yes, it would injure bystanders. But not this way. We're talking about a thin shell that surrounds you, in which the pull of gravity is dozens of times stronger." He flicks off the safety on the Nighthawk. "Let's try it."

"Hey, are you going to give me pointers or what?"

"You visualize what I just told you Brandon, and you make it happen," Frank says sternly, "Just like when you flew. Come on. Forty-five minutes ago, you fell flat when you tried to jump up off this thing. You progressed to rescuing a woman from drowning. I'd say you can handle it."

Okay. Visualize what the man said. "A shell. Heavier gravity inside."

"In a layer, Brandon, not inside, or you'll smash yourself flat. You got it?"

"Yeah, I've got it." I close my eyes, imagine a cocoon of light enveloping me.

"Good. Live fire exercise in three seconds."

"What?" My eyes fly open. He really is aiming the gun square at my face, though he's backed up to twenty feet. "Hold on!"

"Three."

Okay. Focus. Form the shield. I think it's working, but how do I tell?

"Two."

"Frank!" I'm going to find out real soon. Better get it right.

"One."

The gunshot booms, echoing out over the empty base. A burst of sparks a foot from my face startles me, like a camera flash on the tip of my nose. Two more sounds: the *clink* of the empty casing on the walkway and another, harder *bang*.

Frank's smiling. "Well done."

My heart's racing, hands shaking. "You're insane."

"Nope. Thorough. Never had a student get his or her head blown off in this part, so I must know what I'm doing. Now." He holsters the gun and points to a spot in front of my feet. "See what I mean?"

There's a glint of copper in a small crater now dug in the walkway. The bullet he fired is smashed flat as a wafer. "Wow."

He nods. "Ready for Round Two?"

Instantly, I know what he has in mind. "Yeah. I'm ready."

"Good." He sweeps up the Steyr, steadies it in a two-handed grip, and squeezes the trigger.

I flinch at the explosion from its muzzle. A deafening chatter makes it impossible to hear anything else. Sparks batter the shield, scattering across its invisible surface. Thirty bullets later, the magazine is dry, and my ears clear out enough to hear a new sound.

Laughter. Coming from me.

Frank's chuckling, too. "Pretty spectacular, isn't it."

"Are you kidding? Flying and shields?" Reed would crap his shorts.

"Round three?"

"Hell, yes."

"Good. This time, we combine the two. Your targets aren't going to stand still. You shouldn't either, though it's highly amusing to stand there, taking shot after shot, without them making a scratch. You want to see a bully get scared? Watch him unload a full magazine from an M4A1 into your chest while you look as bored as a man waiting for his wife to finish shopping."

I can see that, and also remember it. Seemed like Samantha would be in those dressing rooms for hours "Was Samantha—well, did she do good?"

"She was an exceptional trainee."

"No. Not just that. I mean, at this." I tug the medallion out from under my shirt and hold it up. It's freezing cold.

Frank nods, understanding apparent in the softening of his features. "She was one of the best, Brandon. Never doubt that."

Okay. I can live with that. "Thanks. So, target in motion."

Frank slams home a new magazine.

I put up the shield instantly, and he opens fire. This time, the blast catches me by surprise, so much so that I involuntarily duck. By the time I put my arm down from in front of my face, he's gone.

Footsteps bang down the stairs. I grin. Hunter and prey.

With a shift to the reliable, imaginary rockets, I hop up off the walkway, soaring a hundred feet up and around to my right. There he is, sprinting flat out across the concrete. I barely have time to note his surprising agility when he turns and shoots.

Without hesitation, I put up the shield—and fall from the sky.

"No no no!" Drop the shield. Go with the rockets. Do it!

I hit a tree. A short, stubby pine. Ram is a better word. The impact rattles my brain and dusts me all over with pine needles. I'm stuck grappling in the limbs. But my shields up. Moron.

"Got to multitask, there, Brandon!" Frank's voice taunts me.

Where's he gone? Can't see him from here. Nowhere near the spot where I first saw him.

I grit my teeth. Multitask is right. Watch this.

With a sharp burst, I fly horizontally out from the tree, ten feet off the ground. Brown pine needles spray up around me. Frank's ahead, bolting between an old barracks and a half-collapsed office structure. Funny thing: the images of flight on which I've been concentrating are hazy, less distinct, and it's as if I can tuck them off to the side of my consciousness. So I cautiously bring up the shield again, making sure it surrounds me head to toe.

I don't fall. That's good.

Frank's attack explodes from my right, not from the barracks ahead I'd expected. He must have doubled back. A handful of the shots hit me, but I swoop around the perimeter of the base, skimming close to the rusty walls.

Finally.

I catch sight of him, maneuvering into the ruined office. It takes ten seconds for me to bounce to a halt on the ground behind him after one, two aborted landings. He spins on me, Steyr aimed at my chest.

He gets a push with both hands.

Frank flies backward, through a gaping opening in the wall. He disappears into a stand of trees and undergrowth with a crunch.

Here's hoping I didn't kill him.

"Frank? You okay?" I take off my helmet and hop through the gap. A quick jog and perusal of the place where he landed reveals small, broken branches, crushed ferns, and the Steyr.

In one instant, I have time to think, "Why'd he abandon his gun?" before something hooks my leg and tosses me off balance. I slam onto my chest and right arm.

"That was pathetic," Frank says from behind. "You check on your target to see if he's hurt? Who do you work for, the Red Cross?"

I scramble to my feet, but he immediately immobilizes me in a hold—arm around my throat, hand and arm against the back of my head and neck. The air's cut off to a mere trickle.

"You screwed up. You can't have compassion. Someone comes for you with a gun, intent on your death, you have to put him down. Let your sentiment get the better of you and you're no better off than if you'd shot yourself."

I gasp, yanking on his arms. I don't know how to break a hold like this. Never been trained that way.

"What's your move?"

With the last effort I can muster, I throw us sideways. We hit the building, go crashing through a wall that's more rust than corrugated metal. Frank releases me, and we tumble against abandoned furniture—him into the side of a sickly green desk, me into a pair of sagging metal file cabinets. Dust and debris settle around us like snow.

Frank coughs. There's a stillness in the air now, like a cemetery, after the roaring with and gunfire and crashing.

"Ow," I say.

Frank chuckles. "Good move. Sloppy, but that's your modus operandi so far."

"Yeah. I've noticed." My body aches, and I'm tired. More tired than I should be, considering we've only been at this for an hour or so. I try to stand, and my legs go rubbery. I slap a hand against the file cabinets for stability.

"Easy. The medallion takes a lot out of you, especially in the beginning. Drains your batteries." Frank stands there and waits, tapping his hand against his leg. Like I'm the dog and he's waiting for me to get up and trot over to my master.

I do regain my balance. But I'm not his dog.

"So. This went well." Frank gestures around at the wreckage. "Bashed the crap out of a building, deflected a lot of bullets. Good start."

"I think I need a lot more work, don't you?"

"Definitely. But we've got work to do before long. We have 48 hours."

"What? How the heck am I supposed to get this all under control by then?"

"Don't care. You need to do it." Frank straightens up, brushes dust off his shirt. "Because, in two days, we're going to stop the Polish mob from taking a shipment of rocket launchers."

Airfoil: Origins

Chapter Nine

Marchand got out of his car and frowned at the sea of red and blue lights ahead of him. Six squad cars? Fire, EMS? You'd think there'd been a homicide, not a near drowning. At least the SWAT boys weren't there.

Stupid woman shouldn't have been sailing alone this early in Spring, anyway.

He straightened his tie. This one was silver; his shirt was powder blue and his slacks tan, both sporting perfect creases. It was cool out; he kept on the navy-blue jacket. His badge gleamed brass on his belt, riding opposite his holstered Sig Sauer P320.

Dillard slammed the door to Marchand's car shut. Marchand rounded on him, finger pointed. "Watch it, kid. She gets a scratch, you take extra weekend shifts polishing and waxing."

"Yes, sir, Lieutenant." Dillard stood a respectful couple of steps away from the door.

Marchand glowered. No way to treat a car. Especially his car, a fully restored 1983 Monte Carlo SS, all white, original rims, red pin-striping along the doorframe, halogen lights and a 5.7 liter V8 under the hood. A hundred and eighty horsepower. Dillard didn't get it. Kid probably drove a Prius.

Marchand strode toward the uniforms clustered by the nearest DCPB black and white. Dillard trailed him like a whipped puppy, his stylus typing notes. He recognized Sutton, the black cop who'd been at the shooting in Nine Square, and a couple other young officers from Patrol. They all looked puzzled.

"Morning, gentlemen." He nodded, indifferent, in their general direction, scanning the staging area beyond for the individual he needed. Bingo. Lady wrapped in a towel, long blonde hair, sodden. There was a puddle around her bare feet. A middle-aged, stocky female EMT with brown hair cut shorter than Marchand's shone a flashlight in either eye.

"Lieutenant," Sutton said. "This one's weird."

"That's what Dispatch said. So why'd you guys rope me in? Besides me being better at the job, that is."

Sutton glanced at the other officers, some of whom had sprouted smirks. They thought this was a joke, did they? "Captain Urquhart's instructions. He said you were to be called in immediately on, uh, any of the weird stuff going on."

Marchand's lip curled. The captain was throwing his weight around. He was trying to punish Marchand.

"Sir. Does this have anything to do with IA?"

"What does that mean?" Marchand snapped.

"Rumor has it they were on your back this winter," Sutton said.

Marchand stepped up to him, glared in his face. Sutton, to his credit, didn't back down. "Well, Sutton, I'm still here and I'm still wearing my badge. Didn't hear about any charges being filed, did you?"

"No, sir."

Marchand made eye contact with the rest of the officers. "Anyone else?"

Heads shook all around.

"That's what I thought. Remember that, when you next speak to the dear captain, ask him about the reprimand on his file." Marchand smoothed his coat. IA. What a joke. They couldn't pin anything on him. How'd they think he'd spent these last few years building his extracurricular income? By advertising on Craigslist? "Report."

"The witness stated she was sailing on the Barron Shoals when the chop tossed her. Too windy for small boats out there." Sutton pointed at the ambulance. The EMT was gone. The woman sat on the edge of the open compartment, clutching the towel near. "That's when it, well..."

"Spit it out, Sutton. Don't be shy now."

Sutton stiffened. "She's saying a guy in a mask flew down and picked her up out of the water. Dropped her by the light."

Marchand stared. "You're not serious."

"That's what she says, sir."

"You order a tox screen? Because she's smoking something."

"No, sir, not yet."

"Right. Who called it in?"

"Another boater radioed the Coast Guard and was on its way to grab her when the flying guy supposedly showed up. Coasties contacted 911."

"Okay." Marchand didn't have anything else to say. "Witnesses?"

"Half a dozen people. We've got Martinez and Villeneau taking statements now."

Over by the lighthouse entrance, six men and women were pointing and gesturing as they spoke with a pair of officers. All of them looked as excited as groupies who'd run in to their rock star.

"Outstanding." He beckoned Dillard. "Come on, kid."

The woman occasionally looked up into the sky, eyes flitting from cloud to cloud.

"You think she's in shock, sir?" Dillard asked.

"I'm going with she's got a massive screw loose," Marchand muttered. "Dig up everything you can on her."

"Yessir."

"Ma'am?" Marchand smiled broadly. He offered his hand

to shake, chest back and gut sucked in. "Lieutenant Dennis Marchand, DCPD. I'm glad to see you're unhurt."

"Oh, thank you, Lieutenant." She smiled shakily. Her fingers, slender and cold, trembled in his grip. "Yes, I'm okay. Just in shock."

"Little damp, too, by the look of things. Your name?"

"Alicia Healy. But I already told the other officer."

"It's fine, ma'am, just procedure." And also so Dillard could run down any record she may have, such as something relevant to her mental state. "The officers tell me you capsized. Start off from right there."

"Well, I yelled for help. I knew if I tried to swim I'd freeze before I could get to shore. A wave swept me off the hull."

Marchand nodded as he scratched details in the ratty notebook. Dillard's methodical tap-tap-tap was a metronome behind them. "And then you saw someone?"

Her eyes lit up. She stopped shaking. "It was a man. He flew down to the water. Somehow, he got me up, out of the waves… he flew me over to the ledge."

Marchand was impressed by her transformation. Gone was the tremulous, pale victim. She stood straighter, made direct eye contact with him, and even had a splash of pink on her cheeks. However, he didn't believe a word of it. "Ma'am, that's not possible."

She recoiled as if he'd slapped her. "No. No, it is what happened! I saw it—he, he carried me up to land! There's people who saw us—"

"Calm down. You see that EMT over there? She's gonna take a blood sample. We'll run a tox screen, and whatever you've got banging around in your bloodstream's gonna show up real fast. So you'd better cut the bull and tell me the truth." Honestly, it would take CSI a couple of weeks to get the tox results definitive enough to prove illegal substances. But often, the threat was enough.

"But I am! You don't understand!"

"Ah, sir?" Dillard shuffled his stance. "You'll want to see this."

"Hang on." Marchand pointed at the woman. "Lady, don't think for one second we won't find whatever you're on floating around in the bay, whether it's a bottle or a dime bag."

She was in tears now. Marchand was ready to nail her down. "Okay, Dillard, tell me what you found."

"Umm..." He didn't seem overjoyed at his search results. "Just...here."

He passed Marchand the phone without further explanation. It listed Alicia Healy's record for everything from one citation for public intoxication and a single DUI, plus a handful of disorderly conduct warnings from her college days. Marchand scowled. He'd seen more condemning evidence on nuns. Two of them, in fact, that he'd booked last year for cocaine distribution.

Dillard reached over Marchand's arm and swiped the screen. It was a YouTube video. Marchand groaned. He saw a shaky image of a windswept, grassy hill. There in the middle was a blonde in a red shirt, a bright beacon against the storm gray horizon. Just beyond her was a small figure clad in blue. That blue figure suddenly streaked up into the air. Whoever took the video tried to keep on it but lost the image. There were startled shouts, and the image bounced around. It stabilized enough to show a black speck headed inland, away from the camera.

"Did you see him? Do you believe me now?" Alicia pointed at the phone.

Marchand glared at Dillard, as if the captured image were his fault. "Ma'am, we're going to have more questions for you. Once you're evaluated by the EMTs, I need you to drop by the Third Precinct."

He stalked off. Dillard kept a safe distance; Marchand could hear the footfalls. It helped slow his churning thoughts. "We need to make a few stops, kid. Starting with dropping you off at precinct."

"There's not much more on her record, sir."

"Keep looking. While you're at it, get me anything and everything that's shown up on this new guy. Who apparently can make movies of himself flying."

"Right, Lieutenant. Are we, ah, pursuing this as a hoax?"

Marchand opened the car door. He rested an arm on the window and looked up at the clouds. "Something's going on, Dillard. Something I don't get. This is my town, so whatever it is, I'm going to find out and I'm going to put a stop to it."

He ditched Dillard at the three-story glass and concrete fortress that was the Third Precinct. It was the rallying point for DCPD in Hull, Nine Square, and Little Warsaw. Dillard had a couple seconds in which he could step onto the curb before Marchand peeled out.

He drove over to Little Warsaw. The neighborhood bounded by Hull on the west and the coastline on the east. It ran for six blocks from 10th to 15th Streets, through the second most rundown part of Drake City; only Westerville out by the airport was worse. For all his departmental issues, Marchand was glad he'd kept the captain in check, or else he'd have been transferred there a long time ago.

Bay Drive smelled of fish and marine engine diesel. He parked outside a grocer's storefront stocked full of vegetables and fruits. The colors filling the window were a stark contrast to the dingy browns and grays of the buildings, sidewalks, and streets. The name of the grocer's changed every couple of years, but the real managers stayed the same. In the bottom left corner, someone had painted a black eagle. Marchand nodded; they made the boundaries easy to navigate.

Sure enough, he'd been out of the car a grand total of twenty seconds when a trio of burly men came out the front door. Tts bell jingling cheerily. They had sour expressions, and wore similar clothing: nice slacks, decent shoes, rumpled Oxfords with rolled up sleeves. The shirts were unbuttoned enough to show off gaudy gold and silver chains. They had tattoos stamped up both sides of their necks.

"Fellas," Marchand said. "How's it going?"

None answered, but Marchand guessed they'd had a good collection day. The tallest guy, who had a moustache so thick it hid most of his mouth and a head shorn clean, counted a thick stack of crumpled twenties and fifties. One of his compatriots, a hook-nosed man with bright blue eyes and curly black hair, rubbed blood off his right knuckles with a red handkerchief. The other man, shorter and wider, with gel-slathered brown hair, stared at him from behind very 1980s black sunglasses.

"Cezar, come on. Don't be bashful," Marchand said.

"You are not welcome here," Cezar Stajnik mumbled. "You have worn out welcome. Friend. I ask you leave."

"That's not how it works. I let you collect, you answer my questions and give me my intel. Also, you give me my cut. A thousand, once a month. You know the drill."

Cezar chuckled. It was listening to a bear's stomach grumble. "Your cut. You are not of us."

"No, but I am of police. The same police you want kept off your operations in these blocks, Cezar, and the same police who will show up the second I don't get paid. You want to pass that along to your boss?"

Cezar stopped chuckling. His expression was carved in stone. "Careful. Friend. No one will mourn your passing should you die."

"Only you guys, because that's when DCPD will come down on you like a bag of bricks." Marchand waved his hand dismissively. "Let's talk."

The man with the red handkerchief snapped off something in Polish. He put himself face to face with Marchand. "You leave. Boss is not going to speak. No money."

Marchand scowled at him. He looked over at Cezar. "You're

kidding."

Cezar shrugged. "Perhaps we have changed our deal."

"Okay then." Marchand patted the man on the shoulder, friendly as a frat brother. Then he slugged him in the gut. The man gasped, reached behind his waistband. Marchand hit him in the throat. He gagged, his hands clutching his neck.

The sunglasses man drew a stubby, black Glock 42 but Marchand was a second ahead of him, pointing his Sig Sauer in his face. "Nope. Drop it. Cezar? Put your piece on the ground too."

The sunglasses man didn't move. Neither did Cezar.

Marchand shot the curly-haired man in the leg. He collapsed, shrieking incomprehensibly, and then lapsed into sharp rapid hissing between his teeth. Blood seeped through his fingers as he clutched his leg.

Cezar very slowly put an identical Glock on the sidewalk. The sunglasses man followed his lead.

"Good choice." He nudged the fallen mobster with his shoe. "Stop whining, you wuss, it's just your calf. And it's also what we in law enforcement call a justifiable shooting. If you report it. Which I strongly suggest you don't."

Cezar shook his head. "You could have been *wilki*."

"Hell, Cezar, I'm practically a junior member." Marchand lowered his gun, slipped it back into the holster. "So, tell me what you guys have on this shootout over in Nine Square, and what you know about the other stuff going on. You know, the YouTube hoaxes."

"We hear of mugging. Saw video, as you did. Two punks. No affiliation of ours, you see. Probably Sheehan and his Micks." He said it *meeks*, but Marchand was clear enough—Irish mob. Danny Sheehan. Undisputed rulers of Hull, and not so cozy neighbors with the Poles. "My boss, Mr. Krol, he is curious. Wants to know if there is truth to new rumor."

"Rumor?"

"Of man who threw them, man who made them fly into air and into wall."

Marchand kept the heel of his hand on his gun. None of them had made for their weapons, but he wanted to make certain they knew who was in charge of this Q & A.

"We question men further. They cannot help us identify man. Did not see details, only that he rode bike and was white."

"That only describes tens of thousands of males," Marchand muttered.

"We think nothing of it, after that. Until we are hired by a man to be assistance for an abduction. Things go wrong."

Marchand nodded. "So, it was your crew in on that pursuit. The Uzis...you guys should branch out when it comes to weaponry, you know. Did you supply the triggerman?"

"No, I do not know anything about this. Only that we were to stop vehicle from escaping. Whoever drove car—very good. But we put together a swift blockade on Broad Street. Then—" Cezar made a noise like a balloon losing air, *pffft*. "Trucks move."

"You're seriously buying into this nonsense."

"Your hearing is bad, no? I say again: Trucks. Move. We do not know how. You think my drivers are infants? They can handle cars, trucks, whatever vehicle we need driven. One moment, they are behind wheel, the next, their trucks are pushed out of way."

"Like the muggers."

Cezar nods. "Boss, he is concerned, but he tells us not to look further. Suddenly, he is no curious. I think this strange, no?"

"Very, Cezar, very." Marchand filed this all away. "This abduction. Who hired you? Who was the target?"

Cezar reached into his pocket. Marchand had the gun halfway out of the holster before he could wave him off. "Is only phone, friend, relax."

He tapped on the screen several times with his thumb, then

turned it so Marchand could see. There was a lady's face, gorgeous, big full lips and bright eyes, long black hair. Wow.

"Her name is Consolata Acciai," Cezar said. "Has big reputation for hits and takings."

"Good. Look, I don't care about some mumbo jumbo involving magically moving muggers and trucks."

"Do not forget, man who flies. Yes, I see the news. The videos."

Marchand ground his teeth. These people and their social media. Solving these cases were the captain's idea, but he had a hitman to collar. "I'll deal with that."

"I would take caution. Things like this—there are stories from old country. Good men and bad, hiding in shadows, playing with powers that make brave men cross themselves."

"You should be more worried about the powers of the DCPD. Can you tell me who this supposed super guy is?"

Cezar shrugged.

"Then you're no help. Acciai. Where can I find her?"

"What will you give me in return?"

"Continued assurance we stay off your backs. Plus, you keep the grand this time."

Cezar chuckled. "I will need to tell Mr. Krol you offer something more substantial."

"Fine. I won't show up at your shipment. How's that?"

Cezar didn't reply.

Marchand continued, "Oh, yeah, that's some hefty hardware you guys are importing. You'll make a ton of cash. So get me Acciai and no one will muck up your delivery."

"Very well. I shall consult Mr. Krol."

"You do that. And tell him I'm upping my fee to twelve fifty, because you guys are becoming problematic."

Cezar grumbled. "You push too hard, considering you stand on our land."

Marchand stepped up to Cezar and poked him in the chest.

"This is my precinct, Cezar. My rules apply. You boys have a nice day now."

He got back in his car, careful to not turn his back to either man, and ignored the renewed whimpers of the guy he'd shot. As Marchand drove off, he considered Cezar's words about the old country and folklore. Whomever was playing these stunts was of far lesser importance than catching someone of Acciai's stature. Let Captain Urquhart try to take that arrest from him.

Cezar would come through with an address. He always did. So Marchand got on the dispatch radio to precinct. He'd need backup.

The Sullivan Crown was the premier hotel in Drake City. Seated atop a long, low hill on the north end of Daniels Drive, surrounded by dozens of high-end retailers and ritzy restaurants, it was fifteen stories of Gothic granite grandeur. Brilliant crimson awnings decorated the windows and entrance, blazing against the white stone. Men, uniformed in maroon coats, opened doors and moved luggage; women in black skirts handled every reservation, answered every request. Service was top shelf; even the janitors got tips.

So Consolata Acciai was understandably furious when the concierge's call on her room phone woke her from a deep sleep to alert her that the police had just barged in downstairs, looking for her.

She slammed the phone down and threw aside the sheets. Her mouth was dry as a desert, and the sides of her head squeezed together. Vodka martinis last night, and a man.

The man was still there, snoring. Garrett. The sculptor. A lovely guy. She could have sworn he left late last night. No matter. Fun times were over.

First: clothes. She slipped into the black, spaghetti strap cocktail dress. Second: shoes. Found them under the bedside table. No, forget them. She could move faster without heels.

Third: gun. It and its holster, complete with shoulder rig, were stuffed behind her pillow. Lastly: cell phone and card holder. The card holder slipped neatly into her bra; the cell phone, on the strap around her thigh.

She didn't want to leave the room—plush cream carpet, dark wood furniture, massive flat screen TV, fully stocked minibar, original oil paintings of Drake City Harbor—her last regret was that she'd have to find a new hotel in which to spend her money.

"Angela?" His voice was high pitched as slurred the more popular of her many pseudonyms. He leaned on his elbows, his arms bulging and stained with white dust, revealing chest and abs as chiseled as the work he produced.

Acciai was sorely tempted to rejoin him, even with the police riding the elevator to the 13th floor this instant. Instead she gritted her teeth and went for the window. It didn't help matters that Garrett smelled like her favorite cologne. "Gotta run. You were fantastic. Don't call me."

He frowned, eyes bleary. "Call? I don't have your number, babe."

"Sorry. I'm not on the hunt for a relationship. My last one ended badly, when I had to shoot him in the face." She smiled sweetly and blew him a kiss. Then she opened the window, planting one foot on the sill. Garrett shouted but she'd already tuned him out.

Acciai locked her mind into evade mode,. The burst of noises from the street below held her attention. She cast one last glance at her lavish room.

Onto the fire escape it was.

Wind lashed at her. The air stank of garbage and rain. Sunlight glared from behind clouds. Car horns and engines rumbled beneath her.

Beyond the window, her room's door slammed open. Garrett screeched in alarm.

"DCPD!" a gruff voice shouted.

Acciai swung over the railing with smooth grace and little effort. She got a fleeting glimpse of four police in Kevlar rushing toward the bed. Three were in uniform and the fourth, the man in front, wore what Acciai considered a quite trendy and flattering suit. Mustachioed, thinning hairline, tubby waistline.

Acciai landed with a bang on the twelfth-floor fire escape. She sprinted, feet padding on the grating. The metal dug into her bare soles, but she pushed the pain from her awareness. Down to the eleventh and then tenth floors. En route, she did a quick inventory. All she'd left behind were clothes and hotel toiletries. Nothing that couldn't be replaced.

Footsteps clanged above her. "Consolata Acciai, stop!" It was well-dressed cop. Surprisingly quick, given his paunch.

Acciai grabbed a railing as she swung down yet again, to the ninth-floor landing. Something sharp ripped at her hand. The metal she'd just touched was jagged. She sucked at the blood on her palm to staunch the flow and was instantly aroused.

Delicious.

Now she was fully awake, fully enthralled by the chase. Her senses were keen. At the seventh floor, the squawk of static from a police radio made her aware that footsteps were coming up the fire escape. Very well, then.

She halted at the nearest window and bashed it in with her gun. Glass shattered, allowing enough room for her to reach in and unlock it.

No one inside, she slipped in. The room was a mirror image of the one she'd left, down to identical linens on the bed. Only that bed lacked Garrett. Acciai felt a pang of regret she'd left him behind. He was hot, after all.

She made for the door. No sign of anyone in the hall. She exited and closed the door behind her. A set of upholstered chairs flanked a mirror and a wooden magazine table two doors down, at the bend in the corridors. She jammed one under the handle, wedging in it tight enough to prevent the door from opening out—at least temporarily.

Acciai found the emergency stairwell at the opposite end of the hall and padded swiftly down. Her footfalls were soft on the concrete, barely echoing off the cinderblock walls. This part of the hotel had undergone recent renovation and was brought up to city fire code. Which meant that she should find—

"Down there! Stop!" Another cop. Very young face, fairly handsome, tall and lanky. There were two others with him—a small, dark-haired woman with olive skin and a stocky, square-jawed man with a fringe of a beard.

Acciai grabbed the railing at the sixth-floor landing and vaulted over it, into the open stairwell. Midway across, she twisted and fired three shots. She landed hard on the steps below, to the fifth floor, catching herself before she slid on her stockinged feet.

The shots hit the square-jawed cop dead center in the chest, knocking him down. No blood, sadly. Kevlar vest. Took all the fun out of a successful shot.

The lanky cop and the young woman opened fire. Bullets ricocheted around Acciai as she took the steps two at a time. Found what she was looking for at the next landing, behind a red hatch. She bashed in the glass with the butt of her gun.

In seconds, the lanky cop was after her. The woman must have paused to check on the downed officer—Acciai could hear her talking into her police radio, cool and composed as a teacher taking morning roll in a classroom.

"Put your gun down!" the lanky cop shouted.

Acciai did, letting the gun drop to the floor. In that second of distraction, she whirled around, pulled the pin on the fire extinguisher and blasted him full in the face with the spray. In no time at all, she'd filled their entire corner of the stairwell with hazy white foam. His face was completely obscured. He sputtered foam and gasped.

Acciai swung the extinguisher around in a full circle and

cracked it across his forehead.

Satisfied he was out, she retrieved her gun and kept running downstairs until she reached the door to the underground parking garage. With her weapon ready, she eased the door open a crack.

Again, her way seemed clear. The garage was small by most hotel standards, built into the original foundation when the hotel was renovated. Rows of three dozen luxury automobiles awaited her—Bentleys, Mercedes, Lincolns. Among the black and gray and white was a single red Lamborghini. Acciai licked her lips, relishing the remnant of blood there, but restrained herself. A sports car like that would make it far too easy for the police to hunt her down.

Voices. A policewoman, with blond hair tied into ponytail beneath her cap, was giving orders to a tall, burly parking valet as the pair walked into view. The black man in his maroon uniform jacket kept pointing at the cars behind him, arguing about something. They stood by the nearest car, too close to the door for Acciai to sneak by them.

She pushed the door open and walked straight for them.

The cop turned, and her eyes went wide. She unholstered her gun. "You! Freeze!"

Really? Freeze? Acciai aimed for the valet and kept walking. "Shoot me and I kill him. I won't miss, I promise."

The cop didn't fire. Neither did she put her gun down. Acciai counted down the distance, judging the right moment to strike.

Ten feet out, the valet lunged for her.

He was too big to successfully grapple with, so Acciai shot him clean through the skull. His head jerked back, neck cracking, and his body slammed onto the pavement.

The cop tried to fire, but Acciai bent her gun wrist down. Two shots went into the nearest Lincoln, shattering the windshield and setting off a shrieking alarm. She swung a punch at Acciai, who ducked it easily and jerked the policewoman around. The cop's gun went skidding across the pavement.

Acciai went down onto her back, scissored both legs around the policewoman's neck, and flipped her over onto her side. Her head bounced off a Rolls Royce and she slumped, out cold.

Acciai got back up, smoothed out her dress. She hitched the left strap back up over her shoulder.

Keys. The valet had a pile of them. They were sticky with his blood. Acciai wiped her hands along his jacket, not wanting to get any on her dress. It was one of her favorites, after all. But the sickly-sweet metallic smell was enough to make her giddy.

She clicked the car alarm until she found her ride—a black Bentley Flying Spur. All leather interior. Acciai adored the feel of the seats on her legs. Like Garrett's skin, only better. She got the engine purring and kicked up the sound system. Marvelous.

Her car was on its way up the exit ramp into the bright rectangle of daylight as a pair of uniformed officers sprinted down it, guns drawn. Acciai was grateful for the tinted windows, and she slid right by them onto the street.

The mustachioed cop burst from the nearest alleyway just as Acciai put the pedal down and roared off into traffic. She blew him a kiss in the rearview mirror.

Marchand spat onto the sidewalk. "Dillard," he hollered into his radio. "Dillard! Let's move! She's out, driving a black Bentley! I've got the plates—"

"Lieutenant, Dillard's down, sir. Out cold." Sutton jogged up to him, panting. "We got two more down—Maretti in the south stairs and Emmons in the garage. Parking valet's been shot. EMS is en route."

Marchand nodded. His side ached, his right ankle throbbed, and sweat stained his shirt. He'd have to get it dry cleaned. And have someone polish his shoes. "Come. Get all available units in pursuit. We can still catch her."

If he found out the Poles had tipped off Acciai, he was gonna have a long, painful talk with Cezar.

Acciai sat in a coffee shop eight blocks away, reading a copy of the *Messenger* and its report on the YouTube videos of two would-be muggers accosted by an unseen force. Squad cars screamed by, followed by a white Monte Carlo with a growling engine.

She sipped a latte. They would find the Bentley, eventually, but only after a convoluted drive south of Drake City where a now well-paid vagrant was taking it for a spin. For $200, she considered it a bargain escape.

Her phone rang. She answered the call. "Good morning."

"You are needed at the mine," her employer said. "Did you forget our appointment?"

"No, I didn't. And I'm not late, either. I'll be there in ten."

"Have you run into difficulties obtaining surveillance of the subject?"

"Not at all. He's boring. Handsome, but boring. Home, library, occasional stops in the city. No visitors. One son." She glanced up at the TV, positioned over the door. "Have you seen the news?"

"That is what I would like to discuss. I have additional assignments."

"My pay?"

"Ten thousand apiece."

Acciai smiled. "I'll see you soon."

She hung up the call, then played back the video on her phone taken by the three cameras she'd positioned around Brandon Tusk's apartment. Nothing exciting, yet.

Acciai killed the video and settled back with her beverage to watch the TV again, drinking in the footage of a man flying off through the sky.

Chapter Ten

The lady from the *Messenger* is nice enough. Short brown hair, glasses, intense blue eyes, and the ability to pin down an individual with questions—everything I expected when Reed described Suzanne DiStefano as "Woodward but cute."

She's talking with him and Kelly about our children's programs, limited as they are by lack of space and materials. I'm on the front desk, checking out a stack of Anthony Horowitz teen novels to a boy who's as tall as me and weighs half as much. Can't see his eyes for the shaggy mop of blonde hair and blazing green hood pulled down low.

"Those are due back in two weeks," I remind him.

"'Kay. Later."

Back at you. He ambles to the door and gets it open. Don't know how. He looks like a sheepdog.

"Brandon?" Kelly walks over from where Reed and Suzanne are reviewing photographs on her phone. "I had an idea for a fund-raiser."

"Oh yeah?" The phone next to my keyboard buzzes. Not my phone, the untraceable one Frank gave me. I ignore it. "What kind?"

"A dance, over at the old Legion Hall on Sixth."

"On the waterfront? That'd be a great place." The phone

Airfoil: Origins

stops after five rings. Good.

"I think so. We can get a good deal on the rent—Suzanne's editor has an uncle who's a member. When I mentioned my idea, they said the paper would be one of the sponsors." Kelly smiles. "But we'll need music."

"Live music's better than canned."

"I know. That's why I was thinking of the blues guys you talked about."

I puzzle that one for a moment. Blues guys? Oh, the trio, the ones who biked with me last summer. They needed a fourth man on their ride. Call themselves Moldy Upholstery. It's a terrible name, but their music has soul like you wouldn't believe.

What puzzles me is that she remembers. I'm impressed. "Yeah. That's a great idea. It's the kind of gig they'd love to play. You know, for a good cause. Sure, I'll give them a call."

The phone buzzes again.

"Great. Thanks. I'll make the arrangements for the hall."

"You don't need to run it by Reed?"

She wrinkles her nose. "Oh, I think he delegated that to me. You know: if you volunteer an idea, you volunteer yourself to run it."

I chuckle. Sounds like Reed. He gives me a sour look from across the room. I scratch my chin with my middle finger and smile back.

Kelly laughs, too, though it's more subdued.

"That's a nice change," I say.

"Oh?"

"The smiling and laughing. Ever since Mark Vanchev showed up here with his closing warning, you've been pretty quiet. Quieter than usual."

Her cheeks get dark red and the smile slackens. "Dan got offered a recording contract last month."

"No kidding? Well, good for him." This I say as I consider my paltry paintings tucked away in the office at the apartment.

"Not so good for us. We had a huge fight about it. Not the

only one we'd had, lately, but the worst by far."

I nod, but don't find any of this surprising. Dan's got a tendency to hit the bottle. As far as I know, he never hit her. Good thing. He's lucky she stays with him.

"So, he moved out and took a one-way flight to Los Angeles to sign with some studio."

I have a split-second mental image of hurling him that far with the medallion's power. "Wow. Sorry, that sucks."

She shrugs.

"That'll make for a crappy week."

"And my grandpa...he has fluid building up in his heart. The doctor's not very optimistic. As if he was optimistic about Grandpa losing his mind."

She exhales, a deep shuddery breath. Poor kid. No wonder she hasn't been herself. Boyfriend ditching her is bad enough. But this? It was messy when Samantha's grandmother died; I remember the Samantha's bedside anguish, the days of waiting.

"Tell you what," I say. "Any time you want someone to come along with you to see him, let me know."

"You would?"

"Guaranteed."

She turns back to her screen. "It's okay. You don't have to."

The phone's buzzing again. Frank, give it a rest. Does he think I forgot what today is? "Hey. You're my colleague, and a friend. That's all there is to it. I'll be there."

"Thanks."

She doesn't say anything else, so I take that as my chance to get Frank off my back. "Hey, watch the desk for me. I need to take this call."

"Of course."

As I walk from the desk, phone pressed to my ear, I know exactly who's my choice for a date to this dance fund-raiser idea of theirs.

"You took your sweet time," Frank grumbles into my ear.

"What's the problem? You said ten o'clock tonight."

"I said twenty-two hundred."

"Same thing."

"Shut up. Thought you should know: the police have your attacker's name. Consolata Acciai."

I wait. "Is...that someone I'm supposed to react to?"

"Nope. No reason a librarian should be familiar with an assassin who has more than thirty kills under her belt and a penchant for disappearing."

Goosebumps rise on my skin. I turn back toward the front. Kelly sees me staring and smiles sheepishly. Not the purpose of my stare. "Ah, no."

"Now that I have your attention, listen close. Acciai is a contract killer and kidnapper, but she's not familiar with the Ashen. She's paid to bring you to her boss, plain and simple."

"Why would her boss want me?"

"Our adversaries have a time-tested tradition of trying to recruit medallion holders into the Ashen. By treaty, they can only do it *before* the Garrison reveals itself. They also are forbidden from striking against that called person and his or her family if the attempt fails. Right of first refusal."

"And you're telling me this now?" Irritation gnaws at me. "He could come back for me, or for my son..."

"Again, shut up. And listen. They won't try again. They don't violate the agreements. You don't understand what these treaties mean. They're the bedrock on which modern civilization stands. So, when I tell you Acciai won't go after you or your kid, trust me."

"Okay. Fine. So why bother telling me?"

"Because Acciai will continue to watch you. Which means, we have to be careful to conceal your newfound role from her. Even if she suspects something about the Ashen that employs her—and she'd be an idiot not to—we can't have her stumbling onto the medallion's true nature. This would be a lot easier if you'd stop getting yourself put up on the Internet every five seconds."

"It's been three times. You see the latest one?" I don't really care, but it's amusing to hear Frank's teeth grind over the phone. Besides, if I'm going to clean up around Hull neighborhood, I need a reputation. Smacking muggers and rescuing pretty boaters are good starts.

"Make sure you're ready to go at five minutes before twenty-two hundred. Come out the back entrance, by the dumpster. I'll have the car ready. You be suited up and ready to fly."

"Yes, sir."

"You're not taking this seriously, are you? These men we're dealing with tonight, they won't show any restraint. They will try to kill you when we go after their guns. And you think you can hack it? You'll be lucky to do half as well as Samantha."

It's a blow to my gut. "Quite the pep talk."

"She was the good soldier. Don't forget that." *Beep* and he's gone.

I dig my wallet out. In it is a carefully folded piece of paper—the note Samantha wrote. Making sure Kelly still has her back to me, and Reed's nowhere to be seen, I read it again.

She loves me.

And yet, the words "sacred duty" hammer at me. I nod, fold the note back up. "Okay, Samantha. For you. Not him."

Nine thirty rolls around that night, and I'm a bundle of nerves. Sean and I ate our dinner in near absolute silence, which is the norm. I'd made the spaghetti and garlic bread. He got the salad prepped and mixed the dressing. Aside from "Pass me the parmesan" and "Got any more bread?" we didn't say anything constructive.

Tonight, I power off my phone and thus eliminate the lure of Facebook. There's an itch, a pervasive need coursing through my mind. I flick on the light in our home office. It's a simple square of a room, small, with a tiny window up on the far wall. Bookshelves are crammed with novels, history volumes, and a handful of art instruction books. But I don't need those. I pull up a stool. The paints are where I left them.

An hour later, Sean pokes his head in. My brush hurries back and forth, filling in the green blotches that will become the forests around Mount Stafford. The sky, for now, is a big blue smear across the top of the canvas. I've left a wide space as thick as my hand stretching across.

I turn around. "Need something?"

"No. I was just—you're painting." He leans on the doorjamb. "That's, like, rarer than me doing my homework."

"Sounds like you've been catching up on that."

"Yeah, well."

"It was time to make a change." I smile at him. "What about you?"

Sean shrugs. "Dunno. Didn't think I needed to screw around with that stuff when there's more important stuff going on. Big things. You know?"

No clue what he means. "Sure."

He watches me for a while, from the door, and I can see the two of us in here five years ago. Him sitting cross-legged on the floor, doodling on a drawing pad of his own, while I paint. Samantha calling for us to get dressed, because it's Saturday morning and she has the day off, and we're all going for a hike on Cape Ashwin.

With that, the memory fades, and vanishes. When she left again for her shift, was it really work, or was it her duty for the Garrison? Was she dodging bullets while I played video games with Sean?

He's gone. Probably in the living room. My phone's timer chirps at me. It's 9:40.

"You're headed out?" Sean's sprawled on the couch, a pile of comic books slumped by one leg. He's reading *Amazing Spider-*

man. Where does he get these from? His comic book store? Reed? It doesn't matter. He's got them, and they're his idols.

I gather up my fleece, and my backpack. It bulges some with the helmet inside. "Yeah. Frank and I...we're going to stop a few places."

"Find some women?"

"Sean."

He frowns. "Or not, because you've got your backpack. Weird."

"It's family stuff," I say. "He just wants to catch up on old times."

Sean's face goes flat, devoid of emotion. "Have a blast."

Frank and I drive out through Old Town, under the glittering lights of Drake City, and across the wide, gradual hill of Slidell Memorial Bridge into Newport. From the top of the old vertical-lift bridge I get a great view of the city lights on both sides of the river, stretching out to Rittenhouse Island. Dannersly Bridge arcs across the night sky far in the distance, a jeweled spray of stayed-suspension magnificence between Rittenhouse and the Newport shipping docks. Red and green lights blink on the tips of gantries dangling out over the water. Monstrous container ships sleep in their berths.

Frank takes us south on Slidell Road down the shoreline, headed directly to the ports. Drake City Newport Terminal is a huge collection of six docks and stacks of hundreds of shipping containers, each rectangle a massive blue, red, white or green LEGO atop another. These are hemmed in by a dozen long, wide warehouses, each belonging to a different shipping concern. Dozens more smaller warehouses, repair shops, and offices cluster about their bigger siblings. All of this is bordered by chain link fence, its north side bordered by the sprawling railyards. From there, cargo is shipped north to Canada, or by following the loop around the northwest side of Drake City, beyond Mount Stafford, down south to Boston.

We park in the shadows of an alley, far as possible from streetlights without being more than two blocks from the terminal. I don't know why Frank bothers; he's got the Camaro back, but it looks nothing like its original shiny, silver state. Instead, it's glossy black all over, with a different set of license plates and not a hint of damage. It's the same car, though; I can tell from the way the leather seats feel.

"*Wilki*," Frank says, as he drags his duffel bag out of the back seat. "Polish mob. Interchangeable terms."

"Yes, I know who they are." I pull on the helmet, secure it. Vision is clear. Heart's racing, though, and stomach churning. Yet there's anticipation behind it, not fear.

"Don't sass. These boys won't be low-level street thugs shoving old people and women around for money, Brandon. These are the upper tier enforcers. The ones Nikodem Krol relies on to handle high-level, expensive deliveries."

There's an edge to his voice when he says the name. You'd have to be living under a rock—or at least ignoring every print and electronic news outlet in Drake City—to not tense up when you hear Nikodem Krol's name. Murder, extortion, kidnapping, prostitution, drug trafficking, and illegal weapons acquisition; kingpin was an understatement. "So, rocket launchers."

"That's the deal. Specifically, thirty-six of these." He holds up his phone. In the glowing screen is the image of a long tube with a trigger and grip near the front, sporting a conical warhead on the tip. "RPG-7, Russian made, subsonic speed of 294 meters per second, delivers high explosive or fragmentation warheads up to a thousand feet away. Sturdy, and as shoulder-mounted rocket launchers go, cheap. Four hundred bucks gets you one. Throw in fifty grand more and you get a bunch of warheads."

"How many?"

"Enough to turn every squad car in the DCPD into a

smoldering heap of scrap metal." Frank tucks the phone away. He pulls a weapon from his bag, the Steyr. Loads it, puts a round in the chamber, straps it across his left hip. Then he goes for another one. And it's bigger.

"I take it you're coming with me."

"Automatic SCAR-L, a weapon made by FN Herstal for use by the U.S. Special Forces. They're barely five years old. Thirty rounds in the magazine." Frank smirks. "You'll need backup."

"Okay. So, I go in, I find the rocket launchers, and I get rid of them."

"Exactly."

"By dumping them in the river?"

Frank shrugs. "This is your operation, Brandon. You make the call."

"Right." I nod. "Good luck, then."

"Luck is for idiots who don't have a plan. Good hunting."

I form the field around me and take off. It's a bumpy start, likely because I'm finding it hard to concentrate on the mechanics of flight when thinking about the layout we reviewed. Frank had better be right.

I soar up high over the river, bank left out toward the bay, and fly beyond the reach of the shipyard lights. There's no one around, so far. Plenty of container ships moored, plenty of forklifts and trucks parked here and there, but no people.

Until I reach Berth 3.

There. A trio of U-Haul style moving trucks are parked in a loose circle, back ends toward a Maersk vessel. Eight containers are stacked nearby. Only the bottommost one nearest the truck is open. Black stick figures are busily moving crates from the open container to the three trucks.

That's it then. A grin spreads slowly across my face. Wait until they see this.

I come around slowly, down over the water. Close enough I could trail my fingers across the black surface. My approach to the dock is no louder that the breeze coming across the bay.

Their positioning is smart. With the containers stacked such, you can't see what's going on from the harbor. Sure, the Coast Guard could spot them, if they were patrolling near here. As it is, there're no boats in the vicinity, no signs of police. Nothing.

I come up just before the stack and land gently as possible on the topmost pair. The clunk of my shoes on the metal is terribly loud, my senses heightened. The men down below are so busy banging boxes around and yammering in Polish I doubt they'd hear a grenade going off. Or say, a SCAR-L.

I walk slowly, lightly toward their end of the containers, and crouch by the side. It's dark up here. The few lights shining down illuminate the deck of the ship, and the circle of trucks below, not much else. Perfect.

"Morons! Do not drop these! You will paste all our guts along dock!" The man in charge is black-haired and sporting a black moustache so thick I can't see his mouth from this angle. He's thick necked and wide bodied, wearing gray slacks, black shoes, and a maroon shirt with the top unbuttoned. I have an unfortunate view of a rat's nest of black chest hair tangled with so many gold chains he could lasso a horse.

"Cezar, it's not problem," a smaller, wiry guy with a bald head snaps back. "When we're dead, we not have listen to you whine."

That brings rough chuckles from the rest of the crew. My count is an even dozen. There's three standing guard by the trucks, wearing sport coats, plus Cezar and eight others—including the bald whiner—loading the crates. They're all armed. Uzis appear to be their weapon of choice. The three guards and Cezar all hold one; the others have them slung over their backs.

The sight is not comforting. My memory slides back to the hair-raising chase from my apartment. Same guys?

"Shut up and finish. We move. Mister Krol is not wanting long wait," Cezar says. "He is wanting to give present to Sheehan's Micks as soon as he can. To be neighborly."

More chuckles. I brace myself on the container. Cezar slurs it "*Meeks*" but I know what he means. The *wilki* are going to use the rocket launchers against the Irish mob. They were hostile, yes, according to Reed and the news, but this? This will be an all-out war.

My radio hisses in my ear. "Brandon," Frank murmurs. "You're in position."

It doesn't sound like a question. I glance up, around the shipyard. No idea where he's ensconced himself, but wherever he is, he can see us, and I can't see him. "Yes. Frank, these launchers—they're going to use them, not sell them."

"I figured as much. Odds were better that way. Krol isn't hard up for cash; selling these doesn't make a huge profit." There's a soft click. "Whenever you're ready."

"Okay."

"Remember. Focus. Keep your shield up. Move fast. And break stuff."

I grin. "Got it."

Below me, they've got more than twenty crates loaded, split between two trucks. The third's door is shut; looks like no one's made a move to load it yet. Everyone's wary, checking their perimeter. Cezar chews on a bright green toothpick.

No one's looking up.

I compose my shield and stretch out both hands. Instantly, I see a huge shovel, invisible to everyone else, larger than a man. It's sideways and ready to swing. So, I swing.

The blow knocks two men over and drops the crate onto one's legs. He hollers. Wood splinters, and the crate spills its contents.

Wait. Those aren't rocket launchers. They're guns. Assault rifles, all black AK-74Ms, and another weapon that looks like a much bigger machine gun. Standard Russian military issue.

"Morons!" Cezar growls. "Up, up! You break and Mister Krol has your intestines for supper!"

"Something hit me!" Baldy snarls. "Knock me right over!"

Yep. Let's do it again.

The second blow topples two more men. This time, Cezar and the three guards get their guns up, aiming out from their position. They scan the ships and the deep darkness of the yard.

Okay. Now.

I jump down from the boxes and catch myself in midair halfway down. Then, I push outward with both hands. The field pulses around me; I can feel it convulse and the sharp stab of ice into my chest from the medallion.

The reduced gravity front flings men and crates like thrown toys. A few boxes go end over end, smashing wood and splashing into the harbor. The men react quickly. They grab onto the trucks and slow their tumbling with their limbs.

A few look up.

"*Mój Boże!*" Baldy says.

Now they're all looking at me. No one moves. That makes it my turn. "Put your weapons down and surrender!" I shout as loudly as I can. The helmet still muffles it.

Cezar's the first. He bites down so hard on the toothpick it snaps. Then he opens fire.

The shots veer off, just like they did when I practiced with Frank. They chip the concrete below me. Baldy adds his fire.

But once I get used to the sparks flashing around me, my spike of fear dissolves. This is power. This is strength. They're going to get more of it.

First thing I do is go for the nearest thug. I dive at him, colliding at full force with his chest. We both grunt, and he jabs at me with the stock of his Uzi. Nothing doing; the shield reacts to it the same way it does to the other incoming projectiles. I get sparks and the Uzi gets crunched down into the concrete.

Why didn't it do that to the guy I hit? No idea and no time to wonder. I punch him across the face, breaking his nose in a spray of blood. A second blow to the ribs bends him over, and my elbow to the back of his neck flattens him to the ground.

Shouts. To my right. An impact throws me off my feet—but also throws the two men who slammed into me right onto dock. One's out cold, his left arm bent back at an impossible angle. The second screams, clutching at his leg. Bone protrudes from the torn pants.

I'm stunned into inaction. What have I done? This is more than a simple blow dealt to a mugger.

And the wrong kind of distraction. More gunfire sprays over me. The shield holds, but the flashes are blinding. I'm so disoriented I can't sense my left from my right. So, I push off into flight, throwing myself into the air. Within seconds, I curve back around toward my opponents, eyes filled with purple blobs from the flashes of gunfire.

Suddenly, there's the fast report of an automatic weapon's burst. Three shots in quick succession. Then again. One of Cezar's men, Baldy, goes down. Blood smears the concrete. Cezar is livid, neck and nose crimson. He's pointing far off to my left, toward the next dock, where even more crates are stacked. A pair of men hunker down, work their way in that direction.

The rest take shots at me, albeit at the same time they seek cover, so their attempts are akin to guesses. I watch them carefully, preparing my next attack—

And glimpse, out of the corner of my eye, the same stack of crates I'd stood upon coming up way too quickly on my right.

Idiot! I've flown right into them!

With a frantic twist, I roll left, and it's just enough I don't collide head on with the uppermost crate. My left leg smacks against it. Pain lances from my shin through my knee. My flight is abruptly less than graceful.

I come down right in front of the middle truck, one of the ones that's partially loaded. My leg buckles beneath me, but I grit my teeth and push upright. The driver is in his fifties, balding with gray sideburns, thick beard and moustache. He stares at me, eyes wide as the headlights.

Only hesitates a half second before he fires up the engine and hits the gas.

The truck lunges forward. I tuck and roll to the right, avoiding my damaged left leg. The truck rumbles by, picking up speed. The crates rattle in the open hatchway as it goes by.

I reach out with my left hand, toward the last thing I see passing—the rear right wheel. Turns out it's as simple as picturing Sean as a toddler, yanking the plastic wheel off his favorite toy, a lime green pickup. It's considerably better secured, so it takes more effort. My arm strains and hand aches.

There's a sharp squeal of metal rending and the tire leaps outward and up from the side of the truck. It rolls madly away, bouncing and skidding. The back end of the truck slams onto the asphalt, crumpling that corner and spraying sparks and smoke. I can hear the driver shouting in Polish as he struggles with the wheel, but the truck only veers worse to its left. The truck smashes into a stack of containers, its front end crumpling. Steam rises from the engine. No sight of activity from the driver.

I'm ducking in front of the first truck. More gunfire. The Uzi bursts stitch a line across the truck's fender, barely missing me. Then comes three more bursts of three shots each from the other, louder weapon. I swear the bullets come from behind me this time. Gotta hand it to Frank. The man can get around stealthily. Though, with the racket, these goons are making he could drive a semi through the library and nobody would notice.

The gunfire slackens. Cezar shouts more orders. Footsteps coming, at the back of this truck.

Perfect.

I marshal the field behind both hands and plant them on the hood of this truck. It has no driver. If the parking brake is on, this will be more difficult. But I push. Hard.

The truck skids away from me, so fast I have to jog to keep up. Cries of surprise echo behind it, followed by a heavy *whump*. Two men go tumbling away, one to either side, their weapons clattering across the docks. I let go. The truck continues its manic skid, black streaking the dock, until its open cargo hatch bangs into the stack of containers I used as my perch.

The Poles are scattering. The ones that can walk, anyway. The third truck rumbles to life, starts off away from the docks. I'm worn out, working to focus on keeping that shield up and not get myself shot. I scan for my next target.

Cezar's there, hanging off the back of the last truck, holding on to the rail. He's pointing one of the RPG-7s right at me. Can't be more than a hundred feet away.

He shouts something I can't hear over the roar of the truck's engine. He squeezes the trigger. A flash, a puff of smoke and a screech.

I drop to my knee and put everything I have into the shielding. Funny. I don't want to die.

The explosion blinds me. My body tumbles over the concrete, limbs slapping against impermeable surface. Heat and smoke and pain. Sound is deadened. Someone who might be Frank shouts in my ear. Muffled gunfire comes from—where?

A large, metal object stops my flight with a heavy bang, but I still only see blurs. Bright blurs. Dark blurs. Rectangular, colorful blurs.

"Brandon! Brandon!" It's Frank. He's shouting in my head, and at my face. I blink as hard as I can, shake away the cobwebs.

He kneels in front of me, SCAR-L resting across his knee. He's got a ski mask pulled up from in front of his eyes and a microphone similar to the one in my helmet strapped around his neck. He's also grinning.

"You did it. I knew you could do it. But an RPG at point blank range..." He shakes his head, chuckling under his breath.

Beyond him is a strange, crescent-shaped crater of blackened and glassed concrete. No sign of the third truck. I get to my feet and, just as soon, wish I hadn't. Everything spins like an amusement park ride, the kind that you enjoy because they make you throw up.

"Steady. Deep breaths." Frank stands, rifle held down and finger off the trigger. "The last couple of them are gone. That one who shot you dropped his RPG."

"The truck. We have to stop it."

"No, don't worry. That one didn't have anything on our list."

"But—I saw some guns in one crate..."

"Yeah, I caught them. AK-74Ms. Not a problem. Just something extra Krol must have ordered, it's rounded up."

"Did we get all the launchers?"

"Yeah, Brandon, you got them all. Whatever ones you didn't douse in the harbor." He grins again. "Ready to take care of the rest?"

There're moans from all around me. Injured men. One guy still sobbing, blood congealing under his horribly mangled leg. "Yeah. Then I'm ready to go home."

The cleanup is simple.

Despite my fatigue, I gather the RPG crates in handfuls and mash them together until they're unrecognizable as weapons. The warheads themselves, well, Frank has me stack them all in a pile in the middle of the knocked-out and wounded Poles.

"Anybody gets the urge to walk away, you won't have time to tie your shoes before this pastes your innards all over the docks." Frank tosses a metal box into their midst. He waves a device that looks like a walkie-talkie. "I'm watching, gents.".

Sirens blare outside the shipyard, and we make for the fence.

"You know, if you'd have flown us back, we wouldn't be out of breath." Frank pants heavily, leaning against the car. "I'm getting too old for flat out sprinting."

"Try taking a grenade to the face first," I gasp. "It's invigorating."

Frank chuckles again.

"You really going to blow them up?"

"Nope. The box was for Altoids, wrapped in Duct Tape. This is just a standard radio. Doesn't even have batteries. They don't know it."

As we climb into the car, Frank gives me an approving nod. "The Garrison's going to be proud of this one, Brandon. Your first mission was a success."

"So now what, I just wait for them to call me again?"

"Yes. But that doesn't mean you're sitting around. It means training."

I'm about to groan when a thought strikes like a lightning bolt. "If I'm going to do that, I want it to be field work."

Frank's frown returns. "Okay. Explain."

I think of my library, Vanchev, Reed, Kelly and Sean. I think of the mess the neighborhood has become and the threat to close one of the only safe places people there have to go. There's more than one way to stop it.

My turn to grin. "We're going to make me into a superhero."

Part Two

Summer

Chapter Eleven

It's a hot day out, this afternoon of June 11. But up here, I barely notice. The sun cooks the top of my helmet, the black plastic soaking in the rays. But the wind is cold enough to make me glad for the fleece zipped to my neck.

Besides, whoever heard of a superhero fighting crime in a short-sleeved shirt?

"You got them?" Frank snaps into my ear. "They turned onto Broad Street three blocks ago."

"Yes, I see them." The red pickup truck is hard to miss, especially since there are two men with handguns hunkered in the back. Dull gray duffel bags, bulging against their zippers, are sandwiched between them. Fifteen minutes ago, they walked into First Northeastern Bank at the corner of Fourteenth and Hull and demanded all the money they could carry. Tellers gave them thirty thousand.

But that wasn't enough. The four robbers took every ounce of cash and jewelry they could find on the customers. The same people who were fighting rising taxes, epic bouts of unemployment, and otherwise daunting crimps in their cash flow.

Then they shot a guy who tried to stop them. A carpenter with three kids. He's on his way to intensive care.

"Police are en route," Frank says. "They're not going to make it before these jokers disappear. If they do it's going to be messy."

"So, I'll fix that."

"Watch yourself. This is a two-ton Ford moving—I should say swerving—in excess of sixty miles an hour."

"What, is that it?" I grin. "Feels like a stroll."

"Stop being a smartass and do your thing."

I'm just needling him, because he makes it so much fun. But then, this is already exhilarating without that bonus. It's quarter past four on a Thursday. Having your best friend as your boss has its advantages. With the Hull Branch's doors closing at 6, Reed's happy to validate whatever excuse I use for bolting from work to fight crime.

In my haste, I left my bicycle locked up outside the library's back door.

Dipping my right shoulder, I corkscrew down a couple hundred feet, until I'm soaring above and behind the truck. I could have slammed right into them, but I didn't. Two reasons. One: there is a lot of traffic around, including parents driving minivans and SUVs laden with kids going home from school.

Two: I want them to see me first.

One of the men in the pickup's bed is their spotter. He shouts a warning and raises his pistol. Muzzle flashes come in quick succession. My shield's already formed, not that it matters much. This guy couldn't hit the broad side of a shipping container with a snow shovel if he were standing next to it.

His buddy digs behind some of the sacks and comes up with a rifle, complete with a scope. There's a resounding crack, and sparks shower the left side of my face. The impact with the shield, just over my left shoulder, wobbles my flight path, but only a minor deviation. Bullet impacts are nothing after two months.

I boost my speed and zoom in low over them. Close enough that I can see the wide-eyed fear in their faces, the sweat stains on their white tracksuits with black stripes. As I pass, I reach out with both hands and yank.

Their guns flip out of their hands, end over end, and smash into the opposite robbers' face. The crack those noses make is as loud as the rifle's report.

I loop over, climbing high, and dive back down in a blistering Immelmann. Always wanted to try that. This second pass, no small potatoes—I hover above the truck bed and marshal as much of the field as I dare into two imaginary clamps. Both men jerk limply into the air, dangling like shirts on clothes hangers. As soon as they're secure in my grip, I put on the brakes. The pickup races out from beneath my feet.

"Nicely done," Frank says. "Drop them at the next light. I've got some zip ties and duct tape to decorate our present for DCPD."

"Roger that, and wilco."

Frank snorts and signs off.

I take him literally and dump the men in a heap while going about forty miles per hour. Then I blast off down the road, the red pickup's bumper square in my sights. Dodging cars by mere feet and hearing horns protest only fuels my adrenaline.

Yes, it's broad daylight. Yes, this is not a Garrison-sanctioned mission. Yes, Frank is mad. Our deal is simple: He trains me for action against the Ashen, and I can fight crime, or else he can find himself another person to use the medallion. He's given no indication he wants to do the latter, so, for the time being, I'll do what the Garrison wants.

But this is my town.

The passenger window rolls down. A slim guy, clean shaven from his chin to the top of his head and clad in the same black and white tracksuit, climbs out with the agility of a spider. He clambers into the truck bed and starts shoving aside duffel bags.

Whatever he's up to, he's run out of time. I focus the field to grab around his body, same as I did with his two buddies that got dropped off.

The last bag, full of money, slides over, revealing a big, black machine gun sitting on a tripod.

"Uh oh."

"What's 'uh oh'?" Frank asks.

"Nothing. No problem." The machine gun explodes with fire, clinking and shaking. Bullets slam into my shield with tremendous force. I go spinning off to the left, struck dizzy, spots in my vision from the hailstorm of sparks. Even as my brain panics, a cold hard set of facts pop up from the regimented librarian part: UKM 2000, Polish made machine gun, capable of firing 600 rounds per minute. Thanks for the weapons-familiarity, Frank.

I can block this weapon. But the combination of flying and keeping my shields raised is draining my strength. Even after a long bike ride, I rarely feel this tired. I stay up high, keeping myself on a swerving course, adding in a few sharp twists. This gunner's good. He stays on me.

I don't dare get lower for fear of what he can do to the people in the crowd of vehicles with that gun.

"Report, Brandon."

"Machine gun, Frank. Imported."

"Watch it. I'm tying up your buddies down the street. Can't provide fire support yet, but give me a couple minutes and I'll be there."

"It's not me I'm worrying about." I bank around the side of the truck, making sure the gunner stays on me and doesn't go for any other targets. My angle has to be precise, like a perfectly straight row of books on a shelf. If those bullets slam downward into another car, the results will be catastrophic.

Let's see how adaptable this guy is.

I slowly lead him down, as close as I dare to the road. Asphalt blurs by six feet under me, now five feet, four feet...

Suddenly there's the harsh punch of metal through metal. The machine gun's shooting right through the side of the pickup's bed. Light streams through a neat row of holes—and then the left rear tire explodes.

The pickup fishtails, but the driver's good. He avoids a sedan by inches, keeps his truck racing forward as best he can. I swoop up, around the nose of the truck, and fly backward. Fortunately, I remember to keep those imaginary rockets aimed correctly. I don't want to flip onto my backside at seventy miles per hour.

The drive glares at me. He doesn't produce a gun, which is a good move on his part, considering it appears he needs all five fingers on both hands to wrestle the steering wheel. Behind him the slim gunner is jerking at the UKM. Wonder how he figures he's going to shoot me when I'm flinging along in front of his ride's cab.

"The police are closing in on your location, Brandon." The harsh growl of the Camaro's engine in the background cuts the volume of Frank's voice. "I'm two minutes out."

"Thanks." I plant my hands on the hood of the car. "But I've got this."

I redirect the field, picturing myself as a towering statue of solid steel, weighing tons more than the pickup. The truck slows, not much, but it's noticeable.

It also starts into a spin.

He's going to sideswipe someone. Throwing caution aside, I change tactics. The pickup's heavy. How light can I get it?

Feathers. I see dozens of them, floating. Instinctively, I project the field under the pickup.

It's too effective. The truck leaps up off the pavement, hurtling ten, twenty, thirty feet in the air. Duffel bags shoot out like baseballs, bouncing off cars and bursting open on the pavement. The machine gun crunches into the ground. Somehow, the slim gunner hangs on, screaming what I can only assume are prayers in Polish.

Seconds to react. Use your surroundings! That's Frank's lesson. But all I see are buildings, cars, more buildings—

And Diamond Park.

I plant my feet on the hood of the car and both hands on the roof, stretching across the windshield. This is going to hurt.

From feather to baseball bat.

A tremendous force wallops the bottom of the truck as we change trajectory, tumbling over the roofs of cars. The blur of black asphalt is interrupted by a strip of white and turns brilliant green. The park grounds.

My energy is spent. The field barely reacts to my commands. The shield is gone, and my imagined rocket's failing fast. In the instant before we hit the ground, I can see people, but they're far off, under a copse of trees. I hurl myself clear of the hood.

The truck rolls once, twice, and slams, belly first, into a broad oak. Metal crumples, windshield shatters. The pickup scrapes bark clean from the trunk as it drops the last four feet to the ground.

My landing is less damaging. I hit with my shoulder first, but the last dregs of my strength go into a cushioning field. It feels like landing on the softest, most comfortable mattress, the one you bounce off when you're playing Superman on your bed. I rebound, orient myself upright and come down hard on both feet. My knees buckle with the impact, but I stay upright.

Good thing too. No sooner has the truck come to a complete stop than half a dozen onlookers come running: a pair of young women in skintight running gear that has way too much neon splashed across it; a mother clutching at her infant as a tall, thin and bespectacled husband hurries ahead; an elderly Asian man stooped over at the waist; and an overweight Latino with a thick beard who drops a couple bags of groceries on the way. They all stop moving when they catch sight of me.

"Dios mio! It's him!" The big guy, eyes wide and sweating more than I am even though he's got only a Dragons T-shirt and black shorts on, whips a phone from his pocket. Here comes a photo or another video. "The flier guy!"

"Stay back." My warning freezes him in his tracks. The librarian-slash-parent voice has applications outside the workplace and home, it seems. There's no sign of movement from the truck, but I'm not going to risk it. There's the slim guy who fired the UKM, spread-eagled in the grass ten feet from the initial point of impact, which is marked by a huge brown gash in the green. His eyes are shut. Driver appears incapacitated, too; he's slumped over the steering wheel.

"Brandon! Brandon, report!"

"Relax, Frank." There's no fuel leaking from the truck. No smell of anything burning. I climb inside the cab and shut off the engine. Driver's got a pulse. And in here, I can talk with Frank without sounding like I'm having a conversation with myself. "I'm okay. The truck's stopped."

"No kidding. I saw your backwards acrobatics." He chuckles. "Nice landing spot, too. Listen, I'm three hundred yards south-southeast of your position, on Renaissance Boulevard, engine running. You holding up?"

"I think so."

"It's either yes or no, Brandon. Using the medallion wipes you out. Trust me. I remember. You've got five minutes. If you can't fly by then, I'm coming to get you and we're driving out of here."

"Stand by." I get out and check the condition of the gunner. He's out cold, too, but alive.

"What can we do?" asks the toddler's dad. "How can we help?"

I consider him. Could be a white-collar office drone for all I know, eyes squinting behind thick glasses, but he's right in front of everyone else. If he's afraid, he doesn't show it. Actually, by the way he's looking at me, he seems more worried than anything.

I ease out of a crouch, so the vertigo doesn't topple me. I dig zip ties from my pocket. "Here. Secure his hands and feet. The police will be here soon. Thanks."

He nods. "Sir, I've seen what you can do, even before today. Thank you for watching over everyone."

My strength's returning, which is good, because I can't stick around. Black and white cars speed, sirens blaring, speed down Broad street. I reform the field, carefully, until I feel the familiar sharp cold from the medallion. "Everyone, stay clear of that truck."

I rise ten feet off the ground, testing my flight. From here, I can see cars in a tangled mess with people on foot milling about, snatching up bits of green paper. The police arrive, some waving after the people who try to escape with their newfound loot, but most of the people bring it over voluntarily. That swells my heart with pride. That's Drake City.

"Hey! Flier guy!" The Latino man's waving at me with one chubby hand, the other aiming his phone. "Who are you, man? Everyone wants to know who you are!"

I turn back toward them, rising up. The dad has successfully tied up the bank robber. A quartet of DCPD patrolmen sprint between the trees. I've thought about this moment a lot, and after crossing a bunch of possibilities off my list, I settled on only one.

"Call me Airfoil," I call out, and with that, I boost off into the north sky.

"You're kidding me."

Frank's voice echoes up from the cavernous confines of the abandoned radar tower. That's the only statement I can make out. The series of mutters that follow are indecipherable.

"I like it," I say back down to him. It's brilliantly sunny up here, so bright the pages of my reading material would blind me if not for my sunglasses. The helmet makes a passable pillow, especially with my fleece balled up atop it. I'm laying down, knees up, resting. The medallion's an ice cube on my otherwise sunbaked chest. Any longer out here and I'm bound to get burnt, but for now, the sun feels great on bare skin.

"Airfoil. It's a dumb name."

"Hey, it was your idea."

"What?"

"At the start of flight training. That's how you described the medallion's field, remember? How the air moves around me while I'm flying..."

"Dumb name." His shoes clunk on the stairs. Soon enough, he comes up onto the walkway, wearing khakis, gray sneakers, and a navy-blue polo shirt. He slides on a pair of mirrored shades. "And now you're what, sunbathing? This isn't Club Med."

"Nobody even knows Club Med anymore, Frank," I mutter, and turn a page.

"Reading again. Last week it was Sea of Glory."

"That was a great one. American Exploring Expedition of 1838. Did you know—?"

"Still don't care." He gestures to the book. "So what's it this time?"

"The Good Book."

Frank snorts. "Here I thought you were broadening your mind."

"Never been broader."

"I meant with history, not fantasy."

"Seriously? I'm flying around with a medallion that lets me defy gravity."

"You're not going to find any answers to its origin in there. Nobody has them."

"I'm not searching for those answers, Frank. I'm reminding myself of the answers to questions that matter."

"What matters is stopping the Ashen move for move. If you're done, come downstairs. We've got to review your performance."

I tug on a green T-shirt, follow him down the stairs and into the cool shade of the abandoned tower. It's dark around the edges, with a huge circle of light in the center streaming down through the middle of the tower. A pair of ruggedized laptop computers sits on a rusted metal table, giving off a pale blue glow from their screens. Frank's ever-present duffle bag rests on a second table, with a cornucopia of weaponry laid out beside it—the SCAR-L, the Steyr machine pistol, his T4, a huge revolver, a small Walther P99 and assorted magazines of ammo, plus an open .45 caliber ammo box.

Frank stands in front of one laptop, pointing at the screen. "Right there. See? You got sloppy."

It's me and the truck flipping through the air toward Diamond Park. Can't see the landing, but I wince as I remember it. Fairly clear image, too.

"You can't just go slamming things around, Brandon," Frank says. "Most times you're not going to need a sledgehammer. All you need is a scalpel. In this case, you should have redirected the field more slowly, eased off the weight of the car."

"Yeah, well, I was operating on the fly." What's his problem? "I don't recall this sledgehammer business being a problem when I wrecked the RPG deal a couple of months ago."

"That was different. That was combat. Here? There's greater chance for collateral damage."

"That's why I had to do something! They could have shot other people to pieces!"

Frank shakes his head. "You'd think your limited exploits would lead to you having a better grasp on the medallion and its uses. You don't have to just smash things around! You think the Garrison's medallion holders stayed secret for centuries by breaking stuff?"

I sit on a crumpled, half-rusted file cabinet. "What's this really about, Frank? You taking me off patrol? Looking for an excuse to keep me locked away until the Garrison comes calling?

Which, by the way, they haven't."

"Patrol." Frank snorts. "Listen to you, talking like you've been a soldier for the Garrison. You're too green, Brandon, and you're going to get yourself on YouTube, cause heaps of property damage, and generally be a nuisance."

"No. No, you're wrong. Here." I grab the other laptop, pull up a search engine. Type in "Crime statistics" and "Drake City." The results are instantaneous and can't be argued. Within seconds, I'm in the DCPD public reports page, pulling up a PDF. "This. These are the crime stats for every neighborhood in Drake City, by month. Look at Hull. There's a ten percent dip in robberies, muggings and assaults."

"So, you stopped one out of every ten crimes. You don't get a medal. All you get is exhausted, and sloppy."

I slam the lid down. "Sloppy? Let's talk sloppy. Let's talk about how that machine gun got in the back of the pickup."

Frank shrugged. "I assume Krol and his boys have done some more ordering online."

"I told you there were military weapons in that other truck."

"No, no there weren't. I told you I took care of the crates that had AKs. No clue where they got a UKM, but my guess is not through the shipyards, since they'd gotten throttled by you once. Any more questions?"

"Yes, one that's been bothering me." I let the medallion hang outside my shirt. "The rattlesnake. What's it for?"

"Probably personal decoration, somewhere along the line of ownership. Medallion holders try to add their own symbols. The Garrison discourages it."

"Who used to own this one?"

"Besides Samantha? I don't have that information." Frank takes the second laptop back from me. "What I do have is your next target from the Garrison: the Otte-Vaughn Corporation mine."

I frown, digging back through the information filed in my brain. That sounds familiar, like I'd seen it in the Messenger or heard one of our library patrons talking about. "A guy stopped in last week, talking about the work underway to reopen the mine. Something to do with new ownership. Think they're looking for tungsten this time around, but I don't know why they bother: those mines in the cliffs outside Newport have been dug at dozens of times since the city's foundation, and no one's brought up enough of anything to make sustained extraction worthwhile."

Frank raises an eyebrow. "I didn't realize that."

"That's because you're not a librarian who's obsessed with history." I gesture at the laptop. "So, your secret society sent an email?"

"Our secret society, and yes. It's an encrypted electronic communication. You'd prefer messenger pigeon or coded scrolls?"

"They could have just left it in the book drop."

"Smartass." Frank scrolls down through the message. "There are no particulars as of yet, but the Garrison is convinced this reopening, and the renewed interest, has the Ashen's fingerprints all over it."

"Okay." I pause, waiting for further instruction, but Frank's as silent as the shadows around us. "That's it?"

"Until they give us more intel, yes. I recommend we go take a peek at their reopened facility, for reconnaissance purposes only."

"Not tonight. Sean's home and we're going to stay in."

"You keep spending time with your son and not going to bars, you'll run out of excuses to hide your crime-fighting on the evening shift," Frank says sourly.

"Let me worry about that."

"You've been taking the parent thing pretty seriously as of late. Why?"

"Again, let me worry." I get up, scoop up my helmet and jacket. "If we're done, I've got a bike to retrieve and dinner to cook."

"Hold on." Frank grabs his car keys from the table and powers down the laptops. He tucks the Walther into his waistband, muttering apparently to himself, "Stuck with the peashooter."

I point to his car. "Want to race?"

"Funny guy. Get in. I'm driving. Last thing we need is another daylight appearance this soon."

It's a quick drive to Hull Branch and a fantastic ride on my bicycle back to the apartments. The streets are busy this afternoon, with lots of locals out enjoying the nice weather and on their way home from work. A lot more cars with out-of-state plates around, as tourists trickle into the city. By August, I'll see licenses from most of the lower 48.

Outside my building, my neighbor Coolidge Darrow is watering the flowers in the first-floor window boxes. Petunias, planted by his wife. He's bald, save for a fringe of white hair over his ears and down the back of his head, and wears huge, gold-framed glasses that were last in style in the 1980s. I think he's in his eighties, but he can keep up with me on a bicycle.

"Afternoon, Brandon," he says, voice croaking like a frog. "Day like this makes you glad there's more to creation than rain and fog."

"Sure does, Mr. Darrow." I can't call him Coolidge. Makes as much sense to me as calling my grandfather Ralph. The tattoo on his forearm, sagging with the folds of skin and looking more like a bruise by now, reminds me he was—is—a U.S. Marine. "How's your day?"

"Lots of busy work. The Missus, she has her list for me. Needs all the heavy lifting done, I suppose." He makes a show of shaking the watering can until drops splash on the steps.

I laugh. "Well, it's good to see you. Thanks again for keeping an eye on Sean last weekend."

"Sure thing. You and your buddy have been quite busy lately."

"Oh, yeah, busy."

"Glad to see you home more in the evenings, though. It's

good for Sean. A boy should know his father's there for him—not holding his hand, mind, but around." Mr. Darrow eyeballs me, all jocularity evaporating faster that those drops of water on the steps. "There's not enough of those these days, and the kids get into trouble. I'll help, but your boy's outcome is your responsibility."

I nod and smile. "I know, Mr. Darrow. I know it more and more. Thanks."

Inside, I've barely gotten the door open when Sean beelines for me from his bedroom. One of his earbuds dangles off his left shoulder, blaring music. "Oh, hey."

"Hey, Sean. How was school?"

"What? Yeah, good. Hey, where are the bills?" He glances around, as if the documents in question are preparing an ambush. "I can't find them."

"That's because they're paid and in the mail. As of Wednesday." I pat him on the shoulder and plant my backpack by the door, next to the weight set. That's new to the apartment, courtesy of Frank's urging that I increase my upper body work. "Speaking of mail, anything interesting?"

"Messenger, and junk." Sean frowns. "You did the bills. Again."

"Yes, I did." I grab an orange soda from the fridge. After sucking down cold water all day, it's a jolt of lightning.

"That's like two months in a row now."

"Careful, you might faint. If you do, aim for the couch." I grin at him and grab the Messenger and plop myself onto a cushion. "There's chicken defrosting. What time you want dinner?"

"I...uh..."

"Oh, sorry, do you have plans with Tucker? Or Leon?"

"No, no, tomorrow night but not..." He stops himself, sits opposite me in a chair. "Are you staying in?"

"Once again, yes."

"Weird." Sean's tapping on his phone. It's a practiced nonchalance. "So, no buddy Frank."

"Not tonight."

"What kind of stuff do you guys talk about? Must be interesting, you hang out a lot."

"Well... he's family, in a way." I don't like fudging the truth with Sean, but the medallion—and especially its abilities—has to stay secret. True, Reed knows, but that was revealed before Frank caught up with me. Were anything to happen to Sean, I'd never forgive myself. It makes it easier to see why Samantha kept this responsibility hidden.

"You guys talk about Mom?"

"Sometimes."

He goes cold after that, sullen. I sigh. Should have said no or shrugged. "Sean..."

"Hey, check this out!" His mood changes faster than lightning flashes. He's grinning and flips the phone around for me to see. "I can't believe it! Who is this guy?"

That's me, hurling the pickup truck.

"Huh. That's pretty wild." I go back to my paper, hiding my mirth.

"Wild? It's insane! Dude can fly and now he can throw a truck! Or roll with it, or whatever it is." Sean shakes his head, fingers tapping the phone. "I'm sending this to Reed. He's gonna love it."

"Where'd you find it?"

"Leon texted me. So did Sasha."

Leon's one of his best pals, right after Tucker. But... "Who's Sasha?"

"A girl. In Social Studies." The tops of Sean's ears get red. Just like his mother's used to.

"Oh, I see." I flip the next page in the paper. "Cute?"

Sean shrugs, but that grin's back, creeping around the corners of his mouth. "Maybe. Yeah. And nice."

"Good deal."

My phone buzzes. It's in my bag, so I cross the room to get it. I should say they're in my bag, because my Frank phone is tucked into the outermost compartment right along with my cell. Two buzzes, then nothing. A text. I dig for the phones.

No indicator light on Frank's, but mine shines a pulsing light.

I open the message. It's not from Reed or Kelly.

<You have the medallion of Tobias Rankin.>

My heart thuds. Cold sweat beads along my forehead.

A double buzz. Another text.

<Tobias Rankin can tell you much about its purpose. Maritime Museum. Local History Archives. Find his message. He's left it in plain sight.>

I type furiously, stumbling over letters. <What message?>

Send it. Nothing. Seconds tick by. I set the phone aside and resume reading the *Messenger*. Then another buzz. <The rattlesnake.>

No. How would this person know what's on my medallion? Only Frank and Reed have seen it.

I text back, <Who are you?>

This time I only have to wait a few breaths. And then— <Go. Maritime Museum. Or else when the dark falls, you will be blind as the rest.>

Instantly, I type back, <Tell me your name!>

But no sooner have I sent it than it bounces back with an error, "Invalid number."

"Hey Dad?" Sean shifts in his chair. "What's up?"

"Ah, nothing." I slap the phone against my hand. "Let's go get started on dinner."

"Okay. Was that Reed? You got big plans for work tomorrow?"

"No, not really. Should be an easy Friday."

Of course, that plan now includes heading to the museum. If Frank thinks I'm letting this rattlesnake business go, he's wrong.

Besides, there's someone I know who should have the answers I need.

Chapter Twelve

The next morning, I'm up, showered, and cooking pancakes by the time Sean comes out of his bedroom. He stands at the table, eyes bleary, hair disheveled. "What're you doing up?"

"Making breakfast. Hungry?"

"Duh. Always. I mean…" He shakes his head. "I'm gonna get showered."

My smile fades once he's gone. Somehow, I thought this would help out with things between us. Taking care of the bills on time, getting more rest, not hitting the snooze button on the alarm for twenty minutes. Those failures robbed me of Sean's respect. Hadn't they?

We still eat breakfast in silence. Obviously, my conclusions were wrong. Whatever's gnawing at him goes beyond the lackadaisical routines that I've now improved. He's not doing his homework as a last-minute rush in the morning; today he's got a New 52 Batman under his nose. The stash in his room is piled high under his desk.

"That a good one?" I ask.

"Hmm? What?"

"The comic. Is it a good one?"

He frowns, like I've just asked whether the sun rose this

morning. "It's Batman, Dad. They're all good."

"Ah." My knowledge of these characters has always been spotty, even with Reed pushing them every chance he gets. "So what's up for today?"

Sean shrugs. "School. Leon and me are going over to...we're headed to the Lightning Bolt Comics store after school."

That pause. That's his oh-crap-I-almost-told-Dad-my-real-plan pause. "Sean."

"What?"

"Where are you guys really going?"

"Comics store."

"No."

"Yeah, I just said..."

"Can it. I know what you said. What were you going to say before you caught yourself?"

Sean scowls.

"Never play poker, Sean. Spit it out."

"We're gonna swing by Diamond Park," he mutters. "I want to see...you know, where it happened."

It. The video of yesterday's wreck after the robbery. "You're chasing this flying guy around? That's not safe."

"So what?" Sean pushes up from the table. "He's doing stuff nobody else can. He's taking it right to the bad guys."

As pleasing it is to hear my son say it, there's no way I want him sniffing around my trail. "You need to just stay away from all this flying guy stuff. You're doing so well at school I don't want to see you slip, you know? That happens when you get locked onto an idea."

"Homework? This isn't about homework." He's got his backpack and shoves his comic into the open compartment. "This guy's real. I know it. Everyone knows it now. There's like fifty thousand people who've watched that video. They know he's real. And I want to do something more than—like—get my grades better. Important stuff."

He slams the door. Just me and the soggy pancakes. I jab at them with a fork. Smoothly handled, Brandon. Can't believe the kid. All this effort, all this hard work...no results. He thinks I'm more a tyrant than ever. A competent tyrant, instead of an incompetent one, but a tyrant nonetheless.

Great way to start a Friday.

Less than a half hour after I get settled in at work, I'm hunched over a Samsung tablet. The lady on the other side of my counter waits, arms folded, watching me with that gaze that implies I have no clue what I'm doing. Which is mildly amusing, given she's just given me the device clean out of the box and has never touched it herself. I've already spent more time playing with it than she has.

"Well, Ma'am, it'll take me a while to install the catalog program. The e-reader software functions just fine, but it's a pain to set up, probably twenty minutes," I say.

"Are you sure you're doing that right? That screen looks wrong." She frowns.

I look up at her. Twenty-nine. That's how many e-readers and tablets I've installed in the past year. Every single one of them took longer than expected, because of some glitch, some incompatibility, and four times because the owner didn't charge the tablet. Only one patron had all their ducks in a row when we started. That was a fourteen-year-old. And this lady's talking to me like I'm the one with half a brain. Plus, I'm surly because the air conditioner's in a state of disrepair, and being sweaty doesn't make one better oriented for customer service.

Before I can say anything close to what's on my mind, Kelly's here with a smile. "Brandon, can I talk you a second? We'll just be a moment, ma'am."

The lady squints but doesn't argue. Kelly pulls me over to the other end of the desk, and whispers, "You looked like you needed a diversion."

I keep my back to the lady so I can grin at Kelly. "Nicely done."

"Payback for when the drunk guy kept asking for my number last fall."

"Point." I glance at the woman. The tablet's going to install for at least the next ten minutes. "Still, glad you were there."

"It's not all friendly assist. Reed needs to talk to us about the benefit plans."

"Right. When's Director Vanchev coming?"

"In a few minutes. Patty and Myra are going to watch the front desk for us."

We have our volunteers in shelving for us every other day, two former librarians who divide their time between here and the city's historical society. They're in the back right now, our storage area, swapping out old, worn books with new donations. "Nice. So you can lay out your plan for the benefit to us all."

Kelly nods, still smiling. "Just so you know who's running this show today."

"Thanks. For this, I owe you lunch. Place of your choice."

"Oh." She's suddenly distracted by the lady behind us. "That would be, um, nice."

"Saturday work?"

"Sorry, I can't. I'm going to visit my grandpa. He's at St. Andrew's Home."

I know the place. Across the street from the Catholic Church with the same name, up on Third Street. "Okay then, I did say I'd go with you next time. Why don't we grab a bite before then?"

"I told the staff I'd be there at ten."

"So we get coffee." I grin. "Nine thirty?"

"That sounds nice." She tucks a strand of raven hair over her ear, just enough to drive me nuts, and smiles. "But I don't drink coffee. Tea only. Your brain must be pretty full if you've forgotten."

"Mea culpa."

"There's a café down the block from St. Andrew's. It has outside seating, lovely trees for shade. Dowlington."

"Sounds like a plan."

"Good. Remember to be your usual chipper self, and this lady won't bug you too much."

She handles the patron in question with the typical unflappable Kelly calm, not flinching when the lady peppers her with idiotic questions while fanning herself with one of our brochures. I head for Reed's office, grinning like a dope.

Reed's typing furiously and muttering. There're spreadsheets highlighted in streaks of green and red on the screen before him. That mound of papers looks as unruly as my hair, especially with the tiny white fan mounted on the desk rustling them. He's got a stapler as a paperweight. I knock on the doorframe. "What?"

"Reporting as ordered, Skipper." I sit in one of the two chairs opposite his desk. The office is comfortable, with a single wooden desk and a leather swivel chair for Reed, two pale blue upholstered seats for his visitors. Most of the office is windows out on to the rest of the library, with Venetian blinds that can be drawn for privacy. There's a calendar on the wall to his right—Star Trek spaceships. The pair of photos on his desk of Caroline and the kids are framed in black.

Reed reaches for a mug emblazoned with the Superman crest and sips. The fragrant orange spice tea wafts across me. "Spill it, Brando."

"Spill what?"

"Um, gee, let's think. Spill about the part where you threw a pickup truck into Diamond Park, or the part where you took on a guy with a machine gun. Who shot at you." Reed grins, though it's not as carefree as his usual expression. There's strain there, around the eyes. "I've been a good boy and not bugged you about it since, oh, the second I saw it online."

I shrug. "What can I say? Airfoil: One; Bad Guys: Zero."

"Nice." Reed leans back in his chair. "That is completely

badass. I can't believe I've got a superhero sitting in my office. And he's my employee!"

"Okay, that's great, but how about we keep from shouting this thing to the whole world. Especially since your door's open."

"Duh. I know a thing or two about secret identities. Everybody in the comics hides them. Except Tony Stark. Bad example to follow. You don't want to hold a press conference and tell everybody what you've been up to." He laces his fingers behind his back. "What was it like?"

"Exhilarating. To use that much power," I pause. "That part, well, unnerves me, when it's all over. When the adrenaline wears off, you think about it more."

"Man. That's got to be insane. Superman-insane."

"Superman doesn't get dog-tired, I'll bet. What about you?"

"What about me?"

"You, sir, look terrible."

"Nice. Your concern's touching." Reed taps the papers. "This last-minute budget nonsense. I was here until eight last night. Caroline was upset. But she still let me eat, so that's a win. I don't know if we're going to pull off this thing. Sure, crime's down—thanks to you—but the council's still divided. Our doors could get shut next month."

"That's what Kelly's benefit idea's for."

"I know, I know. Doesn't help me sleep any. And then the air conditioner's out, again. Third time this month. Maintenance dude swears he fixed it, but if he can't get it right this morning, I'm going with someone else. Plus, the roof's still leaking, and the bathroom plumbing's a mess."

"You need to get that stuff off your brain for a while. Get in gear for ComicCon, Mr. Fantastic."

"Actually..." Reed scratches at his hair. "I'm thinking about not going."

"What?" He might as well say the moon was dropping out

of orbit. "You're kidding."

"No. There's another project soaking up a lot of my discretional cash, and with this stuff, you know, the timing's bad."

"What could possibly be more important than ComicCon?" I put my hand over my heart and feign shock.

"If you stop being a dick for five seconds I could..." He freezes in mid-sentence, face going pale. "Mr. Vanchev! Come in, sir."

Mark Vanchev breezes into the room, smelling of suntan lotion and sea salt. His khakis are immaculately pressed, and the coral pink polo shirt is all the more noticeable next to his ridiculous tan. He beams and shakes both our hands. Kelly's right behind him. Through the glass, I see our white-haired volunteer ladies are in full command of the library. "Gentlemen. Please, don't get up for me. Let's make this quick."

I am standing, not for him, but to give Kelly the chair. She sits, with Vanchev next to her.

"Now, I believe Miss Quirke has all the final details in order?" Vanchev smiles in her direction.

"Yes, we're ready." She blushes. "The caterers will have the food there in plenty of time to set up. The mayor's office has been very helpful with parking availability, and the band should be all lined up."

"Definitely." That's my responsibility. "And I've got the posters created. The Friends group will put them out this weekend."

"I talked to Suze yesterday," Reed says. "We're good as far as Messenger PR is concerned."

"Well then. You all hardly need the system director stepping on your toes." Vanchev chuckles. "I should let you know that we have an evenly divided city council with which to contend. It has helped matters that violent incidents in Hull are on the downswing—and bigger crimes are getting, ah, interrupted by this vigilante who's made the news."

"Has anyone seen him in person?" Kelly asks, leaning in

her chair.

"Nah, not me. You, Brando?" Reed grins.

"Not since this morning." I say it like I'm kidding. Everyone chuckles.

"Good, good." Vanchev pounds the arms of his chair. "You folks have done great work. If we pull this benefit off, and things keep the way they are going, I'm certain we can get those swing votes on the council on our side. You leave the political mess to me. Just keep up the great work. You're a fine team, and I promise I'll do everything I can to keep Hull Branch open."

His phone beeps. "Sorry, I realize I only just arrived but this job..." He shrugs. "As you know, Reed, it keeps a man running. Off to brunch with the city comptroller. Ms. Quirke, email me with an update this afternoon and a list of anything else you need on my end."

"I'll do that," Kelly says. "Thanks much for your help with the parking."

"Any time." With that, he blows out of the office as fast as he arrives. Bet he wishes he could fly.

"Brando." Reed snaps his fingers. "Earth to Brando. Now that our meeting is finished up a good twenty minutes early, why don't you go take care of the bathroom."

"Bathroom?"

"Yeah. Guy came in while you were tablet training. Said the men's toilet is backed up. Again."

Kelly wrinkles her nose. "Good thing I have to go over the benefit's schedule with you, Reed."

I sigh. This is one of those things that will be on my resume if I ever leave: catalog books, help with technical training, unclog toilets. Too bad I can't add, "Foil crime."

It's a two-mile ride to the maritime museum, and the weather's perfect. The thermometer at the corner of Eleventh and Hull tops 80 by the time I get there, but the breeze coming off the bay makes up for the sun beating down on my back. The sandwich cart guy shouts for me to stop by for "the usual.". I give a two fingered wave as I race by, promising to grab lunch on the return trip.

Two miles means I cross the railroad tracks on Fifteenth Street about ten minutes later. A slight downhill takes me past the scattered businesses, mostly small warehouses and a long strip of brick buildings dating to the turn of the last century. Those were shipping offices, opened in competition with the Old City stalwarts. Now they're home to artisans and bike repair shops and consultants and yoga studios.

The Sculpin Maritime Museum is a twenty-acre spread on a bulge of land that was once the brash competition's docks, the newcomers who battled it out with the old shipping families of Drake City starting in the 1890s. It was short lived, however, and once the Newport docks opened, both areas fell into disuse and disrepair. The museum bought up land there in the 1960s and slowly rebuilt the area into a well-maintained tract that includes a replica fishing village from the early 19th Century, a long barn-shaped art gallery, a huge boat restoration shed, and the main exhibit hall itself. The sun gleams off the glass front and sides of the building with its signature wave-shaped roofs.

I slip my bike between the dozens of cars in the lot, most of which bear out-of-state plates and lock it up at the rack by the main entrance. The view is fantastic. Not counting the pair of restored tall-masted schooners anchored off the pier, or the old lightship and steam tug opposite them. The glassed-in front of the museum shows off the full-size replica of privateer Jonah Keene's sloop Incorrigible. He was Drake City's hero of the American Revolution, with eighteen confirmed captures of vessels flying the Union Jack.

There's a tour going on, so I bypass a knot of men and women wearing very loud clothing and snapping pictures of everything with their phones. On the right are the staff offices. The one I need has a brass plate outside the open door that says "Registrar Eliana Dachton." I knock on the wall.

"Brandon? Where have you been!" She's up from her desk in a flash, bringing along with her a curious mix of a faint, flowery perfume and the sharp spice of the shawarma she's having for lunch. Eliana Dachton is five-six with curly, dirty blonde hair and blue eyes so pale they verge on gray. "I haven't seen you in ages."

"Not since the community resource training that our bosses put us through."

Eliana rolls her eyes. "That's right. I'd almost forgotten."

"Because you slept through the first class."

"I did not! I did, perhaps, close my eyes to rest...or was it a headache?"

I chuckle. "It's good to see you again. How's Chad and Liz?"

"Doing well. Liz started kindergarten. Chad got promoted at the bank, assistant supervisor."

"Good for him. Hard to believe Liz is that big now."

"Hard to believe Sean's what, thirteen?" Eliana's expression saddens. "I bet he looks even more like Sam. I'm sorry we haven't kept in touch."

"Hey, I'm just as much at fault. You and Samantha were close. It had to have been hard."

"Nowhere near as bad as it was for you." She rubs at the corner of her eyes, nudging her glasses.

My chest tightens. I force away the memories of the car wreck. Focus on the present, not the heartache. "I'm actually here to do some research."

"Oh? Still looking for that merchant captain who built your home?"

"No. A different name. Tobias Rankin."

Her face goes blank, but I know this look. It's her scanning through the heaps of information she stores in her head. If I ever meet a computer that can do it as fast as she can, without freezing, I'll buy the computer lunch. "The last name's familiar, but I don't know why. Let's take a look."

Her desk is the opposite of Reed's. Being a leftie, she's got nothing where I think it should be: mouse, water bottle, even the fork for the recycled paper container of shawarma she shoves aside. Plus, she has the kind of organizational skills a librarian envies. There's not a scrap of stray paper or speck of errant dust anywhere. The photo of her husband, bearded and bald, grins at us from an office boardroom in the frame perched next to her 30-inch computer monitor. Her daughter's smiling from the smaller photo next to it, all pigtails and rosy cheeks.

Eliana taps keys without glancing away from the screen. "Tobias...Rankin." The search comes back immediately. "Nothing in our collection. Did you try Googling it?"

"Yes. A couple of hits on that name, from Midcoast Maine." I join her on the other side of the desk and perch on the edge.

"Hmm. That's it? There has to be more." She dives in, opening multiple tabs in two browsers, eyes flicking from page to page. I'm impressed. I can never stay this organized on a search. That's why my initial foray into hunting down the medallion's origins ended so quickly. "You know, Sam and I used to have these contests, to see which one could find a specific document first. That was senior year at Boston, of course."

"You gals were nerds."

"That didn't stop you and Chad from marrying us."

"Never said you were bad-looking nerds..."

She tries to elbow me, but I dodge it. "Now here's something."

The page before us is an obscure document from a private collector's local history page of Knox County. It's a handwritten document, some kind of invoice judging by the text. "Is that a price for ink?"

"It is. From the Camden Light. A short-lived newspaper in

the town of the same name, early 19th Century Penobscot Bay region. See the signature?"

I turn my head sideways. "It's illegible."

"I'd say it's better than your scrawl. No, it clearly says T. Rankin. The blogger says a man with that surname ran the paper, right around the War of 1812."

"T for Tobias?"

"No idea. But it's closer than anything else I can find. Plus, the proximity can't be coincidental." She frowns up at me, eyes shooting a searching stare over her glasses. "What are you looking for?"

I shrug. "It's just a question. Historical curiosity. Speaking of which, rattlesnakes."

She shivers. "Ooh, I hate snakes! Can't stand them."

"Really? But you've scuba-dived and touched eels."

"Very different. They swim. They're not creepy like snakes."

"If you say so. I mean rattlesnakes as in historic symbols."

"Well, there's the Gadsden flag, if you're looking Revolutionary Era. Don't tread on me and all that. It's rumored that around Drake City there were people who used that symbol to denote a covert network, one that included Jonah Keene. Some say it survived in the decades beyond. There's no proof."

I reach to the medallion under my shirt but pause. Surely there wasn't harm in showing someone the medallion, if they had no clue of its true purpose. It's just jewelry or will be to her. "This is what's sparked my interest."

She stares at it, gets close enough I can feel her breath on my neck, but doesn't lift a finger to touch it. "It's old. Very old."

"That's what I gather."

"The symbol, that definitely fits to the Revolutionary War period. I can't be precise, but I have seen other etchings like it. Some very similar." She frowns and pushes her glasses back up her nose. "Some extremely familiar."

Now we're talking. "Such as...?"

"I can't place it. Somewhere in the vaults—you know, the secure, climate-controlled storage for fragile pieces of our collection. Does this necklace have to do with the Tobias Rankin person?"

"Possibly." Very probably, according to my mysterious texter. I consider telling Frank. He'll likely confiscate my phone or tell me to forget it. Well, there's no harm in waiting on informing him. "I thought you already searched your holdings for references to him."

"I did, but there's many items in the vault that haven't been properly identified yet. I'll need some time to go through them."

"Okay. I was hoping to get an answer sooner..."

"Brandon, don't worry." She pats my hand and gives me the same confident smile I remember from the first time we met in Boston. "If it's important to you, it's important to me. I'll find it."

"Thanks Eliana. You're a good friend."

"I am great, aren't I?"

It's nearly ten that night. Flying over the city, spread out like a blanket of jewels beneath me, is awe-inspiring. The mine buildings of Otte-Vaughn Corporation's latest acquisition are sadly less so. The yard is dominated by heaps of rusting metal and towering smokestacks. Hulking trucks are lined up alongside lumpen storage buildings and hulking trucks. Towering chain link fencing topped with shiny new razor wire surrounds the yard. There's no sign of machinery active, or of another living soul, for that matter.

"What do you see?" Frank's right there, muttering in my head.

"Ah, a mine." I bank north, watching the collection of buildings, at five hundred feet up. "Not sure what you're looking for Frank—or what I'm looking for, since I'm doing all the legwork. There's nothing going on. Everything's dark except for a handful of lights in the yard."

"Odd. There should be some activity. Our intel was clear on that."

"I'm guessing someone screwed up."

"Circle for a while. I've to check in with a contact."

"Circle...? Are you putting me on hold?"

The radio clicks off. I roll my eyes with enough emphasis to make Sean proud, even if no one can see it. I continue a long, slow loop around the mine property, heading out over the deep darkness of Burnt Clearing State Park. There's nothing to see out there; the forest is darker than the bay, reflecting no light back at me. Occasionally, an owl flits from tree to tree. Other than that, it's hard to spot anything.

When I glance back at Drake City, the urban lights explode in my vision. Something streaks by. Was that a drone? Way too small to be an aircraft, and way too quiet.

There it goes again, crossing low over the treetops. Not a plane. But far too fast to be a bird. A pair of owls burst up out of the pines, startled.

This time it shoots by, higher, from the opposite direction. Only reason I see it more clearly is the flicker of city lights as whatever it is races toward the mine. It's leaving.

For now, that is. I hone in on the flicker and pour on speed, leveling out my flight path a couple hundred feet above. Whatever it is, it's difficult to catch. I'm gaining but not nearly as quickly as I expected.

The radio cuts in. "Listen. New plan. We need to get a good look inside the mine. I'm talking down in the newest excavation shaft. I'm going to need you to—"

"Frank, it's going to have to wait. I'm tailing a target. Airborne, a quarter mile or so out, heading toward Newport."

He doesn't respond. Whistles by my helmet. "A target. Flying?" His silence drags on. "There's nothing showing up on SCIA radar. Not even city news or police helos."

"You never see police helicopters anywhere outside Westerville unless there's a major incident." Besides, this thing is making turns that are far more severe than anything a helicopter can handle. And it's not large enough.

We race out to Dannersly Bridge, but no matter how much speed I put on, it still stays a quarter mile out. My target weaves between the suspension cables with the ease of a veteran slalom skier. I grit my teeth and follow. It's a tight fit, and I lose valuable speed making turns with enough clearance so I don't slam into anything, but I make it through.

Now, this thing shoots across the water, skimming the surface and kicking up a trail of spray. I get higher, force more speed, struggling for a clearer look. The distant Braddock Island Light beacon flashes, and its beam sweeps over the target.

It's a person.

"Frank. Frank, we've got a serious problem."

"I know. It's the Ashen."

"I...What? How do you know that?"

"Can't be anything else at that speed, Brandon. That isn't mechanical and doesn't show up on radar. Silent, right?"

I nod, then dumbly remember we're using radio. "Right."

"Fits with Garrison intel. They've had rumors of an Ashen operative in this region, but no visual confirmation. Not until now. And here."

"Wish I could have had that intel sooner."

"It was delayed by the fact that our man in Boston was found dead yesterday morning," Frank snaps, "Smeared like paste under a dumpster. So show some respect the next time you're going to trash my information sources."

My heart's pounding. What am I supposed to do? Follow? Intercept? Attack? This isn't a pair of mob-backed bank robbers or street thugs.

This is someone who wields a medallion.

"Watch him. Maintain your distance and report. If he

strikes, you take him out."

No pointers on how to do that, I notice. "Roger."

This Ashen is fast, staying just slightly ahead of me as I rapidly approach my top speed. When I get to that 300 mile an hour threshold, the buffeting and jostling around makes it impossible to maintain an even flight path. I can't seem to smooth out the ride, no matter how intense my concentration. I drop to 200 and keep up that clip.

Suddenly, he veers toward the Braddock light, cutting across the next beam as it flashes through the night sky. I get a much sharper silhouette of him—black outline with flowing cloak or cape. A cape? Reed will go catatonic with glee when he hears this.

He swoops up sharply, climbing until he's a couple hundred feet over the peak of the Braddock lighthouse.

I fly around to the northeast, and he slowly rotates, watching me. He hovers there, still as an oak, his cape billowing. He's wearing all slate gray, black boots, and his head and face are covered by a formless, faceless mask that gives him the appearance of an unfinished, stone sculpture.

Before I can issue a challenge, he reaches out with his left hand, curling his fingertips.

From below us, there's a great crunching, crackling sound. A dark, sloped shape shudders and rises from below the lighthouse. I'm perplexed, wondering at the thing slowly lifting into the air. That's when I realize it's the roof of the old lightkeeper's house, long neglected and original to the 1913 structure. The crunching is the wood braces snapping. The brittle shingles shatter.

He brings the roof up between us, and I can clearly see graffiti scrawled on the main beams. Without a word, without so much as a chance in stance, he flicks his wrist.

And throws the roof at me.

It moves with such stunning speed, like the owls I startled from the trees, that I barely overcome my awe to dodge. As it is, a hailstorm of shingle fragments pelt me, scraping my arms and battering my helmet. The roof whooshes by, the wind of its passage tossing me off course.

That does it. I ball up my fists. He's still hovering there, left hand raised, waiting. Not for long. I muster the field into a battering ram, a giant fist, whatever mental image will cause the most havoc.

He doesn't flinch or prepare. Instead, he lifts his right hand and pulls in, with grasping fingers.

The sensation reaches me a moment before the roof does. I spin myself over, rolling in midair, as the roof hurtles back at us on its return course. Near miss.

"Brandon! What's going on out there?"

"Busy, Frank! He threw a roof at me. I'm okay."

"I saw the roof."

"What?"

"Radar."

The roof continues on past me, past the light house, curving away and down toward the water. I launch myself at this joker, arms extended, the field ready to do damage.

Two sounds register. Deep laughter. And a distant foghorn.

I pause. It's the 10 p.m. ferry from Cape Ashwin to Braddock and Rittenhouse Island. It's a behemoth vessel—450 feet long, three decks. Looks to have more than 50 cars aboard, plus ho knows how many passengers. I see them, milling amongst the deck lights and as shadows behind bright windows.

The roof spins down toward it.

I lunge, wind whistling by my helmet, arms outstretched. Visualize giant hands grabbing the roof, pulling back on it. Nothing. It doesn't even slow.

"I broke into their radio communications," Frank says in clipped, harsh tones. "Warned them to change course."

"Okay." I barrel on, coming up even with, and now in front of the roof, so that I'm against the flat, spinning surface of its belly. There're plenty of rafters under here to grab on to, so I grasp the nearest two. Every ounce of my concentration goes into keeping us both aloft and stopping its headlong rush.

"Lower gravity. Less weight. But don't forget, it's still got mass. Inertia's a killer."

"Duly noted," I grunt between clenched teeth. With everything I can muster, I push back.

The force is immense. The roof pushes me down, shoving me towards Earth. Come on. Come. On!

A rush of sensations all at once: Cold wind. Sharp, hot pain in my left arm. Lightning jolts throughout my body. The ferry foghorn, louder, insistent.

The roof's too big. Too much mass.

But maybe I can turn it.

Splitting my concentration is tricky at this point, but I give myself a push from those trusty imaginary rockets, hoping to alter our trajectory. The roof is stubborn, big—but it slowly bends to the field's grasp. We tumble over twice. All of a sudden, the bay surface is close enough for me to see a quartet of ducks scatter.

"Pull up!" Frank thunders.

I let go and fly off, arrow straight away. The roof hits open water, throwing up a tremendous splash. As I turn over on my back, I exhale with relief. The ferry's starboard side gets drenched, but that's it. Judging by the wake lines, it had already altered course. Not enough that it could have avoided the roof without my intervention.

"Get back to the barn, pronto," Frank says. "You're out of your league."

"Not a chance." I spin back to the lighthouse. To my shock, he's still there. The Ashen operative. I barrel on to him and unleash what I hope to be a sledgehammer of gravitational disruption.

He sidesteps in it midair as if it were an annoying little

dog. And he speaks the only words he's said throughout our confrontation.

"That's all I wanted to see. Well done."

He's gone in a burst of speed that sends a sonic boom thundering across the bay.

Chapter Thirteen

Dennis Marchand slugged back the coffee and gagged. Nasty. Could've been motor oil. "So, you're telling me there's two of them now."

"Yes sir. That's what the witness statements corroborate." Dillard's phone lit up his face as he tapped commands into it. "Seventeen, Lieutenant. All on the upper deck at the time of the incident."

"Right." Marchand dumped the remainder of the brown sludge on the asphalt, crumped the Styrofoam cup and flung it into the grass by the park. Right next to the bright white and blue "NO LITTERING" sign.

Everything on Rittenhouse was like that. Signs for don't do this and don't do that, side by sign with immaculately trimmed lawns and huge, multi-story McMansions. Every car in every driveway sparkled. Marchand couldn't throw his badge without hitting a luxury sedan.

Except here. The little dog park at the corner of Havenshire and L'Amour was empty, devoid of people and canines. The grass looked laser cut. It would have been a nicer image without the two stiffs slumped over the bench.

Rostek and Salkowski. Two of Krol's enforcers. Big guys, big guns, big responsibilities. Now they, their nice shirts and slacks, and one city-funded green park bench made of recycle trash bags were shot through with a dozen holes. Blood stained the grass.

"Witness walking her dog half a block away heard yelling. Couldn't make it out. Everyone else heard the gunfire," Dillard said.

"Yeah, I'll bet. Haven't had a shooting in Rittenhouse since the Eighties." Hmm. Blood was pooled underneath both victims. Marchand shone his flashlight over the area. Shell casings, mostly .45 caliber. A handful of 9 millimeters. Dark splotches off to one side caught his gaze.

"Both victims apparently drew their weapons."

"You think, Dillard? The Glock in Salkowski's hand wasn't a giveaway at all."

Dillard ducked his head and examined his phone with renewed interest.

"Hey. Get off the screen and down here." Marchand knelt by the spots. "What do you see?"

Dillard mimicked Marchand's pose, right down to the flashlight. His eyes went wide. "Blood trail. From the shooter?"

Marchand put a finger to his lips, gestured with the light. They followed it, slowly, toward the trees rimming the park. He drew his Ruger. A second later, he heard metal brush leather as Dillard copied him.

The flashlight beam caught a glint of white behind a tree. Someone wheezed. A shiny black shoe, then a leg clad in crumpled gray slacks, protruded from behind the trunk. Marchand held back his flashlight, signaling Dillard to stop. "DCPD. If you're armed, drop it."

A grunt answered. Something clunked on the grass. Marchand checked with his flashlight: an old M1911. Probably a throwaway gun. He eased in a half circle around the tree, keeping the person—and the discarded weapon—in his sights.

The guy was short, with a rounded, pale face and auburn beard. His hair was curly at the back, slicked down with so much gunk on top that it seemed black. His eyes were glassy, unfocused. His left hand was tucked below his chest, pressing against a massive, gleaming red stain on his shirt. He'd torn off one of his jacket sleeves to try to staunch the flow.

"Ronny Boyd. Sucks to be you." Marchand holstered his gun. Dillard would be vigilant enough for both of them. Besides, he needed both hands free.

"Last breaths I draw, and I get a cop." Boyd laughed, his voice gravely, but it devolved into hacking coughs.

"Sheehan order the hit?"

"You figure it out."

"I'm betting it's retaliation for O'Hanlon and Murray getting bullets in their respective foreheads this summer."

Boyd shrugged. "Where's my ambulance?"

Marchand tsked. "That's not how I do it." He knelt beside Boyd and shoved the back end of his flashlight against the wound.

Boyd screamed, an animalistic sound, his eyes rolling up into his head.

"Who ordered the hits, Ronny?" Marchand shouted. He had to, to be heard over Boyd's screaming. "Make it quick. You're gonna pass out soon."

"Shee—Sheehan!" Boyd hissed the name through gritted teeth. "You—got it."

Marchand backed off. Boyd's screams subsided into choking sobs. Eventually the mobster calmed down, still grasping at his wounds, his drained of all remaining color.

Dillard didn't move the entire time. Marchand glanced at him; yeah, he was staring, openmouthed.

Get used to it, kid.

"Well played, Ronny my boy. Officer Dillard, call our new pal here an ambulance."

"Yessir." Dillard snapped orders into his shoulder radio, and hurried back to the crime scene.

"Let's keep this between us, Ronny." Marchand lifted Boyd's chin with the barrel of his Ruger. "Give Mr. Sheehan a message from his friendly neighbors at DCPD: back off. The Poles aren't killing your boys. We know who is."

"When we find her, she's…"

"She's mine. My arrest, my collar."

"Tell that to the Polacks. Them and their guns." Boyd hacked. Sounded like a lung was coming up. "Sheehan's orders: we go for two of theirs for every one of ours."

Marchand rubbed his face with the palm of his hand. "You take care, Ronny. I'll send you flowers."

He headed back for Dillard and the others. Ambulance sirens wailed in the distance. Good response time. Twice as fast in Rittenhouse as anywhere else. "Dillard. You ready? We've got our shooter. I'm more concerned about the bigger fish."

"I've got nothing new to report on Acciai, sir. Wherever she's been, she's maintaining a low profile. I've been through everything that could provide an electronic fingerprint—credit card transactions, bank deposits, even social media. She's staying off grid."

"Crap. My sources aren't giving me anything better. No one's seen her—or if they have, they're keeping quiet." Marchand ticked off items on his fingers. "First she puts a bullet in Colm Murray's face on the first of May. Four weeks later, she shoots Ralph O'Hanlon point blank, double tap to the head. Each time, there's no warning of her getting ready to act. Sheehan's convinced the Poles hired her."

"And the Poles?"

"Krol was interviewed. Categorically denies having hired her. Which is fake news, because we know both them and she were involved in that gunplay in the spring. They've worked together before." Cezar wouldn't let Marchand anywhere near Krol, not since that official statement was taken. Marchand hadn't told the Irish that bit of intel; but they weren't stupid. Just ham-fisted.

"What about…our other case, sir?"

"What case?"

"Airfoil."

"Don't call him that," Marchand snapped. "I'm sick of hearing it. Everywhere I look, everywhere I listen, there's the flying guy."

Dillard looked abashed. "Well...he's saving people, sir."

To Marchand, that meant doing the things he couldn't. What was he doing instead? Scrambling around, trying to keep the Poles from igniting an all-out gang war with the Irish. He'd had to put more pressure on Krol to keep his cash flow intact, especially after that botched bank heist. But he had to step lightly. Couldn't afford to make the Poles his enemies.

Then there was this Acciai chick. She was a ghost. Knocking off the Irish enforcers...of course Cezar would deny it. Even if the Poles weren't paying her to off their competition, they'd look the other way when it happened.

"Sir," Dillard said cautiously, "I'm tracking all Acciai's known accounts. I'm also running facial recognition software on social media and...uh, a few assorted other programs that may help."

The kid meant well. Reminded Marchand of his rookie days. "Clean up here. I'm headed out. You call me as soon as you hear anything."

Marchand got into his car and swatted the steering wheel. That was the major downside of not having friends. No one to jaw it all over with. Dillard didn't count.

So why did it all bother him? Marchand was used to playing sides. He thrived in this chaos. No, it was the flying guy that bugged him. Whoever he was, he was clean. He was doing good.

He was a hero.

Marchand dug into his pocket. Found the tarnished copper chain. His Dad had been a cop, one of the best. One of Patterson's Precinct, the squad that swept crime off Drake's streets in the seventies. He'd given Marchand a St. Jude's emblem on his commissioning day. The old man had even prayed over it and kissed it with the gentleness you reserve for babies. He was a sap, full of emotion, hot joy and cold rage. But he was a cop and a Catholic. Good at both jobs.

Marchand lost the emblem years ago. One drunken bender, after he'd first gotten in with Cezar and the Poles. When he'd learned the rules of the new Drake City. They weren't his father's streets. They were his. And they were dark.

The chain was his reminder, his crown of thorns.

Marchand turned the key in the ignition. Screw this. He was going to go see his sister.

Caroline Reed, nee Marchand, met him at the apartment door and hugged him hard enough to cut off his air. "Dennis! I'm so glad you came by. Thanks for the text."

"No problem, Sis. It's not too late, is it?"

"No, no, I'm just reading. Catching up on my blogs. The kids have been asleep for a couple hours now. Come in."

Marchand leaned up against the kitchen wall. He scanned the visible rooms with the same intensity he reserved for entering a potentially violent encounter with Cezar's boys. Coast was clear. "Where's Reed?"

"Work. Some late-night meeting with city officials and the library director." Caroline poured herself a glass of red wine, frowning at the bottle. "Budget season's hard on him, but he's never been this bad. Never had to be out this late this often. The possible closing of Hull Branch is hitting him hard, I think. He won't say it, but I think he's worried it'll actually be shut down."

"Huh. Heard about that." The Poles were watching the possible closure with interest, because it was right smack on their border with the Irish. Hull Street might as well be a barbed wire trench—at least, it used to be. Hadn't the wilki been shaking down people on both sides of the road? Of more interest was the report of late nights for hubby dear. "You sure that's where he's at?"

Caroline shot him a sharp look. "Don't insinuate that about my husband again, Dennis. We've been over this."

Marchand shrugged. "Due diligence."

"Call it whatever you like, just quit it. Do you want something to drink?"

"Just soda. Don't touch the other stuff."

"I never understood why you stopped drinking, Dennis. It's not as if you were an alcoholic before. You barely had a couple of beers a week."

"Drop it, Sis." He accepted a bottle of root beer and made for the living room.

"Here." She followed, holding out a plastic cup filled with ice.

"Thanks." Marchand poured his root beer, leaving a thick layer of foam on top. He sipped. Sharp and cold. Perfect for a hot day.

"You've got some on your lip broom." Caroline curled up on the couch

"Funny girl."

"It reminds me of Dad's. Looks nice."

"Mm-hmm." Marchand poured the rest and set the bottle aside. He stood staring out the night. The view of Drake City was gorgeous, like a bejeweled blonde in an evening gown. His town. The good and the bad.

"So, spill." Caroline patted the cushion next to her. "What's wrong? You said you wanted to talk."

He turned but didn't sit. "Work's... rough. The fighting between the mobs is escalating. I've got a hitman offing people on one side, which seriously pisses off the other, and I can't keep them both from wanting blood. All over, they're pulling strings and crime's up."

"Well, not in Hull, from what the news is saying."

"Yeah. That's the other part of it. The flying guy."

"Airfoil?" Caroline's expression lit up. "That's so exciting! Reed and Thomas have devoured everything the news has run on him, watched every uploaded video they can find. You've seen him?"

Marchand scowled. "No. Okay, not in person, but there's footage…probably doctored."

"There's a lot of people who've seen him."

"Yeah. A lot. Like tonight." Caroline opened her mouth, like she had another question, but Dennis waved it off. He sagged onto the couch next to her. They used to watch Saturday morning cartoons like this. "Forget it. Your hubby will tell you plenty whenever he shows up, fanboy that he is. Let's just say that, while I'm persuaded one person could be stoned out of their mind enough to hallucinate the flying guy, a shipload of people can't be."

He squeezed on the cup, scraping the ice together. "I think he's real."

"I think so too. Is that awful?"

"It's worse than you marrying Reed, and that was pretty stupid."

"Dennis, watch it." She poked him in the ribs.

"Sorry. Look, it sounds idiotic, but this guy—if he is real—then he's a hero. He can do things we can't possibly achieve, or even imagine. He makes the police as effective against crime as an old man with a walker."

Caroline rubbed his shoulder. "Just because someone's out there helping people doesn't mean Drake City doesn't need its police. You and your people are the everyday heroes."

Dennis cringed inwardly. He'd hid a thousand dollars from a handful of Old City businesses in his jacket. He'd collected it this afternoon, in return for him keeping a roving band of taggers away from their neighborhood. If they missed a payment, Marchand would send word these boutiques were fair game, and they'd wake up to fluorescent graffiti all over their storefront windows. His knuckles were still bruised from the pounding he'd administered on a mid-level heroin dealer, a vain attempt to find Acciai.

Yeah. Hero.

The front door banged open. "Hey, babe, I'm back! Did you see the news? There's two of the flying guys now! Airfoil stopped the other one from sinking the Rittenhouse ferry, out by the light! I'll find the link with the report from—"

Reed froze inside the entryway, keys dangling from his fingers, messenger bag slung over a shoulder. He stared at Dennis.

"He came by a few minutes ago." Caroline was up off the couch. "I was going to text you, but I knew you wouldn't answer or look at it in the middle of a meeting."

"Okay." The keys jingled into a pocket. The messenger bag thumped against the floor. Reed moved into the kitchen, not saying another word. The refrigerator door whooshed open. He came into the living room with an open bottle of hard cider. "Hey, Dennis."

"Reed."

"How's policing going? You guys busy with the whole not-stopping-crime thing?" Reed snapped his fingers. "Oh, right. There's a superhero rounding up bad guys now. You're probably not busy with anything."

Marchand squeezed on the cup until its rim snapped. Fortunately, it was near empty. "We're busy enough. And how's your job? The one where you babysit romance novels for old women. Tell you what: stop by the precinct when you want to see what real work looks like. I'll bet you'll find it fascinating. Just as much fun as the comics."

"Super. How's about I get you another root beer. Better yet, let's skip the second drink and you try flying off a roof like Airfoil, only minus superpowers."

"Reed! Please, don't." Caroline put herself between the two

of them. Good thing, too, because Marchand knew if he were anywhere else, getting talked to by anyone else, Reed would be in pieces on the floor. He'd have smashed the bottle and gone for his face.

"Sorry, hon. Dennis just surprised me with his less than welcome appearance. Kind of like coming home from a lousy day at work and finding Magneto in your living room having a cold one." Reed tossed back a huge gulp of his drink. "I get it, though. He's family. There's no way I'd ever take that from you. But you ever show up around here again, Dennis, I'll go to your supervisors and make sure you'd not allowed anywhere near the building."

"A restraining order?" Dennis chuckled. "Please. Don't worry, Reed, I'm on my way out. Have fun with your funny pages."

"Stop it." Caroline was near tears, and she bit off every word. She glared at the two of them. "Dennis, don't you talk to my husband that way. You're both awful! A pair of idiots."

Marchand set his cup on end table. He kissed Caroline softly on the cheek. "Sis, I'm going to go."

"No! You stay here. I invited you." She whipped around, facing Reed, and put a finger under his nose. "This is my brother. And you're my husband. I love you both. You will learn to tolerate each other."

"Really, Sis, I should go." Marchand hated seeing her upset. He cast about for an excuse, anything. "Reed's not far off—I need to track down whatever leads we have on this flying guy before he causes any more trouble."

"Causes?" Reed snorted. "Airfoil saved eighty-nine lives tonight. He's a hero. You—you and cops like you are part of the problem. Just as corrupt as the guys you're supposed to bring in but who walk away after every crime they commit. Don't think I don't hear the stories people bring into the library, Dennis, even while I'm busy babysitting: the graft, the intimidation, ignoring crimes that hurt innocent people. I know who you are."

"Yeah? Who's that?" Marchand's phone buzzed. He snatched it from his belt, revealing his gun at the same time.

Reed didn't blanch, though. Had to give the guy credit. "A criminal." He stormed off to the bedrooms.

Caroline hugged herself. "Dennis...why do you have to do this? It never ends, back and forth. Are you two going to circle each other and take cuts until you both bleed to death?"

"It's...Sorry. I just..." He trailed off as he read Dillard's text. <Acciai. Ethier Court. The Pearls. SWAT en route.>

"Gotta go. Cop stuff." Marchand kissed her on the forehead. "Thanks for the Doctor Phil time."

Caroline wrapped her arms around his neck. "He's right, you know," she whispered. "You can be better. You can be—like Dad."

Not a chance. Not in this city. Marchand's list of sins was too long. Still, he smiled. "Thanks. I'll remember that."

His knuckles still ached.

Acciai checked the hallway. No sign anyone had heard her. She closed the door and admired her handiwork.

Greg Sheehan's private penthouse at The Pearls casino was everything that came to mind when she though the word "opulent": rich wood furniture, marble counters, gold filigree, a bar stocked with more exotic liquors than most downtown restaurants, a sauna, and sliding glass doors that opened onto a rooftop pool.

Sheehan wasn't enjoying it. He was dead. And not in a dignified pose, either. No, she'd left him uncovered, all 200 lily-white pounds of him, wearing black satin boxers and black socks. He was overweight, but not fat like his Uncle Danny. Blood dripped from the bullet hole dead center between his eyes.

Acciai smiled. He'd been too busy staring at her beauty—

and she was gorgeous, she had to admit—to notice the muzzle of her pistol, until a second before she shot him.

She wiped the droplets off her chest, intoxicated by the metallic smell.

Something beeped.

Acciai pulled her blouse back on. The sound came from nearby, whatever it was.

Under Sheehan's pillow. She pulled it up, making his head loll sideways, and making Sheehan stare blankly at the wall. A phone. The status light blinked.

She turned it on.

Unbelievable. He Tweeted.

There was a picture of her. Mostly of her backside as she disrobed. But her face was turned sideways.

She swiped her purse from the floor and shoved her gun into to. She wasn't dolled up, this time: a short-sleeved, clinging black blouse, and tight gray pants. It would help her blend in better.

None of Sheehan's stooges were at the door. He'd dismissed them to the casino floor, to get him food and leave them in privacy—at Acciai's whispered insistence. Men. Thinking with everything but their brains.

She walked to the main hall and rode the elevator to the casino floor, making it there completely unmolested. The Irish were so sure of their safety in Ethier Court, deep in their own territory. That security beyond the main entries was laughable. Really, who would threaten to rob them? Not her.

The casino floor was a huge, gaudy spread of roulette wheels. Blackjack tables and poker players crammed together in a motley assortment of garish dresses, suits, ties, and blue jeans. The noise assaulted Acciai. She focused on the door and the positions of each security man. One of them, a tall, handsome blond with a crooked nose, smiled and winked at her as she sauntered by.

Perfect.

She was thirty steps from the front door—walking between the gaudy twin statues of oyster shells, open to reveal opalescent pearls—when the police burst through.

The man in front was instantly recognizable. He'd led the charge this spring at the Crown Sullivan. The one she'd narrowly escaped.

She sprang left, her hand tucking into her purse. Bullets exploded, ripping the leather apart.

Shouts of alarm followed the gunfire. Acciai ducked behind a pillar, dropped the ruined purse, and flung herself around the other side. She shot again, twice this time. Both shots hit a black police officer square in the chest, dropping him to the floor.

A blow struck her side, sending her reeling. She slammed against another pillar, dropped her gun. Acciai lashed out with her hand, intending to hit the soft cartilage of a neck, but got only air. Another blow hit her deep in the stomach. She gasped, unable to catch her breath.

The lead cop, moustache and all, loomed over her. "You're under arrest," he said, and brought the butt of his pistol down on her head.

Acciai came to in the back of a DCPD squad car. Her vision was a blur of hazy colors. There were two people in the front seat, silhouettes beyond the protective grille. Where were they? She was shackled, no weapons within reach or sight. Out the windshield, wipers swiped away the light rain falling on the city. Another car was just ahead; the taillights and bumper told her it was a vintage Monte Carlo.

"Ma'am, are you awake?" The voice was mellow, soothing. It belonged to the black officer driving. "I'm Officer Sutton, ma'am. We're taking you in to the precinct for questioning."

Her thoughts coalesced at the same speed as her vision. The attempt to leave the Pearls casino, the interception by police, the brief and painful fight... "I see. Did the arresting officer skip reading my Miranda rights? I don't recall them."

"Ah, yes, Ma'am, they were read." Sutton's voice had a dry edge of humor to it. "Lieutenant Marchand insists you were competent to understand them."

Competent. It was unlikely that she was even conscious.

She wriggled in the backseat. There were only the two men. Their attention was focused on the road outside. If she could get her cuffed hands out from behind her back, she could use them as a garrote against the one in the passenger seat. Sutton read as very by the book—he'd likely maintain control of the car, while trying to signal dispatch. The other officer would provide her with a weapon.

Acciai bent her arms, forcing them into a painful position that stung her eyes. But she didn't whimper. She didn't utter a sound. Her breathing barely increased its pace.

The car jerked to a halt. The officer in the passenger seat swore, rubbing at his forehead. Of more interest to Acciai was the fact that the car's engine was still running—and the tires were squealing on the asphalt.

Acciai tensed, shrinking back into her seat. Sutton blurted a warning into his squad car's radio, and the other officer spun around, glaring at her, as if the car's noncompliance were her fault.

It wasn't, but she had a guess.

Her seat lurched. She felt a curious sensation, like riding a slow elevator. By then she'd brought her bound wrists up and around her legs, over her knees. A light blazed in her window, and she rubbed the accumulated fog of her breath off the glass, cold and wet, so she could squint for a better look through the rain.

That was a streetlamp. At eye level with her.

Metal groaned, squealed. A rift split down the centerline of the roof. Both the front and rear windshields cracked, dropping glass onto her. She covered her head, keeping the largest chunks from her face. Warm rain spattered down into the car, like a sprinkler gone full force. Sparks showered down, mingling with the rain, and tendrils of smoke hissed as the emergency lights died and the car's wiring was ripped to useless copper and plastic. The front and rear axles tore free on the left sides. They dangled like dropped dumbbells.

"Need backup!" Sutton hollered, his voice deep and angry among the cacophony of sounds. "All units, respond!"

There was no static. Not a light on the dash. The engine gasped, a sudden last cough, and plummeted to the ground, crunching into a dark mass of metal and spraying fluids everywhere.

"Sutton, look at that!" The other officer raised a hand, his finger shaking, to the rain-soaked night.

Hovering just above the globes of amber light from the streetlamps was a figure, a man in slate gray and a billowing cloak, face obscured. Everything about his body, the way his muscles undulated under the tightfitting clothing and the posture of his frame, radiated control. It seethed with power.

He held out a right hand, fingers flexing.

Acciai smiled, rain streaking her face and utterly ruining her makeup. She clicked off the seatbelt, and the car tipped slowly sideways, so that she was standing on the closed door, facing up and.

"The prisoner! She's going!" The other officer had his gun out and threw himself across the three-foot gap between the jagged halves of the squad car. His left arm fastened like a vise on her ankle.

She was ready.

Acciai had a shard of glass from the windshield grasped in both hands. With a snarl, she stabbed it into his wrist, hard enough to feel it bounce off bone and sever tendons.

The officer screamed. His gun went off, the reflexive shot deafening Acciai. She released the glass and, using the handcuff chain, yanked the gun out of his grasp. She caught it in hands slick with blood and rain, flipped it around, and shot the other officer three times in the face and chest.

Acciai turned the gun on Sutton. His eyes met hers. Surprisingly warm, though wide with—fear? Anguish? No, sadness. Acciai wondered if he had a family.

She put a bullet between those eyes.

The car shook. Acciai looked up at her rescuer. With his left hand, he pointed a finger at her then lifted two. .

Something invisible and strong grabbed her from all sides. Her breath fled. The feeling of power was euphoric. It jerked her free of the left half of the car, pulling her up into the rainstorm. She floated, staring down at the chaos in the street below--the squad cars jostling, officers racing.

This was how the angels felt. The angels, or the demons.

She licked the blood off her pinkie.

Shouts came from below. Gunfire, from four different weapons, exploded in bright flashes. Acciai flinched.

Nothing hit her. Or him. He floated there, serene, head cocked to one side. Sparks glittered all around their feet, but none reached them. Without a word, he flicked his right hand.

The halves of the police car tumbled, dropping ten feet onto one of its companions. That car's windows exploded in glass shrapnel, its roof crumpling. A blaring siren died in a mournful wail.

Together they rose into the air. The man pulled Acciai close to him. She caressed his chest, her body heaving with adrenaline and lust. His physique was as powerful as this invisible strength. She wanted both.

"I owe you something," she purred, "And when I pay you back, I'll..."

Her words cut off in mid-sentence, in a rasp. He'd fastened his right hand, gloved gray, around her throat.

"You are a failure," he said. "You must be corrected."

They flew away so fast she lost the rest of her breath.

Marchand dragged Sutton from the car. There was no point calling for EMTs. The dark hole between his eyes proved that.

He'd have to call Marcie. She'd have to tell their son.

Marchand holstered his Ruger and wiped water from his face.

Dillard ran over, splashing through puddles. "Sir, Officer Bates...he's dead, sir." his chest rattled with a sob.

"Sutton's gone, too."

"N-no. No. What happened? What was it?"

Marchand glowered up at the night sky, his face burning with rage and soaked with rain. Rage, at these flying freaks and their pet assassin. "Get Captain Urquhart on the radio. Tell him our assassin's a cop-killer now. Tell him we're going to break down every door we have to stop them all."

Acciai hung from the ceiling, a cold, damp chain wrapped around her arms, her legs and her throat. The links writhed, a metal serpent bruising her flesh and pummeling her bones.

"You failed, Consolata. The penalty for failure is punishment, followed by death," her employer said.

"No...No, I killed him! I got Sheehan!" She gasped the words, the heavy chain intermittently cutting off and allowing her breath.

"Yes, you did. You killed Sheehan and the other two. Those were your assignments." He floated in front of her, still masked, always hidden, and jerked at air with his right hand. The chains wound even tighter. Acciai knew she'd black out soon. "Then the police caught you! You were their prisoner. Would you have told them of our arrangement? Would you have given me up to preserve your skin?"

"Never!"

"Ah, but I suspect you would. I suspect you would do and say anything to preserve your own life."

The chains loosened. Acciai sucked in a breath and managed a cutting laugh. "You're insane. You're completely crazy. We're through. I'm not anyone's dog to be unleashed."

The chains rattled. "Unless you're bound to me like one," her employer said. "You have no concept of what is to come to fruition."

She shook her head, weary from it all—the pain, the anguish. "You won't even give me your name."

"A name?" He hovered closer to her, close enough he could lift her chin with his hand.

She bit his fingers.

He didn't cry out. Didn't even flinch. But those chains! They pressed down on her with brutal force, until she sobbed for release. Not even the tease of blood on her teeth could ward off fear. She knew what was coming. She would die. And then... nothing. Black. Darkness.

"There is only one name you need know. Domitian," he whispered. "I am the emperor of old, the one come to lead others from their misery and usher in a new age of peace, of strength, and of glory. Are you afraid to die?"

She clenched her teeth, cheeks stained with tears.

"Yes, you are. But you needn't be. Not now. I spare you."

The chains abruptly slackened. She dropped into the shadows, past rusted catwalks, waiting for the solid impact that would break her legs and her spine.

Nothing. She stopped mid-fall and settled gently to a rough floor of dirt and broken concrete, as if lowered on a cloud. There was only the feeble light from a flickering fluorescent bulb, somewhere high above, to illuminate anything around her. The reopened mines. This was one of the shafts.

Domitian settled to the floor. He stood there, watching her.

"Domitian." She laughed, even though her throat burned. "One of the five good emperors of Rome. Not going for grandeur, are we?"

"You are weak, Consolata."

"How can I be strong?" she snapped, her knees creaking as she pushed up. "Nothing can beat the power you have. I ply my trade with sex and blood and weapons. None of that works on you."

"I will make you stronger."

"Give me your power." She didn't care how deadly he could be. She wanted what he could do. That was the only way she'd be safe from him. And imagine how many others she could kill. The contracts she could fulfill. The blood that could be spilled. It made her dizzy with anticipation.

"Good. Very good. You are not ready for the burden of this strength, but I have something else. Something more fitting, that will help prepare you for our mission." He strode to a nearby table, hidden in shadow. With a tap, he activated something—a laptop computer. A glowing technical readout filled the screen.

Acciai approached cautiously.

"You have been disciplined," Domitian said. "Are you ready to start over?"

"I am."

"Excellent. Then this will be yours."

She stared at the image, and brushed blood off her lips with the back of her hand. "Ooh, I want one."

Chapter Fourteen

It's past nine on Saturday morning when I get on my bike and realize the front tire's as flat as a library card. I'm supposed to meet Kelly at the Dowlington café at 9:30, and I'm out of spares. Somehow, between being preoccupied with impending joblessness and fighting crime with a superpowered medallion on late nights, I neglected to get some spares from my local shop.

So, I take the subway instead. I don't have a car—never needed one, don't particularly want one. Most of my family is accessible by train or plane.

The subway's the most ramshackle part of Drake City's public services.

DC Transportation Authority puts a lot of money into their administrators' and managers' salaries; not so much into repairs and maintenance. The car that takes me up to Third Street has a window with a large crack patched by duct tape. There's more graffiti on the formerly silver exterior than on the big train cars that roll out of Newport's freight yards across the bay. The floors are chipped, laminate the color of vomit, and look like they were installed in the 1970s.

Then there's the smell. Unwashed humanity and damp mold. There's a lot of said humanity crammed aboard today—and in the summer, in this heat, the smell gets worse. Add sweat.

None of the surly-looking youth try anything like assault or robbery. I run through a dozen scenarios, all of which end with me using the medallion very publicly to fling them like plastic Army men through plate glass windows. There's lots of cheering from the crowd in those fantasies—right up until Reed's brother-in-law Dennis, and the rest of DCPD, show up to arrest me.

I wonder. If I blow it, would Frank put a bullet in my head? I'd rather not experiment.

The nearest stop is Third and Palisade Avenue. Puts me two blocks from the café and gives me a good, short walk to check my phone. I've got it set to alert me the instant catastrophe strikes, and the news organizations can get it up. What I really need is a police scanner. I'm not at all surprised Frank hasn't pulled one out of his magic bag; he'd rather I kept my nose clear of general crime-fighting as long as possible.

But there's no way I'm sitting around as the Garrison's attack dog.

The Dowlington Café is a former boarding house, built in the decade after the Civil War. Used to be a home for crippled veterans. Now, that character is preserved in polished wood floors and small sitting areas still separated by the original narrow, wood-frame doorways and plaster walls. Each has a pair of tables and an octet of chairs. The lady behind the long, wooden counter in what used to be the family room is tall, reedy and fully in command of the three college aged girls making drinks and serving pastries. "Good morning. Can I help you?"

"Yeah, I'm supposed to meet a friend," I say, readjusting my backpack. My helmet and a long-sleeved Under Armour shirt are stashed inside. "She's a tad shorter than me, black hair—"

The woman smiles. "The part-Chinese girl? She's in the front parlor, left front window."

"Part-Korean, and thanks." I eyeball a stack of newspapers by the nearest table. The lead photo of the Messenger is of the Rittenhouse ferry and the damaged lighthouse roof, with the massive headline: "Airfoil saves ferry passengers." It's subtitled with the ominous, "Faces opponent, second flier."

Wonder how the police are dealing with all this. Frank tells me to lay low; whatever the Ashen is up to, he doesn't want me in any further confrontations. Not yet. But nor will he tell me what this all means. The fact that there's someone out there with greater control of a medallion that I can muster—

Still, things have been quiet since last night. I'm on my guard. But there's only so much I can do. I cannot, as Frank reminds me, be everywhere at once.

Kelly waves as I enter the parlor. She's a portrait of vibrant beauty framed against the warm sunlight from a window. Her outfit is summery, and only lends to her elegance: flowery purple and green skirt, chocolate brown blouse with lace eyelets at the sleeves and collar. Her hair gleams like a raven's feathers, curling about the nape of her neck.

"Hey, Kelly." I sit opposite her, setting my backpack aside. There's a pair of daguerreotypes framed on the wall, behind her head: a thin man with a huge beard and a woman with a round, pleasant face. Owners of the old boardinghouse? Probably. Tough audience.

"Good morning." She cradles a steaming mug of tea in both hands. The scent of fruit and flowers wafts across. "You really do pack that thing everywhere."

"This?" I kick the bag. "Oh, sure. I keep my sketchpad in there. For emergencies."

She laughs. It is true—the sketchpad stays on me most always. She doesn't need to know about the helmet. "How was your ride?"

"Took the subway. Had a flat tire and a severe lack of spares. I didn't want to be late." It occurs to me I could have flown. That's a tricky proposition in broad daylight, though.

"Oh. Desperate times. Speaking of desperate, did you elbow someone too hard in your rush to get here?"

"Hmm?" She's talking about the Ace bandage wrapped around my forearm. Forgot about that. It's still sore from the encounter with my rival last night. Frank was understandably anxious to avoid a visit to the hospital. "Sprained it. Sean and I were shooting hoops over at the YMCA, and it got too rough for his old man."

"I'm glad to hear you two are getting along better."

"Yes, we are." I smile. It's painfully easy to disguise the lie that way. But the shorter the list of people who know my secret, the better. In fact, Reed emailed me late last night to remind me:

Anonymity's what keeps you safe, Brando. You and everyone you love. Don't be like Iron Man. You're not invincible.

He of the comic book wisdom.

"Anyway, the subway ride had its usual charms. It's got more graffiti than passengers. We won't go into detail on the smell. Especially if you're hungry."

"I already ate. Do you want something?"

"Nah, I'm good." Between the pile of frozen burritos I scarfed at midnight and the pancakes Sean and I made a couple hours ago, food's the last thing I need.

A dark-skinned woman with wildly curly hair stops by, takes my order for a plain old decaf coffee, and speeds off to the next table. There's a pair of middle-aged men in athletic gear, still sweaty from whatever exercise they've been at, sitting at the table behind us. Other than that, the room's empty. "How's your morning been?"

"All right, I guess. I was going over the benefit planning—actually, I have been since about 7."

"Early riser for a weekend."

"It was bothering me."

"Ah. Right, your standard operating procedure."

She nods, albeit sheepishly. "All the details are stored on my phone."

"Wow. You know it's Saturday, right? Reed doesn't pay

overtime. At least, he doesn't pay me."

"No, no, this is strictly volunteer. I can't leave something this important unfinished all weekend. My brain won't allow it. You know how it goes—"

"You want it done your way or the right way."

"Exactly."

The coffee arrives. Smells perfect, and immediately clears any lingering cobwebs. I raise my mug. "Great minds and all that. So, what've you got?"

She pulls a bright yellow smartphone from her purse, which sits down on the floor by her legs. Man, what a pair they are. Whatever exercises she does work. Never heard her say she rides; wonder if she runs...

"Brandon? Do you agree?"

"Hmm?" Shoot. "Yes. Yes, I do."

She arches an eyebrow, her index finger poised over a screen full of notes on her phone. "You were daydreaming, weren't you?"

"Also, yes."

"Another scenic view for your paintings, I take it."

"Something like that." I chuckle. "Anyway, repeat that one for me."

"I was saying, we've got the caterer contracted, and she's agreed to be there two hours ahead to be ready in case any guests show up early. Invitations are mailed out, thanks to the Friends of the Library and our volunteers pasting postage."

"So's the email list."

"And the Facebook page?"

"Been running updates every day."

"Oh, good."

"Aren't you following it?"

"I don't do any of that. The social media stuff, I mean."

"Duly noted. What else?"

"I spoke with the fire marshal's office and he assured me we can get a waiver if our crowd exceeds the 320-person capacity rating for the Legion hall."

"I doubt we'll get that many but nice positive thinking."

"Really? If the band you're bringing is as good as you claim, I'd think we'd have people lining up along the waterfront."

"Touché."

She frowns suddenly, peering at her notes. "Do you think it will work?

"What, the benefit? I think it'll bring a good crowd. People like the daycare lady and her family, the older residents who come in every day, the story hour moms who will bring their husbands along for a date away from the kids—that's our crew."

"I mean, will it change the minds of the council?"

"That's tougher to figure. The benefit's only one factor. Budget woes are another—and we can't do anything about that. I leave it to prayer." Not that I've been to church in a while. I should go back. It's good, they say, for what ails me. But whenever I try, I see Samantha and the hurt blocks me.

She seems to consider this. "How did Reed say the meeting went last night?"

"Don't know. I haven't talked to him about it. You know, busy at damage control." I wave my bandaged arm.

"Oh, okay. He seemed really tense before the benefit planning."

Forgot about that. I was busy foiling a bank robbery. "Back up to your original question. The only way we can help stave off the closing is to get a healthy influx of new patrons and bring back old ones. That won't happen unless the crime continues to taper off."

Kelly stirs her tea with a spoon. "Well, our local hero seems to be doing a great job in that regard. What do you think of him? The news is calling him Airfoil now."

"Oh, him? Interesting, I suppose. If everything they say he's done is true, that is. Reed's got himself a major man-crush. I don't know how Caroline puts up with it."

She laughs. "A real superhero patrolling our neighborhood and saving people's lives all around Drake City? I'm surprised he hasn't closed us for a day so we can all go sky watching."

"Nice."

Her laughter fades. Her mood's been a pendulum for weeks now, even from minute to minute.

"Earth to Kelly."

"Sorry."

"Don't apologize. What's going on? You haven't been yourself in a long time. You look worried. And don't say it's the benefit—I know you better than that."

Kelly tucks a strand of hair behind her ear. "Every time I come here, to see Grandpa, he's worse. I'm terrified I'll show up one day and he won't have any idea who I am. You have no idea. In some ways, I'd rather he had a heart attack and passed away suddenly. Isn't that awful, to even think that?"

"No, not at all. I can understand that."

"Even if he were taken in a car accident, I could handle it better than constant deterioration, him losing his mind in little pieces every day."

Instantly, the flaming wreck of Samantha's car blazes in my memory. My insides freeze up, and it has nothing to do with the medallion. It's all I can do to keep the pain off my face, which I accomplish by making like stone.

It must be too evident, though, because Kelly's eyes widen and her hand flies to her mouth. "Oh, Brandon, I'm so sorry. I didn't mean...I shouldn't have said that."

"Hey, don't worry about it. You're right. The long wait is worse. If I'd had to watch Samantha suffer—well, I wouldn't wish it on someone I hate. Let alone someone I care about."

Kelly's sudden very concerned with the contents of her mug. "Oh. I see."

"Yeah." The medallion's rough edge scratches at my chest,

sending a jolt of ice through me. "Samantha's gone, but she's always a part of me. I'll see her again when it's my turn."

"In heaven."

"Well, yeah." I smile. "Not Disney World."

She perks up again.

"Kelly?"

"Yes?"

"That's not what I meant, though, when I said people I care about. That includes you."

Back she goes to the tea. "Thanks."

We lapse into silence for a while. Some date, Brandon. You'd better quit talking about your dead wife.

"It was a nice idea, to get together like this, Brandon," she finally says.

"I told you, I'd be there if you needed someone."

And that's what Sean, and Reed, and everyone else in Drake City need to remember.

St. Andrew's Home is just across the street from the church. It's built of the same sandstone, a soft, pale red hue. Its slate shingles contrasts sharply with the brightly colored houses and the glass and steel businesses. This portion is where Old City and Center mingle, where the modern and the historic coexist. The church, home to the first Catholic congregation in Drake City, towers over the home. A sharp spire casts a shadow on the small, squat two-story place that was once a convent.

Inside the worn exterior gives way to cutting-edge medical technology. Everything about St. Andrew's Home is new: the furnishings are metal and soft mesh; the walls and carpeting done in cool colors without being sterile; the tablets that the mostly female staff carry as they tap inputs with their styluses. The only piece of paper I see is the visitors' sheet Kelly and I sign at the marble and glass arc of the front desk. A cheerful nurse with curly blonde hair, and far too much mascara, leads us down the leftmost of three halls, past evenly interspersed wooden doors. Each room has a nameplate, and none are blank.

Kelly's grandfather is in the last one on the left. His nameplate announces "John Riley Quirke" in plain black letters on burnished metal. He's in a wheelchair, hunched to one side. The apartment's very spare: a bed in one corner, a dinette table and two chairs, small kitchen, TV screen running silently through commercials and the news above the refrigerator, a second door leading I assume to the bathroom. A cluster of small, framed photos on the ledge between the kitchen and dining table watch us. There another photo of a couple, this one with bent edges and muted in sepia tones. The slim, fit young man in a U.S. Army uniform, I figure is our host; he stands with a gorgeous Korean woman in a wedding dress. The ribbons on his chest, I'd wager, come from the conflict fought in her homeland.

John Quirke doesn't look at it. He's staring out the corner windows. There's a breathtaking garden out there, tucked between the neighboring buildings and the alley. The colors are riotous compared with the calm tones of the home—brilliant greens, reds and oranges and yellows and purples. More flowers and plants than I see in the florist near work. Peonies, roses, daffodils—the kinds of flowers Samantha loved in the flowerbox outside our apartment. She and Mr. Darrow would trade care tips all summer.

I shake off the memory. This is Kelly's visit, and I'm here for her.

"Grandpa? It's Kel." She rubs the back of the neck and kisses him on the cheek. "Good morning."

"Kel? My Kel. I'm watching the Earth move life." He turns and smiles at her. He's got a strong face, long and narrow, with a squared chin and drooping jowls. His face is as weathered as the sandstone, taut and pale. He's got most of his hair; it's neatly buzzed and shock white. The red flannel shirt he wears fits loosely on a thin frame. Khaki pants are bunched at the knees, revealing one brown and one black sock.

"That's good. I'm glad you enjoy the garden."

"Best place to see Creation in action." He points with a gnarled finger, his hand shaking. "Watch the bees. They move in a pattern. And the wasps are working on a hive under the angel statue's left wing."

"Grandpa, I brought a friend. This is Brandon."

I offer a hand. "Brandon Tusk, sir. Good to meet you."

He eyes me with unabashed critique. "Kel said something about a man. Yes, the nice fella from the library. Good man. John Riley Quirke."

We shake, and his grip's far more iron than I would have expected. The medallion cuts me with cold then, sending pins and needles down my arms. I jerk back, wincing.

"Are you okay, Brandon?"

"Sure. Wrist aches." He shook the hand on my injured arm. But I'm puzzling over the medallion's surge.

John massages the center of his chest. For a moment, Kelly's talk of heart trouble resurfaces in my memory, but he doesn't seem perturbed. "No harm done," John chuckles. The sound fades as quickly as a water evaporating. "You're...Brandon?"

"Yes, sir."

He glances at Kelly. "And...oh, hello, Kel. It's nice to have you visit again."

Kelly's eyes, the same shade of brown as John's, gather tears at the corners. "Yes, Grandpa. How are you?"

"Good, good. When will the kids arrive?"

"Mom and Dad...they're in Boston, Grandpa. They won't be here today."

John acknowledges this with a curt nod. He stares out the window at the garden again, eyes flicking from side to side as he tracks the wasps. "They move so fast," he murmurs. "Look at how they fly."

As quietly as I can, I move closer and place my hand on Kelly's shoulder. Without looking up, she reaches for my hand and grasps the fingers.

John looks over at me and smiles. I smile back, wholly unsure of what to say. The man's losing his grip on reality and confined to a wheelchair. Were I him, the freedom of an insect's flight would be equally inspiring.

My phone buzzes. I reach down for it. "Excuse me."

Before I can read the alert, a news banner flashes across the TV screen. The announcer looks as serious as a preacher at a funeral. And the headline makes my heart stop: "Airplane Crisis."

Kelly catches me gawking. "What is it?"

"Don't know." I move for the TV, punch up the volume.

"FAA officials insist there is no need to panic. However, our sources have learned that Flight 2626 from Baltimore is reporting engine failure and a complete loss of power. The 737's last known location was 200 miles northeast of Drake City."

Oh no. I scoop my backpack up off the floor. I need to call Frank.

"Emergency responders are en route to SCIA. We have word the pilot intends an emergency landing at the main runway. Stay tuned for news from the scene with Brittany..."

John swivels in his chair, arms shaking. He stares at the screen, his posture stiffening. "May the angels catch them."

"I, ah, got to go, Kelly. Got a message from Sean. He's upset about something...you know how teens get."

Thankfully she buys it. As low as I feel abandoning her when I said I'd come along, this is life and death. "Sure, go ahead. Thank you again for coming. It means a lot to me."

"Welcome." Then, with the enormity of what I'm about to do pressing down like—well, heavy gravity—I swoop in and kiss her on the cheek. "Good-bye."

I'm halfway down the hall when I hear John call out,

"Brandon."

"Yes, sir?" Make it quick.

He wheels toward me, eyes steady. "The man who flies. People have been talking about him. Will he come, do you think?"

"I hope so."

He grabs my arm. "God go with him."

I run for the nearest alley and stash my backpack behind a dumpster. It takes me less than twenty seconds to strip off my T-shirt, pull on the Under Armour, kick off the sneakers, and shove my feet into rugged hiking shoes. The helmet goes on.

There's no answer from Frank.

Too bad. The field forms around me, and I blast skyward, sending litter rustling like leaves.

Northeast. The plane's that way. I arc up and over, climbing, putting the sparkling waters of Sculpin Bay and the grimy buildings of Newport under me in a blur of colors. That abruptly cuts off from gray to green as I cross over the state forest.

Go, go, faster, faster!

Soon, I'm at that 300-mph threshold. I throttle back, avoiding a major mishap. It's not long before a white speck appears on the horizon. No clouds in sight, nothing else coming, so I climb higher.

Cold even seeps through the field. No idea what my altitude is. Could really use my personal air traffic controller about now. "Where are you, Frank?"

No response from the radio but crackling static.

Here it comes. A 737. Nothing looks amiss, until I get closer. The plane's descending way too fast. Right engine's out. So's the left. No smoke, so no fire. That's good.

But it's going to crash.

The terrified faces of the passengers are plain in the windows. At least one, a small boy, sees me and gapes. He waves. I wave back.

There're no lights inside. None on the wingtips or anywhere

else on the fuselage, either. Total power failure, like the news said. Is that even possible?

"Brandon." Frank's voice sounds subdued. "Stand down. You're to await orders."

Where's he been? "Are you crazy? This thing's coming down!"

"I've got you on GPS and I'm hooked in to SCIA radar. There's nothing to be done. Get out of there. Now."

"No! Frank, these people—"

He cuts off the signal. I grind my teeth. "Frank? Answer me, Frank!"

There's no one to hear me, so I press on with my half-assed, spur of the moment plan. Need to get ahead of the plane. I push forward, accelerating through one of the few clouds in the sky. Everything goes startlingly blank for a moment.

It only takes a few seconds to position myself under the plane, a mile beyond its nose. Shaping gravity like an invisible catcher's mitt? Well, that's complicated. I picture it as best I can. With my imagination, should be a cinch. Then again, I wasn't that good in Little League . Mediocre. I dropped a lot of pop flies.

The plane barrels right on for me. Here's praying I've got better hand-eye coordination now.

I put my hands out and alter my trajectory, slowing rising. Decrease the field propelling me, so our speeds start to sync. The fuselage looms closer, curved, white belly scratched and stained.

Easy...

My hands get right up under the cockpit, where the nose curve ends and straightens out into a clean line. Weight increases. Manageable. But that's with me moving along with the plane. I keep doing that and we'll both crash.

We have to slow. Together.

I picture the invisible glove expanding, coming apart, reshaping into a blanket, or a net, something that can wrap around the airplane. That'll do the trick. I ramp up the gravity, flipping it around like a deck of cards.

The full force of ninety-five tons of airplane, clipping along at three hundred miles per hour, slams into me, slapping my body against the fuselage. If not for the gravity field encasing me, it would have done a lot worse than pound the air from my lungs. I gasp, struggle to regain my breath and concentration. The net holds.

It had better. This is no pickup truck.

We keep right plowing through the sky. I level out, feet facing the wrong way, hands pressed against the plane, and will the gravity to reverse. It has to. There could be a hundred and forty people on that plane. I imagine their wives waiting at home, telling the kids Dad will be home soon. Or their brothers standing at the airport, checking their watches, grinning about the old times they'll rehash with Sis.

My arms tremble, the muscles burning with fatigue. Why can't I get the field to reshape faster? More!

We still auger down.

This is insane. I should be able to stop it. I beg for help. My strength alone isn't enough. The plane isn't slowing enough. Wind still howls past me, flapping my clothes and freezing my body. All the time, my brain's screaming at me, What's wrong with Frank? He's seriously not going to help me. I can't believe he told me to turn away from all those people. But the plane. There should be a way to slow it, even if it weighs—

Weighs. Weight.

I'm doing this wrong.

Sennebec County International Airport sprawls out beneath my feet, the perfect railroad modeler's creation from this height. The terminal's arms reach out to the flock of aircraft nestled off to one side of the long tarmac lanes, wide strips of concrete laid out perpendicular to the hangars and parking lots. It's all getting bigger fast.

I refocus and bleed off some of the power from the invisible net I've fashioned around the plane. All it takes is imagining two bars, like the battery level on a tablet. Siphon some of the charge away. Use it for another purpose.

Like lowering gravity inside the net.

Instead of concentrating all my effort on turning myself into an opposing force to slow the plane, I make the plane lighter. Its mass remains the same, but its weight—that drops with each passing second.

The runway looms large under us. I shove against the airplane and want to cry out with exultation when the nose tips up. We're still going really fast. Can't tell if we've slowed down enough.

But it's working.

Almost down. Almost there. I angle the gravity field into a wedge. In my mind, I see a sled. A big one.

I can feel it immediately when it hits the ground.

Dust blasts up a couple of feet under my boots. Invisible forces gouge runway, ripping up chunks of concrete and flinging pieces the size of my head like baseballs.

The plane's weight presses me down, closer and closer to the tarmac, until the field under my feet is smashed into a thin coating. My legs throb.

Make it lighter. I have to. Decelerate and maintain the grip.

If Reed were here, he'd make a crack about my multi-tasking abilities.

The plane and I rip along the ground. A huge mound lies just off the end of the runway, glistening with green grass. A giant speed bump. Slowly, gritting my teeth and ignoring the taste of sweat on my tongue, I let the tail of the plane settle.

Too hard. It bangs down on the tarmac, a terrific grinding sound joined by the squealing of metal. The passengers' screams are muffled inside the body of the plane.

I can't support it anymore. I just can't. Every part of my

body quakes from the exertion. Sweat drenches me.

Do it.

I slip out from under the right side of the plane. My concentration shuts off like a light switch. The gravity fields vanish. I tumble along the runway, barely remembering to cover my helmet. A wide, dark shape whooshes by overhead. That would be the right wing, cutting by a foot away.

The plane showers me in a cloud of debris, completely obscuring my visor.

All I can do is throw out one last surge of gravity to halt my flailing roll. It's good enough to smack me into a sudden stop, hitting an invisible wall. That doesn't hurt as much as it could have. But there's gonna be a giant bruise on my shoulder.

The rumble and hiss of the airplane's slide subsides, fading into the silence of a winter's night. The plane stops, nose angled up on the embankment. I'm a hundred feet away, lying flat on my back on the tarmac, panting.

They can't see me. I can lay here forever, letting the cold seep into my clothes, chasing the heat burning my skin.

Huge yellow slides inflate and burst from the side of the plane. Voices. Some crying, some shouting, some letting out exuberant cheers. Sirens wail, growing louder. A herd of fire engines and police cars race down the runway.

My cue to fly.

I roll over, and stagger onto my knees. Then push to my feet. Focus. The gravity field flickers. I stumble-step and wind up back on a knee. So much for a quick escape.

Restore my strength. Please.

Don't know what possesses me to reach out for God then. Would have made more sense during the rescue. But the field builds around me, and I'm lurch into the air. The ascent is fraught with turbulence.

Below and behind me, the plane is a discarded toy, with Matchbox cars swarming it. There's a huge scar down the center of the runway, veering toward the embankment. Good thing no one's going to bill my insurance company. I chuckle at the thought.

Soon, the field returns to full strength. I'm grateful for being alive and being able to save lives. The immensity of what I just did catches up to me. "I caught a plane!" I holler into the wind. Screw Frank.

My whoop echoes across the sky as I spiral a dozen times.

Chapter Fifteen

I take a roundabout route to the Barn—I like that name for our base of operations, come to think of it—keeping low to the river. It's not as low visibility as Frank instructs, but it's daylight. As soon as I can, I swerve up into the forested hills to the east, surrounding the state park, and weave among them. Then, it's a simple sharp bank to the west to zoom up on Mount Stafford.

There's no welcome when I arrive, nor is there anyone waiting atop the tower. I don't bother with the roof. Instead, I land with a thud in the circle of light at the bottom. Dust billows up around me.

Frank doesn't say a word. He's at that long table, packing up some of his gear.

"So, that went well." I yank the helmet off. "The catching of a fully loaded passenger airplane, I mean, because the part where I communicate with you for assistance didn't happen at all. Want to fill in any blanks?"

He scowls.

"Okay then. Well, I could use a ride back into town. Unless you think it's better I fly back. In broad daylight."

Without any further words exchanged, we're in the Camaro, driving back down the mountain roads. "You have a misconception about what the term 'await orders' means."

I frown. "You're kidding. I just saved an airplane full of a hundred people, and you're lecturing me on following orders."

"You weren't supposed to rescue them. The situation was monitored. You honestly think the Garrison is unaware of stuff like this?"

"Monitored? If I hadn't called it in, they'd be burnt up inside a fireball on the SCIA runways!"

Frank doesn't respond. He glares down the road.

Something occurs to me. When I called in, already en route to the airplane, he had it tracked on radar. In the rush of the moment, I put it down to him being anal retentive and overly organized—like me. But now, with his comments about monitoring... "You knew it was going down. Before I called you."

Frank keeps driving.

"Hey." I twist sideways in the seat. "Did you know?"

"What do you think I do all day? Troll the Internet for cute kitten pictures? I was monitoring the aircraft's approach from the second they reported engine trouble. I've got SCIA tower communications locked at all times, so I can make sure you don't go splat against a really fast-moving windshield."

"I could have been there faster. There would have been more time to—" I shake my head, angry at second-guessing every action of the last half hour. "Were you going to tell me?"

"What, and interrupt your date?" Frank snorts.

"Quit screwing around."

"I wasn't. I was going to sit there and let the airplane crash. Does that make you feel better, to have figured it out?"

"No! What's the matter with you? You'd let all those people die because the Garrison says not to interfere?"

"Yes. Don't be a moron. I had standing orders not to touch Flight 2626."

"Why...? Wait. How did the Garrison know it was going to crash?" A sickening though jolts me. "Unless they sabotaged it. The Garrison intentionally damaged the airplane so it would crash."

"They tasked me to track the flight because of a man who was on it. A man who finances the Polish mob and has some connection with the weapons shipment they received in the spring. He's from Poland, Krakow to be specific, and no one's sure why he came to town. Changed flights after arriving at Logan in Boston from Heathrow." Frank glances at me. "That's why I wasn't to interfere when the plane's engine crapped out. Our potential problem would have been wiped out. Nice and neat."

"Neat? Tell that to the families of the other passengers! Their wives and husbands and kids." Horrific images of Sean screaming as an airplane cabin explodes around him fill my vision. "I can't believe it."

"Why? What's so hard to believe about the Garrison ignoring short term causalities to let one man die so that a long-term endgame can be fulfilled?" Frank asks. "If this guy had gotten plastered all over the runway—which he likely would have, if you hadn't butted in—whatever plans he had with the mob here would have been ruined."

"And hundreds..."

"Shut up about the possible dead! It's been avoided," Frank growls. "You need to get your head in the game. Quit listening to your heart."

"There's nothing wrong with acting to save others out of compassion." I might be lapsed, without a clear memory of the last time I sat in a pew, but I'm not going to turn aside from the greatest commandment—to love other as I am loved. What better way to show that love by rescuing complete strangers?

"Grow up, Brandon. Your own Bible says the heart's wicked and lies to you. It's better to go cold. We're going to start now. I've let you horse around this summer, and that's done. You stay out of the skies until the Garrison calls."

"You're serious? I've put a dent in crime in Hull and been helping people all over the city!"

"Irrelevant. The Garrison's severely irked by your showboating. You think they want to see you all over YouTube every weekend? They're not medieval monks, Brandon, they stay up to date. The Ashen are working on something big. I'm not privy to all the details, but what I am privy to is the pressure the Garrison's putting on me to keep you in line. The more you run off unauthorized, the more I have to explain to them why I'm not keeping you on a tighter leash. So, mind that leash."

"Well, that's not going to happen. I've got a responsibility to the people of Drake City—and that includes my friends and my family. I won't abandon them."

"Let me ask you something: Do you really think stopping petty crime for a couple months in a neighborhood no one cares about will make any difference? Compare that to the Garrison's goals of keeping the Ashen at bay throughout centuries of covert chess with entire nations. What does it matter?"

"It matters to the people who suffer," I say, "If I can stop their suffering, if I can give of myself so they can live in safety, it's worth every second."

"You're an even bigger fool than I thought. Samantha never gave me grief like this. She knew what it meant to serve in the Garrison. Do you remember reading stories or hearing rumors about a flying woman fighting crime?"

"No."

"Of course not! That's because she only did Garrison-sanctioned missions, and she knew how to keep a low profile—not only for the Garrison's sake, but for her own safety and that of her family. Including her idiot husband."

I glower but can't rebut. He's right. Samantha kept her secret incredibly well. How can I dishonor her memory by not doing half as good a job with the medallion as she did?

Yet, I can't let people in Drake City suffer. I can't sit by and let innocents die. That's not how I'm wired. But I don't say anything further to Frank.

It's such a brilliant, sunny morning when I get out of his car that I can't believe he had a gun to my face minutes ago. The alley is cool and quiet. It isn't until I turn away from the door that I notice the spot discolorations on the brick, in corners usually hidden in shadow.

"You finally noticed." Frank's leaning against the hood, tossing something small and black in his hand. He throws it to me.

I catch...a small camera. Rather, a clump of them, tied together in wires that have been expertly cut. Each one is barely the size of a marble. There're some matte gray box in the mess too, no bigger around than a credit card.

"This is what our dear Miss Acciai's been doing while you've been out saving your city." Frank buffs at something invisible on the hood.

He's barely said anything about my would-be abductor and killer all summer. "How did I miss that?"

"Because you've been busy, and you've been inattentive. Focus, Brandon. This woman has ties to the Ashen. If she's trying to run surveillance on you, that means their operative in Drake City is taking an interest beyond the usual. Don't misunderstand: It's not uncommon for the Ashen and the Garrison operatives to find out each other's identities."

"That's comforting."

"Shut up and listen. It simply means that your actions have brought more heat than necessary, more exposure. Exposure is the enemy of both the Garrison and the Ashen. Remember that."

I rub my temples, feeling a headache building like a summer storm. "So, she's still out there."

"Yes. Eluding police."

I frown. Something I'd read or seen in the news. A prisoner transfer gone wrong? "She got away from them. There was a news post, said a suspect was freed after being arrested at a casino. Gunfire, some wrecked police cars…"

"Again, yes, but this is why you should be worried." He holds up a phone, and I can't quite believe the image of a DCPD squad car split clean in half, its innards splayed across rain-soaked asphalt. "This operative and his assassin are dangerous, Brandon. She's after Irish mob leadership. He's got a connection with the Poles, and judging by our initial foray, the Otte-Vaughn mine too. So you'd better be prepared."

I nod. "Call me when it's time to go back there. I'll be ready. You coming in?"

"No. I have to meet someone over in Newport. Old friend." He jabs a finger at me. "Stay sharp."

"Always a pleasure, Frank."

The apartment building's back door is always locked. I let myself in, come up the steps past the laundry room, and find Reed walking toward my apartment. He's wearing a blue T-shirt with the Captain America shield on it and khaki shorts. Something's bundled in a plastic bag under his right arm. He grins. "Hey, Brando. How'd it go?"

"How'd what go?"

"Right, busy morning." He ticks off two items on his fingers. "How about A, the coffee date with your hot co-worker—"

"We visited her sick grandfather, Reed."

"Belay that talk. Or B, where you caught a freaking airplane!"

I can't suppress the smirk. "Yes, that was pretty amazing."

"Amazing? Insane! I saw the replay on Channel 14. They got you tearing up the tarmac with your feet!" He looks down. "They're still attached."

"Think I would have noticed if they weren't," I murmur, hoping he takes the hint and keeps his voice low. "Tread's a little worn."

"A little worn." He shakes his head and slaps me good-naturedly on the shoulder. "Man. It's a good thing you're okay."

"What, you worried?"

"Duh. Who else is going to clean up my messes at the library if you get squashed under a plane?"

I unlock the door and head inside. Sean's sacked out by an open window, music screeching out of earbuds that dangle free from his head. Snoring and drooling.

Reed sighs. "Oh, the life of a teen. How I miss the whole sleeping 'til 11 on a Saturday."

"Uh-huh. I doubt Caroline would let you restart that habit." I slam the door shut.

Sean snorts, jerks upright. He glares at us bleary-eyed.

Reed guffaws. "'Morning, shorty. Here." He tosses the bag. It lands with a slap on the carpet. "Goodies from Uncle Reed."

Sean tugs at the bag, and his mouth drops open. "Sweet!"

I don't recognize a single comic book title, except for Invincible Iron Man. There must be a dozen new characters on the covers.

"Ungrateful hairless monster says...?" Reed gestures with a rolling motion of his hand.

"Thanks!" Sean's already got one of the new titles out, and plugs one of his earbuds back in. "Hey Uncle Reed, while you're here, ask Dad how he hurt his arm."

"Oh yeah?" Reed glances sidelong at me, mischievous grin forming. "Rough night on the town, eh, old man?"

"Nah, just stumbling on the boardwalk in the dark. Hit it on a railing." I make a show of the bandaged limb. It aches worse now, with occasional, stabbing pains at the wrist, after wrestling with an airplane. I realize my error: When Sean had asked last night, I'd fed him the same story about injuring the arm while visiting with Frank out at the boardwalk bars and restaurants. But this morning, I'd told fed Kelly a lie about basketball with Sean. This was the part of superhero life that took the most practice, more so than learning how to fly: the lies.

"Looks like it hurt, whatever it was," Reed says. He turns so Sean can't see his face and mouths the question, "Roof?"

I nod.

"Yep, bummer." Reed grabs a Coke from the fridge. "So, your morning was eventful, in summary."

"Indeed." We sit at the dining room table. I'm certain Sean's left one earbud dangling precisely because he means to eavesdrop, so I keep things sotto voce. "Leaving B aside, A went pretty well."

"Yeah? You realize it's gonna make personnel matters painful if you two are dating."

"We're not dating."

"Hooking up?"

I glare at him, and he holds up the Coke can as a shield. "It was a nice time spent together, that's all. Let's call it the beginning."

"Okay, then."

"Also, I kissed her."

Reed grins. "Details?"

"Not appropriate for her manager to hear."

"You dog."

"Never mind that. You're here for more than enabling my son's comic book addiction, right?"

Reed's smile slips. "You got mind-reading powers now? Yeah, that meeting the other night sucked. Round and round with the council, nobody agreeing on anything, except that they don't want to change their positions. The council's split six to three for closing Hull Branch hull. The Rittenhouse crew, as you can imagine, is firmly in the 'No' camp."

"Leaves three to work on."

"Well, not the guy from Westerville. He's on about the fact that he doesn't even have a branch. But Vanchev thinks we can get a sympathy vote. Maybe." Reed taps the can on the counter.

"I tell you, Brando, Vanchev's mostly been sitting there smiling through these things."

"He's lost some of his star power?"

"Don't think he ever had it," Reed muttered. "Comes across as a big shot and gets people ready to follow him and then...big nothing. He insists he's doing all the talking behind the scenes, you know, one on one."

"Sounds like he's smooth-talking you, Reed."

"No kidding." Reed downs his Coke. "What about you? How's your new boss doing?"

"Ah, we've had some mixed communications." I get out my wallet, and uncrinkle the note. Sean's got his other earbud back in, thankfully, and fully engrossed in his comics. We must bore him. "The thing is, the more I object to what he wants me to do, the more I keep coming back to Samantha's plea. I have to do this for her, Reed."

Reed glances at the note. "You know, it's great that she was able to leave that for you, Brando, but...isn't the timing odd?"

"How so?"

"She's been gone two years. All of a sudden, this Frank guy's giving you a medallion with superpowers and Samantha's note? Why not sooner? Why'd he hang on to them?"

"Don't even, Reed. This is her handwriting. It even smells like her." Lilacs, and the sea.

"I mean, you're going on like it's gospel truth. Last time I checked, there was only one set of written words you were that impressed with."

He's right. I've thought of all these things. But I've pushed them away in the race to save others.

"Just saying, man. Be careful." Reed finishes his soda. "I don't trust your buddy Frank."

"Any concrete reasons?"

"He's a dick."

"I'll take that into consideration."

"Uncle Reed! Dad!" Sean's up on his feet, heading right for us. I hastily stuff the note in my pocket. He's got his phone out, and Iron Man is abandoned halfway to the kitchen. "Look at this! He was at the airport! A whole plane! Can you believe it?"

Reed grins at me. I try to look skeptical, instead of puffing up with immense pride.

Frank's text comes in after 11 that night, as I'm combining two shades of blue and white for the right color of the sea. The painting's the bare bones of the boardwalk, from a far-off aerial image. Unlike most painters I don't use a photograph taken from a plane—it's all from memory.

<Round Two at the mine. Groundside infiltration. Walk over to Bennett. Fly from alley at Gennessee.>

No backdoor pick-up this time? Apparently, the penalty for arguing with your Garrison handler is hoofing it two blocks. It makes sense to fly from there. Fewer chances that this Acciai lady has surveillance.

I leave the light on in the office and a note on my easel explaining to Sean that Reed and I have gone out to a late movie. I peek into his bedroom. The boy's half out from under his covers, one gangly leg and arm hanging over the edge. He won't even notice I'm gone: the boy could sleep through the Apocalypse.

Two minutes later, I'm airborne, sticking to the low-lying clouds that now crowd the skies. It's a cool, overcast night. No moonlight.

I belatedly get my phone out and punch in a text to Reed. <You and me are at movies.>

It buzzes back. <Dude. Superheroing? I'm alibi? Excellent. Good luck.>

The radio in my helmet crackles. "You're not supposed to use that phone for any communications except with me."

"Well, Frank, you're only half the total of people who know how I spend my nights, and Sean's going to get suspicious if I keep going out late with you."

"Use your own phone."

"Roger that. What's the plan?"

"Fly straight and meet me on the south side of the mine, Gennessee Street."

As before, there's no signs of life around the mine. The buildings are lifeless hulks, brooding and drooping in deep shadows. Here and there, a few lamps cast circles of harsh white, throwing concrete and rusted metal into sharp relief. In contrast, the chain link fence surrounding the property is shiny silver, still bearing half-torn manufacturer's labels. The handful of dump trucks parked in the front lot are painted bright red, brand new OshKoshes with the black Otte-Vaughn logo emblazoned on the doors.

Frank's waiting for me in the shadows, halfway down the block, with the Camaro tucked around the next corner. I see the butt of the Steyr tucked under the light gray windbreaker he's wearing over a navy-blue T-shirt.

"Get in and follow my orders," he mutters. "Nothing fancy."

I still have s a lot of questions for him, but he doesn't strike me as in the mood to bother with any of that. Instead I nod and vault the fence. And when I say vault, I mean as in Olympic pole-vault. It puts me forty feet in the wide open, empty yard.

Nothing and no one impedes my progress—no alarms, no guards, no guard dogs. The main mine shaft is ahead, a long, metal structure jutting from the side of Van Buren Cliffs like a massive tin can, half-buried in rock and dirt. A pair of huge metal doors tower over me.

"Locked," I report into my radio.

"Figured that. Let's try something roundabout. Go to the right edge of the building. There should be a seam where the walls join and overlap."

I peer at the corrugated metal. "Found it."

"Pull it open. Peel it back and get inside that way."

I put up my right hand and picture a larger version of my fingers, unpeeling a sticker or separating a plastic wrapper. With caution, I extend the field through my body. The metal whines, buckles, strains at its rivets. Six shoot off like champagne corks. The siding bends back until it reveals a black, triangular opening, a gaping mouth with crooked edges.

"It worked!"

"Good. Get in. Watch yourself."

I creep inside and release my grip with the field, letting the metal sag back into place. It's enough of an overlap to conceal my illegal entry. The darkness envelopes me. I snap a glow stick, and a sickly green hue illuminates a small circle around me. That goes to a clip on my belt. For more, detail visual inspection, I light up the red MagLite that usually makes its home in my backpack.

"What do you see?"

"We could just put a camera in the helmet some time."

"Funny guy. Report."

"Right. There's a lot of rock, of the pale gray variety. Mine cart rails. It's damp. This thing goes a way, back into the cliffs, probably a quarter mile or so."

I follow the tracks, slick with condensation. My footsteps are deafening. There's a steady trickle of water from somewhere I can't see.

"Elevator should be 600 feet ahead." Even Frank is whispering. Paper rustles over the radio signal. He must have plans for this thing, or ground penetrating radar. Neither would surprise me.

The cage doors of the elevator shaft looms ahead. There's a new, shiny elevator car in the left side. The right side, however, appears unfinished.

"Shaft Two should be vacant. Take it all the way down."

I open the cage door, rattling metal and squealing wheels on their tracks. My flashlight shines down, down, revealing only more black. "That's ...deep."

"So, don't fall. Get down there."

Yeah, yeah. I form up the field and step off into nothing. The sensation of descending into a monstrous void makes me want to step right back onto the ledge. Instead, I gradually modify the gravitational pull I'm experiencing inside the field. I settle, drifting past at least eight horizontal shafts that seem to be cut brand new from the surrounding rock. Otte-Vaughn has been busy.

At the bottom are two horizontal shafts. One looks roughhewn and stretches off across uneven heaps of rock. There's rusty equipment strewn about. The other's as new as the shafts I saw above, with three dozen feet of fresh cart tracks laid down. "Which way?"

"The old caverns. Your left."

I inch over broken, rotten wood and metal, so corroded it blends with the rock. There's a half a glass bottle. Green. I kneel, making it blaze in the combined lights I carry. Bauer-Hoffstra? "Frank, how long ago was this part of the mine dug?"

"No one's certain. There's been recorded diggings as far back as the late 1800s."

"It has to be older than that. I found a bottle. The company that makes it only used green glass between 1810 and 1840, before their competitors started doing the same thing."

"That's not relevant to the mission."

"No, but it means this place is older than we thought, and that also means the structure's bound to be less stable." I breathe musty air through the vents of my helmet. My mind fills in the clanking equipment and salty language of 19th Century miners, slogging in the darkness, chasing after rich men's dreams of mineral wealth.

"Focus please."

"Understood. I'm moving." As I explore, following the winding cavern, the ceiling height decreases until I'm hunched over. There's a steady but shallow descent. Questions pepper me. Otte-Vaughn's buildings above were constructed in the 1950s, the start of the last great mining craze. Prior to that, there were several shafts that dug into the cliffs and the outskirts of Newport. Where did this one originate?

"Now, you should come out into a larger chamber."

The ceiling suddenly opens up, arching well out of my sight. I stand on an outcropping of granite the size of a dining room table for four. I cast light about. "Ah, Frank?"

He sighs. "What now?"

"I think your charts misuse the term 'larger.'" The cavern that stretches out before me has to be at least a thousand feet long. It's as wide as a football field's length, with a curving ceiling that's festooned with stalactites. It's an upside-down bowl, concave, and the flat part ahead is full of thick, muddy water. Stalagmites cluster shoulder to shoulder like armies.

I step down—and instantly regret it. My foot goes right into the semi-solid looking muck, with my leg following all the way up to the knee. It takes a great deal of effort and a sickening squelching sound to withdraw it. Good thing my shoes stay fastened.

"What was that?" Frank demands.

"Nothing. Some mud. No problem." My right leg and shoe are coated with thick, light gray goop.

"The cave floor's probably a mess."

"I noticed. Doesn't look like any improvements have been made to it."

"Can you see the far end?"

The flashlight doesn't seem to illuminate that far, but there's a tiny glitter. "Yes, there's something down there. Think this time I'll take the high road."

"Watch the stalactites."

My mother is less micromanaging. I tuck the flashlight away—and that's when another glitter, right by my feet, catches my attention. Some shard of glass or crystal? I bend and retrieve it. No, it's metal. Like tarnished silver. Tiny, no bigger than a toothpick. But strong. Barely bends under my thumb.

It's also freezing cold, far more so than the mud.

"Brandon. Move out."

"Roger and wilco." I tuck the metal into my pocket and zip it up. With a gentle push off the ground I launch into a slow flight over the water, barely a hover.

There's nothing ahead but those stalactites, and I stay ten feet below them. That still puts me the height of a four-story building over the water, which is now deeper and darker. There's far less of the murky muck around, and far fewer stalagmites.

"Anything to report?"

"Nothing. More giant cave." There is something ghostly just below the surface, about ten feet ahead. "Hang on. Might be a submerged mine cart. Let me take a closer—"

My helmet hits something. Strands of wire cling to the visor. I reach up to clear them off, but my arms get entangled. Got to reverse course. I swing my legs around, and they're caught too. "Frank!"

"Brandon? What is it?"

"Caught up in something. Wires."

"Get out now! Cut the wires!"

"Hmm, great idea. How do you suggest I do that?"

"Focus with the field. You're going to have to—"

I don't hear whatever the rest of his suggestion is, because there's a sudden rumble of sound that might as well be thunder in the deathly quiet of the cave. The wires tangling me yank back, and down, drawing my arms behind me and my legs aside. I lash out with the field but, given my hands are tied backwards, all I manage in my panic is to shatter a handful of stalagmites.

The rumble increases, and I'm pulled swiftly down. Got to

keep the field intact. Stay...up!

No good. The wires jerk abruptly, doubling the speed of their pull. My concentration shatters. The field dissipates.

I plummet.

"Brandon! Brandon!"

That's the last thing I hear before I hit the surface of the water, and everything disappears in a dark splash.

I'm underwater. There's barely a green glow from the stick floating from my belt. The wires drag me down.

Water's rising in the bottom of my helmet and leaking around the edges of the visor.

It's not watertight. Thing's supposed to be pressurized, for high altitudes, and it's leaking. Somehow, I've damaged it. Probing fingers reveal a gash along the bottom, under the laryngophone.

I'm going to drown.

Chapter Sixteen

It's hard enough collecting my thoughts and resisting the urge to have a full-blown panic attack while struggling against the binding wires without hearing my radio malfunction at full volume.

"Brand—static—espond to if yo—static—an't reac—"

Mercifully, it shorts out, and I'm left with relative silence. Water gurgles, churning outside my visor, streaming in around loose seals on either side and rising around my neck. I sputter, straining to angle my chin so I don't swallow mouthfuls of the cold, turgid water.

No matter what I do, the wires don't budge. They're tighter now, cutting off my circulation at the elbows and knees. Struggling turns out to be the worst possible options. Every pull and twist only make the wires tighten their grasp.

The water throbs with the pulse of something mechanical. I recognize it as a muffled version of the sound I heard right before I was yanked from the air. Where was it? What is it? Cyclical. An engine.

I go limp, let the slow currents drag me around. The wires pull me in one direction, turning me over, as if I'm rolling over in bed. Water floods into my helmet. Rushes up my nose, stings my eyes. I can barely see through it. Without the feeble glow from the stick, I'd be blind. I wrench my neck, hold my breath, tip back my head, everything I can think of to keep the water out of my face.

There it is: the point of origin. All the wires around me also wrap around and down to a single point. It's a net; the whole thing is anchored to a block of machinery ten feet below. The water is hazy around it, and the image ripples, but I can make out a box that periodically releases bubbles. It's at one end of a slowly turning spool.

There's a motor in there somewhere. Must have a power source. With my hands bound behind me, I can't aim. How do I use a change in gravity to remove a net? Will the field shear the wires? Trying to raise myself isn't working. No matter what image I put into my head to reduce my weight, the cable keeps dragging me down.

Wrong approach. I need more force, not less. It's getting stuffy inside the helmet. My vision's swimming, even if I can't. I visualize my trusty rockets, the same thing that let me keep place with a plummeting airplane. My body strains against the wires. They cut into my skin. I can see the main cable go taut, vibrating like a guitar string. It's not pulling me deeper, but I'm not getting away from it either.

I shift back and forth, tugging against the cables, thrashing with the field. I picture a large sword, then six blades, but all of them miss. In my frenzy, I lose focus. The icy cold of the medallion melts away. There's only the frigid water. It surges higher in my helmet. I choke on a mouthful, spit it out. My heart's racing, and my head's spinning.

Don't. Panic. Think. Think.

Too afraid. I'm going to die.

Don't be afraid. How many times have I heard it? How many times have I read it?

Always, always repeated, my addled brains sing. Don't be afraid. Don't. Fear. Not.

Terror fades. Slowly. Very slowly. I see the water sloshing up and down in front of my face. Count it. Time it. Deep breath... now.

Not enough. It has to be enough.

The spool. The motor. I twist as far as I can, pulling against the wires. My left arm sears with pain. Doesn't matter. Over I go. Bend my legs up as close to me as I can, as if I'm sitting for tea. With Kelly.

Sunlight through a window. A bright yellow goes pale green. Focus. The field. Focus it on the motor.

I can't.

You can. You have to.

I picture myself grasping at the other flying man, the Ashen agent. I picture fighting the Poles with their rocket launchers. I see the fleeing robbers. I'm strangling every thug and thief I've tussled with.

I can only pray I've got a hold on the motor and not some submerged stalagmite.

There's a muffled crunch. The water shudders with it.

It'd better not be a stalagmite.

Hard to see through green murk.

The cable suddenly goes limp. It drifts away from the bottom of this pond, dragging with it the crushed remnants of the spool. The box to which it was attached is mangled, its outer housing mashed to a quarter its former size. Fuel oozes out, black blood that fouls the water even worse than I thought possible. Bits of machinery flutter outward in an arrested spray, dropping into the muck around the winch.

Get. Out.

The field. I will myself to rise. Blackness presses in on my vision. Water fills my ears, my nose, my eyes. Lungs burn. Air. I need air.

My body rockets up, bubbles all around. I can feel them streaming against me.

Explosion. Sound returns with concussive force. The water's gone. Drains from my face, from my helmet. I soar up in an arc, rejoicing.

Short flight. Everything's in pieces. Stalactites. One grazes my arm. Not a cut. Enough to knock me aside.

I hit mud at the edge of the pond. Face first.

Dark and cold.

That hurt.

I push myself up with both hands—and shout as pain lances fresh and sharp through my right forearm. Okay, then, let's not use that one.

The wires are still wrapped around me, still binding my legs, but they've loosened enough that I can bend my right hand forward and dig for my pocketknife. The blade opens easily enough; there still remains the question of whether it's sharp enough to cut the wire.

I start sawing. Meantime, I shake the helmet, watching the last dregs of water spill out. The rest comes spraying from my mouth as I retch all over the front of my jacket. The ragged coughs go on for an eternity, echoing in my ears as loud as foghorns.

I get my breathing back under control. My vision's clear again.

The knife is sharp enough, but this is taking forever. I try the radio as I work. "Frank. Frank, are you there? Do you copy?"

Nothing. Not even static.

It takes me a minute, but I get my arms freed of the wire. With that, the rest slides off my legs, though it takes some wriggling for me to get completely free. I yank off the helmet and scowl—the tiny indicator lights are all green. It's working. It's getting power. So, the trouble must be on Frank's end. Am I deep enough we lost signal? No, that can't be, he was talking even as I went down.

I have to get out of here. Legs, operational. So, I stand up.

Shakily, but I stand.

The water in the center of the pond swirls. A sheen of fuel oil spreads from the center. The full magnitude hits me with lightning-strength clarity: this was a trap. The Ashen set a trap in this cavern.

They set it for another medallion user.

I look up, staring toward the ceiling. Other strands crisscross the upper reaches. They dangle between the stalactites, waiting webs for me, the proverbial fly. There's a great gap where I flew right into the trap like an imbecile.

Frank needs to know. But the radio's down.

The cell phone. I dig it from my pocket. I know it's a slim chance—by my watch I was under for several agonizing minutes. First thing's first. Have to power it down. There's no way it can recover if I can't stop the battery—

Never mind. Screen's black. Doesn't respond.

I stagger away from the water's edge, slogging through the muck. My landing's very close to the small outcropping from which I entered this cavern. Need to get back up to the surface and warn Frank. But I'm not going to fly. Not until I get clear of this Sheol and its snares.

The cold seeps in as I walk, shoes squelching, every part of me soaked and frigid. Only the medallion's spike of ice is welcome, because of it's familiar. It means power and protection.

How could I have failed so utterly? I've handled worse situations than this. But it feels like it was only the grace of God that got me out alive.

I trudge back to the elevator shaft and stare up the long, dark reach. Was that what this was? A necessary reminder that, despite these miraculous powers, I have limitations? Because I'm always aware. I know I'm not invincible. My arm's throbbing ache over the past forty-eight hours is reminder enough.

I call up the field. The medallion slashes at my chest, a pickaxe of ice, and I can feel gravity changing around me. My fingertips drag at the very pull of the Earth. I leap from the mine floor and fly straight up.

The floors flicker by with increasing speed. For one split second, I close my eyes. This has to be His will. Nothing else can explain it.

The unfinished elevator gears loom above. With inches to spare, I roll onto my back and burst into the mine entrance, shooting out of the elevator shaft and flying three feet off the ground.

There's light pouring into the mine.

Without a moment's thought I bring myself to a halt, upright and hovering just inside where the massive locked doors had been when I arrived at the mine. They're gone now. The light is from the lamps that provided the only circles of illumination at the Otte-Vaughn property.

This is…odd. A better word is alarming, because I take five steps outside the entrance and find the doors. They've been broken off their hinges, discarded like a pair of old magazines.

"Frank?" I call out.

"He's otherwise occupied." It's a female voice—a familiar one. Very bland, very smooth, with more than a hint of sultry.

The woman who tried to abduct me. Acciai.

A pair of brilliant blue-white lights flash on, blinding me. Standing in front of a pick-ups high beams would be less painful.

Silhouettes come from either side of the lights. Six of them. Blinking away the blotches as rapidly as I can, I see a motley assortment of thugs—a couple of whom I recognize from that night at the docks when I made my debut. Cezar. One of Krol's enforcers. The other six are young, wearing T-shirts and baggy athletic pants, with varying percentages of their arms and necks concealed by garish tattoos. Skinny, fat, burly—all body types. Besides the clothing, they are similar in their firearms. AK-74Ms. Same kind I destroyed at the docks.

I grind my teeth. Frank. You said you'd gotten rid of them

all. I just keep finding more, don't I?

Cezar snaps his fingers. One of the men ducks beyond the light and shoves a seventh body forward. Even without seeing his face right away, I can tell from his posture it's Frank. Nobody else's shadow would look that angry, even with his arms bound at the wrists in front of his waist.

"Well, well. You've been a very busy boy." A woman's voice comes from the center of the lights. She moves toward me. It's a plodding, thudding sound, makes me think of a jackhammer in slow motion. "He's right. You are powerful. So I was more than pleased to find you friend skulking about. He and I didn't get off on the right foot, what with the exchange of bullets."

"Lady, I don't know what you want, but he won't give it to you, and neither will I. He doesn't appreciate being tied up. Let him go before things get messy." There's far more bluster behind those words than I can back up. My throat's raw, my legs leaden, and my arms sore. After all this, now I get a head to head with a professional killer?

"I guarantee it will get messy. That's what I want." She steps forward again, and the lights flick off. "I know who you are, and I know the power you share with Domitian. It's mine to take."

It's her. Consolata Acciai, according to Frank. But it's only her face I recognize—the face, and the shapely curve of her limbs. The rest of her is obscured by a contraption. My brain takes a couple of seconds to put a name to it: exoskeleton. Black armor is strapped to her arms, legs and chest. Silver pistons and slate-gray, artificial musculature connect the motorized joints at her shoulders, elbows, hips and knees. Her armored boots look like they're size twenty fours. The helmet she wears is split open like a sideways clamshell, dim red lights illuminating the pale skin of her face. Beautiful, in a vampiric kind of way.

Domitian? I file it away, aware of the implications but with no time to search for them.

"What do you think of my new outfit?" She parts ruby red

lips, revealing an alluring smile. "My employer wanted only be best for me."

She lifts her arms. I'm not up on the latest exoskeleton research; my knowledge is restricted to Popular Mechanics and Science.com articles. But none of the prototypes I've read about sport two shining blades on the left armored sleeve and a pair of mismatched gun barrels. One's got the appearance of a thick, black pipe, with a trio of wires or tubes connecting it to the back of her suit. The other is slender with a long ammunition clip protruding from the far end.

"It's definitely you." I let my arms settle at my side. Careful not to let on, I marshal the field about me. It doesn't respond as quickly as I like. The cold at the center of my chest flickers, instead of holding strong and steady. My thoughts crystalize as I inventory what I'll need: a shield for myself, a strike to free Frank, a method to stop Acciai. That last one takes longer to formulate than the others.

"You're sweet. Did you know the prototype was developed for emergency rescue? Hence these." She waves the right arm. Her hand's tucked under an armored sheath; when she moves a control I can't see, a trio of thick metal fingers with rough grips pinch shut with a clang. "It even carries transfusion equipment. Or it used to. I love that smell."

"What do you want?"

"To dance," she purrs. "I promise you'll like it."

She aims with her right arm and a gout of fire streams at me.

I instinctively dodge—or I mean to, but find myself thirty feet to the right, a cloud of dust around me feet. A pair of gouges are dug in the ground, leading back to where I was a second ago. Flame washes across them.

High speed dodge without flight? That's new. I grin behind the helmet. "You'll have to catch me first."

"Play nice, now," she says, petulant, "or your friend bleeds."

"Your mistake." I lunge for her with both fists out. Without dropping speed, I wrap a portion of the field around my right hand and arm, draw it back—

She spins away, gears whirring, and strikes me on the shoulder. The blades don't penetrate my shield, but she may as well have hit me with a steel girder. I slam into the dirt like so much dead meat, skidding and scraping to a halt.

"Don't get winded this soon. I need you to show some stamina." The gun on her arm makes a clacking sound.

I throw up both hands and block the explosions of gunfire. Whatever she's got, it's some kind of automatic weapon. Frank could tell me the caliber, I'm sure. Sparks block my vision as she closes in on me.

Ice stabs my chest, and pain lances through my left arm again. My teeth clench. She wants stamina?

I stand, force myself against her onslaught of gunfire. Two steps. Four. Six. The distance closes, bullets pounding furiously but impotently into the shield, winding up as glittering craters. Halfway to her, Acciai opens up with the flamethrower instead. Fire wraps around me. The shield does its job, yes, but there's not a remedy for the intense heat.

Almost there. Need to free a hand to shove her back.

She hollers something lost in the roar of the flames and thunders toward me. At the last second before impact, the fire cuts out. Her blades slash at me, and I shoulder beneath them. The chest armor has as much give as a concrete wharf. But the field surrounding me pile drives her backward. I'm already reaching around her to grab hold and fly her off. Dropping her in the bay's my best option.

Except she suddenly becomes as immobile as Dannersly Bridge. Pistons whine and metal spikes jab into the yard, ripping up dirt and asphalt. She pounds on me with the mechanized claw, again and again. There's a flash of a picture, half-rubbed off the underside of black armor plating: the outline of the Earth, and a crooked line? Her punches hammer my shoulder and puts me flat on the ground.

Not good. Got to get up.

I shoot forward, skimming a half foot off the ground. Behind me, I hear the twin blades punch into the asphalt. Rolling over onto my back, I let off a disruption of gravity from my left hand, intended to reduce the pull around Acciai to less than a twentieth of Earth normal.

She fires with her arm cannon. Instead of hitting her, the burst sprays bullets everywhere but at me. The thugs she's brought along holler in alarm, ducking their heads and scuttling aside.

In the midst of getting airborne, I realize none of the Poles have shot at me. Besides dodging Acciai's errant shots, they haven't so much as twitched. They're positioned around the yard to block an exit on foot. In spite of the pain and dodging weapon fire, I grin. Wonder if Cezar decided that Frank warranted six men to be his jailers. Like that'll be enough.

"Don't run off!" Acciai ceases fire and jumps at me. I'm talking a thirty-foot bounding leap, moving faster than I thought possible.

I spin out of her way. We graze each other—her slashing with the blades, me pushing out with a burst from the field. Her blades tear at the sleeve of my shirt, but my blow connects, knocking her aside and sending her down onto the top of a cinderblock shed. She tumbles across the roof.

Suddenly, there's a choked cry. Frank's shouldering a guard into the ground. I touch down in time to hear a sickening crunch. He jams his hands into the man's face, and the come up bloody. The second guard looks stunned, but points his AK at Frank nonetheless.

I lunge ahead, replaying the same sudden burst of speed across the yard. In a second, I ram into the guy, breaking his gun from his grip. A single punch slams him ten feet backward.

Frank scoops up the first guard's abandoned AK. "You

didn't respond."

"I was busy drowning. And you're welcome." I widen the field in front of me, forming an invisible shield arcing between us and the rest of the gunmen. The timing's perfect, because they open fire. Sparks litter our position.

"Hold this position. There's a hole I cut in the fence, back fifty yards. Move toward it."

I keep the shield steady but glance up toward roof of the cinder block shed. A dust cloud's still settling. "What about her?"

Gunfire explodes to my left. Frank's firing at them. He must be just beyond the edge of my shield, because his bullets aren't deflected. One man's chest explodes in dark gouts of blood. Cezar shouts an order. The remaining Poles redirect their fire. But it's worthless because I shift the field toward Frank, keeping him protected.

Car tires screech. Red and blue lights erupt down the street at the front of the mine yard. As they close, headlights flood the night.

"That would be the police," Frank says. "Let's move."

Motor's whine. Acciai's standing now, on top of the shed. She whirls in the direction of the approaching police cars.

"We can't leave now!" I holler. "Have you seen her rig? She'll tear right through them!"

"Not our fight, Brandon. Not anymore. Stick to the mission parameters."

Acciai leaps down from the shed, landing inside the gates. Seconds later, a huge, armored Bearcat truck bashes them in. Five squad cars roar from behind. The truck slams its breaks and cranks sidelong, aiming its broad side at us.

"This is DCPD!" a voice bellows over a loudspeaker. "You are under arrest! Lay down your weapons!"

Acciai laughs. She immediately opens fire with her mounted gun, spraying bullets across the side of the truck and down the line of cars. Police officers dive out the opposite sides of their cars. The Poles ignore Frank, and I and join the fusillade, spreading throughout the yard for shelter behind outbuildings and dump trucks. Acciai sends a huge gout of flame searing across the truck. If there's any SWAT team guys inside, they're not making a move to exit.

Leave now? Not a chance.

"Don't wait up at the Barn, Frank!" I leap ahead, going for the nearest target: a bald Pole with a thick blond beard. He's firing his AK on full auto, draining a clip, as he shields himself behind a dump truck. Idiot's acting like I'm no longer here. I reach for him and use the field to form a disc of lesser gravity under his feet. He flips up a dozen feet, pinwheeling over the truck and slamming down on a heap of gravel.

I'm certain Frank's made his escape, citing operational secrecy. But as I turn toward Acciai, I see him bashing the jaw of another Pole with the stock of his AK.

That leaves Cezar. He vanishes into the shadows of the mine buildings. I start after him.

"Leave him!" Frank says. "Get her!"

Nearby, an ATV is parked beside the row of dump trucks. I put my concentration into lifting it. After straining to slow an airliner's descent, it's a breeze—may as well be lifting a twenty-pound box of books. My arm hurts, but that's for later.

Acciai turns just as I heave the ATV in her direction. All force and no subtlety, minus the element of surprise. She blasts it with fire, melting plastic and igniting the tires. Before it can hit her, she lashes at it with the blades and sends it spinning off onto a squad car. It bounces off the hood, exploding in a shower of burning metal and plastic bits. The cruiser's front end is scorched.

Gunfire. From only a handful of what sound like shotguns. Dennis steps out from around the armored truck, wearing shiny gray pants and polished black shoes, a blue shirt and brilliant red tie under Kevlar. He's pumping shell after shell from his 12-gauge Remington Model 870P shotgun. Acciai turns her left shoulder to him, and the thick plating I thought was fixed armor unfolds like a leaf, spreading out into a clumsy-looking barrier. Dennis's shots were well aimed, until that.

I soar in, driving with all the speed I can build over that short a distance. I grab him around the waist, helmet burrowing into his gut, and gun my invisible rockets. Dennis shouts, and the flamethrower roars. Searing heat washes over me.

A second later, the heat's banished by cool night air. I angle up, spinning so fast I disorient myself, until I catch sight of the mine's winding tower. I make for that and set Dennis down on it.

Suddenly, my legs cut out from under me. I topple in a heap, half-dangling from the edge of the tower. Steady. Still weak from the near drowning. The cold spreads from the usual jab at the center of my chest to my torso, my shoulders. Is there a recharge time for using the medallion? Some upper limit I reached?

"Don't move. You're under arrest."

I get up onto my knees. Dennis aims a Ruger at my face. He's pale, hair disheveled, tie askew. But there's no mistaking it.

I shake my head. "You've got to be kidding me."

"Remove your mask and place your hands behind your head. It's about time I got you in my sights. Whatever your game is, it's over tonight."

"You think I'm behind this?" I stand up. "How'd you get here so fast, anyway?"

Dennis doesn't take his gun off me. "We received an anonymous tip that you were breaking into the facility."

Acciai had to have contacted him. She, or her Ashen overseer. I put my hands out in front of me, palms down. "Look. I'm not the bad guy here. You know that."

"All I know is that you and your pal, the other flying freak, have started breaking things in my city, and I'm going to stop you before someone else gets hurt."

"Me? The one hurting people?" I can't contain the snort. "Try the girl with the flamethrower."

I glance back down to make my point—and she's gone. No sign of her whatsoever. The police have fanned out into the yard. They're rounding up the injured Poles, and a knot of them seem to be inspecting a smoldering portion of the chain link fence. Great. Just great. Frank's probably on his way back to the Barn. Wouldn't know, what with my shorted-out helmet radio and dead cell phone.

"I'm gonna tell you one more time," Dennis says. "Remove your mask. Put your hands on your head. Or I will shoot."

I glare at him. Reed's brother-in-law. He's always been civil to me, but now I see what gets Reed's goat. However, if he is the guy hunting down Acciai and her boss, it behooves me to not make him an enemy. I'm amassing enough of those. "Lieutenant, I'm not coming with you. But I'm not your enemy. I'm after the people who are. If you want my help, you'll have it. The people of Drake City already know that. I need the police on my side. Be ready when I come to you for your help."

Dennis squints. The muzzle of his gun dips...

I push off with the field, launching into flight.

No bullets chase me as I soar up through the sky. The mine property shrinks into a collection of amber lights. The police vehicles and flames create a miniature bonfire of color at one end. Arcing back to the southeast, I take several passes over Newport's docks, rail depot, and industrial complexes. No sign of Acciai.

What a fiasco.

I roll over and pour on speed for the Barn. Frank had better have answers for me.

He's waiting at the Camaro, by the entrance to the radar site. None of the lights are on, save the dome inside the car.

"Well, that was a mess," he says. "What did you find down there?"

I yank off the helmet and toss it at his feet. He stops it sharply with his shoe, as expertly as a soccer player, without looking away from my face. "I found a trap, Frank: a net rigged for a flying person, plus a whole lot of water in which I almost drowned. Anything else I should have been looking for?"

"Calm down. Obviously, our target knew you were coming." He picks up the helmet and taps at the radio switch. "Have to replace this set."

"Can we stay on topic?"

"Such as..."

"Such as the assassin who now has her own flame-throwing, bullet-shooting, blade-wielding armored robot suit!" I snap. "This is insane! You've got me diving into these messes with no hint as to what's coming. It's a miracle they didn't kill us both!"

"There's no such thing as miracles, Brandon. We're alive because of tactics and training. You're forgetting your obligation—"

"Obligation. Right, yes, the obligation to serve in a secret army with secret rules, run by people I never see, who give me stupid orders like I'm a mindless grunt!" I poke a finger at him. "I didn't sign up for this! I signed up to help people."

"And it's all I can do to make sure you don't botch that!" Frank's right in my face. "When are you going to get it through your thick skull? We don't maintain our advantage by seeking celebrity! A century ago, we could erase our appearances. Burn the right newspapers, bribe the right publisher, make it go away. But now, there's no stopping it. No way to undo the damage. When your moronic self is up on YouTube, it's viral, and it's out of our control."

"Tell me again why that's a bad thing. These people need a sign of hope, Frank. Something that will show them the evil isn't going to hold sway over them forever."

He shakes his head. "Listen to you. Evil. You're talking like those idiotic cartoons your kid and your buddy read. Wake up, Brandon. This is the real world. There's only two groups seeking balance."

"That's your word for giving the Polish mafia an army's worth of fully automatic Russian weaponry?" I snap. "Balance? Come on. You're blindly following the Garrison's orders and making me do the same."

"That's enough. I'm tasked to keep you in order."

"You don't even do what I do anymore!" I poke him in the chest, connecting this time. "You can't do this! You're washed up, and I'm the guy now. I'm the one saving people and deflecting bullets and getting beaten! Excuse me if I don't care what you think about how I do it!"

Frank hits me. Hard. Knocks me back. But he's been training me, so I don't go flat on my back.

"Touch me again," he says, voice icy and low, "And medallion or not, you'll get the beating you need."

I rub at my jaw, and glare, seething. But I'm not stupid enough to go after him.

"The Garrison knew those guns were incoming, yes. That's why your mission was to stop the rocket launchers. Mine was to ensure the Ashen got the AKs to the Poles. The only way to find out the Ashen's endgame is to let the gang war between the Poles and Irish unfold. All of that was and still is irrelevant to your tasks as a medallion holder. Understood?"

"Yes."

"Good."

"That doesn't mean it's right. My job saving people doesn't get any easier when the bad guys are heavily armed."

"Deal with it, Brandon." Frank sighs. "I'm not arguing this again. Not now. Focus on the business at hand: the mine. Did you find anything at all that might clue as to the Ashen's interest?"

For a moment, I see the blurred image on Acciai's armor. That's for me to investigate, when I've rested. Then I recall the shard stuffed in my pocket, before the trap was sprung. Mercifully, it's still there. "Here."

Frank takes the sliver. He examines it closely, holding it up to the Camaro's dome light. His eyes go wide. I've seen Sean look less terrified when we watch late night horror movies. "Were there more?"

"I don't know."

"Remember harder."

"I didn't see any, Frank. What's the problem?"

He holds it up in front of my face. "The problem, Brandon, is that this is a fragment of a medallion."

Chapter Seventeen

It took Drake City Fire Department six and a half minutes to get a ladder truck from their Newport station to the Otte-Vaughn mine. Marchand noted every passing second on his Rolex. It gave him far too much time to pace and fume.

"Sir? It's Dillard." Marchand had his phone out and set on speaker mode. That level of high-tech he could handle. "The captain said he'll have the ladder in place momentarily."

"That's great, Dillard. Because I'm stuck on top of this tower wondering why you idiots left me stuck on top of this tower!"

"Yes, sir." Dillard's voice went an octave higher, and the words doubled in speed. "The truck's getting into position now. We've secured the perimeter. All suspects are in custody."

Marchand glared over the edge of the tower, down at the miniature emergency vehicles and people the size of toy soldiers. The ladder truck edged its way through the squad cars, a flashing red beacon among the whites and blacks of the police. The ability to see the whole area was perfect, but the inability to have his hand on the tiller down there drove him nuts. "Run it down."

"Five casualties, no fatalities. Two men with gunshot wounds to the chest and upper arm; EMTs stitching them up. Three have second degree burns. We're lucky it wasn't more."

"Yeah, I know."

"If Airfoil hadn't stopped them—"

"Our suspects."

"Right. Near as we can tell, there were six gunmen. Two dead, one from severe cranial trauma, one with a cluster of hits to the chest. Three more wounded; out cold, in a couple of cases. One gone."

Marchand knew that last bit. He'd spotted Cezar in the cover of the trucks, shooting at the police. Yet, during Acciai's onslaught he'd gone AWOL. And the chick in the robot suit herself...He gritted his teeth. "Acciai's gone."

"Yes, sir. We've got people out on the surrounding streets. There was a sighting north of here, up along the river."

"Send a pair of squad cars up there."

"Yes, sir."

The ladder truck was set up below, its ladder crawling upwards. Acciai was far more dangerous than she'd been before. Whoever the flying guy had been, who literally busted her out of custody, he'd seen to that. If it hadn't been for Airfoil...

Marchand growled. Airfoil. Listen to him. He sounded like Dillard, and everyone else in Drake City. Not only had the freak intervened to keep him and his men from getting barbecued, but he'd flown Marchand to the top of the tower. And left him here. He'd had the guy in his sights and failed to arrest him or shoot him.

Didn't mean Marchand wasn't impressed with what the guy did. It took guts for one man to take a bullet for another. But to dive in front of a flamethrower—and bullets—and blades—for someone he didn't even know...

None of it made sense. Crime, graft, payoff and blackmail. Marchand understood those. But flying people? With the power to lift things that no man should be able to? Powers that went beyond the realm of possibility.

"Sir? They've got a firefighter coming up for you."

"Nice to hear, Dillard. Listen: Acciai's suit. Tell me you

know something about this tech."

"Yessir. There's not that many agencies and private companies experimenting with exo-skeletal frames—at least, not many who can field something that far beyond the prototype stage." Dillard stared off above the screen. "You know, I can compile a whole database of sources. I've been following the newest designs for possible law enforcement applications—"

"Easy, Dillard. There's dash cameras on all the cruisers, right?"

"Yes. Got it! I'll review the footage."

"Someone had to have made her gear. I want to know who. If we can track the maker, we can get to this other flying menace."

"What about Airfoil, sir? I mean, we're supposed to be tracking him, too."

"Yeah, I know." Captain Urquhart was going to have a field day with this. "We keep looking into that. But Acciai and her boss—they're the priority."

The edge of the ladder reached over the rim of the tower. A firefighter in full black and neon green turnout gear appeared at the top. He grinned. "Evening, Lieutenant. Nice and cool up here."

Marchand followed down the whole way in stony silence.

Sunday morning dawned hot and muggy. The soupy air clung to buildings, vehicles, and especially people. Drake City reeked of sweat and refuse. Marchand wiped his brow and doffed his sunglasses. This was the last year he put off restoring the Monte Carlo's air conditioner. Really?

The interior of St. Andrew's Catholic Church was cool and dark. Mass was ending: the priest's voice boomed from the front of the sanctuary. Half the pews, dozens of mahogany benches arranged like soldiers, were empty. Marchand craned his neck to take in the sweeping wood beams and soaring white ceilings. The twelve stations of the cross, depicted as granite friezes three feet across, decorated the sanctuary walls. Stained glass windows between each frieze let in soft, multicolored light on either side of the church.

Pews creaked as the congregation rose for the final hymn. Cezar was one of them. He wore a red polo shirt and black pants. He stood among three families with his face bowed and his lips moving to the words.

Marchand had on short sleeves, too, but refused to forgo a tie. Some things were non-negotiable. He stopped at the marble font and dipped his first and middle fingers into the consecrated water. Ice cold. He made the sign of the cross, murmured, "In the name of the Father and the Son and the Holy Spirit."

He smirked. How many decades had it been? Two? Yet the reflex of piety was still as ingrained as the squeeze of the trigger.

He stared up at the life-sized crucifix behind the priest, occupying the focus of the nave. Christ himself, arms spread, legs pointed, sightless eyes lifted to Heaven. No longer on a cross; instead, the sculpture was inset in a large circle.

Marchand shivered. Made Him look like He was flying.

He stood aside as mass ended. A couple hundred people filed by, giving greetings to the priest and deacons. Everyone ignored Marchand. Happy conversations between neighbors, laughter among friends, horseplay by children and chiding by parents—the sounds flowed over him. He caught snippets here and there; listening when no one noticed was valuable.

After the third time the word "Airfoil" occurred, he gritted his teeth and blocked out the noise.

A handful of older parishioners stayed behind, heads bowed in prayer. The last scattered reeds. Cezar was among them, stock still in the center of his pew.

Marchand joined him. As soon as his knees hit the padding on the kneeler, a memory slammed into him: he and Caroline, dressed to the nines, scolded into remaining still, as a priest's homily rolled over him like a summer's thunderstorm.

Reality snapped back. He folded his hands together, pressing the heels into the top of the pew in front of him.

"Ah. Friend. You join me in prayer. There is hope for the lapsed, eh?" Cezar said.

"Don't know what you're talking about."

"Come now. I see the signs. You were at home in place as this. Now, you walk different path. Is common."

"I didn't come here for a homily from a killer and a thug, Cezar. This is neutral ground, per your rules."

"True. Is no place for violence in house of God. Not by likes of us." Cezar chuckled.

"Shut up. You were there last night. When Acciai went fire-crazy on us."

Cezar's joviality faded. "Ah. She was breathtaking. The wilki, they are calling her Aniol Smierci. Angel of Death."

Marchand snorted. "Stupid name for someone who didn't manage to kill anyone. Where is your angel?"

"Is not my place to reveal. Sorry."

Marchand glared sidelong at him. "That's it? No negotiating? Come on, Cezar. You've got plenty of infractions racked up that I can wipe away. Don't tell me Krol's backing out on our arrangements."

"I think you misunderstand. Friend. I can tell you nothing about the Angel. Even if not orders, I would not say."

"You didn't take anything from the mine."

"No."

"Why were you there?"

"Was test for the hero. The man Airfoil. She was to face him, single combat, no interruptions."

"Yet someone called us there. Anonymous tip."

Cezar shifted. "I do not know that."

"Shut up," Marchand hissed through clenched teeth. "I want Acciai and her boss. You're gonna give them to me. I know she's working with the wilki to take out the Irish leadership. What, are you itching that bad for a gang war? What's Krol doing?"

"Shhh!" Cezar's gaze locked on to him, ice cold. "This is house of God."

Marchand kept silent for a moment, organizing his attack. Cezar was being unusually cagey about the whole thing. By now, he should have asked for money, or favors, or both. Instead, he stonewalled. "What about the guy who was with Airfoil?"

"Ah."

"Yeah. Someone else was there, someone I saw talking to him. Didn't get an ID."

Cezar grinned, a wolfish expression. "Too much smoke in face, yes?"

"Try a wall of fire. You got a name for me?"

"No. Man is ghost. No one knows him. He disappears with great skill. Even from first we saw him, in spring when we were to help Acciai with abduction."

Marchand twitched. The shooting. The one at Brandon Tusk's apartment? "I want a face."

"Perhaps I help. In turn, you must never ask of the Angel again. Is Mr. Krol's wish."

"His wish? I'm not the genie in the lamp, Cezar. This is a business arrangement. Get me the picture. You tell Krol I will find Acciai. I don't care if I have to bring the entire da—the whole National Guard on him."

"You threaten wilki?"

Marchand laughed at the absurdity. "What's with the sudden case of honor? You forget who's in charge here."

"No. You do not see it, do you?" Cezar swiveled in the pew. His alcohol-tainted breath made Marchand wrinkle his nose. He was all too aware of the loose-fitting polo shirt Cezar wore—

plenty of room for a gun at the waist. He let the heel of his hand rest on his holstered Ruger. "Your time is finished. Mr. Krol. He will not deal with you anymore. The wilki have a new champion. The Angel and the man with the blank face have shown us true power. Is power of God. Nothing police can stop."

"Don't do this, Cezar. You walk outta here, I'll have cops on every street corner in Little Warsaw," Marchand growled. "You won't make five bucks, let alone rake in the thousands you take every week."

Cezar chuckled. He didn't sound like a man under threat. "Yes, very good. Mr. Krol will be very scared to hear that. Tell me, friend: can you kill man without touching him? Can you lift roof from building, throw it like plate? No. You have nothing." He leaned in. "We will have this city."

He rose. Marchand followed, blocking his path. There were still people in the sanctuary. Cezar wouldn't shoot him. Not with witnesses. Right? "I want a picture of the guy who helped Airfoil."

Cezar sighed. "You hear, but not listen. I will get. Send a message to you for old times' sake, yes? A favor. Friend." He made the sign of the cross, knelt at the exit to the pew. "But the next time I see you in Little Warsaw, Lieutenant, then I will honor my vow to the Angel and kill you."

Acciai had never seen anyone as overwhelmingly gray and cold.

Nikodem Krol ran white fingers through steely streaks of his hair. His black shirt only illuminated the silver in eyes that reminded her of shards of flint. His skin was pale as ash; his beard looked like wiry charcoal wool. He was dressed in a black shirt and pants, black shoes, black belt with a gold buckle. He bore no tattoos. He wore a fine chain of silver visible at his throat.

Acciai leaned against the windowsill, watching him from

the corner of the quiet, dingy bedroom in a tenement building. She disdained being stuck in the recesses of Newport where few people ventured and where foreclosures outnumbered vermin. The pasty green wallpaper had long ago peeled, revealing sickly white plaster. The floor was bare wood. Two rusty metal chairs sagged at an equally corroded table

Krol sat at the table, watching, listening. Cezar prowled behind him, chewing on a toothpick, grunting occasionally. The brute was all muscles, bluster, and pain. Acciai smiled at him, and he instantly froze, his eyes widening. Good to know her reputation carried import.

Domitian stood on the other side of the room, clad in gray business clothing and wearing his mask. Acciai would find him utterly ridiculous if not for the fear screaming in the back of her mind.

"The terms of our agreement are clear," he said. "The key targets of your opposition have been eliminated. It is your turn."

Cezar snorted. "You already have our allegiance. Have our guns. Our blood. You cannot demand more than that."

"Mr. Krol, leash your dog," Domitian said.

Cezar stiffened, but Krol held up a hand. "No. He is correct. Be silent, Cezar."

"Yes, Mr. Krol." He sulked to a corner and seethed, casting irate glances at Domitian and Acciai.

"Now. Domitian. You have hurt the Irish. For this we are thankful. But they have struck back at us, have they not? You think I do not see what is happening: this conflict between us, this is what you desire."

"I believe I have been up front in that regard."

"You have. I have lost wilki—six of my best. More will die."

"Death is a part of war, Mr. Krol. You must reconcile that with the rewards of such sacrifice."

"Rewards? Money, I have. It is security I seek. You promised this. You have not delivered. Therefore, I do not see that the wilki owe you and your...associate anything."

"Let's speak of your promises to me. Your promise of allegiance—and thank you, Cezar, for pointing that out." Domitian pointed to the window. "Out there is a city which I have promised to deliver into your hands. I will keep that promise. But I cannot achieve my aims without the necessary manpower. You promised to provide me with that manpower."

Krol sat, impassive. "It is many men you would have me bring here. Many whom I have...not fond dealings with."

"They are brothers, are they not?"

"They are of the same organization, yes. When I arrived in Drake City as a youth, decades ago, I was alone. I carved out my land here with my fists and my knife and my money. Then—only then—would they send me men. We quarreled as to whom should be in command here."

"I want seventy men. The best you can bring. Enforcers."

"And I tell you, I will not do it. I will not beg to them, those fools of the old land." Krol spoke in an even, measured tone. Without raising his voice, he put intensity behind the words. Acciai understood how he brooked no disagreement among the wilki with his rule. "They have never given me the support I need. Even our weapons, we had to get those from the Ukrainians and the Russians. No. I will not beg. You find some other way to give us the city."

Domitian didn't respond. Instead, he crossed the room and joined Acciai at the window. She had her cell phone resting on the sill, next to her arm. "This is disappointing, Mr. Krol," he said. "Your refusal to cooperate doesn't bode well for our future endeavors. You must reconsider."

"No. We are at an end of our talks. Come, Cezar." Krol stood, slid his chair back. "Good day."

"You are not going anywhere, I'm afraid." Domitian turned to them. "Please, be seated."

Krol laughed, a cold, hard sound, like metal banging on

metal. "You would make demands of me? My patience is at an end. So is our partnership. Cezar..."

There was a rustle of fabric. Cezar pointed a small Glock at Domitian. Acciai stepped in front of him, aiming her Springfield pistol. She'd much rather have had her exo-skeleton frame in place, instead. The memory of the searing flames and the gunfire teased her.

"This is inadvisable," Domitian said. "Have your man lower his weapon."

"You get rid of your so-called 'Angel's' weapon first," Krol said.

"Fair enough. Consolata, if you would please...and step aside."

She stepped aside first, and it still took her another ten seconds to comply. She felt like a fool standing there with Cezar holding them at gunpoint. But then, they had no idea what Domitian could do.

Acciai knew, and the anticipation was murderous.

Domitian raised both hands, lazily, palms up and with fingers splayed. Krol and Cezar froze in place. Acciai could see their muscles twitch, especially their eyes flicking back and forth.

"Do I now have your attention?" Domitian murmured. "Speak."

"You will pay," Krol snapped. "You will pay with your blood! I will have you torn to bits and those pieces scattered from one end of the harbor to the other! Your woman will suffer. She will..."

Domitian pinched his right forefinger and thumb together. Krol's lips clamped shut, his eyes now bugging out. "Obviously, I do. It pains me to do this, but there needs to be reorganization in order for me to achieve our goals."

Acciai didn't know what he meant but aimed her gun again when Krol moved. Rather, he slid—his feet never lifted but his entire body pivoted 180 degrees, bringing him to face Cezar. At the same time, Cezar shifted 45 degrees to his left, leaving Cezar poised with the muzzle of his Glock three feet from Krol's chest.

Cezar's eyes widened. Acciai could see the pulse pounding in his neck. His face went crimson and he grunted, cheeks puffing. Domitian's control was absolute. No words escaped.

Domitian nodded, and Cezar's arm raised until the gun pointed at the center of Krol's forehead. He glanced sidelong at Acciai. She stiffened beneath the piercing sensation. "Do well to remember, Consolata. Such is the price of disobedience."

Cezar's gun fired once.

The shot echoed, banging off the walls, and only Acciai's training kept her from returning fire. Krol shuddered, brains and blood exploding from the back of his head. The bullet lodged in the far wall.

Cezar screamed, a ghastly sound muffled into a choking sob. Tears streamed from his face.

Domitian held them both a few seconds longer. When he released both, Krol's corpse slumped to the floor. Cezar staggered back, slamming into the wall. He stared at the body, at the gun in his hand, and finally at Domitian.

"It is a shame," Domitian said, "To have to kill such an able leader. However, Mr. Krol made it clear he is not willing to share power. I am. Do you know why, Cezar?"

Cezar only continued to stare. Acciai wished Domitian would do something about his gun. Her employer was in no danger. She couldn't say the same about herself.

The sweet smell of Krol's blood made her mouth water, but she didn't want the same fate to befall to her. Acciai forced a smile.

"I am from God. You have seen my power. Who but He could grant such things to a man?" Domitian placed a hand on her shoulder. She shuddered. It was ice cold. "With my Angel of Death by my side, I have been chosen to bring order to chaos. To do so, I need strong men. Men who are willing to follow me without question and lead without fear. You, Cezar—you can do this."

Cezar's mouth worked as he thought. At last, he croaked out, "I—I kill Mr. Krol."

"No. Not you. It was the tragic outcome of a hit ordered by Danny Sheehan, in retribution for the deaths your wilki have inflicted on the Irish mob. I have set up convincing of this. Consolata here will even procure the body of the assassin, slain by her when she uncovered his identity."

And she looked forward to it. Danny Sheehan's youngest nephew, Martin, was tall, auburn-haired, and heavily muscled. An athlete at Gunnison State. Acciai needed only two things—her body and her blade.

"No—no one will believe." Cezar shook his head.

"They will believe it. You will tell them it is so. I will corroborate." Domitian gestured to Acciai. "If you do not comply, we will show your men what really transpired."

Acciai held up her phone and played back the video she'd recorded of the entire meeting. The replay was only of the last twenty seconds or so, a snippet of Cezar shooting Krol.

"Easily doctored to make your face appear murderous, instead of shocked. We have replacement footage ready," Domitian said.

Cezar collapsed to his knees. Acciai swooped in and plucked the gun from his grasp. She kept her weapon trained on him. Cezar put up his hands. "Spare me. Please. I do what you ask. Have mercy."

"I can be lenient. But my patience has limits. You will convene the others among the wilki here tomorrow night. Tell them of me. They will bear witness to my power—if they have not already. Go."

Cezar stumbled from the room, fumbling for his cell phone. Whatever he said in Polish was not good, judging by the panicked shouts. "He's certainly selling the hit well," Acciai said.

"We should leave. Come."

Acciai followed him up to the roof the tenement. She held on to his side as he lifted them both into the air. They soared across the sky at blistering speed, with him shielding her from winds that should have torn her apart. Within moments, they were atop a ridge in the state forest, hidden from the rest of civilization beneath the pines.

Domitian set her down. She could hear only birdsong and the chatter of squirrels. Even traffic was a far distant lull.

"Cezar will succeed where Krol would not acquiesce," he said.

"I didn't say he wouldn't."

"But you have doubts."

Acciai shrugged. "You could just as easily recruit from around here. There's plenty of organized crime, and the prisons are full."

"Local options draw too much attention. Krol's people are reliable and thorough. I want more of them. Having them brought directly from Poland simplifies matters. That, and many of them cling to old superstitions. Much as Cezar does. Now, it does help matters that a Mister Kondrat Serafin has recently arrived from Krakow. On a flight that very nearly crashed at Sennebec County International Airport. He would have died, were it not for the interference of the flying stranger. Krol relied on this man for supplemental financing."

"I take it Cezar will rely on him even more."

"Precisely. Serafin owes me a great deal more than Krol and his men do. It is the perfect combination."

"And then…what, exactly. You escalate the war with the Irish?"

Domitian stared off into the forest.

Acciai scowled. That much was not new. He was not terribly forthcoming with any of his long-term plans. Only his immediate ones, like her task this evening. Seduce Martin Sheehan and kill him. She smiled. Two of her favorite activities.

"Now, about your performance the other night…"

She folded her arms. "You didn't really expect me to beat him, did you? Not right out of the gate. I'd only had eight hours training in the suit before you let me loose."

"I was not disappointed with the results, do not be mistaken."

"I will improve."

"Yes, you will, because I have more tasks for you. And once we bring our new friends into the fold, you won't be alone."

The prospect of doing further damage was outweighed by the taste of blood. She savored the fantasy. "Look, why don't you just let me kill him? It'll solve all our problems."

"Oh? You think you can manage that? A moment ago, you confessed at your inability to defeat him."

"But that was a direct fight. I'm talking about an ambush. Like when I first met him. I should have shot him in the face right then."

"No."

Acciai threw up her hands.

"You have your assignments, Consolata. You will have plenty of opportunities to indulge your need for killing. But you may not touch Brandon Tusk."

"Why not?"

"Because he must remain alive." He moved in closer to her, looming over her. She cringed at the waves of his power that poured off, pressing her away, a steady, invisible wind. "Because I must have Airfoil as my ally."

Chapter Eighteen

Bad Mondays are universal. This is one of my worst.

People stream in the doors as soon as they open. We are go, go, go from the moment the first person hits the desk with a stack of twenty children's books to return. Donated magazines, DVDs covered with unidentifiable sticky substances, a dozen teen vampire novels that have been missing since February. Then there are people who want to request materials from the main branch, irritated that we don't have what they need.

Throughout the first three hours of constant movement—shelving, discharging, checking out, more shelving—Kelly handles it all with aplomb. She never misses a chance to smile at a patron or lend a hand where needed. Of course, she hasn't said a word to me about our abruptly terminated visit. Or our kiss. Or about anything else.

Halfway back to the front desk, with an armload of maritime history books and a middle school teacher who's yakking my ear off about his research into mid-19th century smuggling, I catch her looking my way. She blushes and goes back to filing DVDs. I didn't text or call her this weekend; neither did she contact me.

Frankly, I wasn't expecting anything. That, and I was busy. Which is why my body still feels like I was run over by a Broad Street bus. My legs are sluggish enough to have been dipped in steel, set in concrete, and used to hold up a skyscraper. My head swims a few times, and I stop to brace myself on a wall when no one's looking. Reed spots me, though, and sidles over from where he's shelving magazines—it's that kind of busy. "Hey. You holding up? Yourself, I mean, not the wall."

"What a comedian. Yes, I'm good."

"Really? You look terrible."

"I'm good." I plunk the books on the counter, start checking between pages for foreign objects—ah, one tissue, thankfully used only as a bookmark. "Can you believe this? I'd have thought we were closed all weekend for a holiday."

"It's the regulars. They're coming out to support us, Number One." Reed grins. "Vanchev's not saying anything about the vote next week, but the benefit's on Friday night. They're excited. Kelly's sold a dozen more tickets this morning, and I've got a stack of donation checks to turn in to the trustees. Eat that, City Council."

"That's—whoa." The library tips forty-five degrees. I plant my hands on the counter. Ice cold stabs through my chest. The dizziness fades, faster than it came on. Wish I knew whether the medallion was causing these spells or enhancing them. "Maybe I'll take that break."

"Go sit. Stuff your face. Feel better." Reed claps me hard on the shoulder. "Or you're fired."

"Your benevolence astounds." I bow.

Within five minutes, I've indeed stuffed myself with a leftover burger and soggy fries. Instead of spending time relaxing, I'm on my tablet searching. I yank a small sketchpad from my backpack and flip to the most recent page. There—the emblem I saw in a flash on Acciai's exoskeleton. A portion of Earth's curve, with an odd broken line.

I search every relevant term I can think of, browsing through hundreds of image results. It has to be here somewhere. Some kind of logo. Nothing's come close so far.

A knock on the doorframe. It's Reed. "Better?"

"It's only been five minutes."

"Uh-huh."

"You abandon Kelly and the volunteers out front?"

"Okay, A, the crowds have abated, for the most part. The shelving's done, thanks to me, you're welcome. And B, Kelly hinted I should come check on you." He smirks. "So here I be. What's up?"

"Searching for answers." I rub the bridge of my nose.

"You look haggard."

"That worse than crap?"

"Look, Brando, this thing—this business with being Airfoil, of using the medallion, it's running you ragged." He's inside the doorway now, murmuring. "All summer. You stepped up your game at home with Sean, and that's great, but—"

"My game." I shake my head. "Yes, he and I are getting along better. But you know, I'm gone more often than when I was just out late at night wasting time. No, Sean's not okay. Neither am I. But I have to do this. This isn't a matter of hiding or running, Reed. I'm not doing that, ever. I owe it to Samantha. I owe it to Drake City and everyone in it."

"Look. I'm not saying you being a superhero isn't cool, but think about Sean. And Kelly. And me. People who count on Brandon Tusk a lot more than they count on Airfoil. I mean, why do you have to do this? Give the medallion to Frank."

"Come on, Reed. Samantha's letter—"

"Don't get me started on that. You've got your own set of responsibilities. This Garrison of flying people or whatever—they've got to be able to step in, right? I mean, why does it have to be you?"

I press my palms against my forehead. Five months ago, I would have enjoyed my break. I would have talked with Reed about movies and video games and women. But I would have also been a worse father, an aimless man, without purpose, drifting from one sunrise to the next. "This is my chance to do what's right. I won't give up. Not now. Not with Domitian and Acciai out there."

"Who?"

"The other one. The bad guy who can fly faster than me."

"Oh."

I face the screen, picking up the search again. Reed's silent for a moment. Being Reed, it's a short moment. "She really suited up like Robocop?"

"More like Edge of Tomorrow."

"Yeah, great flick." Reed's eyes widen. "Oh. Wow."

"Yes, exactly. I—" My sentence evaporates. There, halfway down the umpteenth page of search results and off to the right. "That's it."

"What?"

I poke the tablet screen. "The symbol I saw on Acciai's exoskeleton. Same one, I'm sure of it."

Reed leans in. It's a navy-blue stylized outline of a globe, with the Atlantic Ocean and continents surrounding it. A black wrench slashes across it horizontally.

I click on the image. Rigel Research & Technologies. They have a facility about thirty miles up the coast. Another click brings me to the homepage. I grunt in surprise.

"Advanced robotics and human improvement systems," Reed announces. "That sounds like exo-skeletons to me."

"It sure does. Look at this: powered prosthetic limbs, automated scout aircraft, search and rescue support." I jot down notes, bookmark the website. Frank's got to know about this.

My phone buzzes. My personal phone, not the new one Frank gave me as our coded communications link to replace the one that drowned in the cave. And the message is from Eliana at the maritime museum.

<Can u come by? Got something for u. Right now.>

I hop up from the chair, shoving my stuff into my backpack. At the last second, I snag the helmet. "Got to go. I'll be back before break's over."

"Yeah, better be." Reed shakes his head. "Man, can't you just fly there?"

"In broad daylight? Without a mask?" I snap on the helmet. "It'd be pretty obvious if I left from here."

"Also, that Frank guy'd probably kill you."

"No probably about it."

Reed makes a compelling point.

I bike a couple blocks, but faced with dwindling time and increasing traffic, my limited patience fails. I ditch the bike in an alley, behind a dumpster, and lock it to a fire escape.

I remove the bike helmet and trade it for the flight model. My departure scatters scraps of refuse and sends pigeons fleeing. No other witnesses.

Three minutes later, I swoop in behind the museum, skimming the water and landing between two boat storage warehouses. I'm sure lots of people saw me. No doubt there will be photos up on Twitter any second. But, as I jog around to the front of the maritime museum, the groups of tourists and occasional locals don't pay me any notice.

Eliana pops out the side door, several paces from the main entrance, like a jack in the box. She waves me over.

I veer off from a gaggle of children hectoring their grandparents for ice cream and meet her by the open door. "Hey. Do I get to use the entrance to the Batcave this time?"

She frowns. "The Batcave? Mold and running water and bat feces. I keep the vaults immaculate."

"I'm kidding, Eliana."

"Oh, I know. It wasn't funny."

She leads me inside and immediately up the stairwell to the right. We're at the far end of the collection of rooms that include her office, a single door on a landing two floors up. It has only a small, rectangular window. Eliana takes her museum badge and swipes it across a flat, black square set in the wall atop a silver panel. A trio of red lights switch to green. Locks click open.

The room beyond is white, with a glossy, black stone floor, and a pair of soft LED lights. Opposite the entrance, there's another door, sans window. A box of disposable gloves rests on the center of a long shelf across the right wall. "Leave your backpack here. You can take a notepad and pencil for research. Nothing else. And wear a pair."

"All right." I deposit my bag, careful to remove my small sketchpad and a pencil without letting her get a peek at my helmet. We don our gloves. "Lead on."

She swipes her card at the second door. Locks trigger again.

The vault is a long, broad room with a sloped ceiling. I assume it's tucked up above the offices and beneath the roof of the museum; you'd have no idea it was here viewing the building from outside. Everything stretches out for sixty feet to our left. There are rows of glass cases, three shelves apiece, containing rusted relics and tarnished tools. The opposite wall is full of file cabinets, with hundreds of labeled drawers. Huge tables fill the middle, between two aisles. Each table is stainless steel, with a countertop big enough to seat a family of six. Below are nine drawers on one side, and three big cabinets on the other.

Eliana leads me past sextants, pistols, swords, bottles, coins and a myriad of other artifacts to the third table from the end. She opens the middle cabinet. There's no label on it. "This took a while to find, Brandon. It wasn't indexed with the other journals, nor was it filed under the family name, 'Rankin.' Someone kept it well-preserved in a box at the back of this drawer. I knew we keep uncatalogued items in this table."

"Well I appreciate the effort."

"It means you owe me lunch."

"Next time I'll bring a baggie from Stransky's."

She gently lifts a metal box from the drawer. It's got olive green paint that's chipped in several places. Eliana sets it down, flips the latches, and opens the lid.

A musty smell hits my nose. Old paper and leather. Inside the box is a book of thick paper with tattered edges and ruddy leather binding. The cover is worn in spots and stained on the back. My eyes are wide. "So...you're sure this is it?"

Eliana lifts it from its resting place among crumpled red velvet. She turns it over and beams. "You tell me, Mister Librarian."

The cover bears a faded impression of a coiled rattlesnake.

"Unreal." I take the journal in my hands, cradling it in gloved fingers. Gingerly, I open the cover. Scrawled on the first page in long, looping letters is the splotchy ink signature "Tobias H. Rankin."

Eliana smiles. "I told you I'd find it."

"Never doubted you." I page carefully into the book. "Why didn't this show up in your searches?"

"I don't know. That's what bothers me the most. This is an important primary source for New England history from this period. Do you have any idea how rare it is to find a first-person record from the early 19th Century, let alone in this good condition?"

"It's very rare. We have a couple of diaries at the main library, but they're from the 1890s. You can't get much of anything from the War of 1812. Not surprising, given the fire here in 1814."

"That's what happens when the British do a replay of Washington, D.C. on Port Drake." Eliana inspects the book's binding, as if she's an electrician searching for faulty wiring. "They burned two thirds of the city. No, this should have been given the utmost priority. Instead, no one knew we had it."

"No one?"

"I've worked here ever since I got my masters. Call it eleven years." Eliana touches the cover of the journal. "I had no idea it was in this cabinet. My boss didn't either. Even Mrs. Akers, who's been on staff since the 1970s, knew about it."

I whistle. At this early stage of the journal's pages, Rankin records mundane day to day events: Weather was cloudy with light mist, replaced rusted gear on press, had boy ride to Rockland for more ink, et cetera. It's baffling. That mysterious text was insistent I find this and read it. For what purpose?

Eliana's gone silent, standing beside me. "Brandon? Is there something specific you're researching? Something I could help you find?"

"Well, ah, there is, but it's not..." I glance at her. "Wait. You've read this."

"I did. Why shouldn't I? It's museum property. What I want from you is an answer." Eliana's scowling now, an expression as rare as this book. She gently flips pages in the journal as I hold it. A date appears in the upper left corner: October 4, 1814. "This is recorded while Tobias Rankin is at Camden. Most of his early entries are; that's where he ran the newspaper if you recall. You read it."

I squint at the tightly packed words, the penmanship flawless. It takes me three passes through the first couple sentences before I can get into the tale:

A crew of eight men from Lincolnville were chopping wood in the forests off Norton's Pond. Their axes banged out a steady rhythm...finally came the moment the tree swayed, creaked. A crack of thunder. The men hollered and scurried, mice under a giant's feet. One man tripped and lost his hatchet. He stopped to retrieve it, but the tree fell faster than anticipated.

He looked to the sky and mouthed an entreaty, his face so clear I could see the words of the Lord's Prayer.

I answered without permission or knowledge.

With one hand I used the gift given to me to suspend the fall of the tree. It slowed its rush to the ground, coming to a full stop six feet over the logger's head. Black and brown needles showered the ground. He darted from the shadow, as my hand shook.

He was out from underneath. The tree slammed into the dirt with the force of a volley of cannonballs. The men were silent in the aftermath.

The questions came quickly, drifting up through the forest branches to my ears. Has the Lord done this? What miracle has He wrought? They are the same I have asked myself, as I fly above the trees where only birds and insects trod.

Secure in the observation those men did not see me, I put the medallion away and flew toward home. Slate gray clouds of the early morn conceal my return. I gave thanks for a life saved, though I knew there would be questions asked by the Garrison as to my outing. For, doubtless, the loggers will tell the tale, and someone will spread it further. This is where we differ. They would keep me confined to military action—sabotage, intrigue, and the like. I know my purpose is greater. There is more danger and evil than those things which are known. The darkness we keep in check knows no limits, grasps into all corners of our world. By the Lord's grace alone do we persevere with the strength to confront it.

That's...not possible. Tobias Rankin. He was one of the Garrison. He used a medallion, two hundred years ago. I stare at the pages. Frank told me of the ancient age of the medallions, of the Garrison. I suppose I believed him. But seeing the written word is something else entirely.

"Brandon. You know what that is, don't you?"

Oh boy. I fold it closed. "Well. About that..."

"He's like Airfoil, isn't he? You're trying to find out more about him. The superhero. Except now there's someone out there who's the bad version of him. I've seen the news: the lighthouse roof, the attack on the police, the fight at the mine." Eliana has her hands on her hips. I take a step back, waiting for the rest of the storm. "Don't lie to me Brandon, not anymore. You come to me with that old inscription on your medal or whatever, and it matches only one thing: the cover imprint of the two hundred-year-old journal of a man who writes about the same powers these two use."

I stand there, frozen. Frank's warnings of secrecy pound my head. But this is Eliana. Aside from Reed, she's the other person in this city I trust implicitly. Who else was there for my family after Samantha died? She introduced us, for pity's sake. She's as kind and faithful as they come.

She was there with me at Samantha's car wreck.

I don't say anything. Instead, I pull the medallion out, letting it dangle in front of my shirt. With my left hand, I extend the field around the nearest loose object I can find: a dolly, leaning against one of the file cabinets. It's a simple matter to reduce the gravity and lift it clear to the ceiling.

Eliana watches, mouth agape, as I send it in a loop around the room, flying it like a remote-control airplane. I make sure to move my hand to mimic the flight pattern, so there's no mistaking what's causing it. For the encore, I halt it at the far end of the room. Dividing the field, I rise up, careful not to bash my head on the ceiling, and swoop to the end of the room. I grab the dolly and fly back, depositing it and myself on the floor in front of her.

"You...it was..." She waves her hands around.

"Yes. It's me."

Eliana stares. Before I realize what she's doing, she hugs me, standing on tiptoes to put her chin on my shoulder. "Thank you."

"For what?"

"For everything you've done. You've helped so many people." She backs up, teary-eyed. "And thank you for trusting me."

"You see why I can't tell anyone. Tobias Rankin didn't, as far as we know. His journal was undiscovered."

"Yes. Probably, the less I know, the better—that's what you're going to suggest."

"Correct."

"Okay. I'll leave you to read. But if you need any help—anything at all—"

I smile. "I know who's got my back."

She departs, and I dive into the journal again. Rankin was a busy member of the Garrison. The fact that he kept this a secret from the organization impresses me, I admit, as is his willingness to bend or outright break orders. His encounters with the British Navy—with agents provocateurs from Napoleon's army—with hidden members of the Ashen. Several pages, though, are missing. Time after time, I come across yet another ragged end of a page torn from the binding.

After an entire sheaf of lost entries, one of the last pages makes me sit upright:

...perhaps the last I shall record. If the Garrison were to find this, heaven knows, even my life is forfeit. The task is complete. They are buried beneath the surface, none will find them. It is best this way. I am certain those in leadership over me disagree, but the fact of the matter is: the Ashen have lost badly. Their cause is wounded; America is safer. The earthquake I made should be passed off as Nature's wrath. The harbor folk of Lobban's Cove will recover, though sadly, their shanties and boats are in such disrepair from the quake that little of material value can be redeemed.

But it is His will. The secret is hidden. My enemies will not triumph, not today. I pray it never comes to light. When the medallion passes to its next holder, I trust that person will know the right action to take. For I tire greatly. And my beloved is of far greater worth than the power I have buried far below Sculpin Bay.

Sculpin Bay? Rankin was here? Somewhere in the vicinity of Drake. What did he hide?

Suddenly, I recall the shard of medallion I found in the cave. Lobban's Cove. There's no such place in Drake City. Something's missing.

I glance at my watch. Have to get back to work soon. And I have to talk to Frank. Whatever this discovery means, coupled with the mines, there has to be a missing connection. Eliana... I can't tell her all of this. All I can do is have her keep the journal secret.

She's waiting for me in the airlock, chewing on the end of a pen. "Are you finished?"

"For now. Thank you." I grab my backpack. "Look, Eliana, you can't tell anyone, understand? You should know how vital it is that this remain a secret."

"I know. I'd never say anything." She touches my arm. "If you like, I can scan the journal. Make a digital copy you can have."

I wonder. Frank doesn't know about this journal—because if he did, I'm sure he'd have destroyed it, given our prior conversation. A digital copy would be efficient, but the chances of someone finding out about it are greater that way. "No. Let's not do that. I don't want to risk someone hacking into a computer here or at my apartment and discovering it. You can't hack into a journal."

"Okay. Let me know if you need anything else."

"There is one thing." I dig out my wallet and extract the crumpled letter. "Samantha gave me this."

She unfolds it, eyebrows knit together. "Oh? What about it?"

"I need you to verify its authenticity."

After a few seconds, she looks even more shocked than when I showed her the medallion. "She...? Samantha really...?"

"Eliana. Focus." I hold both her shoulders. "Verify it for me. Okay? This is what's pushing me to serve the Garrison. I need to know it's legitimate."

"It's her handwriting."

"I know that. Humor me."

"Okay. Wow." Eliana stares at me. "I don't think I'm getting any other work done today."

Chapter Nineteen

By the time I return to the library, thoughts of Tobias Rankin and a centuries-old medallion spin my brain faster than my bike tires. Focus. The benefit's approaching. Part of me wants to scour the city for Acciai, even with the new threat of her exoskeletal gear looming. But when it comes to seeing Kelly in a dress or pummeling a bad guy, I'm most definitely in favor of the former. I glance inside the front doors. She's at the desk, showing one of our volunteers something on the circulation computer. I glance at my watch. Showtime in three hours.

Inside, I greet Kelly with a smile. "Hey."

"Hey. How was your break?"

"Ah..." Two hundred-year-old medallion wielder? "Eventful."

"Great. My turn." We trade places, and she's gone to the back room.

Tobias Rankin's words resurface in my mind from the pages of the journal: "The darkness we keep in check knows no limits, grasps into all corners of our world. By the Lord's grace alone do we persevere with the strength to confront it."

I seek that strength.

Three hours is gone in a blur. Books and movies, computer troubleshooting and restroom maintenance—they barely register. Next thing I know, I'm suited up, only this time, it isn't my airborne gear.

The American Legion Hall on Sixth Street is packed. I'm impressed. A quick check with the volunteer ladies selling tickets at the door confirms it—there's got to be two hundred people in here. I grin. If this doesn't sway the city council, nothing will.

The hall is long and wide, with a tall ceiling that's had its revealed beams and ventilation ducts repainted in recent years. It's three stories up. There's a stage off to the left, decorated with a broad banner proclaiming "Save Your Future—Keep Hull Branch Open." Kelly's brainchild.

There's Reed. He's wearing the same clothes as I am: black jacket and slacks, black shoes, white Oxford unbuttoned at the collar. It's a thing. We showed up for a gathering at a friend's several years ago, inadvertently dressed as twins. Everyone else found it amusing enough we made a pact to repeat it at any following shindig.

"Smooth," Reed says. "You know, if we keep this up we won't be able to pry the ladies off with a crowbar."

"Yeah? I bet Caroline could burn them off you with her laser death vision."

Reed takes a swig of his beer and grins. "Doesn't hurt that she gets a little jealous."

"Unlike you."

He scratches his chin with his middle finger.

I head for the bar. It's set into the right wall, with a steady stream of guests already imbibing. Stairs lead up to a second-floor mezzanine that covers a third of the floor area, including the bar. On either side of the bar, tucked into the dimly lit shadows, are restrooms, storage rooms, and coat racks behind partitions.

Caroline is chatting with a couple our age; he's an optometrist and she's a dental hygienist. Can't see why Reed would even be scanning for other women—Caroline's got on a low-cut red dress, black hair tumbling down over her breasts, and a silver heart on a gold chain clinging to her throat. Reed gave it to her when they got engaged. I remember her tears.

Tonight, she winks past the chatty couple. I'm all about saying hi, but they're talking incessantly and, from dealing with them at past library functions, they've got a lot of cash to drop. So, I let her keep them happy.

One whiskey sour later, Reed and I are positioned not far from the front door. Moldy Upholstery is in full swing—literally. They're blasting out a toe-tapping swing tune that already has a dozen couples dancing, including the optometrist and his wife. That frees up Caroline to tuck her arm around Reed's waist and whisper something up into his ear. Reed's jaw drops and red streaks across his face.

I gag on whiskey. "Okay, whatever that was, I don't want to know."

Caroline laughs. She kisses me on the cheek. "Why are you walking around here all by yourself? Someone as handsome as you shouldn't be on his own."

"Oh, you know me. Waiting for the best deal." I salute with the glass.

Reed snorts. "Brando claims he's got a date. I say he's full of it."

"Honey..."

"Well, he is."

I shake my head. "I have someone in mind."

"To invite?" Caroline smiles. "Brandon, it's a little late, isn't it?"

"That's my first officer," Reed says. "He's always..."

His beer bottle stops midway to his mouth. He's staring over my shoulder. Like the sun just went nova and he's the only person standing who saw it.

"Reed?" Caroline looks in the same direction and her expression brightens from confusion to joy.

Reed mutters, "Wow."

I turn. Kelly walks through the front door like she owns the place. Sure, the smile is demure, and the way she clutches the tiny sequined purse—how do women fit anything in those?—radiates humility, but then there's her dress. Long, black, strapless, clinging to every curve of her body. Freckles adorn both shoulders. There's a slender, silver bracelet around her left wrist. Emerald earrings sparkle. Her hair's styled up, dark as the night sky.

She stops two feet from me. "Um, hi."

"You're gorgeous." I blurt. Never let it be said I'm not subtle.

Caroline is apparently the only one of us three capable of sentient speech. She elbows Reed and then beams at Kelly. They hug. "We were wondering when you'd get here! You look lovely!"

"Thanks. Your dress is beautiful, too."

They trade tactical pleasantries about each other's wardrobe, long enough for Reed to sidle up to me and whisper, "She's your date?"

"Uh-huh."

"I'm pretty sure I have a policy against this somewhere. You know, dating a co-worker."

"Hey. It's a work function, Captain." I clap him on the shoulder. "Call it professional collaboration."

Reed snorts

"Have a nice evening, Mr. Fantastic," I quip.

Caroline and Reed leave, both of them watching us so keenly over their shoulders and whispering to each other that you'd think it was senior prom. They narrowly avoid a collision with a cluster of couples.

"So. This all looks—amazing." I gesture vaguely at the party swirling around us. "Your work paid off."

"Thanks. I'm glad there're so many people here." She fidgets with the purse.

"Let me get you something to drink. Glass of red?"

"Please."

By the time we get back from the bar, we run in to Mark Vanchev. He's entertaining a cluster of mostly men and a couple women. I recognize the elderly couple who always get their stacks of books from me in the early morning, the ones who always ask about my family. There's a burly, balding man in khakis and an ugly purple polo shirt—Mr. Beletsky, the bus driver. And the round woman in the sparkly blue dress has to be Mrs. Ruiz. There's also a gaggle of far more polished individuals, ranging in age from late twenties to mid-sixties. Library foundation members and a guy who looks oddly familiar...

"Ms. Quirke! Mr. Tusk." Vanchev smiles broadly and grasps our hands. "You've put together an amazing event, especially you, Ms. Quirke." He leans over and kisses her knuckles.

Kelly goes furiously red. I simply smile back and return his iron grip pound for pound. An icy spike from the medallion stabs me—and, though it startles me, I'm grateful, because it's warm in here, despite the air conditioning running full steam. "Thanks, Mr. Vanchev."

"Mark."

"Sure thing. Mark. We're glad to get this great a turnout."

"Speaking of turn out, this is Councilman Jack DiFalco." The man's in his forties, slick black hair, tanned skin, and a smile way too white to be natural. He shakes our hands in turn. "Represents Cape Ashwin. And I think, after tonight, he'll be solidly in our corner."

It takes me five minutes to escape Vanchev's trap of banal chit-chat and get us back to the middle of the floor, among the crowds. Despite all the sound, we're in our own space, where we can speak.

"You clean up pretty well," she says. "Thanks for rescuing me."

I grin. "No problem. I admit, I had ulterior motives."
"Oh?"
"Care to join me for a dance?"
"Took you long enough to ask."

We find a table where several empty drink glasses have congregated and deposit ours. The band's blasting away now, and the center of the floor's full of fifty people dancing—or doing their best imitations thereof. Me? I secure a hand on Kelly's waist and hold her right hand with my left and we're off.

She's good. Not as good as me, though, but I'm the one who took swing and ballroom lessons when Sean was starting middle school. Samantha and I got to be regulars at a gathering of seven couples every two weeks or so...

Inwardly I cringe. Here I am, face to face with a beautiful woman, dancing with her, and she's looking only at me. What's in my head? Memories of my wife. Someday they'll fade.

The music slows. Moldy Upholstery switches to a quiet tune. She presses in closer to me. All around us couples swirl like falling leaves. Her forehead presses against my cheek. Her breath teases at my neck. "Brandon."

"Yeah?"

"I didn't mind when you kissed me, that day at St. Andrew's. I hoped you'd do it again, before you ran off."

"I wanted to. There was...an emergency."

"I know. But you didn't say anything about it, all week."

"Neither did you, actually. I thought I'd done something wrong. You were quieter than usual."

"I didn't know what to say."

"Neither did I."

She looks up. I could fall into those eyes. "What are we going to do about this? About us?"

There's nothing I need to say for that. I lean in and kiss her, full on the mouth.

It's not that I haven't kissed another woman since Samantha. There's been a few. But this is different. She's different. All I want is to put aside all my worries, even superhero nightlife, and just be here, with her.

The explosion is deafening.

One moment we're dancing, our lips pressed together. The next, there's a flash of light that sears my retinas, and a shockwave that lifts me from my feet. How can I be flying? I'm not using the medallion. That's my genius reaction.

I slam down on the floor, shoulders colliding with something narrow and metal. Table legs. I blink in darkness. Where am I? Is the power out?

My ears ring. Gradually, sound returns, my body alerts me to problems: pain in my leg, throbbing shoulders. Screams. Shouts. They're distant at first, but as my hearing returns, they're closer, primal with fear.

"Stay down! Stay down! Nie ruszaj się!" Gunfire. Automatic weapons. Voices and demands, thick with accents. Slavic. Polish?

Kelly? I scrabble around. A flash of the pale blue lights of the dance hall illuminates table. I'm under a table, beneath the black cloths. From there I can peer around the corner.

The front of the hall is gone. Where the door and windows were, only rubble remains. A gaping hole reveals the street, and the rain glittering in the lamps. There're cars out there. Big ones. Inside the hall, people are staggering, some getting to their feet, some fleeing. Others are curled up. Stunned or dead.

Kelly's there, twenty feet away. Her eyes are closed, and there's a bruise on her forehead. She's lost both shoes. Raven black hair spills across the floor.

Men fan out from the opening into the crowd. They're wearing ski masks, black coats, some in blue jeans and some in cargo pants. All of them are armed with AK-74s.

One drags a guest in a torn suit to his feet. "Give us your money, jewelry, everything. Do it now, or people die!"

The guest struggles, breaks out of the grip. He slugs the assailant and grapples with him, going for the gun. Bullets explode through the air. The assailant frees himself, shoves the guest away. Aims his gun.

I put all of my fuzzy concentration into imagining a wrecking ball and hurl it at the thug. He flies back into the nearest wall, hitting it so hard dust settles. The guest he'd been fighting grabs the wrist of a girl pressed against the bar and ushers her ahead as they both run.

"Kurwa!" The nearest assailant raises his gun. "He's here, he's here!"

I strip out of my jacket. With another burst, I send a nearby table rolling across the floor. The attackers open fire.

I'm moving the other way, toward the coat rack. I don't have my suit and need to find something that will hide me while I take these guys down. There. A brown leather jacket. Nothing like the one I was wearing. One thing left.

Careful to stay out of the lights, keeping watch of the assailants as they close in on my decoy table, I yank the one thug I threw against the wall back toward me. His legs thwack against a chair.

"There! Over there!" They start shooting again.

Too late.

By the time a handful of them move into the shadows, all they find is their man knocked cold—and minus his ski mask. I press into the darkness of the ceiling above the light fixtures.

Screams of terror come from upstairs. Some guests must have fled through the back door. But two gunmen are dogging a column of fifteen down to the main floor. Add to that another sixty hostages still strewn about the hall.

Reed. Caroline. They're both in that line of fifteen. Reed's got his arm around Caroline, glaring openly at the gunmen.

"You're imagining things." One gunman stands taller than the rest. He shoves his buddy who opened fire after I flung the other away. "The flier is not here."

"He is! You saw Aleksy!"

"Zamknij się!" The leader rounds on the assembled hostages and fires his gun straight up. I tense. "Listen all! We will take your money, take your jewels, and we will leave. Resist, and die. Mouth off, and die."

Reed's chomping at the bit. In my mind, I beg him not to move. Stay calm. Give me a couple more seconds.

But the leader sees him staring and chuckles. Looks right at him. "So. First contestant."

He takes two steps forward.

That's as far as he gets.

I drop. . Let my shoes hit the floor, startling everyone. Let 'em get a good look.

"You weren't invited," I say.

The leader turns, gun ready. I snap the barrel clean off and throw him into the bar.

"Anybody else?"

The rest of the men shout commands—Polish, I recognize it now—and open fire. Civilians scream and duck down. My shield is in place, and the bullets do nothing but spatter against the floor like lethal raindrops.

Fine. Let's clean this up.

I lunge for the nearest man, grab him under the arms and zip up to the ceiling. He struggles until I slam his head and shoulders into a rafter. Below me, the gunfire trickles off. Footsteps and more shouts. Meanwhile, I tug the guy's belt off. Hope it's sturdy, because it's going around his armpit to keep him suspended thirty feet off the floor.

Next, I zoom down toward another pair of thugs. They don't shoot. When I'm in range, they both swing at me with their guns like they're wielding baseball bats. But then, I'm grabbing the front of their shirts. They get tugged off their feet. One guy loses his gun, the other wings me across the shoulder with the stock. My flight path goes crooked, so I don't bang them off the nearest wall like I planned. Instead, I hurl them into the closest set of tables. They careen across the top, dragging the tablecloth, smashing plates and glasses.

That's four.

A gunshot cracks. Reed's wrestling with the one assailant who'd dragged hostages down from upstairs, pounding on him with one fist and tugging on the gun with the other. It's not an even match: Reed's slim and this thug's got twice the muscle, but Reed fights dirty. The thug spins them around and rams Reed against the bar. Reed cries out, swears, and grapples for a weapon, fingers scrabbling on the bar. He comes up with a half-empty bottle of Wyoming Whiskey.

Something hits me from the side. One of the thugs I threw. Not unconscious, obviously. We roll across the floor. A blade nicks my arm. I grab onto his wrist in time to stop the tip six inches from my chest. The guy's mask is ripped, revealing a line of crooked teeth clenched in anger. Blood mingled with saliva dribbles onto my clothes.

Get off!

Smashing glass, and a scream. There's Reed, slashing at his attacker with the broken bottle.

The guy's hollering, grabbing at his face. He kicks Reed away. This time, Reed's arm hits the bar and there's a muffled crack. The AK's aimed at Reed's stomach.

I finally get my hand pressed against my attacker's chest and use the medallion to shove him off. I'm talking six feet up and clear to the end wall of the dance hall. Freed, I leap from the floor, in a burst of flight that lets me cover the fifty feet to Reed and his attacker in a second.

My head and crossed arms hit the attacker at the small of his back. Together, we pile against the bar. He flips, feet over his head, over the countertop. Bottles explode in showers of glass and liquor. The guy's bleeding from dozens of cuts, lying atop his still knocked out boss. And his gun's on the floor.

Where are the other three?

"Look out!" Reed scuttles for Caroline, who's prone on the floor with the rest of the hostages. He grabs a discarded weapon.

Two more assailants are clustered behind a table, like kids in a tree fort. They start shooting—not at me, this time, but right toward the hostages. "No!"

I hurtle into the space between, praying the shield is still holding, because to say my attention is divided is a severe understatement. The shield absorbs the impacts; the sparks fly again—

Two bullets crease my left arm.

Ignoring the instant pain, I land in a crouch and visualize the shield expanding, growing, bending out toward my attackers like a contact lens flipped the wrong direction. You can't see anything, not with the naked eye, but the effects are plain as day. Tables and chairs break, flitting aside, as sturdy as paper in a hurricane. When the front hits the makeshift barricade, it breaks it into a dozen pieces. The attackers are smashed—literally, they are thrown to opposite walls. They hit, one right after the other, and neither one gets up again.

A shiver runs through me. They could be permanently broken. They could be dead. But I can't control the medallion enough to fine tune my responses, not in the middle of a fight with my adrenaline and temper both burning. Frank's right. If I can't be a scalpel, I'll wind up a sledgehammer.

There's a piercing scream. The last thug's, still in his ski mask, has taken a hostage. She's an older woman, mid-sixties, with shockingly white hair and wearing a dark green dress. The muzzle of the AK is pressed to her neck

"You!" he calls to me. "You let me leave! Right now!" His gun hand shakes. So does his voice. He could kill her by accidentally squeezing the trigger.

"Airfoil! Don't let me die! Please!" She's sobbing.

"Shut up! Shut up or I kill you!"

Reed's voice carries across the chaos. "Go, go, go! Everyone get out!" He's behind me somewhere, shepherding the others to safety.

I hold up both hands. "Easy, pal. Easy. Let her go. I won't hurt you."

"You put your hands away! Do it!" The guy's voice is a tremor. His eyes are wide with terror.

I put my arms back down, fists at my side. This isn't going to work. I need to use my arms to direct the field. I always have. Without direction, I'm the sledgehammer. And anything I do will get that woman killed.

"Please help me! Please don't let him—"

"Shut up!"

My teeth grind. "I'm going to tell you one more time. Let her go. Put down your gun. You can still walk away from this."

But what can I do about it?

What would Frank say? It's obvious. He'd scowl, shake his head, and remind me that the medallion feeds off my body and mind. It connects with my very soul. Whatever I can will it to do, it does.

That means I don't need to use my hands. Right?

I stare at the guy. Stare at his wrist, the silver watch encircling it, black glove over his hand, finger gripped around the trigger. Slowly, slowly I extend the field—not in a sphere, not in an arc, but in a long, sinuous tendril. It smothers the man's arm, hand, and finger.

Sounds rage. I block them out. Reed's shouting, the man's warning, the woman's pleading. All of it becomes near silent. I have to concentrate. Or he will kill her.

The field is ready, like an invisible cast around the man's limb. I get one shot at this.

Only. One. Shot.

With all the ferocity I can muster, I yank on that tendril.

Bones crack, loud as gunshots. The man hollers and releases

the woman. She collapses to the floor, weeping.

The attacker continues to yell. His right arm is bent at a hideous angle below the elbow. The wrist twists in the wrong direction. The watch has crushed it, cutting into flesh and making it bleed. And the trigger finger? Bent out 90 degrees the wrong way.

It makes me sick, but then again, these guys make me sicker. The need for subtlety over, I reach out with the field and pull the attacker over. One punch across the face puts him down.

It's suddenly, awfully quiet in the hall. Then the noises return. Crying, Reed's comforting talk to the woman, footsteps as Caroline runs to…

Kelly. She's still out cold. Caroline hunkers over her.

No sirens. Has someone even called the police? All I hear outside is rain. I brush past Caroline and put my hands gently under Kelly's head. Her eyes are closed.

"Help her, please," Caroline whispers.

I'm already lifting her from the floor. The field wraps around us both, ice digging deep into my chest, and I leap forward. We shoot through the hole in the front of the Legion hall. Rain hammers the ski mask, soaking it instantly.

Drake General Hospital is only eight blocks away. The helipad, emblazoned with silver and blue lights, reaches for the sky like a partially truncated white pyramid. No aircraft in sight this evening. My vision's blurred by the rain, but it makes no difference; I drive through the downpour, cradling Kelly to my chest, praying for more speed.

Seconds later, I touch down in a skid that takes me halfway across the brilliant red H of the helipad. My heart's racing, I'm panting. I calm myself enough to feel that Kelly's still breathing.

She stirs, slits of brown eyes parting. "Wha…what's happening?"

"Shh, you're hurt. Don't move. I've got you."

Her eyes widen, and we stare at each other. I wonder if she can recognize me even with the impromptu disguise. I also don't care. She's safe.

Thirty feet away the double door leading into the hospital slides open. a pair of nurses, a man and woman, hurry out. A burly security guard points his walkie-talkie at us. "You there! Hold it!"

Don't they get it by now? I never obey that command. "She's injured. Possibly a concussion. There was an explosion at the Legion hall."

"We just got the call." The female nurse has iron gray hair and doesn't seem at all bothered by the rain soaking her floral scrubs. "Let us take her."

They help Kelly to her feet. She's shaky. "I'm...I'll be fine."

The security guard's right there, reaching for a baton. "You're coming with me."

"Sorry, can't." I flick his baton from his hand and sent it spinning far over the top of the hospital, where it lands with a distant splash on the roof. Then I'm up, rising twenty, forty feet.

Kelly looks up. "Thank you!"

I toss off a fake salute, and blast back into the night, my insides burning with a smoldering anger.

My muscles quiver. It's all I can do to stay aloft, but I dig deep, searching for strength. Maybe that fury fuels me, because I'm not staggering out of the air. So, I lean on the emotion.

Someone, somewhere, is going to pay for this.

I fly faster.

Chapter Twenty

"This is what happens when the Garrison screws around with peoples' lives, Frank! They get hurt."

Frank's leaning over the laptop on the table in the bowels of the Barn, face impassive as stone and lit eerie blue by the screen. "Calm down, Brandon. We'll find out—"

"There's nothing to find out!" I'm anything but calm. I haven't stopped pacing since I landed five minutes ago. I'm still dressed in my shirt and slacks, except they're soaked to the bone. "It was Krol's gang. With the guns you said you got rid of, the ones you told me you were supposed to let go because the Garrison wanted to play the Poles against the Irish. Guess what! Didn't work that way tonight—unless the library supporters carried their Irish mob membership cards in with them."

"Don't be a smartass. You don't have a clue what the Garrison's plans are."

"Do you, Frank? Are you going to let me in on that secret? I grappled with a crazed assassin woman in robot gear who has now gone missing, and now the people I work with—the people I care about—are targeted."

Frank frowns. He seems to be considering his words, but as cold as his expression is, I have no idea what gears are turning in his brain. "Well. There's a simple logic at play here, Brandon.

It's all your fault."

"I...what?" That stops my pacing.

"You knew the rules of the game. I told you from Day One. You were to follow the Garrison's mission parameters, with my assistance, and keep a low profile. We've been over this. Again and again. And what do you do? Go off like an idiot and rescue people. You know your actions tonight are going to wind up streaming somewhere. You're escalating the problem, Brandon. The more you show up fighting crime, with that ridiculous name, the more you're in the public eye, and the more the bad guys are going to lash out. Tell me why that is."

I glare at him, clenching my fists.

"Because you've made them desperate!" Frank jabs a finger in my direction. Pigeons flutter off in the darkness, feathers flapping, startled by his outburst. "They see you out there, rounding up their buddies, and they think, 'It's a matter of time before he gets me.' The key to hunting a predator is to make it think you're not the slightest bit interested. So, before you lump this all on me and the Garrison, be advised this is exactly the crap-tastic kind of mess we were trying to avoid!"

I don't answer. Just glare back, because all I can see is Reed getting attacked and Kelly knocked out.

"Now. If you're done with your tantrum, you'll be happy to know the police are on scene and have rounded up the Poles. They got the guns, too."

That improves my mood, but only slightly. "How do you know? Is it on the news?"

"No. Their so-called secure server." Frank shakes his head. "It's a lot harder to cover up the actions of medallion holders with the Internet so far-reaching, but that's also made it easier to keep tabs on everything else."

I read over his shoulder. "Dennis Marchand is the investigating officer."

"Yeah. He gets all the fun cases, apparently. You know he's

the one tasked with bringing you down. You think your pal's brother-in-law is amenable to staying out of our way?"

"How did you...never mind." I wave my hand. "Don't care how you know."

Frank smirks. "I've also been in contact with the Garrison, about your discovery at the mine."

"The medallion sliver."

"Yes. There's justifiable angst on their part. Finding a medallion or a piece of one doesn't happen all that often. We're talking, maybe once in a century. Even the Ashen aren't that careless to let one get lost. They pass theirs on like we do, by blood or marriage."

I look at him, the weathered skin of his face, the tiredness behind the eyes. "What did you do with yours?"

"None of your business."

"Family or spouse?"

"I said..." He pauses. His eyes flick sideways at me. "Someone I could trust. Implicitly. That good enough for you?"

I gesture to signal I'm ready for him to continue. If I speak it'll be insulting and likely cause him to knock me flat.

"They want us to go back in."

"Us."

Frank nods. "I've got a few tricks up my sleeve that we can use to take care of potential traps. We should go over the maps again, to be sure we're in the right cavern."

That reminds me..."The Garrison seems to know a lot about whatever's down there. Have they had medallion holders posted in Drake City before? Prior to Samantha, I mean."

"I presume so. Not familiar with this area's history, myself. Also, they wouldn't necessarily tell me. Why?"

"Well, with all this interest in the cave and a possible medallion hidden somewhere beneath Drake City, I figured they must have had information from some time when the mine was operational. That hasn't been for decades."

Frank eyes me. "You have intel."

"I have possible ideas."

"Such as?"

"Such as whatever's down there was deliberately concealed by one of the Garrison."

He doesn't say anything. Instead, he consults his computer. "I'll look into it."

"What did they tell you?"

"That there could be a medallion in the caverns. They had a general idea. The cave into which I directed you was the likeliest route, according to what the Garrison knew."

"They're right, given the trap."

"Listen, Brandon, the treaty is clear: whichever side finds a medallion has claim to it. The trick, though, is finding the right person with whom it can be paired. You can't just hand off something this powerful to any idiot walking the street. Genealogy is vital. Temperament. Mental acuity. So, if and when the Ashen finds it, we'll have time to stop them."

"What happens if we find it?"

"The Garrison gets it. My contact with the overseers will come to get it. There're nine overseers throughout the world. I only know one. That person only knows three. No overseer knows the complete group, except for the Elder. Anonymity keeps things compartmentalized and secure."

It sounds insanely paranoid. But then again, no one's ever made this group public in a thousand years, so I figure their paranoia works. "What's our next step?"

"You go home. See your son. Get cleaned up."

The benefit. Reed. Kelly. "I've got to get to the hospital."

"No. You get home first." Frank closes the laptop. "Stay put while I do some recon. Your friends come by to see you, that's great, but stay out of the public for the night. Tomorrow, go to work."

"You don't get it. They put a woman in the hospital. She

might have head trauma—"

"Still not listening. She'll be there. You showing up right after your flying alter ego dropped her off is too coincidental. So go home."

Sean takes the news of the shooting surprisingly in stride. Doesn't even get up off the couch. "Uncle Reed called me. He, like, said you were at the hospital."

"Kelly was hurt." And I was at the hospital, however briefly.

He looks me over. "Are you okay? Did you get hurt?"

"Nope. Just, ah, very wet." Wet enough to dampen the carpet. Flight number two didn't give me time to dry off.

"Oh. Okay. Good." He goes back to watching whatever is on his laptop that's more important than his father getting shot at.

"So. My almost murder by criminals not spoiling your evening?"

He scowls at the bitter tone. Spins the laptop to face me. "Messenger's got a brief up saying Airfoil stopped them. Plus, Uncle Reed said you were okay. So not worried. Thought you'd be at the hospital with your girlfriend."

"Sean…" I rub my temples. The medallion stabs me with cold. "I'm really, really doing my best to not say something that will piss us both off. But your attitude is unappreciated. There're more important things going on that your obsession with superheroes."

"C'mon, Dad. You saw him! He saved you guys!"

"Of course he did, and I'm grateful." More than he'll realize. I restrain the urge to lift the couch or levitate the refrigerator just to make my point. But he's my son. The idea that something I did could endanger him, that if someone other than the Ashen found out who I really am came for Sean, keeps me sane. "Look, I need your attention focused on home. Focused on us."

"Us. You mean me and you. Like separate. We're roommates, Dad, not a family." He slams his laptop shut. What is it about tonight with that reaction? "If you're going out to play with Frank or try to get laid, don't let me keep you up."

"What do you want, Sean? I made dinner and set it out for you! The bills are all paid. I've come home sober every single night, and all I get is your lip!" So much for keeping cool. Samantha's picture doesn't frown, but the real woman would.

Sean's door bangs shut.

I don't even think. I just head for the bedroom. Collapse in a sodden heap on the sheets, listening to the rain drumming on the windows. Anger and adrenaline peter out, until I'm left with exhaustion.

My dreams are filled with the deaths of people I love. And I'm powerless.

Hull Branch is closed for the day.

That's what the signs says, a single sheet of white 8 ½ by 11 paper taped inside our front door with black text announcing it to the neighborhood. When Kelly makes closing signs for us, they're inevitably decorated with colorful clipart, even if it's only for our semi-annual cleaning.

The image of her asleep in a hospital bed crowds my thoughts. I glanced at my phone. The text message still burns there.

<I'm well. Doctor's saying I can go home this evening.>

My response: <I'll come pick you up. Take the subway together.>

<That'd be nice. Thanks.>

<Just glad you're OK.>

Promising. I haven't been over to see her yet. But she was all right last night, when I flew off the hospital roof. I shove the phone into my back pocket and head for the employee entrance, stewing over the attack and hoping a thug winds up trying to mug me again, just so I have someone to vent my righteous indignation upon.

Reed's here. His pale green Honda Crossfire is in its spot. My watch tells me it's 8:35. Way early for him.

There's another car, a breathtaking Lexus. It's vaguely familiar, and it's not until I unlock the door to the library that I realize it's Director Mark Vanchev's.

The only lights on are glowing from Reed's office. I toss my bag into the break room and smooth out my shirt. I even shaved clean. Haven't done that in forever.

Reed's hunkered behind his desk, staring at his computer screen. The computer's on, but there's nothing on the desktop. His face is stony, and the reflection on the desk in front of him is equally somber. It occurs to me. I can only see that reflection because his heaps of budget documents and policy binders are gone. Cleared away. I spot them neatly stacked on shelves against the wall.

Mark Vanchev sits in a chair opposite Reed, intent on his smartphone. He gives me a sharp nod, accompanied by a tight smile.

"Morning," I say.

"Mourning is an appropriate descriptor," he replies. "Let's not equivocate. Last night was well on its way to being a runaway success for Hull Branch before it became an unmitigated disaster. Thankfully, no one was killed."

"Got Airfoil to thank for that," Reed murmurs.

"Yes, he saved a lot of people," I say. "The city council can't hold what happened against us, though. It was a—I don't know, do the police have a theory?"

"I really don't know," Vanchev says. "The police have kept me in the dark. As for the council, yes, they will hold it against us. Councilman DiFalco for one is appalled. He put considerable support behind us, even touted the benefit in his district, and here he is under gunfire in his suit and tie. So much for his claims of community safety."

I shake my head. "That's crazy. It is safe. Crime's down

what, 15 percent? That's just in Hull. With Airfoil patrolling..."

Vanchev's gaze reminds me of a history professor who literally called me on the carpet for not knowing the correct dates of the Hundred Years' War. "There's been a reduction, yes, but the scale of crime has spiked. Brandon. When have we seen anything like what's transpired?"

"It's become intolerable."

I lean against the wall, folding my arms. Reed shoots me a dirty look, the kind that says, Stop arguing with our boss! Traitor.

"The Messenger is spinning the outcome as positive, referencing the apparent mistaken identity of the attackers' targets—namely us. But we're out of time, gentlemen. The City Council will decide the matter in a week. Budget year starts up shortly after that, on July 1, and the Rittenhouse contingent wants desperately to offer their constituents this victory of cutting vital services to save taxes." Vanchev shakes his head. "Terrible. It could have been far, far worse last night, but I'm afraid the damage is irreparable. A shame. All the work done by you and Ms. Quirke brought our patrons to our rescue."

I push out of my chair. The legs thump against the office wall. "We can't stand by and let these cheapskate dilettantes shut down a vital part of the community," I snap. What I don't verbalize is the snarl inside that says, They won't take this place away from the people of Hull, from my friends, or from me. This place kept me afloat when life was at its darkest. "There have to be remaining backers on the Council."

"There are, but their support is precarious. I have a handful of meetings today with those individuals. Fighting fires, one might say."

"Then we can still do this."

"Brando, get over it." Reed's first words since I arrived are a hoarse imitation of the norm. "We're through. Let Mr. Vanchev do his damage control. It's all we've got."

The silence is thick. Vanchev clears his throat. "In any case, gentlemen, in light of last night and Ms. Quirke's injuries—the hospital informs me it was a concussion—you'll remained closed until Monday. If you need additional staff, I'll get people here as fast as possible.

"Thanks," Reed says. "We'll be fine."

"Yes, well." Vanchev rises and brushes lint, imaginary or otherwise, off his sleeve. "I too am thankful that Airfoil was able to put a stop to the violence. Very clever to dress as one of the crowd."

"Sure was." Reed's avoiding eye contact with me.

"Gentlemen, carry on here. I'll do my best. And thank you for all your service to your community." Vanchev disappears down the hall.

I slide back into the chair. Reed and I sit there for maybe half a minute of pained silence. "So," I say. "That sounds final."

Reed continues his uncommunicative stare at the screen.

"Next time I'll have to be more careful about my choice of costume. Though you have to admit, it was clever."

"Uh-huh."

"How's Caroline?"

"Fine. She's okay. Cried a lot. But she was ready to make breakfast with the kids first thing in the morning." Reed exhales. "That's not the problem."

"You going to spill or shall I continue my terrible attempts at small talk?"

"Option A. She stayed up an hour after we got back to the apartment, waiting for Dennis to show up. He didn't even call or text her. His sister." Reed slaps the keyboard. The ALT key skitters across the desk.

"He could have been deep in some big profile case."

"Yeah. Sure. Deep inside his extortion of street thugs. Busy night."

"So...how're you guys dealing with that?"

"Fantabulous."

"That's not a word, Reed. Also, sarcasm."

Reed gives me the finger. At least I've prompted a smirk. "Vanchev's right. It is a good thing you were there."

And just like that, my mood sours along with his. "Some would disagree."

"What?"

"Let's say that if I followed Frank's instruction and kept the tights in a closet, so to speak, none of this would have happened. His theory."

"No. No way. Do you have any idea how many people would be dead if it weren't for you? Hundreds. Forget it, man. He's wrong. Don't let him get to you."

"Easy for you to say."

"Whatever. I don't care what his little secret society's been doing for hundreds of years. You know what? They screwed things up pretty bad, if you ask me." Reed picks up the ALT key and flicks it at me.

I stop it in midair with the field. It hovers between us. I grin at him and deposit the key neatly atop his keyboard.

"Show-off. C'mon, Brando, you've got the chance to show people there's something better out there. Something bigger than all the petty crap they put up with."

I ponder that for a moment. Reed leans back in his chair, takes a long look around his office, and finally points out at the darkened stacks of the library. "This sucks."

"Yes, it does. We can still keep it open, Reed."

"I know. There's still a chance."

"You want me to sort? Easier to shelf-read if there're no patrons."

"Nah. Take the day. I'm gonna answer a few dozen emails and get out of Dodge. Take the family out to the boardwalk."

"Sounds like a plan."

"You should spend some time with Sean today."

"Thanks, Counselor. I might. I have to pick up Kelly this

afternoon."

Reed nods. "You, ah, got any other activities planned for this evening?"

My mind's eye offers up the image of Caroline, curled up on the couch, her phone cradled by her side, waiting deep into the night for a call that never comes. And Kelly, sprawled in that knock-out dress amidst smoke and violence.

"I think so. Have a few visits to pay."

I'd seen Dennis's car around, and even if I hadn't, it took less than thirty minutes to identify it in the parking lot of the Third Precinct. Talk about a gorgeous ride. I wait on the top of the adjacent building. There're some weathered, granite gargoyles on the corners of the Whaler's Mercantile Bank, atop the eleven-story structure. I run my hand across the tool marks on the wings, wondering at the crews of French-Canadian masons who carved this in the 1890s

The sun is fiery red in the distant hills, sinking low on the horizon. I wait as night falls. Reed is certain: Saturday evening, Dennis leaves around the same time for a card game. Who would want to play cards with him? Most likely a full table of Dennis clones.

Cars empty from the lot. Soon, there're only a smattering of cruisers, disgorging tiny officers. Men and women returning from patrols. Dennis's Monte Carlo is by itself, away from any other vehicles.

The first stars show their eyes, and Dennis finally leaves.

He strides to his car, not talking to anyone. No one so much as waves. Can't imagine working in a building swarming with people, not acknowledging a soul.

Satisfied no one's paying the bank any attention, I wrap myself in the field and fly down to the parking lot. Everything zooms in rapidly, until I land lightly as a leaf on the roof of the

Monte Carlo. "Lieutenant Marchand."

"You!" He's fast. One swoop, and he has a Ruger semi-auto pistol trained on me. Car keys lay discarded by a crumpled coffee cup on the asphalt. "Put your hands up. Get your shoes off my car!"

"Shooting's a bad idea. You miss, you'll break a lot of windows. Probably dig some deep holes in your doors. That'd cost a lot to fix."

"Get. Off."

"This is fun, Lieutenant, but I need information."

Dennis stares at me, then snickers. "You're standing on my car and I'm pointing a gun at you."

"Only one of us is bothered by either of those. Big hint: it's not the gun." I fold my arms.

Dennis waits too, gun still steady. He makes another sound—like a surly dog. He holsters the weapon. "You've got balls."

"Yes, last time I checked."

"Fine. Tell me what you want in thirty seconds before I call for backup. SWAT will have a blast nailing you to the brick."

"What do you know about the shooting at the library benefit?"

"What do I know? Besides the fact that the Polacks claim they were after the Irish? Not much else. Everyone's pretty tight-lipped about it."

"Including you."

"Rigel Research & Technologies manufactured the exo-skeleton used by Consolata Acciai in her fight with me at the mine."

"Rigel Research? How'd you figure?"

"I saw an image on her armor that matched their logo. But there's no proof. That's where you come in."

He nods. Still hasn't called anyone on his radio. But I feel ridiculous standing here atop his car, negotiating with him. I form the field around me, preparing to fly.

"Okay then. Those guys you slapped around? Definitely

wilki. Guns are the same kind they've been swaggering around with for a while. But the Irish weren't anywhere near the benefit. And the Poles are smart enough to know it. So, we're trying to pull info out of them. Worse than pulling actual teeth."

"You've tried it?"

He sneers. "You tell me."

"I'll need more than that if I'm going to stop them. One of us has to."

"What's that supposed to mean?" He plucks the radio from his belt.

And that's my cue. I rocket away. My frustration at Dennis's intransigence is offset by the sight of him shouting skyward.

Kelly and I ride the subway from Drake General to her apartment in Longshore, south of Hull. She looks good—you'd never guess what she'd been through last night. With her hair in a ponytail and having changed into blue jeans, white sneakers and a purple blouse, she could have been out for an afternoon of shopping.

Our seat is near the front, away from the tightly packed confines of the subway car and the bulk of the body odor. Sunlight bursts through the grime-streaked window as the train emerges from the Twelfth Street tunnel onto the aboveground rails. "Are you okay?" she asks.

"Me? Yes, just have a lot on my mind."

"Me too." She touches my hand. "Thanks for coming to get me home."

"My pleasure."

"How did the meeting go?"

I shrug. "Vanchev is less than optimistic, but willing to push on. Reed—poor guy. He's beat."

"I can't believe what happened," she says. "If I'd only checked beforehand. We might have known what kind of people were using the hall. Maybe…"

"Maybe what? There wouldn't have been an attack?" I throttle back my irritation. It's not her—it's them. They ruined the evening, our chances at saving our library, and threatened my friends. And now both of them are blaming everything but the bad guys. "No. There's nothing you could have done. No way you could have known."

"I want to help, still, but I don't know what to do." She scowls, still managing to look cute while being mad. She rubs her forehead. "At least the doctor ruled out a concussion. That would make things worse.

"They could have been a lot worse."

"I know, but... Never mind about that. So, we're left with the council meeting, and that's it."

"Then that's where we make our stand."

"We round up as many of our patrons as we can to come support us. I know they will. Look how many were at the benefit."

"Good plan."

She reaches to the floor and drags up a small duffel bag. I catch sight of a corner of her dress, folded inside; the lumpy shape of the bag's likely caused by her high heels.

"You looked amazing last night."

She grins. "I thought we were planning strategy."

"We did. Briefly."

"You were fairly handsome yourself."

"That old rig? Yes, yes it was impressive." I crook my finger over the edge of the bag. "How'd you get a change of clothes to magically appear?"

"My cousin Neil brought them. He says hi. He also says to tell you he's a firefighter and U.S. Army Ranger, and so you're supposed to be extra nice to me."

I laugh. "Sounds like I'd get along well with him. He come up to take care of you?"

"He's visiting from Boston, some reunion or another. Came over as soon as I called him. We were very close growing up.

He's the same age as me, so we played more often than my siblings and I did."

"Beaumont!" the conductor hollers. The train lurches to a halt at the intersection of Beaumont Street and Suffolk Road. Kelly's apartment is in the three-story brownstone on the opposite corner, the one with the blue and white striped awning. Yes, I've seen it before.

We both get up. I clear a path through the sardines by applying my shoulder and friendly "Excuse me"s.

"You should get back on, catch the train home," Kelly says. "I'm going to rest, per the doctor's orders."

"Okay. I'll see you at work."

"Maybe before then." She kisses me. I linger there, ignoring everything else—which apparently includes the train's departure. When I open my eyes, it's a block and a half away.

"It's okay," I reassure her. "I'm going to take a walk, clear my head."

"Be careful. Longshore's nice, but after the benefit…" She shivers. "We can't always have Airfoil show up to save us."

She walks to her apartment, and I brush my fingers against my chest. The medallion is an unyielding lump under my shirt.

"We always should," I murmur.

Chapter Twenty-One

The first day back at work, and I'd rather be anywhere else. Focus, Brandon. DVDs are not going to get out of their storage sleeves and into the cases all by themselves. I glance over my shoulder, offer a reassuring smile. The two burly men with grease-stained coveralls aren't paying attention. They're pretending not to watch Kelly as she helps an elderly man reach Alan Furst mysteries from a high shelf.

My fingers flip through the file, not needing my brain for this task. We've got upwards of six hundred movies in this collection and I can find every one.

What I'm waiting for is my phone to buzz. But nothing. After five calls to Frank yesterday and three this morning, I gave up. He was nowhere to be found when I flew out to the Barn. I didn't leave a message. What am I going to say? Hey, Frank, wanted to speak with you about my suspicions, now confirmed by police evidence, that you assassinated a woman in broad daylight?

I slap both piles of four DVDs each down on the counter in front of the men. "Here you go. Enjoy."

"Thanks." The clean shaven of the two looks around. "Sucks they might close you guys down."

"Yes, it does."

"We been in here every other day since we got laid off," he continues. "Couldn't pay the cable bill. Or Internet. But we got a couple of prospects. Should be back at work next Thursday."

I blink. Yes, these guys have been in here a lot. Never said more than three words to any of us.

"So, yeah, I guess…thanks. For being in the neighborhood."

"Uh, you're welcome."

They're not gone more than three minutes before a black woman with gray streaks in her hair flags me down as I'm en route to shelf a stack of biographies. "Can you help me? I've never filed for unemployment on a computer before."

"Sure thing." The books go on the desk next to one of our computers. The state's system is fairly complex; I've been around computers since sixth grade and still have difficulty. Once I see her resume includes work flagging for construction projects on the interstate, and watching her hunt and peck on the keyboard, I realize it could take her hours on her own. "Shouldn't be a problem."

Twenty minutes later, we're done, and she's holding a printed copy of her resume in her hand. "Wow! I couldn't have gotten that to work if I live to be a hundred and fifty!"

I chuckle. "I promise it would take less time. It's ten cents a page…"

"Oh, here, honey, you put that in your donation jar or whatever you got." She hands me a crumple of three ones and smiles again. "My hero."

The words ring in my head long after she's gone. Sure, I can catch a crashing airplane, and save a ferry boat of doomed passengers, and foil crimes left and right. But when it comes to the important things, no medallion can fix it. I have to.

During my break, my phone buzzes. Frank picked a heck of a time to call back. I'm two bites into a roast beef and provolone from Stransky's.

Except it's my cell phone, not Frank's, and it's a text. From

Eliana.

<Glad you're okay. Saw what happened at benefit. Envelope coming via courier for you. Hope it helps. :)>

Eliana is taking my warning seriously, I assume.

Five minutes later, Kelly raps on the doorframe. She's got a manila envelope in her hand.

"Courier?" I ask.

"Yes. So, I take it you were expecting a delivery." She hands me the envelope.

"Thanks. You guys hanging in there out front?"

She smiles. "Only if 'hanging in there' means having to reboot a public computer that's having a fit about its new security software. Twice. And then I need an Advil."

"How is your head?"

"Not a concussion, but it still hurts like crazy. Tech support won't help."

"Ouch. Good luck."

Once she's gone, I tear open the envelope. Address confirms it's from the maritime museum, and inside is a thick stack of paper bound in a folder. A yellow Sticky Note's affixed to the front. "One journal, as promised," Eliana's written. "Scanned it and did OCR as best I could. Don't worry—was on my personal laptop, without connectivity. Enjoy the light reading."

I dive into it, eager to find more examples of Tobias Rankin saving his city. While those don't disappoint, I find no more clues about what he buried beneath Drake. Whatever it was, it was enough for him to fear its unearthing. He also mentions Lobban's Cove again.

"I have no doubt the Ashen will endeavor to track me. My identity is secure, however, and they already know the penalty for endangering those dear to me. I have made men pay that price. No matter. For as long as I complete the work God has lain upon my soul, no amount of machinations between the Garrison and my enemies will dissuade me from my path."

The rest of the hour passes as swiftly as a lightning strike. I pack up the printout and its envelope in my bag. I glance at the calendar on the opposite wall. It features an old painting of Sculpin Bay and the coves along the northern shoreline, rimmed with trees and homes and old wharves.

Coves.

My mind races back through the minutes to the reading. I hurry from the break room, edging by a mother with a tall stack of children's books in one hand and a latte in the other. "'Scuse me."

Ignoring her protestations—I'm sure the stain will come out with the right detergent—I find my way to the narrow shelving in the back of our small history section. Right about…there. I pluck our copy of Drake's Port: A History of the Early Settlement of Sculpin Bay.

I'd shelved this book a couple of months ago, for a man who had checked it out and then returned it in the book drop a half hour later. At the time, I'd noted its worn down red cover, the faded gold lettering, and flipped through the index—like I'm doing now/

There it is. Page Sixty-Seven. "Lobban's Cove," I murmur.

It was a tiny fishing dock, lasting only forty years at a small, flat inlet. The map is immediately recognizable, once a modern shoreline is taken into account. Newport's shipping docks replaced those contours. They were dredged and reshaped.

Whatever Tobias Rankin had buried, whatever he'd concealed with an earthquake, he'd done it only a few blocks from the same mine where the Ashen had set a trap for me.

Home, finally.

I drop my bag, weary from a day that seemed filled with funereal expressions and words of condolence. Hard to hold out hope when everyone's given up.

Check my phone. Nothing from Frank. No big surprise.

No sign of my son, either. No matter how I try to concentrate on the Lobban's Cove element of the Ashen's plans, I keep returning to my failed conversation with Sean. I've got to get him to see what's wrong.

I knock on his bedroom door. "Sean?"

He doesn't answer. So, like a good dad of a teenager, I let myself in. Sean's bedroom is littered with stuff. There's a bed, an antique, wooden dresser nicked and scratched by time, and a cheap prefab desk with a chair that's missing one of its five wheels. All three surfaces are covered with comic books, clothing, and food wrappers of every kind. I painted the walls pale green five years ago, but you'd never know it for the posters that hide them: Hulk, Thor, Batman, Green Lantern, dozens more. The roster could fill a barracks.

He's lounging in a Sean-sized hole in the refuse on his bed. I rap on the doorframe. Sean yanks an earbud out and doesn't look up from his homework. "What?"

"How was your day?"

"Why?"

"I'm your father. Standard protocol."

"Whatever. It was fine."

"Lots of homework? Nobody hassling you?"

Sean's face is a mask. "Dad, if this is another mom-talk, just do it and go away."

I sit down on the chair. Boats at sea in a hurricane bob less. It tries to tip me forward, but I prop a foot against the desk. "Things didn't end well last night. We need to restart."

"I'm not a lagging computer, Dad."

"You're still grieving, is what you are."

"Yeah, no, I'm not."

"Don't give me that."

"You're not a psych."

"Right, but lately you've been..." I cast about for a polite way to say it.

"Been what?" He wrinkles his nose. "Surly?"

"A jerk." So much for polite.

"Thanks for the vote of confidence." He's back to his homework. The pencil scratches away at the paper. His Algebra I book is propped on his pillow.

"Sean, give me a break. It was rough for us both. She was taken from us suddenly."

"Yeah, I know. 'Taken suddenly, prime of her life, very tragic, be there for each other, blah blah blah.' You've said it before."

"And you don't listen." I'm trying very hard not to snap at the boy. He doesn't need my recriminations—but he doesn't need a buddy, either. "It's okay to be upset about her death. Really. Something's bothering you, tell me about it."

"Dad. I'm not sad about it. You don't get it. I got over Mom dying a long time ago."

"When you started putting up your posters?" There's all watching me with steely gazes, posing grandly for our benefit. My brain fills in a rare blank spot on the wall with an image of me, in full getup, hands on my hips. Better yet, fist raised, soaring into the sky. "Those didn't go up that long after."

"You get the cookie," he mutters.

My patience is rapidly waning. It always does with Sean. Especially when I do this—try to get him to open up, peel off the armor, see what's got him so mad. "So talk. What's bugging you?"

"Do you wanna start with the not paying bills? Or the staying out late trolling for girls?" The pencil scratches furiously now.

"I think I'm entitled to a personal life. The bills—all right, fine, I'd let things slip. Not going to pretend this has been any easier for me."

"Guess it's easier to pretend you don't have a kid by ignoring him."

"Ignoring—you? You're never here." That comes out harsh,

clipped. He's doing it again. Samantha always advised me never to argue with Sean, even when he was young: "You can't win a war of words with a seven-year-old."

Sure I can.

"You're right I'm not," he says. "Let's play this game: why do you think that is?"

"I have no idea. That's the problem. You need to tell me. We're not getting any better. We've been circling the drain for a long time. Eventually, we'll go down."

"You wanna just fix it and make it go away."

"Of course I want to fix it. That's my job. Can you stop being so stubborn for five seconds so we can do that?"

"Come on, Dad."

"Just be quiet and let me help with the problem!"

"You're the problem!" His pencil rips through the paper, dragging a gouge between equations. He slams the book shut and hops off the bed, fists clenched. "You should have been with Mom! It's your fault!"

Shooting me would have been less painful and confusing. "What? Are you crazy? I would have died too."

It isn't a good idea to call your very upset 13-year-old son "crazy" if you're trying to improve his mental state. The kid's a beanpole, but he's wiry, and only a half foot shorter than me. I stand up, slowly, to remind him who's boss.

"You suck, you know that? You could have saved her! Then we'd be okay. But you were at work, and she was coming back from the hospital. You weren't there for her, and you should have been!"

"Calm down. I know it hurts. Don't you think I wish I could have been there?" But I know, cold and logically, that I would have died in the crash too.

His eyes are brimming with tears, and his face goes red. He's shaking with anger or mourning or both. "You keep telling yourself that. It doesn't change what happened. You were supposed to save her! You're my Dad!"

"I couldn't save her!" I snap. "Just because I'm your Dad doesn't mean I'm some—"

The word gets stuck in my throat, because I see Captain America staring at me. Him, and Iron Man, and Nightwing, and all the rest.

"Superhero," I murmur.

Sean barges past me. I stand there, immobilized by his anger and my revelation. No wonder. All those posters. All those comic books. The sudden fascination with anything caped and costumed. He wanted someone like them to be real, to pull his mother from the fiery wreck when no mortal man could be there.

I rub my face. Here I thought Sean just looked up to Reed, took on his obsession.

The front door opens and then bangs shut. He's gone out. I rush to the window. Sean's on his bike, pedaling west. Probably the mall again. I grab my phone but pause mid-dial. There's no point chasing him now. He'll run farther.

I set the phone on the counter. My pulse calms. Samantha's portrait is watching me. "You would have handled that better. He never got your goat like he does mine. He always understood you."

She smiles back, patient as always. She was always reassuring, ready to back me up, but willing to point out a different path.

My frown deepens. Yet, she had a path I knew nothing about. The scene of her wreck floods over the dams, erected in my memories: the mangled car, black billowing smoke, leaping orange flames, boiling heat and stinking fuel. Nothing left but a twisted hulk of metal and plastic.

Why hadn't she used her medallion? My hand touches the lump under my T-shirt. Was there no time? Did she react too slowly? Or was she as fanatical about the Garrison as Frank, so devoted that she was willing to preserve their silence with her death?

That rankles me. The Garrison manipulates whole nations, and on a smaller scale, the cities among them. But worse than that, they have no regard for the lives they trample.

Sirens wail by, headed farther down the block. My pulse rises. Someone's in danger. It could be a father, or a mother—or a kid like Sean.

Forget Frank. Forget the Garrison. Tonight, Drake City needs me. They need a hero.

As much as I want to chase after Sean, drag him back home, I know that won't do either of us any good. Sean needs to see a hero.

Two minutes later, suited up and helmeted, I leap into the sky from the top our building, chasing those emergency lights. Time for another very public appearance. Frank'll kill me.

This time, that seems far less of a joke.

I thought the sirens were leading me to a fire or a car accident. Instead, I get a war.

Six police cars are arrayed in a starburst at the intersection of Walnut and West Barnegat. They're a phalanx of red and blue lights, with twelve officers wedged between then, guns drawn. Beyond them, the street echoes with the staccato of automatic weapon fire. The far end of the block is stoppered by four white sedans with tinted windows: two Jaguars and two BMWs. The Poles.

I soar by, low enough to see two groups of combatants—then men in slacks and ties near the sedans, and fourteen other men in blue jeans, carpenter pants, and T-shirts and jackets stuck in the middle of the block. Anyone's car unlucky enough to have been parked on either side of the street has become a barricade. They've also lost most of their windows and gained dozens of bullet holes.

The men in T-shirts are Irish. They have to be Sheehan's

enforcers—that's plain from their weapons of choice. I count eight shotguns and an assortment of pistols.

There're already four bodies in the middle of the street and slumped behind cars, with dark stains smeared across the asphalt. Only the Irishmen's superior numbers keep them from getting overwhelmed.

I bend my approach, leaning onto my side. Buildings whip by, blurs of glass and brick lit into garish colors by the emergency lights and street lamps. Flashes of gunfire keep me alert.

First things first.

My flight path blasts down the far end of the block, bringing me to street level—five feet off the pavement. The timing has to be precise. Just as I reach the first man who's blazing away with his AK, I go through the steps for bullet deflection Frank taught me.

I'm in front of the guy for a split second. The expression on his face melts from angry intent and reforms as astonishment. A dozen bullets spark as they impact the field and are driven down under the pull of increased gravity. They leave little, shiny craters in the asphalt.

My passing throws him back from his shelter behind the sedan, wind flapping his jacket and whipping up his tie. His body slides the on rain-slicked street. The AK is still firmly clenched in his hands.

All along their firing line I knock them down like a hurricane making landfall. It's such a thrill to watch them get knocked down I barely remember to bank up at the end of their barricade of cars. Thugs and guns are strewn between and behind their vehicles.

I shoot straight up, arc over, and dive into a curve that takes me toward the Irish. They're a scattered target and require a more personal approach. I land smartly by a big blue Toyota Highlander SUV. It looks more like a giant cheese grater more than an automobile. The man there, his red T-shirt sweat stained, stares at me a full second before raising his Bennelli M3 Super 90 semi-auto shotgun to my face.

Really.

The blast is startling, but the shield holds. It's a Fourth of July display of sparks. The pellets dig a trough inches from my boots.

He gapes.

I give the field double duty—fling him to the left and his shotgun to his right. He hits the SUV's hood, rolls over it, and slaps the ground with a crunching sound which I assume heralds multiple fractures. But I handle the shotgun with a different mental image. A paper shredder. It rips in black shards, spilling pellets like rain and dropping shells like big red crumbs.

Panicked shouts sound from nearby. I shoulder into another car, a little green Chevy Volt. It skids backwards, slamming into the hood of an old Buick behind it. Two men hiding alongside the Buick yelp, diving onto the sidewalk for cover.

Gunfire opens up all around me. I'm still shielded up. Nothing gets through, and the impacts surround me like manic fireflies. It's funny., I chuckle despite my racing heart and drenching sweat. These boys fail at short-term memory retention.

I barrel into the largest group, running flat-out at six men clustered behind a pair of old Ford Tauruses. Right before I'm on them, I imagine a bowling ball hitting pins. The outer edge of the shield solidifies, ricocheting bullets instead of absorbing and redirecting them. When it collides with the cars, the impact flips both up on their tails. The gunmen scatter, shouting curses. The cars bash down, blowing out their remaining windows in sprays of glass. Three gunmen get knocked off their feet.

Unfortunately, I'm thrown off balance, too. I'm too close to the cars; my knee strikes the street. Cold water suddenly soaks my pant leg, and what's even more jarring than that is the bullet that whistles by my head a foot away.

Shield's dropped.

The Poles take advantage of my chaotic run at the Irish to resume fire. But I'm already throwing myself up in the air, re-forming the shield. More bullets buzz by, perilously close, before I can shut them out. Sparks glitter once again. I exhale.

These AKs are the major menace. Should have gotten rid of them sooner. I should have dumped them all in the bay instead of listening to Frank.

I drop among the Poles, all eight of them, without announcement. Half the men goggle, but the other half keep up their fire.

I just wait, letting the shield absorb. I'm getting tired, and the bullets press in closer, shot after shot. Metal splotches ring the ground around me.

Soon enough, magazines go dry. There's the clicking of triggers from a pair of the neophytes. The older, scarred veterans shout obscenities I can't translate at their dumbstruck companions.

I leap at the nearest pair, using the medallion's grasp to slap them together like wet sandals. They go limp and drop their guns.

Another pair rush, trying to hit me with the stocks of their empty weapons. I slip between them, coming up at their backs. A kick sends the first one sprawling head-first into a storm drain. He goes terribly still. The second turns and swings a punch. I block the blow with my forearm and land my own in his face. Don't need the medallion for that.

His head snaps back, and he staggers, but doesn't do down. He gets in a good hit with the gun, rebounding it off my ribs. I move with the impact, let it spin me around, and hook my foot inside his. He trips forward. I loop my arm around his neck and introduce my knee to his face.

Blood spurts onto my knee as his nose crunches in on itself. And he's out.

I turn. The remaining four Poles pile into a sleek, white BMW sedan that's mostly bullet free. It backs up, brake lights glaring red and tires squealing.

I crouch. The field thrums around me, begging me for action. One second.

Two seconds.

The BMW roars in reverse at me. The Poles shoot backward. Go.

I leap up, over the back windshield, twisting through streams of bullets. My boots bounce onto the roof, and I hunker down. With every ounce of concentration, I leach off the medallion's energy from my shield and into something I've never tried before.

A humongous lever.

The BMW screeches to a halt. I jam the end of the invisible lever under the passenger side door and pull, straining with every muscle in my body.

The car flips—much better than I expect. I fling myself backward, shunting the field into my visualized rockets. But the car does a double spin, six feet in the air, and hits the pavement with an ear-shattering crunch. The hood and trunk bang open. The roof crunches a good foot down. Groans echo from inside.

More gunfire. The Irish are still at it! That's all I have time to think before something hot rips across my abdomen, right where the Pole hit me. I drop to the ground. My vision swims. Blood seeps onto my jacket.

Shield's off. Can't focus enough to re-form it. Footsteps running closer.

"He's down! Shoot him!"

It's all I can do to get turned over, and the cobwebs clear enough. I can start the shield steps. But I'm halfway through when a red-faced, balding thug with murder behind blue eyes gets a pistol in my face.

The gunshot isn't as loud as I think it should be. There's no pain, either. Instead the mob enforcer jerks away, a burst of red soaking the front of his shirt.

"Sniper!" One of the others spins around, his gun aiming high for the rooftops. The kill shot takes him in the back of the head.

I'm on my feet. The shield reforms, finally. I daub at my side. Blood, but the pain's manageable.

"You just got grazed," Frank's voice scratches over my radio. "If you're tiptoeing around, you could clear the rest of these bruisers off the street."

He hasn't disappeared off the face of the Earth. All at once, I'm relieved he's got my back and angry that he's been AWOL. "Roger that," I pant, just to tick him off.

I charge the nearest Irish enforcer. To my surprise, I cover the fifty feet in a heartbeat, without demanding a boost from the medallion. He blasts away with a shotgun, sparks spraying everywhere. I rip the shotgun from his grasp and swing it fully around. Batter up.

The crack echoes. He flies back into his nearest compatriot who's running to assist.

There's a half dozen of them remaining. Must be out of range because they don't shoot, merely stand in line, weapons raised at me. Behind them, someone's hollering through a police megaphone, "Drop your weapons! Drop your weapons!"

They don't take the advice. I let go of the shotgun and use the medallion to make it hover halfway between us. My concentration's split between keeping it steady and watching their movements.

"Tell your boss, this city isn't his," I say, loudly enough to be heard past the helmet. "It's mine."

One quick image: a twig snapping. The shotgun breaks in half.

None of them lower their guns, but they don't shoot, either. Most stare back. One gapes. Even with his shrub of a moustache and bodybuilder's bulk, he can't be more than nineteen. This is what Sheehan uses kids for around here. Fighters. Killers.

"You're showing them restraint," Frank says. "They won't give it to you later."

I push with both hands. The gravity shifts under their feet, flipping them up six feet and back another dozen. They hit asphalt with satisfying smacks.

The police stream out from behind their cars. Their guns shift back and forth from the downed enforcers to me and back again. I recognize the lead cop instantly. Dennis.

For once, his gun isn't pointed at me. I consider it progress.

I soar up several stories and arc over the row of buildings.

"Get back to the Barn. I'll patch you up."

"Oh, you'll see me again. When I'm good and ready. You've got questions to answer. But if you think I'm going to hop to any more of your orders, think again. I already said it. Screw you." I kill the radio and wish vehemently I didn't need it anymore. Or Frank, for that matter.

My side aches. Thankfully, home is in sight. I land on the roof, stumbling to a stop against the doorway from the lower floors. There's nothing up here but some clunky HVAC equipment, a couple of ratty plastic lawn chairs, and a cluster of beer bottles discarded by tenants apparently taking in the view. I peel back my fleece and grimace. Not too bad. Bleeding's slowed, though it's a gash as long as the Great Stone River. First Aid kit's in the bathroom. Now, to get down there and hope Sean's still—

"Holy crap."

He's here. He has his phone out, aiming it at me like a paparazzo's camera. I've never seen such a look of wonder and joy on his face. It's everything he's ever wanted to happen in his life for the past two years, come true in one moment. He's standing on our rooftop, staring at a superhero.

"You're real. You're right here! On my roof! Wow. Just... wow." He laughs. "Hey, don't worry, it's not posted. I wanted to ask you first before I did anything with the video."

My boy. The most important person in my life, and he's far more excited to see this persona than his old man. "Sean. Stop filming."

"Sure, sure." He taps the phone, fumbling with it. "Anything you want. I just like wanted to..." His words trail off as the import of what's been said registers. "You know my name?"

"Yes."

"Are you...on Twitter?"

Despite the pain, I chuckle. "Sean, whatever you do, don't fall off the roof."

I reach for the straps under my chin. Hang on. Frank's warned me about this—the dangers of revealing my identity. But how else can Sean and I continue together? If I'm going to be gone at crazy hours, I can't keep lying to him. Sure, I want to protect my son. Keeping the truth from him isn't the way to do it.

Besides, I feel like this was meant to be. I pray to God that it's true.

I remove my helmet.

I didn't think it possible for his eyes to go wider. He stands frozen, phone halfway to his pocket.

"Sean? It's okay. Don't worry."

"Dad? You're Airfoil?"

I nod.

A grin I've seen countless times in my mirror breaks out across his face. "Awesome."

Chapter Twenty-Two

Dennis dropped into a leather chair at the Third Precinct. Patches of duct tape concealed gouges in the cushion. One of the boys had gotten it for him when he made Lieutenant—back when they were still apt to give gifts and play pranks on each other. The chair was as old as he was and as comfortable as his Monte Carlo.

His desk hunkered in one corner of the squad room, behind a pair of partitions plastered over with newspaper articles about his collars. Some were yellowed, others freshly clipped. A careful examiner—and Internal Affairs—would note the absence of any names related to Nikodem Krol's criminal organization. Sheehan's, yes, and some of the minor players. But that was it.

He wasn't the only one tucked into this corner. Dillard had been there for hours, perched on the corner of a metal folding chair that squealed every time he shifted position. He searched on the computer for—well, for whatever it was he thought he'd find there. They had the name of Rigel. All good. The company's webpage was very informative when it came to flashy graphics of robots and exo-whatever suits. But when it came to finding out who was in charge of what, and how a maniac like Acciai could have got her hands on one of those suits, they had zilch.

Marchand took a careful bite out of a hot dog. He had

it secured in a sizeable paper towel but couldn't take chances with the mustard, ketchup, and relish piled on top. His wore a crisp white shirt and khaki slacks, the latter pressed with perfect creases. The smell and taste of the condiments was irresistible. But there was no way he was going to take a stain stick to his clothes when he was done.

Anyway, it was better than dwelling on the real matter. He looked at his phone, sitting dormant on the corner of the desk. No light. So, no messages or returned calls. He'd tried to reach Caroline a couple of times today. She hadn't called back. Surprise, surprise. He'd be furious if she hadn't checked on him if he'd been at a party that'd gotten shot up.

No returned calls from Cezar, either.

"Sir?"

"What now, Dillard?"

"Could you, uh, chew…quieter?"

Marchand stared at him, mid-chomp.

"Sorry, sir." Dillard rubbed his eyes. "I'm having trouble concentrating. There's just so many possibilities out there. Rigel has links with hundreds of other groups, including DoD, Homeland Security, and even state DOT, not to mention private businesses."

Whine, whine, whine. "That's rough. I tell you what Dillard: I can solve your concentration problem."

Dillard glanced over his shoulder, expression brightening.

"Stop worrying about my eating habits and get back to work."

"Right. Sir."

Dillard hunched his shoulders, but Marchand hadn't gotten halfway through the dog before he sat bolt upright. "Yes!"

Marchand fumbled the dog. Mustard dripped onto his knee. "Well, that's great. Perfect. This had better be good, Dillard."

"Yessir. It is. It's not, um, strictly …" He went red in the face.

"Strictly what?" Marchand doused a chunk of paper towel in water from the Nalgene bottle on Dillard's desk. He daubed at his khakis. That one was going to be miserable.

"Legal sir."

Marchand froze. "Now you're talking. Show me what you've got."

Dillard gestured to the screen as Marchand rearranged his chair. What were those, tax exemption forms? "Rigel operates a nonprofit firm for cancer victims call White Heart. I pulled names and ran background checks. Several have minor indictments for money laundering and fraud that were dismissed years ago. Now. Those individuals also have paid jobs at Rigel itself. Which...I only found by cracking in to their personnel division's firewall."

"Hell, Dillard." Marchand kept his voice low. He didn't know computers well, but he knew that what the kid described was bad. As in, bad if Dillard was caught but good for Marchand. "You really got in?"

"Yessir. It wasn't as hard as I thought—took three hours." Dillard frowned. "It's sad how poorly maintained their encryption keys are, considering the sensitive technology they—"

"Don't care."

"Oh, right. Well, once I confirmed that these individuals worked for Rigel, I dug into their backgrounds more to see if anyone had ties with other businesses. There were a ton. But only one that raised alarms."

Dillard clicked through a blizzard of screens, pausing on one that held a familiar logo. "Otte-Vaughn," Marchand said. "The mines."

"It can't be coincidental. Acciai fought Airfoil at the mines, wearing an exo-skeleton bearing the mark of a company that has financial ties to the mine ownership."

"Good. Good work." Marchand slapped the kid on the shoulder. "We need names."

"That's where it turns difficult."

"You just said you got into their personnel firewall."

"I did, sir, but the individual who had links with Rigel

doesn't exist."

Marchand ground his teeth. He glared first at the screen, then Dillard. "How can they not exist if they're getting a paycheck?"

Dillard went red again. "They used a pseudonym. It's a false name—"

"I know what a pseudonym is, Dillard. So, you ran a check on it."

"I didn't have to." Dillard shrank two screens and clicked on a third, which popped into view. It was a payment schedule, with monthly amounts in the $20,000 to $30,000 range. The recipient was highlighted in blue.

"Domitian," Marchand read.

"Yessir. I checked. It's a Roman emperor's name."

"Okay."

"You might find it more interesting to note that an individual with that name bought shares totaling six percent ownership. From Danny Sheehan."

Marchand stared at the records Dillard produced. "I knew Sheehan's family had part ownership in a bunch of businesses on Newport. But not the mine. This transfer—was it before the fight at the mine?"

"Preceded it by several months."

"And Acciai shows up to fight the flying guy. With some of Krol's goons? On property this Domitian guy bought from Sheehan? Using a robo-suit from a company that the same guy who bought mine shares from Sheehan has financial interests in?"

Dillard pondered that. "Yessir."

Marchand nodded, slowly. "Domitian. He's got to be our guy. That one."

"What one?"

Marchand scowled at him. "Think, Dillard. Acciai? We had her in custody. Right after she'd killed one of Sheehan's boys. Remember how that turned out?"

Dillard's eyes widened. "The other flying man?"

Marchand brought his finger to his lips. "You get all this stuff you found printed. All of it. Stash it away—safety deposit box. Wipe it off the computer."

"Yessir. I've already copied it all on a flash drive."

"Good for you. Meantime, we need to find out who else knows about this Domitian character. You peck around, see what other links you can find. I want a name. A real one."

"Okay. What's your play, Lieutenant?"

"I'm going over to Newport, lean on a few acquaintances. Someone's got to have seen something." He got up, found his jacket, and tossed the crumpled paper towels in the trash bin. His knee was still damp. Thanks, mustard.

The phone was still silent. Marchand grabbed it, willing it to ring. He had no excuses for Caroline. The night of the attack, he'd been out pressing drug dealers for intel on Airfoil and Acciai. He got nothing, even after spending a hundred bucks and shaking down three hundred from a pimp with a big mouth who owed him for keeping his brother out of jail. But he'd stayed out of contact with the precinct.

"Nothing from your sister?"

Marchand shook his head. "Didn't even know about the shooting until I got in at 4 a.m."

"She should understand."

"Sure." Marchand pocketed his phone. "Stick to the data, kid."

Marchand drove with one hand on the steering wheel and the other scrawling notes in his red notebook, outlining everything Dillard had told him. Whoever this Domitian guy was, Marchand wasn't about to let him or Acciai go on carving up the city's gangs. Equilibrium had to be maintained, if crime was going to be controlled.

He made a stop en route to Newport. Caroline's preschool was on Adams Street, in Old City, four blocks from the bridge. The buildings here were worn out, like most of Old City, and he knew they had something to do with the original settlement. The preschool was in a gray stone building, looking like it had been an old meeting house. But now it was fenced in on one side with green panels. Brightly colored animals romped on the fencing. Children's voices squealed from the other side.

He leaned against the Monte Carlo, waiting. Waited some more. Rubbed at the faint spot left from the spilled mustard on his pants.

A bell rang, and adult commands rose over the sounds of children at play. He could see them now, headed up the back steps into the school—a row of the tops of heads, black hair, brown, blonde. Caroline stood at the door, smiling and giving high-fives.

Marchand watched, waited for her to look around. Once the last little head bobbed by, she did, scanning the playground and then the street. Her smile froze.

"Let's talk, Sis," he muttered.

It took forty-five seconds for her to come out the front door and cross the street. "What?"

No greeting, no hug, no warmth. She stood by the car, arms folded, eyes blazing.

Marchand rubbed at a smudge on the Monte Carlo's hood. Hooked his thumb in front of his holster. "So. About the other night. I'm sorry."

"All right."

That was easy. Marchand grinned. "You hadn't responded back to me, so I thought I'd drop by for a surprise visit."

"I didn't say you're forgiven, Dennis. I don't recover that quickly from family betrayal," she snapped. "Do you honestly think you can show up here, interrupt my work, give me a one-liner and then everything's settled?"

Marchand frowned. "I'm going to go with 'No' as the correct answer."

"My students could figure that much out. You let me down, when I needed you most. You let us all down. It was all over the news the next day. I had to explain it to my babies. Do you know what Thomas asked me? 'Is Uncle Dennis going to stop them? He's a police officer.' I didn't give him an answer, because I didn't know if you could. Or would."

"I had somewhere else to be. I didn't know about it until later. And then I figured it was too late."

"Save it, Dennis. Just...stop." Caroline poked him in the chest. "Maybe Reed's been right this whole time—about all the things you do that I wanted to deny knowing about. Maybe that's what's more important, keeping your position safe and your little corner of a kingdom secure."

Marchand couldn't come up with words. It was as if he'd been shot and running short on breath. "Caroline. Please."

"No more. You need to go. When you figure out what's more important to you, you're welcome back with my family. But don't...just don't talk to me. I'm sorry." She hurried back inside, not looking back.

Marchand stood by the Monte Carlo. It was only a couple of minutes. He'd intended to make jokes, make light of it, push forward with a more heartfelt apology after. But she'd never given him the chance. Could he blame her? He'd let her down. The one person who had faith in him to do the right thing.

Now it was just him, and the job. He got in the car and slammed the door. His hands twisted around the steering wheel. Why couldn't he do better than this?

The image of Airfoil fighting Acciai flashed through his mind.

Enough. He had to get rid of this crap. Maybe, when it was all over, when he had Acciai and this Domitian nut and yes, even Airfoil taken care of, he could make it up to her.

First thing's first.

The pusher must have seen Dennis coming as soon as he turned the block. A car like the Monte Carlo, at this time of the day, cruising Gennessee in Newport, meant one of three people: a mob enforcer, a high-level dealer, or a crooked cop.

The kid took off running.

Please. Dennis shook his head and stomped on the accelerator. He shifted gears so fast he was alongside the kid in seconds, no matter how fast he ran. And that was pretty fast. But the consequences of using that much dope in three years meant you lost whatever track and field skills you had in high school. Dennis jerked the steering wheel, swerving at the curb.

The kid lost his balance, tumbled, and sent two trash cans spilling. Dennis slammed the brakes. He was out of the car and jerked the kid to his feet by a ragged, gray and blue Sculpin Navigators sweatshirt. The basketball logo had a hole in it, revealing a bright green shirt underneath.

Dennis grabbed him by the scruff of the sweatshirt and hauled him up. "Winchester. Where you running to, my friend? We need to talk."

"Aww, Marchand, let me go. I don't got nothing." Pale as a ghost, stocky and broad, clumpy brown hair under a black knitted cap, Winchester squirmed in Marchand's grip. He smelled like cat piss and old cardboard. "You got enough last month."

Marchand pulled a Ziploc bag from his pocket. Winchester immediately stopped struggling, transfixed by the sight of the small, white rocks.

"There's a good boy." Marchand shoved him away. He waved the bag in front of him. "What's the word on the flying man? The new one, not the hero."

"Airfoil!" Winchester grinned. His eyes were focused lasers on that bag.

"I'm talking about the other one. I've got a nickname: Domitian." Marchand scowled as the word slipped from his mouth. Not possible for him to feel like more of an idiot.

"I heard stuff, sure. Nobody messes with him. He's got pull, man, like with Krol and his boys."

"Krol's dead," Marchand said. "Hit by the Irish. So they say."

"Yeah. Cezar's in charge."

"Old news, Winchester. Gets you zero ice." Marchand started to put the bag away.

"Nononono!" Winchester's breathing intensified. "This Domitian guy, he's the one got Krol killed. That's what's new. Cezar and the wilki, they're scared. Like Domitian's the devil himself. You never seen so many big guys with guns crossing themselves and...and that thing they do, they bow or something."

"Genuflecting," Marchand murmured. "You've seen them together?"

"Yeah yeah." Winchester swiped at the bag, but Marchand yanked it back, holding his other hand out like a battering ram. "C'mon, man!"

"You can do better. I need a face."

"Nobody's seen his face, man," Winchester said. "Always got a mask! Never goes anywhere without his 'Angel.'"

"Angel?"

Winchester's face took on a dreamy expression. "Black hair. Blue eyes. Likes to hurt people."

Acciai. Marchand frowned. "You know a lot about them, Winchester. More detail that you usually give me. Who's the source?"

"I never tell, Marchand, you know that. I seen them."

"You've seen them, where?"

Winchester waved his hand to the east, gaze never leaving the bag. "Eight blocks. Old tannery section, by the railyards. Big old mill or something. One of those. I think."

Marchand grabbed the front of the kid's shirt and dragged him in. He could ignore the stench of Winchester's breath and everything else in the neighborhood long enough to get what he needed. "This wouldn't be the time to screw with me. You're sure about this."

"Oh, yeah. No doubt. I just came from that way, man. Now gimme the goods, come on, I done all right…"

"Wait, they're in that place right now?"

"Yeah, yeah. Whole big crew of Polacks. Cezar's there, and some rich-looking guy. I seen them all when they got out of their cars. Me, I was—"

"Selling again. Anyone see you?"

Winchester frowned. "Maybe. You know, it's not like I was hiding."

"Right." Marchand tucked the crystal meth into his trousers and spun Winchester around. "You're under arrest."

"Huh? Arrest? What're you doin', man!" His voice was shrill. Spittle sprayed over Marchand's shirt.

Perfect. Marchand slammed him up against the building, digging behind his belt for handcuffs. "Don't resist arrest. I'm booking you on trafficking."

"C'mon! We got an understanding, yo—"

Marchand leaned in and hissed, "Yes, we do. That's why I'm hauling you into lockup so that my perfectly good informant doesn't get himself perforated by Polish mob bullets. They saw you. If you want to remain not dead, shut up and get in the car."

He kept a sharp watch on both ends of the street. Nothing except parked cars, all shabby, and the occasional vehicle crossing at intersections. No one appeared to be watching from the buildings across the street, but he wasn't taking chances. He shoved Winchester in the backseat and slammed the door behind him.

"C'mon, Marchand!" Winchester whined inside. He wrapped his fingers through the grille separating the front of the Monte Carlo.

Marchand pulled away sharply from the curb, jostling Winchester back against the seat. He cried out. Marchand accelerated down Gennessee. "Winchester, I swear, you leave so much as a sweat stain back there I'll be the one gunning for you. Now shut up."

There was only the sound of the rumbling engine as Marchand dialed Dillard's cell. "Hey. It's me. What? No. No. Shut up. Listen, get Captain Urquhart on the line. We've got 'em. Right over here in Newport." He paused. "No, I'm not kidding! Now get the Captain on the phone!"

He waited, blasting as he did through a red light and ignoring the chorus of horns. "Winchester. Was she there? The woman?"

"Yeah, man, like an crazy robot chick…"

"Right. Got it." Marchand grinned. If Acciai was indeed there, he'd have a nice surprise for her when he rolled up. Kudos to Dillard for that one.

Acciai had to hand it to her master. There she was, standing in the shadows beneath the very spot where he'd hung her from the ceiling in suffocating chains. She'd been certain of death. Now, instead of death, she was shrouded in an array of pistons and circuits and wires that gave her the strength of ten men. She was a walking arsenal. It was a new life.

Subtle? Not so much. But Acciai appreciated the symbolism.

Before her, Cezar stood in the center of two dozen wilki. They were an eclectic bunch of men. All of them ugly to so-so. Not a single one she'd sleep with. She shook her head and sighed.

Cezar continued his speech, most of which Acciai had tuned out.

"…And it is with the sincerest of brotherhood, Mr. Serafin, that we thank you for agreeing to the late Mr. Krol's request. He was true martyr to wilki. We must seek blood for his blood. Your men, they will help do this."

The man facing him, Kondrat Serafin, was a tall blond man

with a thick, neatly trimmed beard and eyes the color of Sculpin Bay frozen in winter. Muscles shifted under a beautiful charcoal suit. He smiled and nodded at Cezar. Acciai cocked her head to one side and fully appreciated his physique. This one…she'd make time to further her acquaintance before he left Drake City. It was guaranteed. He was hemmed in by six equally tall, stone-faced, well-built bodyguards.

"Yes, Mr. Krol's death is an untimely tragedy," he said, his accent quite softer than Cezar's. "But it does make our arrangement simpler. I was invited here to approve the extra finances he sought. Let me be plain: my superiors were ready to refuse him. But with you in charge now, Cezar…I know you are a practical man. I know you will serve our best interests in Drake City, for quite some time."

Cezar bowed at the waist, his manner so obsequious Acciai gagged. "Of course, Mr. Serafin. Friend. We stand ready to serve you."

"Good. The financing is approved. The men you request? The soonest I can have them here is late August. Possibly sooner, if I apply extra pressure on Customs. Will that suffice?"

Cezar glanced in Acciai's direction. She was tucked back in the shadows, close enough for them to make eye contact but not for anyone to pay her attention. The cloak over her shoulders was ridiculous, but Domitian did have a point when it came to concealing the exoskeleton. She gave a curt nod in confirmation.

"Yes. Thank you. Friend." Cezar smiled stiffly. What a buffoon. "Your support means much to us."

"Very good." Serafin stepped forward and clapped both hands upon Cezar's shoulders, patting them twice. "Let us make arrangements."

Cezar hollered at one of the men nearby, making a sharp gesture with his hand. Another of the wilki rolled a battered metal cart over. Its top bore a clattering collection of glasses filled with ice and a quartet of vodka bottles. Several of the men cheered.

They were so busy imbibing and engaging in boisterous laughter that none of them heard the cars pull up outside. Acciai could have heard them even without the earbuds she had, linked to the monitoring systems she'd placed around the warehouse. It was the gunfire that surprised her; she'd expected something less bold.

Cezar and Serafin reacted first. They shouted at their respective men to draw their weapons, to investigate the chaos outside. More gunfire.

Acciai chuckled. This ought to be interesting.

The far bay door burst open and, in two pieces, slammed down onto the concrete floor. A pair of dark gray Lenco BearCat armored trucks with DCPD SWAT markings rumbled in. Twenty men poured through behind them, black-clad and body-armored. Flashlight beams shone from under the muzzles of M4A1 rifles. A half dozen plainclothes officers and another half-dozen in uniform hurried in behind them.

Acciai recognized Lieutenant Marchand immediately. The man had tenacity. And the way he moved—with precision and a surprising grace—made Acciai wonder if she should switch up her idea for a bed partner. Or maybe she'd be satisfied with his blood.

"DCPD!" Marchand shouted. "Put down your weapons and surrender! You're all under arrest!"

Cezar answered by pulling the Glock from his waistband and shooting. Serafin, too, was armed, with a pair of old MAG-95 semiautomatic 9 mm pistols. Gunfire thundered throughout the warehouse, reverberating off metal walls and concrete floors. Between the AKMs wielded by the wilki and the M4A1s the police used, there was no way to hear a word being shouted along with the roar.

Acciai let them go on for half a minute, watching with glee as a handful of the Poles were shot down. One man took six bullets to the chest, his blood spraying out in a red cloud that fairly glowed under the droplights. A pair of SWAT officers were sent sprawling. Whether dead or wounded, she couldn't tell.

Men on both sides spread out for cover—behind the Bearcats, or among the rows of metal shelving and stacked containers.

There it was. The metallic odor of spilled blood. Iron. Her breath quickened. No more waiting.

She put power to the suit and jumped, a strong leap that normally would have propelled her up above waist height. But with the exoskeleton, it sent her hurtling twenty feet, in an arc, over the nearest shelves. No one saw her. Why should they? With gunfire in every corner, there was more than enough to occupy their attention at ground level.

Acciai landed behind a SWAT officer. His partner saw and shouted a warning. She slashed through the barrel of his rifle, shearing it off, and punched him hard enough to shatter the visor of his helmet. He flew ten feet back and slammed into a steel container, leaving a huge dent in its corrugated surface.

The other officer managed to loose a few rounds in her direction, but she'd already spun away from him. With a single thrust she put both blades through his Kevlar, until her fist touched his chest. She flung him off, a limp carcass that flailed across the hood of the nearest Bearcat.

There went her surprise. More police fired her direction. Acciai extended the armor shield from her exoskeleton and leapt, this time nearly touching the thirty-foot high ceiling and running five truck-lengths along the warehouse wall. She bounded hard enough along the concrete to crack the surface, sending up fragments and white dust. With a flick of her left wrist, she triggered the shield that extended from her shoulder, widening out into a thick sheath. The incoming bullets ricocheted in every direction. She slipped beside the Bearcat and gripped it firmly under the chassis, between the two left wheels. Acciai pushed, grimacing at the effort, breathing hard. The pistons strained and the motors whined. The Bearcat lurched off its tires, groaning. The men behind scattered as it reeled over and bashed into the side of its neighbor.

She strode up onto the side of the truck, opened fire with the autocannon on her arm. The shots tore up the side of the Bearcat, spider-webbing the reinforced windshield.

A huge blast threw her off balance, making her stagger sidelong. There was Marchand again, advancing on her with a squad of six men. He pumped shell after shell into his shotgun, firing at her without caution or restraint. She admired that. He'd be a good one to kill next. But for him, she'd make it special.

Acciai whipped the autocannon up and cut down one of the men in his squad, leaving him smeared across the concrete. The rest, Marchand a moment behind, scrambled for cover again, and she kept her shield between their gunfire long enough to make sure her flamethrower was primed. A dreamy smile crossed her face. Marchand had escaped her fire, but it was only with Airfoil's help, and he wasn't here now.

Marchand leapt from behind a stanchion and fired his shotgun. Acciai didn't bother to block the shot, poised at the armored midsection of her exoskeleton. She triggered the flamethrower. A gout of fire burst forth—and died in a sputter. Her arm froze up a moment later, immobilized. Then her left leg. And her right shoulder.

A malfunction? Really?

It was only then she isolated a new sound—a crackle—accompanied by sparks that spread up and over her exoskeleton. There was something jammed against her armor. Whatever projectile Marchand fired in that last shot was no shotgun shell. It was black and yellow, striped, and stabbed into her metallic gun as if it were a giant, malevolent wasp.

Acciai swore and stumbled backward, but she froze in midstep because her right leg wouldn't bend . Everything on the suit was grinding to a complete halt. She had no displays, no response to switches, no control. She toppled like a felled tree, the armor ringing as she hit the floor.

Marchand planted his shoe on her armor. "Stay down."

"You're smart, bringing backup," she said. "What makes you think I didn't?"

The walls of the warehouse vibrated, heaving in and out. It was as if they were all inside a living, breathing body. The metal rippled, rose and fell in waves. Horrible shrieking reverberated through the building as the roof peeled back in five strips, gouged away from its rafters. The walls bent until they were arches that touched the pavement outside.

Domitian descended through the twisted frame, floating on the air, his cloak billowing behind him.

Marchand swiveled and loaded another shell. "Take him down!"

All around them, police weapons turned skyward and opened fire. Domitian raised a hand, a languid gesture that seemed to Acciai as an afterthought. The air encircling him exploded with sparks. Bullets ricocheted among the police, causing shouts of alarm. Some of those returned bullets found their mark in unarmored limbs.

Acciai took full advantage of her master's arrival. She heaved free of her exoskeleton, no more mobile now than a marble statue. She rolled from beneath Marchand and angled a kick upward, knocking the shotgun free of his grasp. Her next kick took his legs from beneath him.

Marchand scrambled away, sprawling on hands and knees. She was already up and struck him across the face. The blow was hard enough to cut his lip. She clapped her hands savagely onto his ears, making him shout in surprise and pain. In a second, she was on him, a knife angled across his neck. Her left hand's grip entwined in his hair.

"You failed again, Lieutenant. You'll never stop us. And if you try, every time, this will be the result." She pulled his face close and kissed him hard, so she could suck on his lip. The taste of his blood set her heart racing.

The explosion of a gunshot cut her revelry short.

Searing pain lanced through her right shoulder. She collapsed onto Marchand, who grabbed her by both arms and heaved her aside. Acciai slid on the concrete, striking the base of her neck on a stanchion.

She looked around, dazed. Ten wilki were dead. So were police—but she couldn't see how many. Marchand's young officer, Dillard, towered over her, his Glock trained in both hands. "Sir! Are you okay?"

"I'm fantastic." Marchand spat blood from his mouth. "Help me drag her out before that maniac comes down!"

Maniac. Listen to them. They would fight Domitian, their feeble strength against his pure power, and he was the maniac? Despite the pain of her wound, Acciai laughed.

Above them, Domitian reached out to either side, his fingers flexed. Girders screeched.

He bent his hands, and those girders snapped free, dozens of metal spears hurtled to the ground. Two pierced the upright Bearcat. More slammed against shelves, toppling them against the police.

One sliced through Dillard's middle as if he weren't even there.

He gasped, immediately coughing up blood. He was rooted to the spot by the steel shaft. The gun felt from his hands. His body convulsed.

"No! Chris!" Marchand reached for him but was flung sideways.

Shouts of confusion, and pain. Acciai got back up, scooped up Dillard's discarded gun. She didn't see any able-bodied wilki around, but high-powered engines roared to life somewhere at the back end of the warehouse. SWAT officers swarmed into the clearing where she'd lost her suit, yelling at her to stand down.

She shot the nearest man point blank, wrapped her arms around the second officer's chest and shot the third behind him. Then she wrested the second man's M4A1 from his grip, a task made easier after she knelt and stabbed him behind the right knee. She drowned out his screams by bashing his faceplate in with the stock.

A large section of the roof caved in where the police had made their entry. Then another. Then two more. The building was coming down.

Acciai considered putting a bullet in Marchand. But she couldn't see him or where'd he landed.

Another fragment hit the ground near her, and she bolted from the warehouse.

Thunder roared throughout the warehouse. Then silence filled the air.

Laughter. Deep, resonant. Why couldn't Marchand see anything to go with it?

"Your time is at an end," the voice called. "Welcome to my realm."

A rush of wind, a tremendous gust like a storm at sea, and stillness after.

"Lieutenant!" Hands grabbed on to him. Eased him over. Light flooded his vision. That hurt.

"Sir, stay with us." One of the men from the SWAT team. Face sweaty, streaked with chalky concrete dust. "Hold on. We've got EMTs and backup en route."

Marchand coughed. He sat up, shoving the officer away. "Chris. Chris Dillard…he needs help."

The man's expression was nauseated. "Nothing doing, Lieutenant. He's dead."

No. He grasped the sides of his head. This wasn't happening. Everything was falling apart. Caroline was right.

He'd lost.

Chapter Twenty-Three

The Hull Branch Library's fate is decided here, and even though I'm Airfoil, I feel powerless.

The city council chambers are packed with people. There's a great deal of murmuring going on, even as the council prepares to begin. They haven't said a word.

It's a wide, half-circle of a room, with ceilings two-stories high, lit by long, curving glass fixtures that remind me of waves. The nine city councilors sit behind a tall arc of a desk made of granite and wood. The mayor sits in the middle, his chair and podium elevated a foot above the rest. Behind the council hangs a four-foot diameter bronze disc with the Drake City seal on it. The familiar pair of schooners on stylized water rest in front of a mountain to the left and a bridge to the right. The walls are blue and cream, with blue-gray curtains hanging on either side of the hall. Drake City spreads out beyond the windows on either side, the buildings of City Center catching the oranges and purples of dusk.

I'm in the back row with Reed, Kelly, a host of volunteers, and a hundred residents of Hull. Even Sean is here. On my left hand, staring at the masses, he frowns at the council. He types furiously on his phone, tweeting everything that pops into his mind. He's not unlike the reporters and bloggers camped out among us, snapping photos on cell phones or holding massive cameras, taking notes, badgering everyone with questions.

Mark Vanchev sidles over to us, immaculately dressed as ever, but his expression is tense. "I'll warn you now: most on the council have their minds firmly made up about the closure. We'll do what we can to convince the swing voters otherwise, but I—"

The mayor's gavel raps on the desk. She's a stout, stone-faced woman with gray hair wound tightly in a bun, her eyes peering behind slender glasses. "We now call this meeting to order. Our sole item on the agenda this evening: final decision to close the Hull Branch Library of the Drake City Free Public Library system."

One of the councilors from Rittenhouse stands—a thickset, balding man with a paisley tie named Councilor Kameroff. "Madam Mayor, I make a motion to close the Hull Branch Library to the public as of August 1, with staff and material relocation to be completed for final closure by September 30."

"Do I have a second?" the mayor asks the council.

"I'll second the motion." A woman, tall and dark-skinned, examines her fingernails as she says the words.

"We have a motion and a second," the mayor intones. "I'll open the question for discussion."

Vanchev stands straight, beaming a smile at the council. "With your permission, Madam Mayor, I'd like to address the assembled."

"Proceed."

He stands at the front of the room. The podium faces the left windows, so that he can turn equidistant to see both the council on his right and the hundreds of people in the hall to his left. "This is a question we've grappled with for months now. I won't make the same arguments you've all heard. But here are pertinent facts. Hull Branch's circulation has increased steadily since April, on the average gaining 25 percent. Our residents are making more use of our services."

"That's all well and good, Mr. Vanchev, but there're the twin problems of cost and safety," this again from Kameroff. Sweat beads along his brow. "The place drains half a million dollars from our budget annually. That excludes the constant supplementary requests for improvements we keep getting."

"That's not fair!" Councilor Sam Bertrando, a short, burly man with curly white hair and a thick moustache, wags his finger at Kameroff. "I've told you all time and again: Hull has long been ignored by the city, like our brothers and sisters in Westerville. How're we supposed to keep our streets safe when you all won't lift a hand to help?"

"I'm not implying the city's in the right on this, Sam," Kameroff says smoothly. "I'm merely giving Mark a chance to make his points."

Vanchev doesn't flinch. He holds up two fingers. "I'll address your concerns one at time. Costs: if the proper funding for maintenance were approved in my initial proposed budget each year, we would not have to beg the council for supplementary funds. As for crime, I can assure you Hull Branch has never been safer. The whole neighborhood has never been safer. Thanks in no small part to our resident hero, who's done more than could be asked of any one man to protect a city."

Sean nudges me, a sharp, quick motion that Kelly can't see from my opposite side. He smirks. I keep a poker face, because the last thing I need people to see is me grinning every time Airfoil gets kudos for doing his job.

A black woman, Councilor Dalton, speaks into her microphone "For all your promises, this sounds an awful lot like the same arguments we've heard from you and residents this summer, Mr. Vanchev. Our sales tax receipts are down this year. The budget can't sustain this kind of luxury."

That elicits grumbles from the crowd. "So close Rittenhouse Branch, why don't ya!" someone bellows over my head. Whistles and clapping follow the comment.

The mayor bangs her gavel. "Please refrain from comment," she snaps. "The public input phase of this decision has ended."

"Says who? No one ever told us!"

"You all received notification months ago of this possible decision. The time for debate has passed. The council is assembled tonight to decide the matter so we can approve the coming fiscal budget and rein in our finances."

"Then answer the question!" It's Mrs. Ruiz, from the daycare center. Her brother looms over her, arms crossed. She's surrounded by younger men and women, either her family or parents of the children she cares for. "Why is it Hull that must be sacrificed? Can't money be trimmed elsewhere?"

"The Hull Branch Library has long been an underused, poorly maintained, and in an unsafe location," Kameroff says.

"That's patently false." This from Councilor DiFalco, the one who'd been present at the disastrous benefit. "You've heard the comments from Mr. Vanchev, and seen his reports, and those of the manager, Reed Andreen. Hull is on the mend!"

"I'd hardly call a couple of months with fewer shooting and drug deals 'on the mend' in Hull, Mr. DiFalco. That isn't even in your district." Kameroff suppresses a dry laugh.

"So?" DiFalco snaps. "It's in our city, and we have an obligation to the entire community, not just our own neighborhoods."

"I ask the Council once more to reconsider," Vanchev says firmly. "Think of all the good that has been done as of late. We are improving. We can continue this trajectory."

The Councilors begin muttering amongst themselves, gesticulating with one hand as they cover their mics with the other.

I want to say something. But the only words I can muster are snide, sarcastic, and full of anger and disappointment. What I really want to do is lift the council from their seats and use the medallion's power to dangle them a thousand feet over Sculpin Bay for good look at my neighborhood until they acquiesce.

I'm halfway out of my seat, mouth open, when Kelly rises to her full height. "Our library is not a luxury," she says, her voice carrying from the chamber ceiling. All discourse up front stops. Gradually the crowd behind us shushes themselves into silence. "Our library is a necessity for the people of Hull. They need a place they can go to feel safe, and to be safe. A place they can bring their children to read in quiet, without worrying about fights at school or drug dealers harassing them on the streets. That's where we work. That's why we're there—to serve others. Please, don't take this away from us. This is our family, our community. You can't measure those things against taxes and budgets."

The silence lingers on. All I can hear is the whir of the air conditioners overhead. Reed stands up and starts clapping. The applause spreads around the room, wildfire catching in every row, until all of us are on our feet.

Sean climbs up so he's balanced on the back of his chair, one hand on my shoulder, and takes a sweeping panorama around the room with his phone.

The banging gavel interrupts the cheers and clapping. "Thank you for that sentiment, Miss." I can't miss the exasperation in the mayor's voice. "I will now call the vote."

A few surprised exclamations escape the crowd, and even Vanchev appears perturbed.

"All in favor of the motion to close Hull Branch Library?"

Six hands go up, including the mayor's, Councilors Dalton and Kameroff.

"All opposed?"

Three hands go up, belonging to Councilor Bertrando of Hull, DiFalco of Cape Ashwin, and a brunette woman named Case from Westerville. I shake my head. Even the councilors from Longshore and Newport sided with the opposition.

The gavel bangs. "The motion passes, six to three. Hull Branch Library will close to the public effective immediately.

Staff have ninety days to complete the shutdown and to have all materials removed to storage at the main branch library in Center. Is that understood, Mr. Vanchev?"

He nods, jaw fixed, unsmiling.

"Good. We will now tend to the disposition of the property."

I can't stay for this. I feel sick. Reed's already on his way out of the chamber, glowering. Nothing I say I going to comfort him. And this on top of Dennis being in the hospital and his partner dead; Caroline has to be beside herself. The crowd breaks up, people shaking their heads and muttering discontents.

"Let's go, Dad." Sean smiles at me, but it's half-hearted. "We'll go grab something to eat."

"Sure."

Kelly walks with us. "I can't believe this. I—I didn't think it would turn out this way."

"Me neither." There's nothing else to say. We failed. I failed. Months of putting away bad guys and getting shot at and banged up and bruised. It still didn't work.

The crowd ahead of us parts for a new arrival, a burly man in an expensive suit coat and pants, with a black polo shirt underneath. The four men with him can't be anything other than hired muscle. And the man himself...

Danny Sheehan.

I stare, watching as he breezes past with a huge grin and outstretched hands directed to the council. "Thanks for this opportunity, ladies and gentlemen! I'm delighted to be able to offer an alternative use for this eyesore. Sheehan Investments is willing to offer a competitive price for the sale of the closed library property."

DiFalco balks. "Mr. Sheehan, I'm sorry, this isn't protocol."

"Sure it is, when you're talking quick turnover of valuable land." Sheehan pulls a thick envelope from his jacket pocket. "I have payment here in the amount of five hundred thousand dollars. All yours. If said land is similarly mine."

"I believe we can deliberate," the mayor says slowly.

"You can't be serious!" DiFalco snaps.

"I'd hear the proposal from Mr. Sheehan," says Kameroff, smiling broadly.

My teeth grind together.

I barge past the remnants of the crowd, not caring if anyone keeps up.

It's dark. I gaze up at the stars. You can see so many more of them from the top of the tower, here at the Barn.

My back's to the city. I don't need a reminder of how far it sprawls along the bay, its lights like a bag of diamonds spilled on black velvet. Doesn't matter right now. Nothing does.

I want to read Samantha's note again. But Eliana still has it. I pray she confirms everything I've worked for, everything I've made myself do to honor Samantha's memory.

My phone buzzes. <U OK, Dad?>

I smile. Sean wanted to come to the Barn with me. But he doesn't know about this place. Only Frank does Of course, I haven't told Frank that Sean knows I'm Airfoil. I perfectly understand the need for secrecy. But I can't do this alone. Not without the people I care about. <Good. Waiting for Frank. Be home in a while. Thx.>

<K. If u go put smack on bad guys, I want 2 see! :) >

Chuckling, I text back, <Good night.>

Headlights cut through the night. A car rumbles up the road onto the grounds of the abandoned radar base. A red Camaro. The engine cuts. The door opens, illuminating the driver.

Frank.

I fly down to meet him, landing gently to a walk. Ten feet away I stop, arms folded. "You've been AWOL."

"Had business to take care of," he says, setting a roll of papers on the hood. "Heard about the Council meeting. I'm sorry."

"I don't want to talk about that."

Frank runs a hand through his hair. "Don't get me wrong.

You're stubborn. Much more than Samantha ever was. But the Garrison—while they hate your methods, they love the results. Some of them, anyway. You're causing the rest a great deal of heartburn. Never heard them this indecisive."

"What are they going to do about Domitian?" My hands curl into fists. "You saw what he and Acciai did to those cops."

"I don't know."

That's first time I've heard him admit it. "There's no plan?"

Frank starts unrolling the papers. "Apparently, Domitian is operating outside the bounds of the Ashen. That presents us with a problem."

"A problem? Frank, you keep telling me the bounds set by both organizations are the only things that restrain them from... well, from truly terrible actions."

"Bingo. So, are you going to lend a hand here or are we going to keep griping at each other like an old married couple?" Frank says. "All right. I may have something that can help us get an edge on Domitian."

Frank pats the papers, which I now realize are geological charts of Drake City and Sculpin Bay.

"Right. Tobias Rankin. He was a medallion holder operating out of New England in the early Nineteenth Century," I say. "At some point, in late 1814 or early 1815, he buried something beneath Drake City."

"Hence Domitian's interest in the Otte-Vaughn mine."

"Whatever it was, it was near Lobban's Cove."

"Never heard of it."

"You wouldn't have, because it doesn't exist anymore." I walk to the car and lean over the map, then circle the relevant area along Newport's coastline with my finger. "Most likely it's here, buried under decades of landfill and rebuilding."

"The cave system runs under the whole bay—and this entire region, seems—fairly extensive. Look. It's worse than having moles in your front yard."

I grin at him in the dim light. "Wouldn't think tiny moles would bother you."

"Don't underestimate them. They're cunning." Still one hundred percent serious, Frank traces a line along the maps from Newport into the heart of Drake City. "There has to be hundreds of miles beneath here. Cave-ins, collapsed mine shafts, flooded tunnels. It's a mess. Now, if I were this Rankin guy, I wouldn't just drop whatever I hid down a hole, knock down a hill, and call it quits. He had to have stashed it pretty well for Domitian to usurp an entire mining company to go look for it."

"Right." He's just outlined a collection of caves that run east-west under the bay, long strands and twisting curves that spread out again on the other side. "You think it's under the bay itself?"

"That's where I'd put it. But we're going to have to check them. You up for that?"

I nod. "At least we've got a new starting point."

"Yes, we do. Whatever Domitian wants is down there. It's up to us to find it before he does."

"That sounds like a plan the Garrison will like. There's one other thing."

"Such as?"

"Rankin made it pretty clear he didn't tell the Garrison where he hid—whatever it was."

Frank stares at me. "Where are you getting this intel?"

"Not your concern."

"I think it is."

"Look, Frank, this whole time you've been on me to not only trust your word but to blindly follow every order you get and give. This time, you've got to trust me. The information's reliable. Tobias Rankin might have prevented a catastrophe once, but now it's our turn."

Frank drums his fingers on the hood of the Camaro. He's looking out toward the glow of lights from Drake City. "All right. We'll do it your way. I have some gear I need to round up: night vision, motion sensors. Extra ammo. Kevlar. C-4."

"Explosives?" This plan is taking a turn I don't like but should have seen coming. "What're we going to blow up?"

"If a medallion holder hid it, and Domitian wants it, and he's running against the orders of the Ashen, we aren't going to let anyone else get their fingers on it. We'll find whatever it is, then we'll blast it to pieces."

My phone buzzes, repeatedly. Not a text, then, but a call. Sean's face grins from the screen. "It's my son. Hang on."

Frank rolls his eyes but settles on muttering over the map while I take a step away.

"Sean?"

"Dad! Dad, you've got to check the news!" His voice rises an octave and the words bump into one another. They're coming so fast. "Everyone's saying that other guy is—I dunno, he's like just sitting there!"

"Whoa, Sean, take it easy. Who's sitting where?"

"The other flying guy," he snaps. "He's floating over the edge of the city, out toward Mount Stafford. He's not doing anything!"

Hell. "Sean. Stay there. I'll get back to you." I mash the keypad, calling up the Internet browser. "Frank, we've got a problem. You have binoculars or something? It's Domitian."

"What? Where?" Frank moves to the car, starts rummaging in the back seat.

"Not sure. Sean said he saw him on the news—wait." I pull up a video posted on the Messenger's site. Dated a few minutes ago. "Listen."

The sound is tinny over the phone's speakers. "...authorities have been unsuccessful in attempts to signal the individual, whom police have identified as the man responsible for the death of eight officers in Newport yesterday. He's also the one who supposedly ripped the roof from Braddock Island Light. Individuals in the vicinity of Vine on City Center's west side and the neighborhood of Mount Stafford are warned to remain indoors..."

"Got him." Frank's leaning on the roof of the car, with his SCAR-L propped on a small black tripod. He squints through a massive scope affixed to the top. A sickly green glow illuminates the rim of the eyepiece. "Definitely just floating there. Arrogant prick."

I can't see what he does, but I know how to follow directions. "My backpack's up on the tower."

"So get up there and go pay him a visit."

I soar into the night sky, the mountain and city beneath my feet.

"Should be at your three o'clock, couple hundred feet up," Frank mutters through the radio.

"I see him." The gray shadow is nearly indistinguishable from the dark. Then police search lights cut across the sky until they fix on him.

He turns, arms loose at his side. "Ah! Airfoil." We're barely a hundred feet apart, floating a thousand feet in the air. His voice booms with confidence across the distance. "I'm pleased to see you received your invitation."

"Ballsy of you. I didn't think the Ashen went for showy tactics. Between this and your other appearances, I think you're going to get poor marks on your report card."

Domitian chuckles. "They're fools limited by lack of vision. You, on the other hand, you have a boldness I admire. I've been watching you for a while now. I think you'll be far more receptive to my proposal than they were."

"I'm not here to listen to anything, except the sound of me accepting your surrender." I raised both hands. "Now's your chance."

"Bold, yes, but not the brightest. You really are enamored with them, aren't you?" He makes a flippant gesture at the sprawl of city lights below. "Those are the ones who should surrender, to the likes of you and I. Have you no concept of the power around your neck? We are the ones who have authority."

I glare at him. He's talking slavery, conquest. Not of my city. Yet the only counter that blurts from my mouth is, "A servant is no greater than his master."

His laugh cuts me worse than a knife. "A servant? You've touched on the problem. We were not meant to serve. These medallions are God's gift, so that we can lift mankind out of chaos into order. Our kind—both the Garrison and the Ashen—need not be separated by the conflict that has kept our powers barely effective for centuries."

"But there's a balance to maintain. I don't understand."

"Yes you do. You only refuse to admit it." He flings his arms wide, as if to embrace all of Drake City sprawled out beneath us, a heap of glittering jewels for him to scoop up. "Not only that, you've been doing what you claim not to understand—Brandon."

Cold creeps through me that has nothing to do with the medallion's power.

"I know who you are. I've seen what you do in your daylight hours. The contents of your inbox, the receipts of your grocery trips, the color of your dining room linoleum—there's nothing of your life that's a mystery, Brandon. Though you've done a fine job masking yourself as Airfoil."

"That's enough."

"Again, your work is very impressive. No doubt your keeper is furious that you don't adhere to the Garrison's strict interpretation of necessary missions. You, on the other hand, see it as your duty to help others and save lives, to make things better."

"What you're talking about is stripping those same people of their freedom."

"Nonsense. It's taking custody of that freedom, lightening the burden of all their worries. We're not servants, we are to be served. They will be so busy following us they won't have time to fight with each other over the scraps. They won't have to be afraid of crime, because there will be none."

I shake my head. Yet how can I argue with him. Freedom has its perils. There are times I want to take it from others, from those who—according to me—do not deserve it. Hadn't I already done that, playing the vigilante? Hadn't I usurped the powers of the law?

My silence must reveal my turmoil, because he's nodding. "You do see. You do understand me."

"No. This is wrong. What you're proposing is murder."

"Cleansing. Purification. Once we're done, Drake City will be purged of its dregs and only the strong will remain. And what will those few strong ones do when they see us? We, who wield the power of God. They will worship us. With an army at our backs we will rebuild the city into a citadel that can withstand any assault from without and be protected from insurrection inside. From here, we will spread across the nation and unite medallion holders everywhere to our cause."

"The Garrison and the Ashen have their treaty." I can see my watch's glowing hands out of the corner of my eye. Need to stall for more time. Frank's still listening; the radio crackles with static on his end. Where are the police?

He waves off my objection. "Garrison. Ashen. It doesn't matter. All will join us, or they will be eliminated. The more who flock to our banner, the more power we gain. My acts will force their hand: reveal themselves and fight against us, or stay hidden and watch the world they claim to sustain fall to our reign."

"You can't get an army to follow you. How can they possibly stand up to the Garrison? They won't let Drake City be taken over."

"Really. Just as your keeper lets you deviate from your missions to save the locals? Don't patronize me. If it suits the Garrison's grand, elusive purposes, they will allow this city—any city—to be ruined." He points straight at me, an arrow to the heart. "But as it happens, I know they will turn out to stop me, because the secrets hidden deep in the foundation of Drake are too tantalizing to ignore."

"I don't know what you're talking about." If anyone knows the history of this city's founding, it's me. From trading post, to fishing village, to shipyard, to commercial hub for the entire region, I know every era and every industry. There's nothing that could possibly give him the power he claims he'll unleash.

Except...Tobias Rankin's scattered bits of information about the medallion's history piece together in the back of my mind. All this focus on the mines and Frank's comment that they've been dug up over the centuries.

"The mines." I'm muttering aloud, eyes wide with abrupt realization, thankful he can't see into my mask. "You're looking for a medallion, in the abandoned mines."

"Hardly something so mundane."

"It can't be. There's...more?"

"Not a single medallion, or even a cache of a few, but a source. Imagine an object that can been carved and shaped into medallions. The legend has been with the Ashen for the entirety of its existence—whispers of a source that will bring whoever possesses it enough power to upset the balance between our two leagues. When I say upset, I mean one side or the other will be obliterated."

"The Garrison won't..." I can't finish. More medallions. Would the Garrison wipe out the Ashen if it had the means? I'd like to say no, they'd take the honorable route and force a surrender, a confiscation, something. I don't believe it for a second.

"Don't you think they've heard the rumors? I'm surprised they haven't told you or your keeper." He laughs again. "Or perhaps your keeper is keeping more secrets. You've already noticed a few, haven't you?"

"All those medallions—no one could stop either side."

"You're getting it now." Domitian points at the city. "You

understand why things cannot stay as they are. The millennia of hiding, of slipping from shadow to shadow in nation after nation, is over."

There're lights on the horizon, off over his left shoulder. Red and green pinpricks, moving in formation. "Police have three helos inbound," Frank says. "ETA two minutes. Loaded for bear. You're going to want to duck."

That's crossed my mind. But I have to keep him here until they're in range. Keep him talking. "This won't work. I won't join you because innocent people will die, and that's not going to happen in my city."

"Technically, Brandon, no one is innocent. Basic theology. All are tainted with sin. We can harness the fear that accompanies sin as our driver toward rule."

"Don't you dare distort what God says," I snap. "I'm the first to admit I don't have it all nailed down but that doesn't mean you can claim to be in the right."

He laughs. "Distort God? You insolent mongrel, I am God. I'll rain judgment upon you and our inferiors. Why do you think I've entertained you with my soliloquy?"

He's spotted the helicopters. I put out my hand, send a burst his way, enough to tumble an automobile like I did in the mob battle.

But he's turned his left side toward the helicopters and his right toward me. Casually flicks three fingers. My airburst separates in two—I see it clearly in my imagination. Barely ruffles his clothing as it breezes by.

"You savage idiot," he snarls.

A wall slams into me. I erect a shield just in time to avoid broken bones. As it is, I tumble end over end, hurtling down. Stars above and streetlights below meld in a dizzying swirl of colors. My body and limbs feel pummeled.

A voice booms out across the sky, but it's not Domitian. "This is Captain Urquhart, DCPD! Desist and surrender or you will be fired upon!"

Domitian reaches for the helicopters. They're Blackhawks, painted a pale gray and marked with blue police stripes. The first one doesn't have time to respond. It freezes in midair, shuddering. It continues to shake, oscillating wildly, until the props shear off at blinding speed. The helicopter tears itself apart, reduced to fragments of metal and plastic and wire, spraying fuel from severed lines.

Six men tumble to their deaths.

I dive for them, ignoring the approaching lights, wrapping them in a wide field that looks, to me, like an invisible bag. I make it tie tightly, until all six are mashed against each other. With only a dozen feet to spare, I bring us out of a dive, over a high-rise with a rooftop penthouse and the glowing blue outline of a swimming pool. My speed slows enough for me to release the field. All six splash, dead center.

No time to check on their well-being. I corkscrew back up, throwing myself at Domitian, just as gunfire explodes from the remaining two helicopters. Domitian darts like lightning. One moment, he's right in front of me. The next, he's gone. A tremendous fist slams into my right side. I thrash at him, connecting with his ribcage. But instead of being even slightly injured by the blow, he wraps me in a field so constricting I can't breathe. He yells in rage and hurtles me like the world's largest fastball at the two helicopters.

They veer apart, and I do my best to recalibrate my field, to gain a semblance of control over my trajectory. Instead, I graze my shoulder and my head on the side of the nearest chopper. A ringing fills my ears.

The chatter of machine guns and the roar of the rotors obliterate. I see now that both choppers are firing machine guns from their sides. Domitian's field sparks so badly I can barely see his silhouette behind the deflected shots.

The shape of that field, outlined in sparking bullets, distorts.

The sparks stop. The helicopters' cockpits explode glass. Lights shatter and wink out. Bullets tear into the fuselage. I can hear every man aboard cry out.

Their own weapons rip them apart.

The choppers lurch toward each other. There's barely a second to reach, and I throw an invisible cushion between them—but it's gone, because another great blow slaps me down as if I were no more bothersome than a gnat. Fifty feet above me, the helicopters collide and explode in a ball of fire. The tiny fragments that remain could be metal or man. I can't tell as they streak by me, flaming comets headed for the ground.

"You see the penalty?" Domitian thunders. "You've made your choice, Airfoil. It's a foolish one, and I know you'll see the error of your ways. Though it will take some teaching."

My radio screeches with static—and another sound. Gunshots? "Frank!"

"Perhaps this is the first lesson." Domitian points lazily at Mount Stafford.

A flame burns bright on the other side of the peak, the red-gold glow sharp in the midnight blue and black.

A great gust of wind and a tremendous boom herald Domitian's departure.

I hurry for the Barn.

The tower is in flames. The Camaro is a blazing heap.

A trio of black SUVs are tearing down the road, and even as I close the distance, automatic weapons fire on me. They disappear into the forest, and I could care less.

Where's Frank?

I land amidst the burning tower, hollering his name. Small explosions are dangerously near—ammo cook-off. I swoop up and out, arcing over the abandoned radar base. Something moves, near the tree line.

It's him. He's smoke-stained, his shirt and pants burned along one side, and there's a sodden blood spot on his right midsection the size of a dinner plate. I get alongside, pull him gently off the ground.

"Acciai," Frank gasps. "Ambush. Didn't see it coming. Made 'em pay for it."

I look back to the Camaro. Four bodies lie still.

"Brandon."

"Easy. Just shut up for once, okay?"

He chuckles, and it devolves into a hacking cough.

"Don't worry. I got this." I stare at the burning Tower and hear the moan of sirens in the distance. "I got this."

Part Three

Fall

Chapter Twenty-Four

I'm freezing up here, while a ten story building burns below me.

The Ramsdell Apartments on Eighth Street blaze in the night like a torch, brilliant reds and yellows clawing at the sky after a column of thick smoke. The fire department says three floors are fully engulfed, and they can't get any men close enough to rescue the nine people trapped inside. Frank would tell me to stay clear, reminding me of my failure to stop Domitian.

He disappeared again not long after that attack. Supposedly spelunking. But for almost three months? So it's just me left to literally put out the fires.

It's the eighth arson in as many weeks.

I keep the field steady around me as I swoop to the building. Heat assaults me. The street is littered with fire engines, police cars, and news vans. Somewhere overhead, a helicopter blasts by. I don't bother looking to see if it's media or police. Shouts draw my attention; a row of golden-leafed elms ignite, matchheads struck close to the fireplace.

The radio's silent. Frank's not helping on this one. All I get is static when I try the frequency.

A scream carries across the air from the eighth floor. Flames leap through windows on the seventh. Whoever's left inside is

Airfoil: Origins

headed up. I bank my course and auger through an open window at the corner of the eighth floor.

It's a living room so thick with smoke I can barely see. Something shatters, and I look to down, navigating over shards of a ceramic vase surrounding a soggy plant and heap of dirt. A woman rushes past me, yelling at two boys who can't be older than six. All are dressed in their pajamas. Hers are pink and spattered with white clouds; theirs are blue and green camouflage. None seem to have noticed a man in a black jacket and blue jeans has flown in and knocked their begonias off the windowsill. "Hey!"

They stop. The mother stares at me, mouth open. "Oh no. No! Get out! Get. Out!"

She rushes for the bookcase on the other side of the room and comes up with Mace. "Ma'am, please, we've got to get you all out of here. This whole place is going up!"

She's wide-eyed and frantic. The boys cling to her legs, but their expressions are unadulterated awe. The blond-haired one pokes his black-haired brother and hisses, "It's him! Airfoil!"

"You have to help us!" The mother gags. "The stairs are full of flames!"

"Okay. Is there anyone else up here?"

"I don't know!"

Enough of this. I grab her around the waist, and instruct the boys, "Hold on to your Mom tight, okay? We're going to fly."

"Cool!" the blond says.

Problem: the window's too small for all four of us. There is a fire escape but the ladder's ripped free of its underside. If we climbed out and then took off—

The floor shakes hard enough to topple another vase. Flames roar and crackle even closer. I glance down the hall to their apartment door. Orange light seeps underneath.

"Sorry about this, Ma'am," I say, and extend a hand toward her living room wall.

It needs a sledgehammer.

I give the field the image of a massive fist punching out, and it responds as soon as I summon the picture. An eight-foot-wide hole blows outward, spraying sheet rock, shattered studs and broken brick everywhere. The mother and the black-haired son scream. The blond whoops.

"Hang on!" I lurch into flight. Steering myself through the air is instinct now; I'm as deft as any bird, riding air currents, manipulating the slightest quirks of gravity for maximum speed and smoothness. It's something else to throw yourself from a burning building, arms wrapped around a lady you don't know, tuning out the yelling from her and her kids. I'm straining to keep all of us enveloped in the invisible warp.

So, I exhale deeply when we land without a bump on Eleventh, just beyond the line of emergency vehicles. She touches the side of my helmet, tears cutting clear paths down soot-stained cheeks. Everything reeks of smoke. "Thank you. Thank you so much."

"You're, welcome."

The blond kid hollers so loud I worry for a moment he's injured. But he just grabs the front of my jeans and says, between coughs, "Can we do it again?"

"Sorry. Got to get up again." I leap straight off the pavement, leaving him yelling at me from below. In seconds I'm back up on the floor.

The fire's reached the eighth floor. Flames lick under the doorway into the family's now vacant apartment. I skim along the side of the building until I come to a window that looks onto a hallway. With a focused blast from the field, I break the window and hit the floor jogging.

"Hello! Is anyone up here? Hello!"

"Over here! Hurry!" It's a man's voice, pitched high with fear. He stumbles around the corner, mid-twenties, shaggy brown beard and unruly hair, shirt and boxer shorts. He's got a cut on his left arm, dripping blood. He and a shorter, thinner woman with blond pigtails and wearing flannel pajamas have an elderly woman in a yellow bathrobe propped between them. She looks unconscious.

Three adults. I exhale. I can do this. Held an airplane up, remember?

Barely.

A heavyset black man and his wife exit an apartment just beyond them. He immediately takes over from the skinny girl, helping hold the elderly woman.

"Okay. All five of you. Hurry!" I move in, ready to assume the load.

"No. We've got her. Get the ladies down first," the bearded young guy says.

"I can take all five, don't worry."

"Just get my wife to safety!" The black man glances at his carrying partner. "And his. Move it!"

I don't wait a second longer. Over protests from both women—and a flurry of well-placed but ineffective slaps from pigtail gal—I grab them both and fly out the window. It's a much taller and wider opening than the living room panes that necessitated blowing a wall apart. Faster, faster, faster. But can't lose control.

The urgency trips up my concentration. I stumble on this landing, tripping off a curb. Almost drop one of the women but recover enough that we all slump onto the sidewalk. I gasp for breath. "Are you both—okay...?"

Pigtail girl slaps me again. On the mask. "My husband! Save him!"

"And you're welcome," I mutter, without so much as a backwards glance, and soar back up. My limbs and lungs are aching.

The flames spread. I swear the building's twice as bright as when I first show up. I'm thankful to see both men right by the window, clutching their neighbor as if she were their last load of treasure on the earth. The black man grins. "Never seen anything like it! You got to get her down next!"

"No more playing hero, gentlemen." I raise both hands. While keeping my own field intact, I siphon off a portion to wrap their bodies in what I picture as Saran Wrap—tight fitting, enveloping arms and legs and torso. All three are secure. Then I pull them toward me. We hurtle from the building as one lump of humanity.

There's a brief, happy reunion on the ground. Then I shoot back into the building. I have to make sure everyone's out. But with all the smoke and flames, it's near impossible to see anything beyond six feet in front of me.

For all his lies and obfuscations, I could use Frank's help about now.

My cell phone buzzes. Really? But it's not Frank summoned by my wishes. It's Sean. I answer. "This isn't a good time, Sean."

"Dad! I've been watching on the news. You got to get out of the area!"

"Can't. I have to make sure everyone's out alive."

"That's what I mean! The ninth one...there's been Twitter pix flying around. That crazy lady, with the robot suit. Someone, like, saw her coming into the building before the fire started!"

Acciai? Here? There hasn't been a sign of her for three months. Her or Domitian. But I haven't been looking either. Between arsons and gang fighting...

I form my shields. Not a second later, there's a tearing rumble from behind me, and the floor caves in. Acciai bursts up through it.

Word was she'd been torn up badly in the showdown with police in June, and her suit had not only been disabled, but confiscated. Whatever the case, she's gotten a refitted version: same black and silver casings. But this time, there're blades on both of her gauntlets. A helmet with a smoky colored visor gives the barest hint of the gorgeous face beneath it. The blades lash out, but I dodge them.

"Welcome to my party!" she shouts. "I've been hoping you'd get the invitation!"

I give a sharp push with the medallion's power, but she sidesteps it with ease, and all it does is bash a huge hole in another wall. Acciai opens up with her flamethrower—should have expected that—and a wall of fire pushes me down the hallway. Apparently, she's upgraded that piece of equipment, too.

I dodge a collapsing rafter that careens from the ceiling, slamming into the floor. The spray of sparks is as thick as a rainstorm, momentarily showering Acciai's faceplate. I can work with that, and this time, I strike fast with the field. Acciai bangs off the right side of the hall, then the left, then the right again, before I picture invisible claws that yank her right at me.

I wrap my arm in an extension of the field and punch her clean across the face.

It's a testament to the exo-skeleton's manufacturer that the faceplate doesn't crack. It does send Acciai reeling off balance. There's a split second in which I feel bad about hitting a woman—until my common sense comes roaring back and yells at me about her armored robotic suit.

Acciai spins swiftly out of her steps, and the blades tear across my chest. There's a double shock of searing pain. She's ripped open the jacket and left two thin red lines which trickle blood. Before I can counter, she unlimbers a huge weapon, one that swings forward from amongst the machinery on her back. I have long enough classify it as a stubby version of a .50 caliber machine gun when she opens fire.

Nothing hits me. It's because she's shooting the floor, chewing up tile and wood and whatever else is under my feet. It creaks, and groans.

The world falls out from under me.

I flail for something, anything, to break my fall, several

stories into a cauldron of flame. My fingers slap against a beam, slide off, then find purchase on a pipe. It holds. I pull up and grab on with my other hand.

Great. The fire's burned out a hole in the core of the building. My feet are still two stories above the ground, and there's fire all around me. The field is dormant, because my concentration got itself shot to pieces. I marshal it, ready for flight in less than three seconds.

Acciai aims her arm over the hole in the floor, and makes a gesture that, at this distance, mimics blowing a kiss.

There's a puff of smoke, and a blunt projectile drops my way.

Okay. She added a grenade launcher.

I let go, plummeting into the wrecked building. The still-intact third floor rushes at me.

Flying blind, I bank sharply, skimming the hall at three feet. A black rectangle. Window?

The grenade explodes behind me. The concussive wave can't be seen but is as potent as anything you'd experience in a hurricane. It buffets me, and I bash my shoulder against a wall, spiral down the hall, fighting for control., That window is ten, eight, six feet away.

I shoot out, a firework trailing smoke and flames. Everything in my body screams to collapse, to fall and never get up, but I will the field to maintain coherence. Up. Just. Get. Up.

I level out fifty feet away. The building's toast. I struggle to catch my breath.

Acciai. Two circuits around the building and adjacent blocks reveal nothing. She's gone, again, and I don't relish the implication. That was a bold move on her part. If she's been the one setting fires…

My phone again. I punch the answer key.

"Nice job, Dad." Sean's ebullient. "You should see it! They're interviewing the old lady, and those other people. No one got hurt—okay, so some scrapes and stuff. Smoke inhalation. But seriously! You were, like, better than Iron Man!"

I grin. "Thanks, Sean. I'm coming home."

The next day, still nothing from Frank. No text, no call, no email. There is a one old-school communique—a letter in my apartment's mailbox. By now, I know the drill: slit it open, dump out the piece of paper, match it with a section from the mine map he gave me. Another quadrant marked off. He's found nothing.

The handwritten scribble on the backside of the paper answers by next question: "Stay put. He's quiet; we stay quiet. I'll contact you when I strike gold."

So instead, I get some time for real life. I'm over at St. Andrew's, helping Kelly move her grandfather from his wheelchair into his bed. He barely acknowledges our presence. The nurse warned us that he's fading fast. Frankly, I thought the stress of relocating from the wheelchair would send him into cardiac arrest, the way he gasps and wheezes.

Not that I have room to talk. We finally set him down and I break out into body-shaking hacks.

"Are you okay?" Kelly's tucking his sheets around him but her eyes are on me.

"Yeah. Yeah, just got a sore throat." More likely, smoke inhalation. It could have been far worse, though. Grenades and steel blades are equally unhealthy. "Just have to get a glass of water."

"Well, you know where they are." She brushes back her hair. "Grandpa, is that better? Watch your breathing."

His breath is still sharp. "Are you a new nurse? It's too cold in here."

"No, I...The thermostat's at 72."

"Too cold." John shivers. "Are my children coming?"

"No. No, they're not, Grandpa."

I fill a glass from the tap in the kitchen and slug it down. It clears up the tickle, for now. John scowls at her, an abrupt change from the placid, pasty expression he had a second ago. "Don't tell me that. You don't know. Stop calling me Grandpa."

Kelly slaps the wall and spins from the edge of the bed, arms clasped about herself.

"Hey, what is it?" I put a hand on her should.

She shrugs out of it and pushes me away. "Stop it. Just stop it. Don't try to make it seem better than it is."

"He's sick, Kelly. The doctor told us this...he's not improving. His mind isn't—"

"I said stop it!" There's a fury in her eyes I've never seen before. Ever. Not even when the two of us held down the fort after a four-day weekend and everyone and their mother was bringing back a stack of books you could carry in with a forklift. "I know what they said! I'm so tired of it! Tired of coming in here and trying to be family. The only family he has right now. Did you know that? No one else comes here to see him anymore! It's like they're all waiting for him to die."

I absorb the hammer blow of words. They're not aimed at me anyway. But if I stop them, they're only going to build into a bigger explosion. Kelly stalks further into the kitchen, casting a wary, tear-stained gaze at John, but there's no indication he's heard a word. He just stares out the distant window at the garden, replete with red and gold leaves. "I can't do this anymore. I can't come in here and smile and pretend everything's going to be okay when he never remembers me. He doesn't know me, Brandon. How can he still love me if he doesn't?"

"I don't know. I've never dealt with anything like this. But I know you've shown more patience, more love, than anyone I've ever known." I know Samantha comforted a man dying of a gunshot wound, watched her weep as she talked about the light disappearing from his eyes. This had to be just as hard, perhaps more, so for Kelly, because it dragged on and on, a constant torment.

"I need...I need to go outside. For a walk."

"I'll stay with him until you come back." I kiss her gently, wipe away a tear. "I promise."

She hurries from the room, leaving us two guys in silence. No TV playing in the background today. I take a seat on the edge of the bed and cough hard. It's a miracle my hair doesn't still smell like smoke from my bout with Acciai. Only took two showers to get rid of the stench.

John turns his head in my direction. His eyes are glassy, his chest rising in shallow motions.

"Not much for us to talk about, sir," I murmur. "Except maybe the bees. But it's getting too cold for them."

"Cold. It is too cold." He whispers something else, but I can't hear it.

Fatigue and desperation overwhelm me. I can save people from a burning building, risk my neck to break up a gang shooting in a busy street, but this...I can't fix this. Can't fix Kelly, can't fix John. It's adding up to a lot of can'ts, and I'm as tired of them as Kelly is of caretaking. Unsure what else to do, I lean in closer to better hear John. "Say that again?"

He clears his throat, and whispers, "I watch the bees because I want to fly again."

A gnarled hand, shaking from the effort, reaches up and grasps at my T-shirt. The medallion's hanging from my neck, dangling out the collar. His fingers snake around it.

"That's—some dream," I say, mouth dry. "Ah, you'd better let go of that. Personal heirloom."

He closes his eyes. He gets a beatific smile. "Now I remember."

Sharp cold jolts my body—but not like the usual. This feels as if tiny icicles are shooting out from my skin, instead of digging in. I'm expecting the field to coalesce around my body. Nothing.

Instead, John lifts his free hand a couple inches off the blanket. Forget trembling—it's rock solid.

Metal clacks. I glance over my shoulder.

The wheelchair hovers off the floor, its handles bonking along the ceiling as it floats from our side of the room, past the kitchenette, into the restroom. John twists his hand, and it zooms back in, coming to a sudden halt right over my head.

He chuckles, a soft, but confident sound. A handful of seconds pass before he removes the aerial hazard and deposits it in the same corner of the room from which it took flight. John sags against his pillow, chest heaving, with a smile firmly in place.

A stab of cold shoots back into me. I stare at him. "You... how did you..."

"Forty-four years," he wheezes. "I had to give it to another, when I couldn't maintain it any longer. Still...thank the Lord. Forty-four years I served. For God and country and the Garrison. Never forget that. Never. Airfoil."

I can't think of anything intelligent to say. I tuck the medallion back in my shirt. He used its power as easily as I did. Did he have to retire from the Garrison, as Frank did? What else did he know about it?

John's expression shifts, and it's as if the last two minutes were a mirage. He glares at me. "Are you the nurse?"

"No, sir. It's Brandon."

He rolls onto his side and breaks into a fit of coughs. "I don't want to see the nurse."

"But...the medallion. You had one, didn't you."

No response. His body barely moves, rising and falling with each breath.

"How did you use mine? I thought only the medallion holder could access that power. No one ever said—"

"I have to rest." He coughs again. "Go home."

I sit back, lapse into silence, waiting for Kelly to return.

Airfoil: Origins

Monday morning, September 5. Sean and I are quiet while taking an early morning bike ride downtown. Sean has the day off on account of a teacher in-service day at his school, so he offered to join me when I headed out early. What I really need is time alone to clear my head, but since my teen son is deigning to spend time with his old man—unsolicited and without a guilt trip—I alter my plans.

Sean's bike handles are swathed with duct tape; black paint has peeled off, revealing chrome underneath. I cycle through memories, searching for the last time he rode it. I come up blank. Instead, I'm glad for the opportunity to make new ones.

We take 11th all the way to the bay, then head along the shore to the Maritime Museum. This early, there's a substantial chill in the air, frost sparkling along the edges of car windshields. But the sun's rays beaming around Mount Stafford are already melting what little there is.

After a good, long loop down to the boardwalk, we stop halfway up on the return. Our bikes lean against the back of benches facing the bay. A handful of runners sprint the wet sand forming the border between the beach and the waves. Eight women of every age are stretching into yoga poses from which I'd be hard pressed to untangle.

Sean's watching his phone out of the corner of his eye, but as per my request, he doesn't pick it up. Instead, it sits on the bench beside him, dark. I can only assume he's watching for an indicator light that heralds news—another fire, or a robbery, or gun battle. Something he's certain Airfoil should fly off to investigate.

My phone's in my back pocket. Still nothing from Frank. I haven't breathed a word about the incident with John Quirke to him. Not sure how to process it. It's one thing knowing a man such as Frank, who essentially retired from his role and continued on as a trainer. It's another to delve into the history of a man who's ninety and claims to have used a medallion for almost five decades.

Nothing from Kelly, either, for that matter. Just a single text late Saturday: <Roller derby practice. New league starting. See you Monday.>

Fair enough. She hasn't said much all weekend. After the explosion concerning her grandfather, I can't blame her. But I don't press for details. She doesn't want me to fix it and doesn't ask for a solution.

I take a deep breath, inhaling the tang of sea spray. There's a peace here, without the tourist throngs, that comes closest to what I found in the pews. "It's beautiful this morning."

"Yeah." Sean shifts, going all business. "Nothing exciting this morning. Been listening to the news and watching Twitter since like 6."

"What happened to taking the day off. You're going to be a disappointing teenager, Sean, if you don't at least pretend to slack."

He shakes his head, that familiar irritation with my lack of comprehension. "C'mon, Dad. Your buddy Frank's been gone for months now and you need to keep up your guard. Somebody's got to let you know when you've got to fly in and rescue people!"

"And that's you."

He grins. "I've done pretty good."

"Sure have." I get up. Need to do some push-ups before we set out again. I start in, wood of the boardwalk digging into my hands.

"Dad, can I ask you something?"

"Name it."

He's quiet a moment. When I stop after twenty and look up, he's drawing lines in drops of water on the bench. "Mom. She—you said she had like the same power medallion you."

"The very same one. It used to be hers."

"Well...why didn't she use it to escape?" He doesn't meet my eyes, and his words come out in a torrent. "She could have put a shield around herself like you do, or maybe lifted her own car—done something, I don't know. Why couldn't she save herself?"

I do ten more and, realizing he's not going to ponder these mysteries in silence, call it quits. "It's something that's kept me up me plenty of times, since I first got the medallion and Frank started training me. He doesn't know, either. He doesn't even know how the medallion got from Mom to me."

He nods. "I guess. Dunno. I was hoping one of you guys—could tell me."

"If I could tell you, Sean, I would. I trust you. Otherwise do you think I'd have let you in on the big secret?"

That gets another grin from him. "Yeah, right. I found you out. You didn't have a choice!"

I clap his shoulder. "That's what you think. There's always a choice. I could have lied."

"To your kid? Less than awesome, Dad."

"Some would say I should protect you by keeping you in the dark, ignorant of what I was really doing."

"I guess I get it. But don't ever do that, okay? I'm in this with you."

I smile. Didn't expect anything less from Sean.

We bike over to Hull Branch. It's the same route I take every Monday morning, past the same apartments and businesses, down to the same intersection of 9th and Hull. Only difference this morning is that, through the front door, all you can see are empty shelves. There are still books inside, just buried in stacks of boxes down the hallway to the staff room.

Jackhammers jolt me from my reverie. Sean's around the corner, pointing beyond the staff parking lot. "Hey, Dad! You see these guys?"

"These guys" are two dozen workers in T-shirts, jeans and Dickies bearing the logo "Sheehan Contractor Services." No surprise there. Ever since Danny Sheehan's last minute and overpriced purchase of the library property, he's had men working all around the grounds. No idea what they'd been doing. The fact that I couldn't find a single detailed plan, other than the basic permit on file with City Hall, only heightened my suspicion.

Today, it appears they're laying cable. Electrical conduit? That's what it reminds me of. Why they're putting in all that cable from multiple directions into a building that likely won't be standing...

I let us in the back door and stare off into the space. All Kelly's children's program decorations are gone. The paintings that have hung overhead for decades have left behind pale squares. The break room is empty. Even the couch is gone. Shelves stand bare. The whole place is a blank canvas.

Sean nudges me. "So... guess we better finish packing up."

"Yeah. Come on."

It takes us the next couple of hours to dismantle the computers from the public terminals and my workstation, taking care to box and label everything. Reed shows up then, banging the back door open. "Donuts! Got donuts for the superhero!"

"Reed! Secret identity!"

"Relax, Brando. Kelly's not here." He freezes mid-step, giant white bag of Howitzer's dangling from one hand and a tray of coffees in the other. "She's not...right?"

"No, she's not." It's just a jest. I don't want to tease too hard. His mood's been trudging uphill since the council voted to shut us down, thanks in part to Caroline and the kids making sure he's well-loved.

"Sweet." Reed tosses the bag. Sean snatches it midair. "Hey, Sean. Eat something. Let's finish packing up this mess."

His arrival makes the task of dismantling our workplace infinitely more cheerful, especially when his phone starts blasting Stone Temple Pilots. I carry the box containing my workstation clear to the back room. My memories flood back—shelving stacks of books, finding rare volumes for picky researchers, pulling down stories from tall racks for little kids, flying back and forth between the desk for DVD orders, troubleshooting word-processing problems. All those mundane activities that fill up a day and seem meaningless in the moment. Yet now, when this huge portion of my life is done, and my job is at an end, they're vital.

Sean brings back another box. It catches the edge of the door and tips over, spilling paperbacks. "Aw crap."

"Hang on, I'll help." I scoop them up, handing books over to him. A flash of metal from around his neck catches my eye—a gold crucifix, tiny with ornate arms, dangles from a black cord. "Where'd you get that?"

Sean blinks. His hand darts up, tucks the crucifix back into his T-shirt. "I bought it at youth camp. I think I was like eight."

"Forgot all about that. You find it recently?"

"No. I've had it in the same place in my dresser. It's just..."

"What?"

He chews his lip. "Do you think she's really, you know..."

"Keep trailing off and you'll never find out what I think."

"Do you think she's really there?"

"Where?"

Sean rolls his eyes and points at the ceiling.

"Oh. Up there." I rock back on my heels. "Used to be I'd just say I hope so, Sean. Nowadays, I know it. I'm certain. As certain as I can be without being with her."

"Thanks, Dad."

Someone knocks on the front door. "Tell them we're closed!" I holler out front.

"Brando! It's Eliana! You still want me to tell her to get lost?"

I sprint up front. She's waiting outside the front window, wearing a tan skirt and white blouse, denim jacket, and her maritime museum nametag. Her wave and smile are friendly enough, but I can tell by the way her fingers clutch at a small envelope that something's wrong. Her knuckles are as white as her shirt.

The air's warmed up nicely; fall chill is gone. She gives me a quick hug. "Hey, stranger."

"Hey yourself. What's new?"

"It's really empty in there. And dusty. Did you guys find a lot of spiders?"

"Sure."

"Fun. Anyway, I wanted to see how you're doing. With all this."

I shrug. "It's...a lot to process. Physically and mentally. All the books are being divvied up among the other branches. I don't think the main branch is taking anything, except for a few old first editions."

"Are you excited about the new job?"

"Yes and no. It's good pay, comparable hours. Tech services, mostly processing incoming books, and the like. But it's not the same as a small branch like this. My interaction with the public will be minimal. Not quite a dark dungeon they've stuck me in, but close."

She nods, taking in the view of the denuded library. She's not really looking at anything, though.

"Eliana." I gesture at the envelope. "What's up?"

She creases the paper, turns it over in her hands. "You asked me a while ago...it's Samantha's letter."

"You had it analyzed."

"I have a friend who specializes in handwriting. She's a genius when it comes to determining the difference between an individual's styles. It took her a while because...well, because it's so close."

"Close to what?"

"Read her report."

I open the envelope. Samantha's note is the first thing I remove, sealed as it is in its own plastic bag. The other item is a neat printout jammed full of jargon that spells out, in ostentatious verbiage, an undeniable fact.

Samantha did not write the note.

I stare at it, the breeze shaking the paper. Eliana watches me, not saying anything at first, until she apparently can't restraint the flood. "I'm sorry. I thought she wrote it, too. But there's no mistaking, not at this level of comparison. I had some letters and cards from Samantha, all the way back from our days at Bowdoin. My friend used those as reference points. Whomever wrote this, Brandon, went to a great deal of trouble to replicate her writing. The style, the word choices, the flourishes—it's all convincing. But when you subject it to analysis, you see the discrepancies."

"I know. I read them." It's the letter B. In Brandon. It's not the way she would write it, or so the report states. Somehow, that makes sense.

A lot makes sense.

"Brandon?" Eliana touches my arm. "I'm really sorry."

"It's okay." My insides are dull, leaden. It's one more lie. That's what I tell myself. But it's more than that. Everything I've done since I picked up the medallion, all my decisions were predicated by the knowledge that Samantha served a great cause, and I would honor her by doing likewise. Now, my mission and my wife's memory are desecrated.

No. It's not okay.

Chapter Twenty-Five

Frank finally calls me around 11 on Wednesday. "Where are you?"

"I think that's my question for you."

"Don't be an idiot. Meet me at the subway station at Haskins and 8th. Now." He hangs up.

I'm on the move. Sean's back at school but me, I don't have anywhere to be until the new job starts in two weeks. I set down the paintbrush and consider the near-finished work. The landscape is complete, with Newport's bridges in the distance. The figure in the foreground is indistinct. He's flying, but that's all I can focus on...blurred lines form a shadow. It's a question of how I want to portray what I feel. And then there's the question of why I'm compelled to paint this.

That's for another day. I grab my bike instead.

As I near the intersection with Haskins, it occurs to me that the subway station will be near abandoned this time of the day. At least, it will be for the next half hour, until everyone leaves their offices for lunch. I lock my bike to the red railing outside the stairs and trot down into the warm, fetid air.

There's a row of four turnstiles, guarded at the far-right end by a woman in dark blue coat and hat. She glowers at me, then returns her attention to a well-creased newspaper.

Then scratches answers to the crossword with a yellow pencil, sharpened down to a mere stub.

Frank stands on the other side of the turnstiles. He's wearing all black—a jacket, cargo pants, boots. They're all stained with dirt and grease. His face is smeared with gunk I hope is mud. It partly conceals the glistening pink of scars that reach up from the right side of his neck to the base of his chin—his souvenirs from the night we lost the Barn. He has a big, olive-drab rucksack slung over one shoulder. There're scabbed scrapes on his knuckles.

I pay the tokens for the shortest possible ride and cycle through the turnstile. "Frank."

"Come on. We're going for a walk." He gestures at my backpack. "Brought your gear?"

"I assumed you didn't call me for a sightseeing tour."

He scowls and walks down the platform.

There's no one around. Mold and mildew stain the gray stone. The lighted display of the Drake City subway system flickers in a few places. A whole section goes dark. I sidestep a pair of socks and discarded hamburger bag that smells as if it's been there a few days.

Frank leads me down the stairs at the end of the platform, into the tunnel itself. There's a rusted metal gate guarding the way. He unlocks it, pushes it open. Once I'm through, I hear the lock click behind us. The ring of keys he used disappears into his pocket before I can inquire about their origin.

He doesn't speak a word as we enter a small access tunnel that branches to the left; he merely ignites a glow rod and unlimbers a huge, black Maglite from his bag. For my part, I chew over the words I want to use to confront him about Samantha's letter. But my curiosity about our destination keep my mouth sealed.

"Watch your step." He starts down a ladder in a hole in the tunnel. Water trickles down this passageway, cascading off broken stone and dripping onto dirt. I head down, taking care to grip the slick, metal rungs.

The cave extends deep into darkness, and I'm just about to ask Frank how much farther, when I hear his boots stop clanging on metal and splash in a puddle. A small, dim circle of light glows far above our heads. Frank's glow stick lights the room in pale green—ceiling so low I have to crouch, rocks ranging in size from pea to car tire. We head deeper, following a downward slant in the cave.

"Took me weeks to find this extension." Frank's murmur echoes around us. "Those charts don't show half of what's down here. This particular shaft starts out on the other side of the bay, at Newport. Not far from your Lobban's Cove."

"You think Tobias Rankin made it this far? It has to be at least four miles from the site of the old cove."

"There's no doubt. It reached all the way under Rittenhouse. I came up on the side of the hill out there; thought I'd lost the track more than once. There'd been cave-ins, excavations for new construction—lots of modern work." Frank flicks on his flashlight. The ceiling's now a couple of feet overhead, and the cavern has narrowed so that only two people can fit side-by-side. The air is damp and my breath fogs. "But this—this is the only cavern that comes this far under the western mainland portion of the city. Seventeen dead ends. That's how many I found."

"This would be the part where you say I should have helped you search."

He glances back at me. "I made it clear your orders were to stay visible so Domitian would have a target and not worry so much about what I'd been up to."

I grab his shoulder. "Frank, we need to talk."

He stops. Keeps his flashlight forward, but faces me, his expression stern.

Whatever anger I'd been nursing, whatever disillusionment, it all feels strangely muted. I'm suddenly tired of it all. "I know about Samantha's note. That it's a fake."

He stares at me, unflinching.

"You used me. From that first meeting, when you gave your grand spiel about the Garrison and its global fight in secret against the Ashen. You sold me on this...whatever this is, based on the promise that I'd carry on Samantha's legacy. It was a lie." Now comes the anger, cold and bone-chilling as the sodden cave air. "You used my dead wife to con me into being an operative for your secret society."

Frank nods. "That sums it up, yes. I wondered how long it would take you to find out the note's forged. You did much better than I expected—I didn't predict it any sooner than Christmas."

"Enough lying, Frank!" I slap the cave wall, scraping my hand on wet rock. "For once, just tell me the truth. Everything we've done, and been through, you owe me that much."

"The truth. One could make the argument you've earned it. Though in my experience, the truth is hardly liberating. More often than not it's a roadblock." He stands there, flashlight braced behind his back, in military parade-rest. "I was tasked with securing your service as a medallion holder. This required months of observation, during which I reported your activities to the Garrison. After due consideration, and my recommendation, they decided to give you your medallion."

"Mine. You mean Samantha's."

"No, Brandon. Yours. That line I fed you about inheriting a medallion through marriage? As far as the Garrison has determined, it's bloodline only. Unless you have an ancestor who used a medallion, you can never use one. That's not Samantha's. Hers is gone. Lost in the same fire that killed her."

The revelation stabs me square in the chest, mingling with the cold pains from the medallion. Besides the note, it was the only link I had to my wife, the only proof I'd successfully carried on her crusade. No longer. "That means...the other medallion holder, Tobias Rankin, was my ancestor."

"Could very well be. He'd have to be, if you can use it. All I can tell you for certain is the medallion's not Samantha's."

"You could have told me that from the start!"

"Wrong. I knew, after seeing how you go out of your way to help everyone, you wouldn't be satisfied with blindly following the Garrison's orders. I gambled that making up a story about Samantha's desire for you to follow her would convince you of that necessity." Frank chuckles, a mirthless sound. "She'd have told me I was a moron. Yes, I really did train her. My plan backfired, though; not only did you not willingly become the Garrison's tool, you took her note and this medallion as—I don't know, your sign from God that you were meant to help people.

"But as sometimes happens—rarely—I was wrong. Domitian is not playing by the treaty. He openly challenged authorities. He's staged very public events. Not unlike you, actually. The Garrison is deathly afraid of what he'll do next, and terrified that no one from among the Ashen has tried to stop him. You see, both groups are fossilized. They've held the old battle lines so long, in such secrecy, that they can't comprehend doing things a different way."

"How does that concern me?"

"You're the hero, Brandon. You're the one who stepped out of the shadows and showed people in the city that a medallion holder can be more than some enforcer or errand boy." Frank frowns. "You...did good."

I must be a foot taller. Goodness knows my swelled head could bump the cavern ceiling. It's better than when Dad cheered my first solo ride on the bike, sans training wheels. "Thanks."

"Well, don't let it swell your head, or we'll never get back up out of this cave." He prods me in the chest with the flashlight. "If you're waiting for an apology, it's not coming. Everything I did, I did for the Garrison and the safety of our world. Samantha would understand, even if she'd hate my methods."

"Say it as many times as you want, Frank. You lied to me.

The whole reason I got into this mess was false."

"No. Reading Samantha's note kept you going. You would have come to the same decision, eventually. I just accelerated your deliberation."

"Is that supposed to make me feel better?"

"Brandon, I'm tired, and I don't care. What I care about is making sure the Ashen don't get their hands on what's down here—and if that means working with you on superhero playtime, with the Garrison somewhat misdirected, I'm going to do it."

It's enough of an admission to take the edge of my anger. But if Frank think's I'm going to ever take him at his word again, he'll be severely disappointed. "Doesn't matter. I know I did what's right."

"Come through here and let me show you the last thing that has to be done." He shines the flashlight ahead, into a dark opening, and walks on without waiting for my reply.

What does he expect? Forgiveness? He's deceived me from the start. Lied to me about my wife. Played me as a naïve fool.

Yet he owned up to his sins. If I'm to carry on, I can't do it with that kind of baggage strapped to my back. I have to be willing to start over.

I have to take the first step.

The ground ahead is even more rocky, but the cavern feels less claustrophobic. The glow reveals a ceiling twice our height, and the room is wide enough to accommodate a couple SUVs parked end to end. Frank shines the flashlight at the center. Something bright reflects the beam.

There, set on a cairn of white and gray stones, is a medallion.

It's larger than mine—and as my eyes adjust to the lighting, I realize it's two hands across and the same height. A lumpen, misshapen mound of the same silvery tarnished metal as a single medallion.

Domitian was right. You could easily get dozens out of this

thing.

The pull from the center of the room is unmistakable. Bitter cold drags on every cell of my body, from toes to tips of my hair. My medallion—not Samantha's—digs against my chest with a greater intensity than I've ever experienced.

"You can feel it, right?" Frank closes his eyes. "It's—so much. Almost too much. Imagine what we could do with this. The Ashen? Please. They wouldn't stand a chance."

"We have to destroy it, Frank." My imagination is fertile enough to show me shadowy figures cut down by beings of light. The Garrison could easily destroy the Ashen. But how soon after would they use the same power to level whole cities? Power corrupts.

"I know. I know." Frank opens his eyes. He takes a long, deep breath. "It's tempting to carve off a few, though."

"Would you even have any idea where one begins and the next ends?" I brush the surface. Like touching cold itself. My fingertips are instantly numb. A rush comes into the field, so potent, I see the air pulse with modified gravity. A dozen stones of the cairn jerk into the air, free float for a few seconds, then collapse with a clatter.

"That's not ominous," Frank murmurs.

I hope he's brought a container for this thing, but before I can suggest a next step, more stones rattle free of the cairn. The rest vibrate in places, like chattering teeth. Soon, the floor and walls of the cavern shake. I stagger back.

"What did you do?" Frank snaps.

"Nothing!"

The right wall of the cavern rips away, falling back in on itself, tearing a huge gash along the length of the room. Dust billows in. Frank drops his backpack, rummages in strobing motions caught by the flashlight's beam. Metal snaps together.

Domitian floats through the newly carved opening. "Gentlemen. Such a pleasant reunion."

Frank's back up, holding his SCAR-L, which has appeared like magic. No words, no warning. He opens fire.

The shots spark in the air around Domitian, same as they do with my deflection shield. Domitian grasps empty space with his left hand. The SCAR-L bends, its barrel snapping clean off, and flicks up out of Frank's grasp. It mashes against the ceiling, reduced to flattened metal, no more a threat than a crushed soda can.

After this momentary distraction, Frank lunges forward the instant the gun leaves his hand. He ducks a blow from Domitian that slams me against the far wall. But with my shields up, it doesn't do anything more than knock the wind from me. Frank comes back up, crouched, holding an LHR combat knife with a seven-inch blade of flat, black steel. He slashes at Domitian's legs, moving with such speed that his opponent barely has time to swoop to the other side of the cavern, out of reach.

There's a line of red on Domitian's gray-clad leg. Blood drips on the floor.

He snarls, an outraged beast, and seizes Frank with the field. He lifts him off the ground until his feet dangle. But the knife stays gripped in Frank's outstretched hand. Domitian slowly closes his own fingers.

Frank's arm moves, bending in toward his chest.

He grunts, grimaces, sweat pouring down his face. The blade moves, as if of its own accord, propelled by a hand that defies his mind's orders to stop.

I throw my own extension of the medallion's field, enough of a reverse grasp on Frank's arm that the inward motion stops. Immediately, a section of the cavern wall, jutting from above the medallion source, snaps off from the rest of the rock and hurtles at my head.

My concentration splits, keeping the restraining arm image tucked into one corner of my head while I reorient part of the field into a globe of increased gravity. The rock runs headlong into it and smashes to the cave floor, throwing up a spray of dirt.

Domitian laughs. "Good. You're learning. Very good. Let's deal with this matter as equals, shall we?"

The knife flies from Frank's hand, impaling itself in the cavern floor. A flippant gesture from Domitian sends him pinwheeling backwards, into the tunnel we traversed earlier. Another gesture, and the cavern shakes again. A car-sized chunk of the walls collapses across the entrance, sealing it off from us.

I throw everything I have at Domitian. Subtlety has no place; I give him a sledgehammer of a blow.

It may as well have been a sneeze, by the way it pushes him back without so much as rustling his cloak. He throws me aside with minimal effort, it seems, but I'm ready for this tactic. I reorient in midair, feet pistoning against the nearest wall, and I shove off with a burst of speed, like I'd practiced in the fight with Acciai and again on the street gunfight. It leaves me in Domitian's personal space, which I promptly further violate by ramming my shoulder into his midsection.

His hands grasp the back of my shirt and twist, spinning me off. My head careens off the ceiling. My vision goes wildly unfocused. Glad I have the helmet.

"Are you really going to continue this schoolyard brawl?" Domitian sounds more than irritated; there's frustration evident in his tone. He's also pressing his arm across his gut, which could mean that I actually hurt the guy. "Stand still!"

The blast welds me to the wall. I can't free a hand, a leg, any part of my body. Can't even turn my head.

"Brandon. Would you prefer I address you that way? This Airfoil name is unnecessary down here, with a colleague and an equal."

"If I've got to call you by a dead Roman emperor's name, you'd better stick with Airfoil," I snap.

"Fair enough. I see no reason we can't be reasonable." Domitian reaches up and removes the flat, featureless mask of gray that obscures his identity.

"You've got to be kidding me," I mutter.

Mark Vanchev, director of the Drake City Free Library System, beams back at me. Same confident smile on the same rugged features that assured me and my friends that he'd fight to save our branch, who put his political weight behind our benefit. He takes a moment to fix his hair. "I know what you're thinking."

"You really don't."

"Don't I? One thing you should know by now, Brandon, is that nothing is accidental, nor is it coincidental. I am of the Ashen. I've researched the bloodlines. How better to know a potential ally or enemy? My fortune improved greatly when I learned of your application to our institution. I let Mr. Andreen do the hiring, but I made certain you were approved by the board of trustees. I wanted you right where I could keep an eye on you."

I struggle against the invisible bonds. No luck. There's no sound from behind the cave-in, either, meaning Frank's either trapped, or worse, knocked clean out.

"You refused my offer. That's fine. I'd hoped you'd see the error of your ways. It was blindly simple to stay quiet for a few months and let your friend Mr. Belasco bumble about underground. He did me a great service, that—finding the Source. I didn't know where it was. Yet, I doubt Mr. Belasco gets all the credit. You must have figured it out, somehow. Brilliant."

"You can go to hell!"

"You can cease being so melodramatic. You don't see it at all, do you? Your posting at Hull, the closure of the Branch, its purchase by Danny Sheehan...oh, very well, let me be blunt." He reaches up with his left hand.

Rock trembles, rips apart. More rock, thick dirt, comes pouring out. The fissure widens, into a conical breach that must go up thirty feet. White chunks of concrete tumble down, followed by broken wooden trusses, insulation, and finally, carpet. Water-stained carpet. I know that spot.

I stare up, at a distant opening that frames a miniature view of Hull Branch Library's ceiling.

"The Source is here. Right here. It has been all this time." Domitian shakes his head. "I had simply proceeded with the rewiring because I knew it was perfectly, geographically centered. But this…this makes it all the more fitting."

He places both hands on the Source. A hum builds. My bones vibrate along. Something swirls across the outsides—ripples in the air, as solid as the surface of the ocean. It pulses, increasing its diameter each time, until it's six feet across. Vanchev's—Domitian's—face becomes a tight mask of concentration. The bubble explodes outward, expanding at lightning speed. Cold washes over and through me, fading out as fast as it hits.

It's gone. But the Source remains, and Domitian releases it. It hovers at eye level.

"What did you do?" I ask.

"I used the Source to fulfill my ultimate goal. It has created an impenetrable field around the entire city, cutting it off from the outside world. Not unlike how we erect our own shields."

The entire city—trapped by this madman's command? He has to be lying.

Domitian holds the Source as proudly as a father cradling a newborn son "You can't fathom this power, Brandon. With this Source, I will usher in a new era, one that neither the Garrison nor the Ashen both will be unable to stop. Once a new set of medallions is given to new masters, once I have those bloodlines under my aegis, they will be immeasurably powerful. We will be immeasurably powerful. I offer you another chance: stand beside me and rule."

The strain of fighting against his field is wearing down my body, my mind. "No. Never," I stammer through gritted teeth.

He stares at me and removes a cell phone from his pocket.

"I anticipated as much. No matter. Let me do you the courtesy of a final phone call. To check on the well-being of your family, you see."

The phone lights up. A murmur echoes from the speakers, followed by a high-pitched, frightened question. "Dad?"

"Sean?" My mind freezes up. "Sean, what happened? Where are you?"

"Dad, I'm okay. There's these guys, they came and took me out—"

Domitian kills the call. "You see? He's fine. A bright boy. You must be proud."

"Where's my son!"

"He is safely tucked away and will remain so to ensure your cooperation. In the meantime, my faithful servant has unfinished business with you."

The field confining me to the wall contracts, squeezing against my sides, and yanks me forward until Domitian's face is a foot from mine. His gaze burns through me. "Stay clear of my path, Airfoil, or your son dies. It will be painful, I assure you, and when I'm through, I will deliver his heart into your hands."

With that promise, he hurls me up through gap in the ceiling. No sooner do I burst through the floor into the darkened basement of the library and up into the building itself than the field collapses. At least I think to wrap myself in a sheath that cushions the blow of my backside smacking into the roof. I slow my fall enough to land on the floor, shaky but standing.

Through the gap Domitian has ripped, I see cables—the same cables Sheehan's company installed. They snake all over the basement walls, through newly drilled holes. They're pulsing, much the same way the Source pulsed when Domitian enacted what he claimed was a city-enfolding wall.

He flies up through the hole leading to the cavern, soaring high in the air. In the distance, I hear great crashing, the sound of concrete crumbling and walls collapsing, like the roar of an avalanche. The ground trembles with impact.

I have to stop him.

The front of the library explodes in a fireball. My mind slows down—chemical reaction, gases expand and shove a wave front of air and gas, moving faster than sound. But that's not what gets me. An instant later, the air pressure nosedives, resulting in a vacuum. The secondary blast is a shockwave that lifts me from my feet. I tumble like a log, lost in a spray of glass and building materials.

A breeze rustles my hair. There's a crack in the side of my helmet. My ears ring. Voices, muffled. I feel footsteps on the floor rather than hear them. A pair of hands reach down for me. Grateful, I hang on to the arms.

Those arms are covered in black armor and pistons. They jerk me to my feet, and Acciai lifts the bottom of my helmet up. "I missed you," she purrs, and kisses me, digging her tongue into my mouth.

There's an instant in which my mind and body react, lust stripping away pain and disorientation. That vanishes when she pivots and throws me through the broken entrance to the library. I hurtle through, into the bright sunshine and cool air—blessed relief—before I rebound off the wall of the flower shop and skid on asphalt.

My hearing clears out. Words crystalize. "Keep him there! Don't kill him."

Don't kill me? That's directed at the two dozen men in the street. Armed men, clad in body armor and bearing heavy weapons—mostly AK-74s, with a smattering of AK-12s and shotguns. A handful are aimed at me. The rest, outward.

There're sirens in the distance, and three thin pillars of smoke, by my count. I watch them climb higher into the sky...

Then, they are suddenly whisked down and away, by nothing.

Tell me it isn't true. Domitian has to be bluffing. Yet, my eyes don't lie as the smoke continues to dissipate rapidly, streaking down on all sides, following a long curve. Just like the bullets. Domitian's field must be similar to the one I erect to block gunfire—increased gravity. Anything that touches it is crushed to the ground. A ripple passes overhead, catching sunlight and gleaming opalescent.

"You didn't believe he could do it, did you?" Acciai's exoskeleton boots crunch asphalt. She stands over me, hands on her hips. I catch a whiff of burnt air. "I knew he could. With his power, this city is ours now. Our army will root out all opposition, and the blood—there's going to be so much blood. Can't you smell it? Taste it? I'm going to share it with you, if you're good."

A creak of collapsing masonry fills the air. The left wall of the library turns to rubble. Some of it slips down an invisible curve, smashing against the floor.

He's got a secondary field inside. For what? Protecting the library?

No. The cavern.

Waves pulse out from the foundation, through the street, following cables out of the library and into buildings, spreading across the ground and up into the air.

"He's using this as the epicenter," I murmur.

"So, you can learn." Acciai comes at me.

I roll aside, hearing her armored fist shatter the road beside me. With a burst from a hastily constructed field, I leap off the ground, swoop into a tight arc. I shoulder between a pair of the armed men and circle back to Acciai, aiming for her exoskeleton's power supply.

But she's fast, already turning. Crackling bolts of electricity writhe from shoulder to wrist. Metal spikes protrude, four from each forearm, and the bolts leap at me. The strike catches me in midair. There's a thunderclap of white-hot light and I awake on my backside, just inside the ruined library entrance.

I cough, struggle to my feet. She's advancing, taking her sweet time. Why should she hurry? We're trapped in Domitian's playground, and she has an army. This many guns, combined with my exhaustion and inability to keep the field coherent—what is wrong with me?—has me cornered. "Stop!"

"Stop? Why should I?" Acciai spreads her arms wide. Electricity sparks from her fingertips, running up her forearms to her elbows. Every inch of her is covered with armor. Only the faceplate allows me to see her features, beautiful and terrible all at once. She takes a few steps into the rubble, mechanized feet smashing drywall and crumbling stone. "You see what power he's given me."

The men spread out around her, guns aimed.

I burst forward, throwing myself through the air. The shockwave topples the remaining shelves, tosses up papers and breaks the front desk in half. I have a second to realize I've destroyed the last remnants of my workstation before I collide with Acciai.

My field is solid now, a ram that blasts apart the congregated enemy. The armed men scatter like leaves, tumbling end over end. I barely notice, because I'm still shoving Acciai backward, a hundred miles an hour or more. We bash through the windows of the flower shop, exploding glass and bouquets in a blur of glittering fragments and riotous colors.

She frees herself from my grip. Wary, I reach out for her with the field, planning to fling her into the nearest wall. But she's got upgraded equipment. Crackling bolts of electricity, blue-white and hot enough to wilt flowers, leap across the fifteen feet between us. The jolt seizes every fiber of my body, turning me into one giant, cramped muscle.

"You're pathetic." She walks up closer, increasing the wattage.

I don't scream. I grind my teeth until they feel like they're going to crack, but I will not scream.

"Domitian was right. Everyone in this city is weak. Even you, their hero. Well, guess what? Your blood's going to have the sweetest taste. Then I'm going to round up everyone you care about and burn them from the inside out." She laughs, sounding giddy and drunk on her abilities. "Starting with your son. And ending with the woman you love."

I have both hands planted on the floor, in part because of the sheer agony. But it also lets me form a small, concentrated field underneath the floor, stretching three feet wide and ten feet long.

With a yell that burns my lungs, I rip the floor right off its moorings.

Chapter Twenty-Six

Acciai stands atop a half-foot thick panel of tile, wood, and metal,. The astonishment is clean on her face for the second that passes before I spin around and throw her back through the broken windows.

The floor, Acciai and all, spirals across the intersection, taking out the nearest lamppost. She hits one of the library walls that's still standing and knocks it over in a shower of concrete chunks and a cloud of dust.

The pain of her electric strike throbs, but I don't stay put. I'm up on my feet, and with one jump, I land before her. She's dazed, tottering, yet somehow still upright. Blood trickles from the crest of her temple and the corner of her mouth. She licks at it, swipes her tongue across her lips, and shudders.

We lunge for each other simultaneously, my fists dragging the field around them and her hands sparking with voltage. At the last minute, she shifts her stance, banking left. I thrash at her with a blow, catch the side of her suit, crumpling metal. Hydraulic fluid sprays out, thick brown-black. She stabs at my back with twin jolts that steal my breath.

I rebound off a half-collapsed wall and put on speed. This time, I grab on to her with the field, jerking her off her feet. We rocket up into the sky, angling through City Center. The financial skyscrapers flash by, and I catch a glimpse of my reflection—blue and red, the colors of my shirt and my blood.

As we grapple, we turn back toward Hull. Suddenly, the rumbling and crashing I felt when Domitian tossed me up out of the cavern makes sense: the sounds of construction. Domitian is right there, a thousand feet up from the library, motioning with his hands, as if directing an orchestra. Great slabs of asphalt and masonry bash together, reforming into smooth panels and jamming into the ground. He's erecting a massive wall around several blocks of Hull, with the barren sites of the summer's arson attacks as his foundation. No wonder he had Acciai burning them down.

The walls rise higher, up to twenty feet now, with more pieces of rubble hurtling into position.

Acciai stabs at me, and I barely remember to keep her out of arm's reach. She switches tactics; a gun barrel drops down from each armored wrist. No idea what caliber, but it's bigger than a shotgun.

I cut speed and start spinning her like a top.

She screams something I can't make out and opens fire. But at the speed I've got her twirling, the shots go haywire. Gritting my teeth, I release my hold on her with the field and put on the invisible air brakes.

I jerk to a sudden stop in midair. She doesn't.

Acciai flies off in a flat spin, straight toward the harbor—except the Fairpoint Mutual Investments tower is in her way. She smashes into the forty-somethingth floor, disappearing in a shower of blue-green glass and billowing white plaster.

In that split second, I try my radio. Nothing. Not even static. The blow that cracked it must have severed something. I'm on my own.

I tear after Acciai, ramming into the building. More glass and plaster explode around me. She's pulling herself out of a ragged crater that used to be someone's very well-appointed conference room. My next burst slams her against the wall, pinning her up like a tapestry. A short leap later, I have both her arms held against the wall, neutralizing the use of both her blades and her guns.

"Where is he?" I snarl, my visor inches from her. "Where is Sean!"

She laughs, the giddy sound morphing into a hacking cough. Blood stains her teeth. "I don't think I'm going to say anything. Nope. This is way too much fun. Besides, you're my reward for serving my master. Your son's nice and safe as long as you leave Domitian be."

I growl and fling her sidelong, through the wall—and the next wall, and the wall after that. Disregarding Frank's analogy about using the powers like a scalpel, I sledgehammer my way through the office spaces, leaving chaos and destruction in my wake.

She opens fire—literally. Flames blossom, scorching the office walls and setting them alight. Alarms sound. Sprinklers drench us.

With one hand extended, I block the fire, throwing myself through the gap. Next thing I know, we're on top of each other. I wrap both hands around the nozzle of the flamethrower and wrench it from its housing on her exo-skeleton. Even with the field as my extra force and a protective shield, the heat's unbearable. I stagger away, toppling a bookshelf laden with plaques for community service.

Acciai screams, lashing at me with the double blades. I dodge the swipes, losing chunks of my fleece, until a lucky blow jabs through the right shoulder of my jacket. Now I'm the one pinned, up against the wall, my feet dangling.

She slices with her free arm. I grab her wrist with both hands, halting its progress as well as the razor-sharp blades inches from my visor. Pistons whine as the exoskeleton adjusts to the resistance, shoving those blades ever closer.

I pool a portion of the field into a flattened globe between us. This is going to hurt. What else is new?

The reversed gravitational field blasts Acciai sideways, into yet another room of the wrecked office, while flinging me in the opposite direction. From beyond the wall, I hear glass shatter and the long wail of Acciai falling a terrible distance. I pick myself up from the tangle of cooked vines and leaves that used to be an impressive bookshelf plant.

I make for the window, eyes open for Acciai. Wind blasts through a gaping hole in polarized glass, making me pause a foot from the edge. It's a straight drop at least forty stories to the pavement.

A roar echoes from my left. The spray of bullets impact on my shield with enough force to throw me off balance, my field not formed. I fall, tumbling six floors before I right myself in midair.

Acciai swoops in at me, upright and leaning forward, like a woman-sized predator beetle. The air behind her wriggles with heat waves from whatever's giving her propulsion. Apparently, she too can fly. Perfect.

She dives for me, and I dodge, dropping headfirst into the maze of buildings around us. If I can get her low and moving fast enough, I can trip her up. No way she can match my maneuverability. Not judging by the way she barely banks those corners. I aim for a pair of twelve-story hotel towers, willing the field to warp gravity between them. I see it clearly, an imagined net, given form by the medallion.

I have to disorient her, trick her, get her to reveal where she's got my son.

A handful of stories above street level, I realize my mistake. I'm not the only one planning an ambush. Two large SUVs blaze down the road. They swerve into position three blocks ahead, their hoods nearly touching. Eight men leap from open doors and lean out of the windows. Bald heads, tattoos on bear arms —they're wilki. Correction: now they're Domitian's army.

The makeshift blockade erupts with gunfire. Bullets spark

off my field as I take fire from all eight AKs. My flight path wobbles, and the field I've stuck between the two buildings fades from my vision. I grind my teeth. Splitting my concentration has limits. Fine.

I'll clear the road out first.

Putting all my will behind the shields and my speed, I dive for the road, pulling clear with ten feet to spare. Buildings, trees, and asphalt blur as I tear down the block. These guys are no slouches—their aim is dead on, pummeling me as the distance shrinks with incredible swiftness. I've got no idea of my speed. And I don't much care.

One block out, I strip half my shields away, the bottom and back portions, and reform them into a wedge of reduced gravity. Think standing on the surface of an asteroid. You'd float right off. If you happened to be hunkered behind an SUV while shooting an assault rifle in regular Earth gravity and someone suddenly flipped a switch—

The wave catches the SUVs under their front wheels. They flip up—and I mean, twenty feet up. The men go sprawling, terrified shouts interrupting their endless stream of weapon fire. Turning on my back, I reach out with both hands, grabbing hold of the SUVs even as I fly between them. I yank them back. They reverse course midair and smash into one another with a sickening crunch of metal. The combined mass drops to the street.

Eight men are sprawled all around, most of them groaning on the sidewalks, two are tangled in the branches of the chestnuts lining the street.

I land. Here comes Acciai. I brace myself, scrambling for a new plan, even as she lines up her arms. What's it going to be this time—blades? Fire? Electricity? Or plain old guns. She knows what it'll be when I strike back—

I smirk. So, let's change tactics.

Acciai gets within half a block, her jet thrusters giving the appearance of melting air behind her. She shouts something I probably don't want to hear and fires a projectile with a great puff of smoke. Grenade.

I zip sideways and forward, watching the grenade impact in the center of the road. The explosion happens in slow motion, clear enough for me to see the burst of flame, the expanding fireball, and the rippling shockwave. I reach out with the field, pulling my target off the sidewalk.

An AK-74 leaps into my hands. Safety? Flipped off. Switched to fully automatic. Works for me.

I take aim and fire. The sound is excruciating, even in my helmet. Never shot one of these before. A 9 mm pistol, yes. This?

My aim is terrible. But it surprises Acciai, judging from the sudden zigzag in her flight path. None of my shots hit her. After a few seconds, my arms ache.

Acciai swoops low, off to my right, weaving around a row of trees. She skids into a rough landing, tearing twin troughs in the asphalt. She bends over and grunts, pulling something from the surface. She twists sharply and lets whatever it is fly with a scream.

A manhole cover.

At this distance, all I can do is absorb the blow. It rips the gun from my hands, but I hold my ground. I let the impact spin me around in a full circle, ducking as I go. I push out with the field, hands aimed low. The strike rushes along the road, kicking up leaves and refuse. It hits Acciai in the reinforced robotic shins, jerking her feet out from under her and face-planting that crazed expression.

I close the distance in two seconds, but it's still enough time for her to get up. She locks arms with me as soon as we collide. Electricity flares. Heat and pain wash over me in fierce waves. I don't let go. I won't.

"You like to play rough," she snarls. "That's good. I'm going to give you exactly what you want because of that. I'm going to beat you until you—"

I never hear what precisely she wants to do to me, because

the blare of a car horn cuts off her manic speech. Acciai glances over her shoulder. A Honda Crossfire races up on us, top speed, with no intention of braking.

Reed's hollering behind the wheel, hand planted firmly on the horn.

He's going to get himself killed.

I break Acciai's grip—thanks to my best friend's distraction—long enough to tear the source of the electric charge from her exoskeleton. She rids me from her arms as if I had a contagious disease and aims her grenade launcher.

Too late. Reed sideswipes her, the black armor scraping with a hideous screech along his hood.

Acciai bashes into the wreck of the SUVs, but only for a moment. The next second, she leaps skyward, her jets carrying her over the roof tops in a blast of heat.

"Brando, hurry up! This ain't Uber!" Reed lays on the horn again.

I stagger to the passenger seat, collapse against the cushions. My body's got no strength. Everything's so cold. My teeth chatter as the medallion sends spike after spike through me.

"Hang on. Just hang on."

"Sean...she's got Sean."

Reed throws the car in reverse, and we hurtle backwards. then he jerks the wheel and we spin out in a messy version of a U-turn. He drops it into second and we tear off again. "We'll get him back."

"I'm—I'm run out, Reed. No power..."

"Yeah, Frank thought you might. He called me up. Said Mark Vanchev is a supervillain, and you were getting smacked around. He's on it. He said to take you somewhere safe for a couple minutes while he put his plan into action. His words."

I close my eyes, head reeling, stomach churning. "Sean. He's in danger."

"We'll find him. Just hang on."

It occurs to me I have no idea where another of my loved ones is. "What about Kelly?"

"She's gone off after her grandpa. Caroline's got the kids, there's a bunch of people in our building holing up." He slaps my arm. "But you need this. Just wait."

Reed doesn't crack a joke or flash a grin as he weaves us through abandoned cars. His Crossfire is nimble. More than once, we zip through an intersection after lights turn red but before traffic closes in. There are jams everywhere. Somehow, Reed keeps us clear of them.

"I have to get back out there," I say. Even to me, it sounds hollow. My head's still ringing.

Reed snorts. "Sure. You in your T-shirt and blue jeans. You forget the part where that loon bashed your helmet apart?"

"Okay, I get it. Secret identity. I think we're past that." The sky above shimmers, as if a heat wave were passing over asphalt. Domitian's barrier, controlled by the Source, keeping us all his serfs. "But if you're trying to get us out of the city, you're going the wrong way."

We screech to a stop in front of a U-Pak-It self-storage building. We're in Center, on First Street west, between Glassock and Conrad. All the buildings around are five and six-story offices, mirrored glass, gray and white concrete, the occasional red brick. The U-Pak-It has steep sides and bright yellow metal doors and window frames.

"Come on." We burst from the car at a dead run, with Reed leading me up to the locked gate. The air's full of sirens and smoke. An explosion booms in the distance, reverberating between buildings and sending tremors through the sidewalk. He pounds in an access code on the small lockbox and swears. "The lock's changed. Or the thing's glitched. Stupid—"

I put brute force into the medallion's field and rip the door off its hinges. It flies back and bounces off a tree across the street.

"Sweet." Reed slips inside.

Our shoes squeak on the polished, concrete floor of a wide halls. Dozens of yellow doors line either side, each with its own number. We make a couple of corners before we hit 311. This one has a simple padlock. Reed produces a key, opens it with one swift twist and pauses, hand on the handle. "Okay. You'll love it."

"Reed..."

"Aaaand pause for dramatic effect? Check." He yanks the door up.

My jaw drops.

Finally, that grin appears. "Right? I told you."

I stare at a mannequin, same as any you'd see modeling men's clothing, with arms straight at its sides. It's wearing a sleek, form-fitting suit of charcoal gray. A white armored chest plate wraps around the front, emblazoned with a stylized letter "A" in metallic blue. It's shaped to mimic someone running—or flying. There's more white armor, trimmed in metallic blue, at the shoulders, as forearm gauntlets, and running down the flanks and front of the legs to the knees. A white helmet with black trim crowns the costume. Aa wide faceplate of polarized blue and violet, shifting colors like a pair of sunglasses, reflects me with my mouth hanging open.

The whole thing boasts of strength and speed. It looks tough. And it looks like it could step out of the storage room and beat me senseless.

"Reed...what in...where did you get this?"

"Not off Amazon. I know some guys who do work for cosplay—they've helped with a couple of my costumes, when I needed custom pieces. Anyway. They incorporated some, ah, extras into this. Like Kevlar."

"You—they custom made this?"

He nods.

I shake my head, astonished. "And when you paid for it

Carolyn said...?"

"Not a thing. Because it's ComicCon money. And graphic novel money. I've been saving up since—well, since you hit the news, Brando. Came up with the design...oh, about June. Hey, man, I never thought the company would get it to me, but it arrived a couple weeks ago."

"You were planning to eventually tell me that you'd built me a superhero costume, right?"

"Eventually." Reed grins. "Hell of a time for the reveal, right?"

I can't believe it. Rather than say anything else stupid, I pace around the thing, staring. It looks as if it'd fit perfectly.

"You have to stop this guy, Brandon. You're the only one who can. Everyone knows it. But there's more to it than that." Reed scratches the back of his neck. He won't make eye contact and seems to be examining his shoes as he struggles for words. "You've become a symbol of everything right and good. Someone the people of Drake City can look up to. When they see you fly by, what are they looking at?"

I take the helmet off the mannequin and turn it over so my reflection watches me out of the visor. "A man doing what's right."

"Nope. Wrong." He taps the helmet. "They see a guy in blue jeans and fleece and a beat-up paintball helmet. Doing good stuff, yeah, but looking like an amateur. With things accelerating from bad to worse, they need more than just a guy who flies in and rescues people. They need to see someone inspiring. Someone who fills them with awe and makes them feel just as brave as you are. They need a superhero."

I've always known this and have never let myself get there. Figures Reed would simplify by shoving me forward. It doesn't matter what the Garrison wants: now more than ever, it doesn't matter in the slightest. I never sought the medallion, or the responsibility inherent in wielding it, but I have both. I won't let anyone down. I won't let anyone else hurt the people I love.

I won't give up.

I clasp Reed's shoulder. "Thanks. Really. There isn't a better friend alive."

He grins. "No kidding, Number One. Suit up."

"Frank's going to burst a blood vessel if he sees this."

"About that…"

I put on the helmet. A laryngophone presses against my neck. The speaker foam conforms to my ear. I reach up to the blue circle at the corner of the visor, give it a hard twist.

Static bursts. "I think the getup is ludicrous, and waste of money," Frank grumbles. "Both his and mine, your friend should note."

"Frank! Nice to hear you're alive, I think."

"No kidding." There's a rumble of an engine behind his words. "You and Acciai's spectacular mess gave me time to escape. Took a while because I had to go back the way I came. Also gave me the opportunity to retrieve something useful."

"I can't believe you helped Reed with this suit."

"Brandon, I'm never going to admit I was wrong more than once in a day. Get back to work."

Downtown is a madhouse. Domitian's men are everywhere—yet I realize they're not just the regular wilki. Some are leaner, more vicious in the way they loot and destroy. More to the point, in all my dealings against them over the summer I've never seen their faces.

New to town. Someone Krol or Cezar brought in. Frank warned me about the financier whom the Garrison wanted eliminated. Judging by the sheer numbers of these new men and the amount of heavy weaponry they've brought along, the Garrison was right to worry.

I bank over First Street, heading for St. Andrew's. This new helmet has a spectacular field of vision. The suit conforms to my body so that I feel every shift in the air currents and every crinkle in the field.

I dig out my phone and dial for Kelly. "Are you okay?"

"I'm fine. I'm with Grandpa. There's staff here trying to move a bunch of patients to Drake General. But there're men outside. One of the nurses, a big burly guy, tried to get them to clear off. They have guns." Her voice catches, whether from fear, or anger, or both, I can't tell. "They shot him. He's alive. The nurses and I stopped the bleeding, but he's badly hurt."

"Hang on." Am I going to tell her Airfoil is on his way? "The police should be there soon."

"I don't think so. There's a burning police car outside."

Well, she isn't wrong—I've just passed three more in flames. Whatever the local law enforcement is doing to combat Domitian's men inside this force field, it's not working.

"Where are you? Are you and Sean okay?"

"Everything's fine. Don't worry." I don't want her finding out. Sean knew my secret. Now the Ashen has him. That can't happen to Kelly, too.

I have to find him. Stop Acciai. But there's more people in trouble.

St. Andrew's spires rise ahead of me on Third. I see the men gathered down below, a block away. There're seven of them, and they block the way of six cars trying to get by—a pair of cabs, a delivery truck, and three other cars. There's a trio of ambulances parked in a row in front of St. Andrew's home.

"Get out! Get out of cars!" This one, a tall, rangy guy with a black leather jacket and shaved head, glowers at the nearest cab driver. He jabs the muzzle of an AK-74 through the open window. "You get out and give us money! Don't, and you die!"

"Uważaj! Up there!"

The warning draws all their attention skyward, so they get to see me, gleaming white and metal in the sun, as I barrel down on them. I don't even bother to form shields. Instead, I snake out the field into seven tendrils, seven tentacles that wrap around their waists. I pull them up.

The men flip off the pavement, shouting obscenities and crying out in panic. Without stopping my descent, I bring them rushing together until their bodies slap against one another with heavy thuds. They hover upside down.

I float in front of them. "Drop your weapons."

They all look to the bald guy in the leather coat who hesitates.

I sigh. Really? I have them strung up in midair and they still won't listen? I modify the field holding them, peeling off an eighth tentacle that slathers the lead guy's gun until it mashes flat as paper.

He yelps and drops it. His buddies follow suit.

A burly man in overalls and a yellow T-shirt hops down from the cab of the delivery truck. "Airfoil! All right! Hey, man, I got a place you can stash the trash!"

Without any prompting on my part, he hurries to the rear of the truck and rolls up a metal door. Not a bad idea.

I pull the men in close enough to hear them whimpering, and in one case, praying. "Don't go anywhere." And then I throw them in a quick arc that sends them right into that open door. They bang against metal walls, shaking the truck on its shocks.

The driver slams the door shut, locking it. He stands there, slaps the side of the truck with evident glee.

Right. "Thanks. You should get off the streets, all of you. Stay indoors and protect your loved ones."

The truck driver organizes the other motorists into a convoy, steering around them and leading them down the street. I don't much care what plans he has for his prisoners, and don't ask.

I land in the middle of the street, not far from the ambulances. Nurses and a couple of doctors move patients out, pushing wheelchairs and stretchers. A school bus rumbles down the street toward us. Something explodes at the waterfront, and there's the chatter of automatic weapons firing, tinny from this distance but still unnerving.

Kelly's with a female nurse, helping her push a stretcher. John Quirke lays very still, his face waxen, eyes unblinking. Whatever end he meets, I pray it's lacking in pain.

My radio crackles. "Brandon. What's your position?" Frank says.

"Third Street, St. Andrew's Church. Finished cleaning up a group of Domitian's men. They're all over the city, it sounds like—just heard explosions down by the dock. I'm going to check it out."

"Forget that. Head up to the bridge. Word is these punks are coming from Newport." That engine sound is in the background again, only louder. "I'm coming down Chennette Drive from upriver."

"That's not another Camaro, is it? Or have you been busy fixing the old one?"

"Funny guy. Just get over here. Don't wait for police help. Most of them are racing around the city, trying to help people, and getting shot at everywhere they go. Heard at least a dozen calls over the scanner of precincts emptying in response to the attacks."

"We could use some backup."

"I've put word out to the Garrison."

"I'm not holding my breath for them, Frank. We need help on the inside."

One of the ambulances speeds off, lights flashing. As I track its departure, I notice a car parked on the other side of the street. A really nice car, well-restored. Monte Carlo SS, perfect white paint job marred by dents and smudges.

"Hold that thought." I climb the steps to the church and push open the doors.

It's dark inside, and empty. Beautiful. Serene. I want to kneel in a pew, put my hands together, and just be there. It should be the most important place on the planet for me, if I'd been doing things right all this time. I want to bring Sean inside. I need to stay. There's nothing but the whisper of God's presence.

Almost nothing. I spot the lone occupant and remind myself of why I came inside in the first place.

I stride toward my target. He's hunched over, forehead pressed against clenched fists, dressed in khakis and a crisp, blue Oxford. One of those fists clutches a Ruger. My footsteps echo on the tile. It's enough of a warning that he twists in his seat. He aims the gun straight for his head.

"Lieutenant Marchand. I need your help."

Dennis glowers over the gun, his eyes rimmed red. After a couple seconds' deliberation, he lowers it. "Airfoil. Get out. Now."

Chapter Twenty-Seven

Dennis couldn't believe it. Airfoil. Here. In the place he thought offered the last sanctuary in his life.

He didn't have his radio on. He'd switched it off after the last twenty reports of confrontations with armed men, of explosions and firebombs destroying buildings—but the last straw was the call that claimed Airfoil was tussling with someone in an armored robot suit.

"You heard me. Out."

"Marchand, the entire city is trapped under a powerful field put in place by a madman. He wants to control everything inside. This is his kingdom, at least in his twisted mind." Airfoil didn't budge.

Marchand had to admit, he made a much more imposing statue in the white armor, clad over the gray jumpsuit. Almost like the real deal.

"Let me tell you something. You know why I'm in here?"

"I'm not going to guess at your faith. God knows mine is barely a thread of what it should be."

"Wrong. This is why." Marchand waved the gun. "To put a bullet through my head."

Airfoil didn't move or say anything.

"So get out! Get out of here so I can finish it!" Marchand

slapped the pew in front of him and rushed to his feet. "You fly around here since the Spring, saving babies and throwing cars. Meanwhile, I grub around after the real criminals, the real threats. I don't have any of your powers. I can't stop bullets or fight hand to hand with a psycho in a robot suit. Instead, I get dead cops, and my cases pulled off my desk. I get muggers!"

Still nothing. Marchand wished he'd back off. Just leave him to his decision. "Well? You got anything inspirational to prevent me from taking my life?"

"I was sorry to hear about your partner. But you're not going to kill yourself. You'd have done it by now. So, let's move on." He stepped in closer.

Marchand raised his gun again, muzzle on Airfoil's chest.

"Don't bother with that. You'll only shoot your toes off. Look, let me start over. Everyone knows you're crooked."

The words sliced into Marchand, with the same pain he'd dreamt over countless nights, tormented by Dillard's impalement. He could feel the steel gutting him, the agony that awoke him in a cold sweat. "Yeah, I got a certain reputation."

"You know a lot about the Polish mob, where they operate, who they work with."

"I used to."

"Where do they keep kidnap victims?"

Marchand frowned. "It's been a long time since they dealt in kidnap for ransom. Not since Krol was hard up for cash. Once he solved that problem, he cut that side of the business out. Never liked it. Made up for it in gun-running."

"Not what I asked. I need a place."

"There's a couple of rowhomes down in Little Warsaw. Between Sobieski and Kava. Try those."

"I need you to be more specific than that."

Marchand snickered. "I'll bet you do. Drop the hero act, okay? You know what's happening. It's over. Domitian has the city locked down. It doesn't matter what you or I do."

"You're still protecting them? After all this?"

"I'm protecting my future contacts and clients."

"You just said you were going to kill yourself!"

That stripped away the solemnity Airfoil had employed., Now Marchand had a truer insight into the man's emotional state. He was on edge. Marchand prodded him with the gun. "Be a good boy and go outside to play. Have fun throwing things around with your pal. I'm staying put."

The gun's barrel snapped off, with no more effort than a pencil breaking. Marchand stared at it, his mouth dry. The rest of the weapon flipped out of his hand, clattering against a wall somewhere in the shadows of the church.

"Acciai has my son locked away somewhere." Airfoil's voice was low and muffled behind the helmet. All Marchand could see was his own stunned expression reflected in the blue faceplate. "I'm going to pray for help, and in the meantime, you can provide that help. We can end all this. The police, they're doing everything they can to stop the attack out there. Get out of here and do something worthwhile for a change."

The word "son" blasted through Marchand's walls of self-pity. He thought of Caroline's kids, his nieces and nephew. He hadn't seen them in months. Caroline had made it pretty clear he was to have no part of their lives. But how could he hide himself in these walls if they were under threat?

A large part of him still wanted to eat that bullet. It would be so much easier.

But what good would that do? He liked living. Besides, he wasn't entirely sure God would be happy to see him if he showed up with a hole punched through his head. Not with the list of sins he'd compiled.

Then again, his final destination might involve pitchforks instead of halos.

Marchand knew he wasn't ready to end his life. Even with Cezar's threats to keep clear of the wilki, there were plenty of people who owed Marchand favors. He could leverage those on the other side of this conflict, maybe carve out a new existence. Maybe keep Caroline's family safe too.

No. It wouldn't work. If he really thought it would, he wouldn't be cowering in an old church. He wouldn't be making decisions that were all about keeping himself out of trouble. Because if he were watching out for Caroline, he would have come back around to her long before. He would have made sure he was there for his sister.

Marchand stared at Airfoil. This guy, he could be the real thing. Lord knew he'd already saved hundreds of people and thrown down with more scum than Marchand had ever. If there was any chance of keeping his town intact, against people like Domitian and Acciai, Airfoil was the only one who could make it happen.

So, it was an easy call, after calculating it that way.

"I can show you the rowhome. Let's go." Marchand started for the door.

"Good. You'll probably want another gun."

Marchand grinned. "If you think that was the only one I had, you're dumber than you look. Come on."

Marchand gasped for breath as Airfoil landed on the top of the building, near a boxed-in entrance to the stairwell. How long had that taken? He checked his watch. Only a few seconds. Sure, he'd flown before. In his airplane. Never like this, in the open air.

Talk about a rush.

Off to the west, he saw a bizarre structure taking root—a forbidding tower, made from what appeared to be pieces of dozens of different neighboring buildings and rubble from burned out apartments. The sides were smoothed toward the bottom, rougher toward the top, and several sharp spires rose atop the narrowed, pyramidal shape.

Someone floated dead center above it, swathed in gray.

"Your, ah, competitor's trying his hands at real estate," Marchand said. "Shouldn't you pay him a visit?"

He couldn't discern any expression behind Airfoil's blue-plated visor. The voice, however, was solid. "I will. But this is first."

"Okay. So they used the top floor of this building. Made it easier to guard." Marchand jerked a thumb over his shoulder. "Only those stairs and one fire escape on the north side, other than the front door."

"Good to know." Airfoil walked over to a wide open-spot on the roof. "Right about here?"

"Yeah." Marchand drew his gun, the spare Ruger he'd retrieved from the Monte Carlo. "You gonna breach the door and want me as backup or...?"

The roof trembled. Airfoil extended his hands. His arms shook, and the roof's tremors increased in response. A huge crack ripped open, tearing shingles and wood and wiring, kicking up insulation.

Marchand took a big step backward.

Pieces of the roof landed in heaps around the new skylight Airfoil tore open. He jumped down into the room. Marchand moved in, not sure how he was going to follow him down and aimed his gun through the opening.

No one visible. A couple of chairs and an old wooden table, a threadbare brown couch with giant tears in the fabric, stained carpet, dust-covered TV, but no sign of anyone living.

"They're not here," Airfoil murmured. "They're gone."

"Okay, relax. You, ah, want to give me a lift?"

That same strange grip enfolded Marchand, and he was yanked from his feet. He floated down into the room. Once he was sure he had solid footing, he looked. Someone had been here—beer cans, cigarettes. Marchand leaned over the ash, inhaled. "Mocne."

"What?"

"The brand. Mocne. Krol imported them from Krakow for his boys." Wisps of smoke still lingered in the air. Marchand touched the end of the stub. "Warm. They haven't been gone long."

"Where else could they have gone? I need a location."

"I know that. It's not so simple. The Poles own a ton of buildings up and down Little Warsaw. That doesn't count their interests elsewhere in the city."

Airfoil rounded on him. "I have to find my son. I don't care how many places I have to rip open, or how many bullets I have to deflect."

Marchand wondered if anyone had even a slim prayer of hitting the guy with a slug before he used his shield-thing in the air. Probably not. "Relax. I've got an idea."

They went downstairs, out onto the street. Marchand felt vaguely ridiculous, standing on a street corner with a man dressed head to toe in a modern version of a knight's suit of armor. But once he found his target, that feeling faded.

A couple of young wilki stood two buildings over, talking to each other and checking their phones every few seconds. If they were being paid to watch the house surreptitiously, they were doing a lousy job.

Marchand strolled over to them, leaving Airfoil behind. "Hey! Come here."

The two froze. First mistake. They looked to be in their early twenties, maybe late teens, ropy muscle and baggy clothes. One was blond and pale; the other had hair black as coal and a thick nose that had been broken at least once. "Get lost." Black Hair lifted his phone to his ear.

"Nope. Put it down." Marchand raised his gun. "On the sidewalk. You too, Blondie."

They both complied, staring at him. Their mouths suddenly gaped. Marchand sighed. It'd been too much to hope Airfoil would stay out of the way.

Sure enough, here he came, walking right up to those kids like he owned the joint. "The people staying in that house," he said, indicating the rowhome they'd just exited. "When did they leave?"

Both youths stared but didn't utter a word.

"Tell me when they left and where they went, and there won't be any trouble. If you don't, I'm going to have this officer arrest—"

"Oh, for Pete's sake." Marchand punched the black-haired one square in his twisted nose.

The kid staggered aside, into a front step railing, grabbing for his face. Marchand didn't wait to see if it was bleeding. He moved in, grabbed the kid by the collar, and slugged him twice in the stomach. "You heard the man! When did they leave?"

Shoes scuffed on the pavement behind him. A startled shout followed. Marchand glanced over his shoulder. Airfoil held out his left hand, fingers splayed, and the blond kid hovered a foot off the sidewalk, arms flailing, legs cycling. Must've tried to run.

"Okay! Hey!" Black haired kid's voice choked through tears and he coughed, sounding for all the world like a lung might come up. "These trucks—big vans. They pulled up about an hour ago. Took a crew of guys, four of 'em. There was a kid, too. Teenager maybe. Took him in the same van."

"What are you doing?" Airfoil reached for Marchand.

"That's what we call cooperation." Marchand slammed the kid up against the wall, satisfied by the crack of his head against brick. Blood streamed down the kid's nose, and he sobbed. "Grow up. What kind of van? Details."

"Gr-gray van, Massachusetts plates, Ford. One of them Econolines. Brand new."

"Which way?"

"Into the Center. I think. I don't know! There were a bunch of them. Please. They just paid us to watch the place, to call them if anyone tried to get in."

Marchand threw him against the railing. There was a spot

of blood on his shirt. Take a bit of doing to get rid of that. "So, there's your answer, Airfoil."

"You didn't have to assault them."

"Please. Lecture me on proper application of vigilante justice later. Me getting brought up on misconduct charges is the least of our worries right now."

Airfoil didn't harass him anymore, but he didn't pick up the guy Marchand had roughed up. Finally, Airfoil released the other kid. Then he scooped up both phones. "Can we track the calls made on these?"

"Hell yes. At my precinct."

"Let's move."

Acciai wanted badly to finish her opponent. She wiped his blood from her armor, savored the smell under the tip of her nose. He'd almost been hers. So close. But Domitian had other tasks for her. Keeping Airfoil out of his way was just one in which she took special pleasure.

Instead, she flew east, toward Rittenhouse Island and the U.S. Coast Guard base jutting from the west side. It was a cluster of concrete buildings arranged in a rectangular formation. This centered around a pair of three-story brick structures that served as the administrative headquarters. Piers poked long, gray fingers out into this portion of Sculpin Bay. Only two vessels were moored there—a 154-foot *Sentinel*-Class cutter and the much larger *Legend*-Class National Security Cutter. The latter was *USCGC Weskeag*, and was already moving off from the dock. The smaller vessel, *USCGC Passaic*, had yet to cast off.

Acciai pursed her lips. The *Weskeag* carried more formidable weaponry—a half dozen machine guns of the 7.65 mm and .50 caliber variety, a 20 mm Phalanx Close-In Weapons System handy for shooting down missiles or rampaging exo-skeletons. The icing on the cake was the Bofors 50 mm cannon mounted

Airfoil: Origins

on the bow, which was already turning slowing in her direction.

Well. She could handle that. Nothing quite so disarming to opponents like putting your blade to one of their friends. So, she dove in for the smaller cutter still moored to the dock.

Enlisted personnel in dark blue swarmed across the deck of the Sentinel¬-Class cutter. Acciai chuckled as they scrambled into position at the Browning M2 machine guns anchored in four locations around the vessel. The 25 mm cannon at the bow swiveled.

Please. They might as well try to bring down a supersonic fighter with a spear.

She swooped close to the sea, her jets kicking up spray and launched a pair of rocket-propelled grenades. They pierced the hull, exploding up and through the *Passaic*'s superstructure. Acciai pulled up, skimming through the smoke, and dropped with a sudden lurch onto the deck. Her landing put her right beneath the barrel of the 25 mm cannon.

She reached up and grasped the barrel. When she pulled and twisted, the exo-skeleton did the bulk of the work, and she rather liked it that way. The metal groaned beneath her armored fingers, and the barrel bent until it reached a 45-degree angle.

"Intruder!" The voice came from her right. A trio of Coast Guardsmen skidded to a halt, clad in Kevlar vests. They aimed M-16s.

Acciai smiled. She swept her flamethrower across the space between them. The wall of fire obscured her vision and rewarded her with startled cries from her opponents. She jumped, arcing thirty feet over the deck. Automatic weapons fire exploded beneath and behind, but none of the three reacted fast enough to get anywhere near her.

She landed at the side of two men working a Browning. They didn't have time to so much as gasp before she punched each of them with tremendous force. The blows impacted their chests with a horrific crunch. Both men hurtled over the rail, into the water.

Acciai ripped the Browning off its mount and heaved it over after them.

Alarms rang out, and fire crackled across the deck. Acciai jumped again, angling for the port side. As she came down, she fired her grenade launcher again, this time destroying another Browning machine gun. A glance into the distance confirmed that while the *Weskeag* circled out into the bay, it hadn't opened fire. Why would it, when it risked killing fellow Coast Guardsman.

One more weapon to render useless.

She stomped down the deck, armored boots leaving imprints in the metal. A Guardswoman and man fired on her from around the corner of the bulkhead. Bullets caromed off her black armor. Acciai retaliated with her guns, relishing the hammer blows through her arms as the bullets ripped through the thin bulkhead. They tore the two enlisted personnel into chunks of blue uniform and red flesh.

Beyond them was the final machine gun. The man there managed to get behind it and twist around to target Acciai. He opened fire, the shots vibrating the deck.

Acciai leapt sideways, out over the port side rail, and activated her jets. She flew around in a half circle, still upright, and returned fire. Her shots hit the Guardsman in the chest, punching clean through his Kevlar. He collapsed, the Browning machine gun tipping down and away from her.

More crew were on deck now, and she accelerated, flying up and over the ruined *Passaic*. She would have given anything for decent cloud cover, but there wasn't any. *Weskeag*'s fire control crew must have decided to chance hitting her, because the Phalanx gun opened up with a horrendous whine like a great clanking chainsaw. Even from a quarter mile away, having 75 bullets unleashed at her each second made for a hailstorm that she twisted and writhed to avoid. She'd not climbed too high, so the superstructure of *Passaic* and the nearby base buildings offered cover.

Acciai got below those and was immediately faced with more armed men and women. Humvees rolled up, fortunately without any roof-mounted weaponry. She turned her guns on them—

A blast like a gust of wind, hurricane force, shoved the Humvees across the pavement. They bashed into each other, two flipping up on their sides., A third landed on its roof. It was as if a child had thrown his toy cars aside in a tantrum.

She knew what it meant. Domitian dropped down from the sky, fast as a lightning strike, halting above her, ten feet away. His expression was hidden, as always, but that didn't stop the waves of disappointment in his voice. "Consolata, there's no need to play with your food. Your assignment was to disable the Coast Guard forces."

"I've been busy doing that." Acciai gestured at the flaming superstructure of *Passaic*. "I'd have been here sooner if I hadn't fought Airfoil first—which is what you commanded of me."

"Yes, and it doesn't seem you have brought me his broken body, nor have you communicated his defeat."

"No. Not yet."

Domitian shook his head. "I will finish this business."

He rose into the sky, arms outstretched, and flew swiftly over *Passaic*. Out in the bay, the cutter *Weskeag* was halfway through its turn, coming back at the Coast Guard docks. A message blared across a bullhorn—Acciai couldn't hear it but assumed they were demanding Domitian's surrender. She laughed.

She rocketed off, dousing the Humvees in fire. Sporadic gunshots echoed, and though several shots cut through the air in her general direction, none came near.

A series of rapid, heavy cha-thunks shook the sky. Acciai saw the *Weskeag*'s Bofors cannon flash, eight blasts. Shell bursts wreathed Domitian in black smoke.

Yet when the sea breeze cleared the smoke, he hovered in

place, motionless, without so much as a singe on his cloak.

Acciai shivered. Even with all the power wrapped around her body, it was nothing compared to his.

Domitian reached out. His fingers curled as if grabbing on to the empty sky. Water rippled around the *Weskeag*. The cutter's turn halted, its forward momentum arrested. Which, Acciai mused, should not be possible.

The Bofors gun pounded again, this time joined by the jarring buzz saw of the Phalanx CIWS. The Vulcan gun that made up the bulk of the system spun in a blur, sending up a stream of fire that exploded all around Domitian. He vanished behind sparks so bright Acciai had to turn aside, even with her visor in place. She feared, however briefly, that she'd have to provide distracting fire so he could continue his efforts.

But the *Weskeag*'s defenses didn't stop his onslaught. The waves increased at either end of the ship, making it rock along its centerline. It floundered. Weapons fire ceased, accompanied by a metallic crunch that reached Acciai's ears even from five hundred feet in the air. The Bofors gun barrel squashed flat against the mount, which, in turn, crumpled in on itself as if it were a ball of discarded paper. The Phalanx system snapped clean off its housing and flipped off the deck, before splashing into the bay.

Domitian settled from the dissipating black smoke, his boots only a few feet off the water's surface. He brought his hands together, pressed them flat, and then moved them slowly apart.

The squeal of metal shattered the air. Rivets popped off like champagne corks. A fissure appeared just below the port side railing, a black line spreading down the hull to the waterline and up into the superstructure. Klaxons howled the alarm across *Weskeag*'s deck. Crew scrambled up from below, racing to the rails and grabbing for lifejackets.

Acciai's instinct was to pick them off as they abandoned ship. It would be so easy. But that took the fun out of it, really. There'd be no challenge to the kills.

The cacophony of sound from the dying ship crescendoed as the fissure widened into a gaping yawn. The bulkheads snapped apart, metal that was forged to withstand storms at sea tearing free of its welds. Water churned and gurgled, rushing into the hull breach. Sailors shouted, splashing overboard, their cries mingling with the groans of the dying ship.

Domitian lowered his hands. He floated, impassive, as the torn halves of the cutter *Weskeag* sank beneath the surface of the bay. It didn't slip under the water as fast as Acciai would have expected; it was a slow, drawn-out death.

"I think we're alike," Acciai said to him. "You get a thrill out of seeing your opponent die, too, don't you?"

"It's hardly as base an emotion as lust," Domitian said. "My remaining here is for the benefit of the news cameras and cell phone pointed in this direction. I want everyone everywhere to see the power wielded this day."

"I understand."

"Do you? There's strength in using fear as a tool with which you can control others. Fear is as simple as the implied threat of death. But I doubt you consider much beyond blood and pain."

If Acciai could have relinquished enough control of her exoskeleton's thrusters in order to shrug, she would have. "What else is there?"

The ship was now completely submerged, save for the tip of the bow and davits poking up from the stern. The bay around it was littered with gray-white debris and brilliant orange life rafts and vests.

"The convoy with our forces is embarking from Newport," Domitian said. "Rendezvous with it and the hostage. See to it both reach the Hull district intact."

Acciai glowered at him. "I don't need to be reminded of my job."

"It seems you do. Keep Airfoil from those convoys at all costs."

"I thought you wanted him alive."

"It doesn't matter now. I have the Source. The more medallions that can be stricken from the Garrison's arsenal, the better. You have your orders." He took off for Hull, shattering the air in his wake with a tremendous gust of wind and the roar of a sonic boom.

Acciai staggered against the blast, readjusting her jets lest she be flung into the bay. With one last glance around, she satisfied herself that the Coast Guard forces were eliminated as a threat. More vessels prowled the waters just beyond the shimmering edge of Domitian's giant shield. Overhead, a swarm of helicopters buzzed incessantly. She wanted badly to cut them all from the sky—but they were no threat to her inside this new domain. Even as she thought it, one of the helicopters, a Pave Hawk with U.S. Navy markings, pivoted toward her and opened up with blistering machine gun fire from the Browning mounted just inside the hatch. All it did was give her a nice fireworks display as the bullets were smashed aside by the shield.

Acciai boosted away from the Coast Guard base, flying north to Slidell Bridge. She switched on her radio, skipping past the frequency that let her smile at the terror in the voices of police dispatchers. "Cezar, tell me you're en route."

The de facto head of the wilki sounded distant, his voice scratchy in her radio. "Yes. I have men ready. Have crossed bridge. Where are others?"

Off in the distance, Acciai could see the tiny vehicles comprising a second convoy of vans and trucks coming north out of Westerville. "Headed to your position. You'll meet them on Broadway, then over to Hull. Domitian wants us at the Source. He's preparing something special."

"Yes. Will be there."

Acciai circled the City Center a handful of times but saw

no sign of Airfoil. She was both glad and disappointed—glad he wasn't there to cause her grief, and disappointed because she yearned for another bout. He was strong. The same kind of strength as Domitian, but wilder, untamed. The very thought of their last fight set her pulse racing, her breath faster.

She wanted him. Preferably impaled on her blades, so she could kiss the last gasp of life from his mouth as he died.

Even more invigorating was the sight of Domitian's tower. It was complete, so far as she could tell—ten stories tall, gleaming like a metal spike in the sunlight, sides rendered smooth by whatever powers Domitian wielded. Waves generated by the Source pulsed outward with greater intensity, increased frequency, spreading throughout the city and up into sky, reinforcing the field. She couldn't see Domitian or the Source, but the top of the slender tower was sheared flat and dark as if it were open to the air.

Below her, vehicles rolled toward the tower. The first convoy had fifteen trucks in it, including six SUVs and six shipping trucks, accompanied by three military surplus Humvees. Acciai could see six men in each of the SUVs; Cezar had told her he was bringing sixty.

The second convoy turned onto Broadway from out of Center, its five vans full of wilki rolling into formation with the first. A hundred twenty men, most of them hardened enforcers brought over from Poland just for this day. Acciai watched one gray van in particular that contained a very young and gangly bargaining chip.

She swooped down to thirty feet, speeding over the top of the convoy. There was no traffic in the area, and only parked cars along the sides of the streets. Every so often, she glimpsed frightened faces behind windows of office buildings and apartments. Yes. The new regime would come for them later. Let them wait, anxiety rising.

There were no police cars near. Also not surprising. Acciai

cycled through the radio reports of shootings at every precinct and gun battles raging all across the city. Even Hull was a battleground, as Sheehan's Irish mob waged a losing battle against the Polish rivals and what little police presence remained.

She'd clear out their nest of rats soon enough.

The lead SUV in the convoy suddenly braked. Red lights flickered up and down the line of vehicles. Acciai frowned. "Cezar. What's going on?"

"Is not clear. We are calling first truck. They say—"

Harsh static squealed across her radio, piercing her hearing. She snarled and cut the signal. Jamming? Impossible. There was no way the National Guard could penetrate Domitian's shield.

Ahead, a truck rumbled around the corner of Fifth Street. Not one of Domitian's forces. It wasn't like any she'd seen before: high wheel base, drab tan, polarized windows, the chassis covered with armor plates set at odd angles.

What is that thing?

That was when she noticed the very large guns mounted on the roof.

Chapter Twenty-Eight

I have no idea where Frank got it.
There's a lone military vehicle roaring down the street. It pays no heed to stop lights or signs. I'm betting it doesn't brake for crosswalks.

That's because it's—well, I don't know what it is, a military scout truck with tall wheels, a low roof and very futuristic design. It's laden down with armor plating, painted a sloppy tan camo, and sporting an ungainly cannon on the roof, giving it the appearance of an enraged dune buggy on steroids. Plus, there's a Gatling gun spinning in anticipation on the lower right side of the roof, mounted with belts of ammunition coiled behind it.

"Brandon, you read?" He's on the radio, sounding surly as usual, but with extra determination behind the question.

"Yeah, I'm two blocks west, coming behind Acciai." She seems frozen with indecision. Probably wondering about this military mirage barreling straight toward her convoy. "I came with Dennis Marchand."

The Monte Carlo's tucked down an alley. Dennis is in position—or at least, I have to trust he is, because he and an M4A1 and shotgun are somewhere among the stores fronting Broadway.

"Stay clear, I've got this," Frank says through the radio.

"With your...tank car thing?"

"Panhard CRAB. The French built it. Go figure. Perfect scout reconnaissance vehicle for tight quarters. STANAG level 2 armor, with some of my own modifications. Such as the Dillion M-134, loaded with 7.62 Roufouss High Explosive incendiaries." He sounds as happy as Sean did to get the latest batch of comics from Reed.

The van's third from the end, behind Acciai's floating form. Same gray and same plates the wilki watchman told us about. I breathe deep. This has to be fast. No room for mistakes.

This is my son.

I shoot off an arrow of prayer and launch myself for the van. Wind roars by me, barely dulled by the helmet's lining. The van's rear windshield grows larger. There's a pair of burly men in the rear bench seat, sandwiching Sean's much thinner frame.

Two hundred feet. A hundred.

I fashion a blade in my imagination, a great big serrated weapon. With a wrench of my wrist, with every ounce of strength poured into my flight, I cut into the metal.

The roof shears off the top of the van, flipping open like the cover of a book. Thankfully I avoid breaking any glass. There's a split second in which I reach the van, see a crowd of astonished faces staring through the ragged rectangle that used to be the roof...

And Sean.

I pull him out with the field, jerking him into the sky. He tumbles behind me, a puppy trailing its parent, yelling in either panic or exhilaration—I can't tell them apart. I fashion shields out of the field I used to dismantle the roof. A good thing, too, because gunfire immediately peppers both of us. I'm up and out of the street in a flash.

Acciai blazes a path right for us.

"Sean!" I drag him up alongside me, looping an arm around his waist. "Sean, are you all right?"

"Are you kidding?" His eyes are watering, but he's refusing to close them against the wind, hair blasted straight back. Sean lets out a whoop, puts his arms forward. "You did it! You're a superhero, Dad!"

Even with Acciai behind us, likely planning our demise, I grin. "Brandon. You've got him?"

"Yeah, Frank, they're all yours."

The Panhard jukes to the right, scuttling across the empty lanes in a movement that earns it the name Crab. Both sets of wheels pivot in the same direction. The cannon on the roof swings around and opens up with a terrifying staccato that thuds through the air. CHA-CHUNK-CHA-CHUNK-CHA-CHUNK.

The first SUV explodes. No messing around, no cumulative damage, just blows up. There's nothing left but a flaming chassis with white shards of plastic rolling through the intersection.

The second driver swerves, but he's gone in a crimson spray, leaving the vehicle out of control. Flashes of flame and bursts of smoke rip the hood, the driver's side door, the truck bed, tearing plastic off all the way down to the rear tires. They burst like balloons. The gas tank follows a second later, in a brief fireball that tosses the truck into a roll.

By now, the other drivers have scattered. Trucks and vans and SUVs spread out across Broadway, some making for alleyways. Men burst from every one, wielding AK-74s and Uzis.

Those Humvees race up the line, from the rear. A man leans out the rear of one, leveling a Russian RPG at the Crab. He fires a grenade Frank's way, disappearing in a great puff of white smoke.

Frank wheels the vehicle so it drives backwards and sideways, its engine growling. The Dillion Gatling gun opens with a vicious chainsaw sound as it streams bullets at the Humvee. Bullets perforate the steel doors and tires explode. There's no way anyone inside is left alive. The vehicle veers aimlessly before impacting a storefront full of male mannequins in tuxedoes.

My own pursuer is catching up. A pair of explosions rock my flight path, though with my shield in place, they succeed only in tossing Sean and I around in the air. It's not safe for him up here. I scan the area below us. The YMCA is up ahead, a three-story white concrete and blue glass structure in the shape of a truncated "A" that spans an entire city block. At the center of the "A" is a wide triangular courtyard filled with trees, benches, and a pond.

I press my helmet against Sean's head, hoping he can hear and feel my instruction without it being lost to the roar of the wind. "Keep your legs loose! I'm going to drop you off!"

He says something back. I can't hear it, but I see his wide-eyed grin.

I bank right and roll us onto our backs. I throw off a burst of power that ripples through the air along our flight path. It widens to five times its original size, imitating a giant umbrella, right before it reaches Acciai. She tries to avoid it, but it catches her right arm and flank. Bits of metal and armor flake off. For a moment, she's spun around, away from us.

I drop as fast as I dare, the green swath of the courtyard looming below. At the last second, I pull out from the dive and put on invisible air brakes. They rip branches and leaves from the trees around us with a great gust of wind. Sean lets go, ten feet up, and crashes through a row of hedges. He tumbles, swearing with a bunch of words I'd usually chastise him for. But right now, I'm happy he doesn't appear to have broken anything.

On the way back out of the courtyard, skimming the roof of the YMCA, I spot a couple of men and a woman, all three in tight-fitting exercise kit, hurrying in Sean's direction. So the Y is still occupied. How many other buildings are full of people hunkered down against Domitian's takeover? And yet, they still reach out to help those they don't know, in a city of half a million people.

I curve sharply, barreling head-on at Acciai. This ends here.

She's enraged. She has to be, by the way she unloads the blaze of bullets from her gun and pours flame from the thrower. We collide in a blinding sparks, her rebounding off my shield, me gasping for lack of air among the flames. I'm unable to clear my vision among the smoke.

Reed and Frank did their parts well. The suit protects me from the bulk of the heat. I can tell from the expense of dark streaks scoring across the otherwise immaculate armor. The smoke clears in time for me to see Acciai slashing at me with her blades.

I reel out of the way and land a punch across her jaw. Her head snaps back, and something cracks. The bottom half of her black helmet spins off, dropping like a stone to the YMCA below.

Acciai swipes at me again, catching my right shoulder, but the blades only gouge the armor and leave my flesh intact. She's frenzied with anger. If I can stay calm enough, ignore her ferocity and focus on attention to detail...

There. Where the blades protrude.

I manage a deep breath, and of all things, the image of a man in a boat standing amidst a storm pops into my head. The boat's rickety, the companions around him howling with fear, their voices as loud as the raging wind. Yet, He only speaks, and it all goes still.

Acciai's movements slow to a bare crawl.

I focus the field on that junction where the blades are anchored to her exosuit. They bend, warp, shiver, and finally collapse in on themselves until they're nothing more than fist-sized lumps of metal. Now, they resemble lumpy softballs more so than weapons.

Everything speeds up. My stomach lurches from an overwhelming sense of vertigo. Acciai takes a pause as she realizes her hand-to-hand weapon is gone. This gives me enough of a window to seize her by the arm and punch her. She falls like a meteor, away from the Y and back toward Broadway.

From behind and below me, there comes a tremendous explosion. A fireball rises from Broadway, topped by a tower of black smoke and a flaming tire that spins through the air. I pray it's not Frank. Staying within eyeshot of Acciai, I race back at the battle.

It's not Frank. The Panhard Crab wheels about the scattered convoy. The 25 mm cannon thumps out its payload on a second Humvee that's quickly reduced to a shredded chassis. But he's not escaped unscathed—there's a great scar along the right side of the Crab, and the passenger door is gone, replaced by a huge blackened gouge. The right rear tire is half flat, dragging as the vehicle skitters out of the way of another incoming RPG blast.

At least six of the convoy vehicles are wrecked. There're also newcomers to the fight: a dozen DCPD cruisers, in various states of damage, and forty or more police in garb ranging from the plain old patrol blues to full SWAT armor. They engage the mob strongmen, automatic weapons fire adding to the cacophony in the street.

"Frank! You holding up?"

"I'd be doing better if I had three more of these," he says. "And also no RPGs on their end. But it's going well." His voice gets drowned out by the chatter of AKs somewhere nearby. "Your buddy's brother-in-law makes a decent insurgent, for a cop."

I haven't seen Dennis at all, until a blast from a darkened storefront cuts down a wilki from behind a toppled SUV. He sprints to the next building, stopping only to unlimber the M4A1 from across his back and sling the shotgun in its place. Dennis fires on the move, in short bursts that find their mark two times out of three. His tie is gone, and there's a rip in his right sleeve. That forearm is soaked red.

Fire rolls across the street. Dennis dives for shelter as the blaze ripples across the storefront.

Acciai.

She storms into the midst of the battle, screaming through the shattered remains of her face mask. One arm hangs limp, but it doesn't stop her from shooting indiscriminately, the blasts killing wilki and destroying police vehicles.

I swoop in low to the street. The field digs a trough through asphalt, flipping aside a pair of wrecked vans. Cezar's men are thrown asunder like so many downed leaves. My rampage skids the Panhard Crab, ass-end first, through the window of a barbershop—sorry, Frank. I blow aside everything I can, with only one target straight ahead.

The plow hammers her backwards, sending her flying until she slams into the broadside of a credit and loan bureau.

I tear her down from the building, bashing her onto the street. With both hands grasped behind her exoskeleton, I give it all my will and rip at the armor, the wiring, the hydraulics, anything that my fingers reach. The suit collapses, leaving Acciai limp.

She sags against the concrete, tears streaking a face covered with dust and spattered with blood. One eye is bruised a nasty purple, swollen almost shut. She spits.

"Stand down." What do you say when you've defeated your enemy? I'm sure Reed could feed me twenty different victorious lines.

"You can kill me," she gasps, "But you'll never stop him."

I raise my fist. The field builds intensity until the air throbs visibly, pulsing with my anger and my cold desire to smash her from existence.

"No!"

Sean? He's not at the Y, but sprinting up to me. All around us, the sounds of battle slackens. More police arrive

Regardless, I immediately encase him in whatever portion of the field I can siphon off of my fist. "Get back, Sean. She has to be stopped."

"You don't have to kill her. You beat her. She's going to have to pay for everything she did. But you can't—You can't kill her."

I hold my fist over Acciai. Those tears could be fake. So could the look of panic on her face, the whimper in her throat…

"Mom wouldn't kill anyone."

"We—I don't know that." Samantha, a killer?

No matter the lies Frank's fed me, I can't pass that judgment about the woman I loved.

So instead, I leach power from the field and use the dregs to fasten Acciai securely to the pavement.

Dennis staggers up to me. He does have his tie, it turns out—wrapped around his arm, presumably to stop the bleeding. He has his own prisoner: Cezar, limping and in handcuffs. The leader of the Polish mob is bruised, scraped, and half his clothes are charred. Blisters sear his face and chest. "Nicely done," Dennis says.

"Thanks. You had a good catch yourself."

Cezar spits on my armor. "You are all fools if you think—"

Dennis puts the stock of the M4A1 to his back, driving him to his knees. "Shut up, Cezar. Friend."

The explosion shakes the air behind us. I turn, and there're huge chunks of concrete and metal hurtling toward us. Behind that wave of speeding debris, Domitian rides on a wave of air.

"Everyone down!" I put all my will and a quick prayer behind a shield that spreads wide over the street, protecting as many people as I can—Sean, Dennis, even Cezar and Acciai.

The first few chunks of concrete strike, as big as bicycles. The impact jars me, straining my body. Every ounce of my concentration is on holding this barrier. If I could spare just a segment to counteract Domitian's force, to throw the projectiles back at him—

Suddenly, we're blow off our feet. It's as if my shield were just brushed aside. I rebound off a furniture store's wall, landing face down on the pavement. All around me, the concrete crashes down. There's a rending scream from Dennis., He's collapsed over a manhole cover, his right leg crushed beneath rebar and concrete. Sean runs to him. I hastily lessen the gravity under the slab enough so that Sean can shove it aside with no more effort than moving a garbage can lid. Cezar is sitting upright halfway across the street. There's a dazed expression on his face and blood pouring from a gash on his forehead. Acciai—

Her body is mangled in the frame of the exoskeleton. Whatever random appearance this attack has, she was the target. Or else it was sheer coincidence that three huge slabs of concrete have smashed into her. She stares, unseeing, at the sky.

Domitian descends through a cloud of dust. "What an absolute waste. All the time and resources spent to better her, and this is the end she receives." He sighs. "And you. Your stubborn bravery is a thorn I cannot ignore."

He raises his hands. A Chevrolet Impala, long abandoned by its driver, lifts up off the pavement.

And that's where I started this.

I sever the Chevy and manage to deflect its engine block. Domitian tears the street apart in a thunder, yanking subway cars from beneath our feet.

Now they roar through the air at me.

I leap for the sky. Easy enough to get out of their path. But with Sean and Dennis and Frank—Where is Frank?—down below, I can't leave them to be crushed.

The subway cars rush by, dragging a tunnel of wind behind them. I reach down with both hands, fashion invisible cables that loop around their bodies, writhing into tight knots. The grip's firm enough. I heave.

They yank me off my flight path, my shoulders straining and my arms burning from the exertion. Turn. Turn!

The subway cars slow their descent and begin a northern arc, still losing altitude but no longer in danger of crashing down upon my son and my ally. They are still perilously close to the tops of the buildings in the nearest block. A triad of telecom antennae shear off one roof.

I keep dragging, pulling on the cars until they're over an empty patch of Broadway. By now, I've swung them in a half circle. I release.

They glide forward a few hundred feet before crashing down the centerline. Asphalt explodes. Glass breaks, large metal wheels spin off, axles snap. Overall, the subway cars wind up with as much shape to them as a soda can that's been stomped on.

Breathing hard, I spare only a cursory glance to make sure I didn't flatten anyone before I dive back at Domitian. Shouldn't worry about losing track of him, because he's blazing straight for me, moving at what appears to be twice my speed.

Our shields glance off each other, two high-velocity projectiles colliding. Even as I spin away, I lash out with the field, going for a modified version of the invisible lasso I just used on the subway cars. It catches, and I reel Domitian in. Easy.

Too easy. It takes a second for me to realize that the reason is that he's performed a variation of the same hold on me. The sudden pressure on my abdomen feels like a vice pressing the air out.

We close on each other once more, only this time, I dissolve my shield and wrap both arms in extensions of the field. Then I opt for that fast side hop action I'd used a couple of times before—on the ground, never tried it in the air.

Suddenly, I'm right on top of him. I throw a right hook.

He catches my hand.

Just like that, he holds on to my fist, and I react with a blow from the left. It does me no good. He whips me around, is somehow right behind me, and punches me square in the kidneys.

"Such a nuisance," Domitian says, and he hammers me across the shoulders with a blow that sends me reeling. "You had potential to make an excellent lieutenant. Imagine the power we could wield over the rest of mankind!"

I boost up high enough that I can knee him in the face. What I wind up doing is catching his shoulder, which makes a satisfying crack.

"No thanks," I say, "I've seen the benefits package you offer your pals."

It infuriates him, I figure, because he grabs my ankle and throws me toward the harbor.

I don't even resist, opting instead to bank into a sharp curve, pour on speed, and angle the field so I drop close to the ground. I blast through the aftermath of the gun battle, snatching up the straps of four AK-74s. Not enough. A red Prius has been chopped in half by one of Domitian's concrete slabs. Perfect. I scoop the rear up with the field.

Arcing into the sky once more, I fling all but one of the AKs at Domitian, blistering fastballs accelerated by gravitational distortion and, for good measure, I shoot at him with the remaining gun.

He smashes the three projectiles without flinching, crumpling each one like balls of paper. I empty the magazine. The bullets spark off his shield—though I notice a pair of holes punch his cape in the seconds before he can deflect the rest.

Interesting. Break your concentration, did I?

No time to dwell on it, because he's pulled a communications antenna off a building and sent it my way like a subsonic javelin. But I'm prepared—because I've got my half a car.

I swing it around, as if I were trying to hit a baseball bat with the ball and clip the antenna in half. It shreds into arm-length metal spears that stab into the ruined car body. This whole time, I've kept moving, and Domitian's closed on my position too. When he's near enough, I swing the car back the other direction.

The blow connects, but he's done something with his shield, similar to my splitting the Chevy in half. The Prius explodes to either side of an invisible wedge. It showers me in plastic, hunks of metal, and even a tire. The pieces hammer my armor, pounding at my arms and legs. My head rings from the impacts with my helmet.

Domitian grabs me by the throat. "You see what I've done? You see the fortress I've built?"

I gasp out, "That pile of crap? Give my kid LEGOs...he can make a better one."

"Your persistence in agitating me will not alter the outcome."

"No...but it distracts you pretty well."

Shouts echo from the street below. I can't see how many police are gathered there, but when they start shooting, it's an ear-shattering cacophony. The air around us is full of sparks and bullets.

Domitian flinches at the initial intensity, but rather than backing off, he whirls and presents me as the new target, pushing me a few feet in front of him. I'm suspended in the iron grip of his field.

I manage to throw my shield up in time to catch the incoming fire.

There's an explosion below us., The shockwave rockets us another thirty feet up. Frank must have the Crab semi-operation, despite its sitting still like the other wrecked vehicles. The 25 mm cannon looses a trio of shots. I absorb two, the blows squeezing all the breath from my lungs.

Domitian blows the third up in midair before it even reaches us.

"This is why we should rule, Brandon," he growls. "Their reactions are based on fear—the fear that they cannot overcome the medallion's power. But once they are broken, once they accept that it is good and right to fear what they cannot control, then they will be the most model of servants in a new kingdom."

He reaches out toward the Panhard.

"Frank, incoming!" I manage to croak.

Doesn't do much good. The air shakes with the passage of the field Domitian throws. It smashes the Crab flat to the pavement, squashing it under an unseen hammer. Fuel bursts in dark rivers from the rear, and the remaining wheels shoot off.

"Frank!" I yell.

Domitian doesn't let the cops off easy either. He cuts his other hand sideways through the air, heel of the palm first, and a series of smaller waves slash down among the squad cars. Several get cut in half, spraying debris across the street. Police scatter for cover, even as a half dozen of their number tumble away in the onslaught. But some manage to keep firing, hunkered down in corners of buildings or behind squad cars that Domitian's missed. He unleashes more waves at them, simultaneously smashing the Crab's carcass. As if that weren't enough, a pair of ruined SUVs leap into the air, rolling end over end, and coming down against the police cars as giant battering rams.

In the midst of this, as I'm trying to keep my shield from collapsing, the grip on me relaxes. Not a lot, and it returns just as strong, but there was a flicker. A weakness.

"Brandon! Get out of the way!"

Frank? "You're not dead!" I hiss through my teeth.

"No, but I'm hurt, and this is the second ride Domitian's cost me. I'm starting to take it personally. Move out of the way."

"He's got me cold. But I think he's over-taxing himself."

"Well, no medallion wielder can divide their attention between multiple attacks for long." Something crunches loud enough to drown him out for a second. "Although he's pushing the record for that."

Distraction. I can barely move. But I don't need do. "Whatever you're planning, Frank, do it now!"

A pause. "Got it. Just remember our first day of target practice."

"Our what?"

"When you were the target." There's a loud whoosh from his end, and the radio signal dissolves.

Simultaneously, a puff of smoke on the street blooms like a springtime flower in time lapse. It's an RPG.

Oh, come on, Frank.

Domitian sees it too. He shifts position and raises his hand. A perfectly new BMW, gorgeous blue paint job and still bearing temporary tags, shoots up from the street. I don't know if he's fast enough. I hope he is.

The BMW and the rocket-propelled grenade intersect thirty feet from us. The explosion's blinding—but I'm ready. I've been ready since Frank signed off.

Domitian puts something between us and the explosion, a kind of expanding wave front that redirects the shockwave. And with that, his grasp slips from around me, weakening enough for me to move my body

It's not without considerable effort, but It's enough.

I twist and aim both palms at him. My field, everything I can muster, drags him in like a fish on a hook. He makes an exclamation, the first sound that isn't oozing confidence. It ends when I punch him.

You'd think I was hitting a brick wall. He reels from the blow but comes back with his own. My body keeps on going, though I don't know how—everything aches. The impact from his hit hurt worse, even through the body armor.

We grapple, moving across the sky—I can't tell which one of us adds speed to the equation, but we're soaring toward the harbor again. Rocketing is more like it.

I clobber Domitian across the mask with an elbow strike and follow it up by bashing against him with my helmet. He seizes my right shoulder, grasp amplified enough for him to leave fingerprints. I roll with the punch, and we literally spiral through the air, corkscrewing right toward the bay waters. My view alternates powder blue sky, thick white cloud, and dark blue sea.

I hit the waves, torpedoing into the deep. Everything's gurgling water, and cold, and dark. No Domitian. Though I do spot a foggy, orange stripe on a shattered ship's white hull. Coast Guard? What did I miss?

Airfoil: Origins

The darkness closes all around me, but I've been in this situation before, so there's no panic this time. No matter what happens, I know where my soul will rest, so that's not my concern. What drives me is all the other people who depend on me. Sean, and Frank, and Kelly, and Reed—I don't even know what's happened to them all. I flail for only a second before I can redirect the field and propel myself back up. It takes way too long to shoot back to the surface. Light bombards me. Water sprays all around, as if I'm riding the top of a fountain.

Domitian's here. Waiting. Hovering.

There's a ship coming toward us. One of those monster freighters that ply the coastal waters from Drake City to Boston to New York and points beyond. Great big sucker, more than 600 feet long, and from what I've read, they weigh tens of thousands of tons.

Which adds even more awe, because it's flying toward me as fast as a small airplane, soaring over the top of Rittenhouse Island's Coast Guard station

"Stay down!" Domitian shouts, his voice sounding as if it's coming from all the loudspeakers at Coronet Stadium.

The ship's right on me, angling up as if it were a raised baseball bat. Domitian swings his arms, and with a ponderous creaking groan, it drops on me.

No.

I rise to meet it, arms outstretched. I'm exhausted. But I can't let him do this. I will massive, invisible hands into existence, decreasing gravity as much as I can.

The weight plows into me. This is far worse than a lighthouse roof, or an airplane. I gasp for breath, straining for strength. My arms shudder; my whole body struggles. Every muscle and bone are bound together with the field. The medallion's cold impales me. My heart's made of ice.

But I hold. I have to hold.

Despair floods me, welling up from a dark corner of my

soul. A deep murmur: You can't. It's over. You are weak and forsaken.

Even as I hear this, I feel—I know¬—it's a lie. When I'm at my lowest, He lifts me up. All this time, He has been the constant when everything around me as been variable. My soul is content.

The ship slowly bends back toward Domitian. He shifts his position, and whatever he does with his medallion, the ship stops again. I can feel the opposing medallions striving against each other, magnets repulsing each other's power. It must be a strain for him as much as me, because he's not sparing any breath for another of his lectures.

My radio activates. "Brandon, you've got him?"

I grunt. "Sure. No. Prob."

"Don't think about the weight. Concentrate on your will, subvert the field to it."

Great advice. I'm drenched in sweat.

Domitian moves, gliding east, and the ship groans as it twists midair. I feel my grip slipping. The bow turns toward me. I adjust, getting in front of it instead of below. Now we're both pushing this thing at each other, neither budging.

"I'm at his tower. I'm going for the Source."

"You can't! There's a barrier…"

"I know. I'm banking on Domitian being heavily distracted by you, provided you don't die first. Be ready. We'll shut this thing down."

He cuts out. I hope he's right. Because I can't keep doing this, hovering up here over the water…

Water.

The trick is to do this swiftly, so I can still keep the boat from crushing me. I visualize a cylinder, deep in the bay, under Domitian's feet. My arms tremble. The ship creaks, tipping on its side.

Then, I let the medallion do its thing.

Water explodes from the surface of the bay. A column, twenty feet across, roars like a ravenous beast. It surges up, enveloping Domitian. Immediately, I feel the grip on his side of the ship slacken.

I lean in, shoving it forward. I've never killed a man. But this one—unless I can find a way to neutralize his powers, I'll have to.

The ship bashes through the column of water, and just like that, it's wrenched from my grasp as the field around it dissipates. It plummets to the bay, a hundred feet below, and hits with a deafening roar that throws plumes of water everywhere. Waves surge out.

I wince. Someone's going to miss that particular vessel. Good thing I'm wearing a mask, because my salary wouldn't even begin to cover the cost.

In the midst of the crash, I scan the skies and the sea. There's no sign of Domitian.

Better check on Frank.

Chapter Twenty-Nine

Frank Belasco didn't wait for confirmation that his medallion holder was en route. This was part of the operation he was perfectly comfortable handling solo.

He found substantial gaps in the bottom of the spire, left unfinished, but not unguarded. Five hired guns with Uzis blocked the nearest entrance, two of them diligently watching the street, as the other three gaped at something unseen to the east. Likely Brandon fighting Domitian.

Frank dropped into a crouch at the corner of Hull and Eighth. Right beside a pretzel cart that was half-crushed. The smell of stale dough and tang of salt filled the air. So did smoke, and fire. He breathed deep, sighted on the nearest of the keen-eyed men.

With his SCAR-L wrecked and abandoned in the tunnels below, he'd scooped up a discarded AK-108, a pleasant surprise, from one of the downed mercenaries the Polish mob had imported. He'd also made sure to grab a full magazine from the corpse. Now, he flicked the selector over to a three-round burst.

The first squeeze of the trigger put all three shots into the chest of the nearest thug. He wasn't wearing body armor, and a crimson spray indicated a clean hit. He went down in a spasm of arms and legs.

The second swiveled, raised his Uzi, and shouted a warning to his sightseeing friends. Frank duck-walked to better cover behind a flipped-over minivan—not that it would stop the bullets any better than a hot dog cart, but at least visibility would be limited. He leaned around the bumper and fired two more bursts.

The second man went down.

The remaining trio reacted, albeit sloppily. Two of them, jittery young men in their twenties with shaved heads, cut loose with their Uzis, firing indiscriminately. Only a handful of shots hit the minivan. The other man ducked into the opening.

Frank put them down with three more bursts from the AK-108.

The final guard didn't show his face, nor did he try to shoot around the bend of the opening in the bottom of the ersatz fortress. Fine. Frank slunk along the wall, AK at the ready. A couple feet from the opening, the man flung himself around the corner, grabbing onto the rifle and trying his best to yank it from Frank's grip.

He didn't succeed, but he did get it pushed aside so Frank couldn't shoot him. Frank brought the stock up into the man's chin, breaking his jaw with a resounding crack. He let go of the rifle and hit the man in the chest, grabbed his left arm and slammed it against the wall. The gun dropped, and the wrist shattered.

But the man still stood. He threw a wild haymaker with his good arm, which Frank dodged with enough space to feel the breeze go by. He grabbed the guy by the damaged arm, bent it sharply, and punched him in the kidneys. The man collapsed to his knees. Frank struck him on the back of the neck and he was down.

He picked up the AK and eased into the opening.

It was dark inside, tomb-like, except for a shaft of light shining from the opening several stories above. The damaged library sat at the center, the walls having encased an entire city block. It was sheathed in shadow, a dark, barren, broken remnant of its formerly living self.

Frank filed that observation away as irrelevant.

What was important was the absence of the enemy inside these walls. Apparently, Domitian had both underestimated his opponent's ability to distract him from his goal and overestimated his hired thugs' skills.

Frank stepped carefully through the crumped front doors to the library. In the dark, he used a small MagLite, at least until he reached the stream of natural light at the center. It made the hole in the floor that Brandon had described glow with a heavenly aura.

He could see the occasionally opalescent swirls in the field high above the city, through the gap in the pinnacle of the tower. He shone his flashlight toward the hole in the floor. The Source should be right underneath.

Bingo. The misshapen mound of metal pulsed with its power, sending waves rippling up the walls of the cavern and through the gash torn in the floor. It snaked along the wires, poking outward from the basement and into the walls.

Frank's first impulse was to cut those, but he squashed it. He'd waste time, and even if he succeeded, that still left the Source as a threat.

His orders were clear. The Garrison, stunned to find the Source actually existed, demanded its destruction. If he didn't, the Ashen most assuredly would make the attempt, and their brand of clean-up would result in considerably more collateral damage.

Frank unlimbered his backpack. He dragged out a nylon rope, climbing rig, and shrugged into it with practiced ease. The only viable support for the rope was an I-beam that was jammed deep into the ground, and its top end wedged firmly into the cobbled-together ceiling. He looped the rope, tied it off, and applied his full weight. The I-beam didn't twitch.

He retrieved his gun and hung the strap over his chest. Frank rappelled down into the pit, in a swift descent. He hit the ground hard enough to jar his knees—hard enough he'd regret it for a couple of days. The burn scars on his neck itched. Yet another trophy in the endless war between the Garrison and the Ashen.

The Source throbbed in front of him, hovering over its cairn. Frank stared at it. There was so much potential here. How many medallions could be crafted from it? How many more could serve the Garrison?

He snorted and shook his head to clear the reverie. Please. He had no idea if anyone even knew how to craft a medallion, let alone how to carve up something like this monstrosity into little siblings. For all he'd told Brandon of the history wrapped around the medallions and the Garrison, he knew precious little himself. Yet, he'd seen enough of the silent conflict to know it was vital both sides keep each other in check.

That is, until the madman Domitian made his move. Now, it was out in the open—the whole power struggle revealed to the world.

Yet the general public and the authorities couldn't have a clue about medallions themselves. What they saw were two superpowered individuals pummeling each other, with one dealing death to innocent while the other stood in his way.

In that ridiculous white suit.

Frank scowled. He knew what he had to do. He reached into his backpack and removed eight pounds of Composition C-4. Each one was packaged as M112 demolition charge assemblies, those thick blocks he knew all too well. With quick and careful hands, he adhered each one to the Source. Taking care not to touch it, he wired them together and set up a timer for detonation. The Source took on the appearance of a slouched planet, with its own chunky ring of debris.

He readied to set the timer, comparing the time to his watch. Something stopped him, though. The more Frank stared at the Source, the more he noticed his haggard expression reflected in its surface. Thoughts trickled in around the rock-hard barriers of duty and determination that kept his mind focused on the impending task. They prodded him, urged him. Shouldn't you take this? What better way to serve the Garrison than by wielding the greatest power known to Man for the betterment of all that is good? What better way to end the death and dying by overwhelming the Ashen, once and for all, with superior numbers?

"No. There has to be a balance between the two." His reply echoed in the cavern, surprising him with its vehemence.

Lies. You know what's best. They trust you to train medallion holders. Why not trust you with this great power? Take it. Now. It can be yours. It should be yours, after all you've done for them.

Frank's hand rested on the timer, ready to set the countdown. Instead, he let his fingers drift over and caress the metal of the Source. He'd seen how Brandon reacted when he touched it, so maybe...

It was like walking through the front door of his childhood home, except instead of familiar sounds and smells greeting him, a familiar strength awaited. Familiar power. All around him, the ebb and flow of Earth's gravity was as visible as the waves rolling in and out along Sculpin Bay. He could touch them.

And the cold. It was back, an old friend who sat down to visit, cutting into his chest with such force that he gasped for breath. Tears welled. He remembered what it had been like, and it only made him despair all the more that it'd been lost.

Frank grasped the Source fully with both hands, lifting it away from the cairn. His head swam with the implications. All at once, every loose stone, broken rock, and discarded pebble flew away from him at the center of the cavern, sticking as if magnetized to the walls and ceiling. He breathed deep, inhaling and exhaling. The rocks moved in and out, mimicking his breath.

He controlled them. He could feel them, every one, enfolded in fields of manipulated gravitational pull. But that wasn't the sensation he desired the most. It wasn't what he missed.

Frank redirected the fields into a single envelope around his body, showing the Source what he wanted done.

He rose from the cavern floor.

It was—magnificent.

Frank soared up, still clutching the Source, up through the gap in the library floor, up into the shaft of light from the center of the tower's pinnacle. Up, higher. Faster. He knew how to give it speed, and the memories came back—of swooping down the length of the Grand Canyon, of skimming the waters of San Francisco, of perilous loops around the Golden Gate Bridge, of alighting atop the Space Needle.

He flew.

The Source poured out its power, drenching him until all he could see were the shadows of buildings and landforms rippling in the gravitational fields. Off in the distance, though, were two brilliant outlines, two beings aglow in a chaotic mass of writhing fields.

Domitian and Airfoil.

Somewhere, deep in the back of his mind, the duty-driven Frank knew he had to intercede. But the majority of his thoughts were consumed by the beauty of the Source. He willed it to transfer more of its power.

It did. With the numbing, paralyzing cold came the memories, beyond the sheer joy of discovering flight. The memories of the deeds. The results of his following orders for the good of the Garrison, maintaining of the world's balance of power—dodging tracers of Soviet tank gunners in Afghanistan, breaking the spines of Sandinistas in El Salvador, ripping a medallion through the chest of his Ashen opponent in the midst of Hurricane Alicia's howling winds. On and on the images went, overwhelming him with blood and death and the sickening feeling of helplessness as he let innocents die, all for the good of the Garrison.

He cried out, his voice shattering the air around him like a thunderbolt and gave himself over to the Source.

Domitian's not down.

He launches from beneath me, slamming into me with a mass of water, and his own body, and the field. The explosion sends me reeling. I black out.

When I come to, I'm tumbling end over end. City Center? Probably—the buildings look taller than Hull, when they're not upside down. I clamp my mouth shut so I don't vomit inside the helmet. A gray streak spirals in from the southeast. Domitian.

I brace myself for his impact. It arrives, and it's with the shockwave of a bomb's explosion, pushing ahead. He pounds on me with calculated blows, and I block them. Most of them. As for the ones that get through, they're what I imagine a real sledgehammer feels like. If his concentration's been disrupted by my attacks, then mine's been nearly shattered. It's all I can do to stay aloft and maintain some semblance of shielding to lessen the damage to my already battered body.

Then the shout hits us. I mean literally. It's a wave of raw power that trundles across the sky, bowling us both over. My medallion reacts with sharp icy stabs of urgency. From where?

Someone's floating over Domitian's pinnacle.

Frank?

Domitian lunges ahead but I grab his cloak, yank him back, and drop every bit of my shielding into a right cross. His mask splits in half, blood spattering from his face across his chest. I push off with both legs and hurriedly dump the field back into flight mode before I fall out of the sky. With a burst of speed, I leave him flailing and hurtle toward the floating figure.

It's Frank. He's got the Source in his hands—the power flowing from it makes me tremble all over. The Source is also festooned with C4, like a demented, killer Christmas decoration.

And Frank's just floating there, staring off into the distance.

"Frank! Trigger the bomb!" I holler into the radio.

There's no response. No indication he even sees me in approach. Instead, he shouts again, the sound carrying through the confines of my helmet as clear as if I were standing next to him. This time, the shockwave is so substantial I see it rush toward me, leaving me only a second to arc over the wave front that sweeps out in a spreading circle.

Whatever's going on, it's bad. "Frank! Let go of the thing!"

He turns, looking back over his shoulder—and his eyes are all whites, as if someone's erased the pupils and irises. They're as bright as the noonday sun. He lets go of the Source with one hand and aims it at me, palm first.

Oh, boy.

The blast misses, only because he's stationary, and in some kind of crazed trance, while I'm racing for him. It's not the usual Frank—precise, accurate, determined. There's something else at play.

I brake twenty feet from him, at the same time, using concentrated fields to pull him apart from the Source.

The glow fades. A stunned expression takes its place, on a pale face drained of all other emotion. "I...Brandon."

"Frank. You okay?"

He nods. "Domitian?"

He's speeding toward us. "Frank. Trigger the thing. We've got to destroy it."

"I...I tried. I can't."

"You can. Give me three seconds on the timer. That's all I need."

"No. I can't. The Source—it's too powerful."

I grab his shoulders and shake. "Listen to yourself! This isn't the man who showed me how to fight my enemies. This isn't the man who served the Garrison, who both saved me and bullied me. You can do this! Trigger the bomb, and..."

Too late. A tremendous force yanks the Source from my field's grasp. It hurtles away, on an intercept with Domitian.

I lash out, intensifying my own hold. The cold pierces my chest so deep it feels as if it's tearing out my back, out my sides. I cry out in pain. The exhaustion is unbearable. I stagger in mid-air. Use any more power, and I'll plummet. But the Source slows to a crawl, shivering between Domitian and me.

"You will not take my Source away!" Domitian shouts. "You will not defy me any longer!"

Frank floats there, off to the side, helpless in my remaining grasp. I can't let him fall. "I have…to set you…down," I gasp.

He shakes his head, his face set in stone. He mouths two words: "Throw me."

I know instantly what he intends. I don't want to do it, but there's no choice. I nod.

With one hand, I let my grasp weaken on the Source. It leaps ahead, jerking through the air as Domitian drags against me.

With the other hand, I accelerate Frank.

He swoops in at the Source, flying like he must have when he bore a medallion. In that moment, I see him thirty years younger. A quiet, unknown, hidden hero. But a hero, nonetheless.

He reaches the Source, and I barely break his velocity. Frank slams against it, swearing, but he glances over his shoulder at me. Thumbs up. Then he slaps the timer.

Now.

I yank him back and use the last dregs of what my medallion allows to encase the Source in a sphere of the densest gravity I can imagine. Enough to crush a star.

The C4 explodes inside an invisible sphere, barely larger than the Source itself. The small fireball brightens to the intensity of the sun, blazes white hot, blinding, until I can't see anything but white.

Domitian's roar is deafening.

Then there's nothing. A wisp of smoke in the air. The Source is gone. No debris left behind by the C4, not even a shard. Just vaporized.

I'm falling. So is Frank. I put a cushion under him, slowing him as best I can. With only thirty feet before the top of an apartment rowhome, I do the same for me.

He pounds onto the roof. My impact is more jarring. The lighting strike of pain tells me it's a good thing I was able to blunt our fall

"Frank? Frank!"

He lays still.

I press my head to his chest. No beat. No pulse, either. I don't feel any breath passing between his lips.

Tears sting my eyes. Frank can't be dead. He can't be. Not after all this.

"Come on, come on!" I know the drill—clear his airway, rapid compressions, and mouth to mouth.

He coughs violently on the third try. "Idiot," Frank wheezes.

"You're welcome." Relief washes over me.

He stares up. "Brandon..."

"Yeah?"

"You'd better not be crying."

I can't help a hoarse chuckle.

"It can't be!" Domitian whirls about, staring wildly above him. The shield encasing Drake City is gone. No tell-tale flicker. No spikes of cold from the medallion. No surges coming from Domitian's tower.

In fact, it's crumbling, large pieces sloughing off like melting ice.

I lurch to my feet. Domitian's lowering toward me. I marshal whatever strength I can. Pray for protection. Because I'll need it. "It's over. Surrender."

Domitian stares, his blank mask discarded. Blood streaks his face. His eyes are wide, crazed. "You did this. We could have ruled unopposed. Why?"

"Because this is my city, and the people in it are under my protection," I say. "And you won't touch them. Ever again."

Domitian glares. "Very well. Then watch as you fail them completely."

He hovers there, arms out, palms up. He trembles, body wracked with violent spasms.

The roof under me shakes. A tremor at first, building to a vibration that makes me fall to my knees. The rumble grows, louder, stronger. Windows on nearby buildings shatter.

Off in the far distance, the bridges sway.

Earthquake.

"No!" I lunge at him, seeing only Sean, Kelly, Reed, Eliana—Frank. Everyone who I care for. Everyone who can't fight back. Relying on me.

But I need more strength. Could use that Source. Even if I had two medallions instead of one…

Two.

I'm an imbecile. John Quirke, old and near infirm, losing his mind to the ravages of disease, showed me the way.

I collide with Domitian, grabbing on to him and using every bit of the field to hold fast. "You have to stop this!"

"You have to watch as everyone dies!" Domitian says.

With one swift motion, I tear open the front of his shirt, cleaving through fabric and armor and Kevlar and whatever else he has padding it,. There. His medallion hangs from his neck, just like mine. I grab it.

"You cannot wield my medallion!" Domitian snarls.

"Turns out, I can."

The intensity of the field around me builds, growing beyond anything I've achieved.

Below me, the shaking and rumbling stops as suddenly as a flipped light switch.

Domitian sags, his power drained. Because I have it. He's got nothing. In that moment, he's beaten. He can stay that way. I know the police will take him. Maybe there will even be a trial. A jail sentence. A lethal injection.

But there will also be media. Juries. Judges. Bribery. Corruption. Sin tainting everything.

Domitian must sense my hesitation. "I will rise again. You know that. When I do, Brandon, everyone you love will die. I will start with your son."

"No, you won't." I focus the field inward on him with a sharp thrust. The only pictures guiding me are Sean's face—and Samantha's burning car. With those in mind, I close out all other distractions. In that space, I feel Domitian's heartbeat.

No more sledgehammer. Scalpel.

He gasps, face draining rapidly of color. He tears at my suit, clawing, begging with his hands to be released from the field—from me.

I don't let him go. I hold him, arms locked, body rigid, as the field stops his heart.

The last breath from Mark Vanchev's mouth fogs my visor. His head lolls to the right, eyes blank, unseeing.

Dead.

I killed him. It had to be done.

Forgive me.

Wind rushes by, surrounding us in a cyclone. It pushes us up, rocketing us through the layer of thick white clouds, until our surroundings clear into brilliant, azure skies. Is it Domitian's medallion? He can't be doing this—he's dead. But I'm not the one in control.

Suddenly, I'm not alone up here. There are six people. Three float in a loose triangle to the east. They're shrouded in gray jumpsuits and cloaks, faces concealed behind flat masks.

The other three wear an assortment of civilian clothing, including jeans and khakis coupled with vests, long-sleeved shirts and jackets. They wear paintball helmets identical to the one Frank gave me.

The Ashen and the Garrison.

The Garrison man in front floats forward, effortlessly as a leaf. He's wearing pressed khaki pants, brown Keen shoes, a pale green long-sleeved shirt and a black windbreaker zipped halfway. His hands are folded neatly before him, skin as deep brown as fallen pine needles. "I suppose I shall call you Airfoil."

I float there, holding on to Mark Vanchev's body, surrounded by these opposing forces, and this guy sounds as if he were inquiring about our library's movie selection. To say I'm perplexed is an understatement. "Yes?"

"You've handled this unfortunate situation well. The degree of public exposure is regrettable, but I fear we're past the point of arguing that. Mr. Belasco agreed, and that's part of why we're gathered here."

"Vanchev—Domitian—whomever, he's dead." I feel numb, despite knowing I'd taken a life. I use the field to float Vanchev's body out from me. "I assume that's why the gray squad's here."

"They are here only for Domitian's medallion."

"You're going to let them take it? They're the enemy!"

The man frowns, but doesn't seem angry, rather curious, as if he were a researcher with a vexing specimen. "This is how we maintain the balance. Medallions are always accounted for. Domitian's—that is, Mark Vanchev's—medallion must be kept by the Ashen so as to be ready when his successor is chosen. This is how we have preserved the world for centuries. This is how we will continue to do so."

For a brief, anger-filled moment, I consider refusing. However, weighing my exhaustion against three—possibly six—opponents with their own medallions leads me to the opposite conclusion.

I stay rigid, not daring to move, lest I provoke a seven-man gravitational smackdown right here. But the Ashen swoop in silently, and the one in front, who is taller and broader than the rest, removes Vanchev's medallion from his chest. "The body is yours," he says in a sonorous voice, "So that you can present it to the authorities. This mess is his doing; his name should stay attached to it, and we wash our hands of his arrogance."

With that, he nods at the dark-skinned Garrison man. The three, cloaked Ashen soar away at a blistering speed that reduces them to tiny, dark smudges in seconds.

"Mancuso, be a good lad and return Mr. Vanchev's body to the streets below. Discretely," the dark-skinned man says.

The shorter of the two Garrison men doesn't acknowledge the order verbally. He merely flicks his fingers. Vanchev's body moves from my grasp with a pull so strong I can't resist it. The Garrison man dips below the clouds, body in tow.

"You guys sat around and waited to play cleanup," I say. "What would you have done if Domitian had won?"

"It seemed, given your surprising resilience, an unlikely outcome. We did have contingencies in place. Unpleasant ones. But we have experience disguising true events. Take a closer read of the Port Royal earthquake of 1692."

I shiver at the thought of tens of thousands of people, including my son and friends, smothered by tidal waves and debris.

The Garrison man returns without Vanchev's body. Together, he and the taller man soar off into the clouds, leaving me with the one other medallion holder.

"I suspect you have many questions for me. The bulk of them shall have to remain unanswered, for the time," he says.

"Who are you?"

"My apologies. That I can answer. Weld. Christopher Merritt Weld." He removes the helmet. His eyes are pale blue as the sky around us. His hair is curly and black, neatly trimmed, with a scattering of gray over either ear. He offers a hand.

I don't shake it.

He clears his throat. "In any case, our observations proved correct: you are more than worthy to wield a medallion."

"Frank did all the observing," I say, "Even he admitted you guys were wrong about me. About the need to stay hidden."

"Let's not dwell on that, shall we? What matters is, for the present, the balance is restored. The Garrison has reached a decision—albeit, not a unanimous one. You may maintain your guise as Airfoil in service of your city and to our Garrison. For the foreseeable future, however, your activities must be limited to a radius of one hour's flight time. I trust this is acceptable?"

It's more than I dared hope for. I've been fully prepared to have them strip me of my medallion, or outright kill me. "Yes. I agree to those terms."

"Very good. Godspeed to you, Mr. Tusk." Weld dons his mask again and begins a slow rise away from me.

"Wait!" I call out. "You said an hour's radius. How far is that?"

Weld smiles. "The more appropriate question, Mr. Tusk, is how fast can you fly?"

Frank's waiting for me below, sitting propped against the edge of the building. I land next to him, and slump into an identical position. I remove the helmet, swiping sweat from my forehead with the side of a gloved hand.

"You stink," Frank says. "Plastic and body odor."

"You're pretty ripe yourself."

We sit there a moment, listening to the sounds of helicopters approaching from the west. Voices shout orders on bullhorns. In the distance, heavy vehicles rumble.

Frank cranes his neck. "National Guard. They've been hanging outside the shield. Pretty good response time."

As if to emphasize the point, a pair of F-16 Falcons scream overhead. I can't identify the bombs and missiles they carry, but there're a lot strapped to their bellies. Even this weary, my librarian brain can't help store that question to be answered later.

As if there aren't more important things to deal with.

"I think we'd better leave," I say. "Get Sean, find Kelly, and Reed. Then rest. Lots of rest."

"Rest?" Frank winces. "I could use a beer."

Chapter Thirty

Two weeks later, I stand next to Kelly at the memorial service for her grandfather. John didn't last through the attack. The hospital was never targeted, only overrun with victims and refugees from the battle-torn neighborhoods.

Kelly doesn't say what triggered his death. She doesn't say much of anything. Her eyes are rimmed red from crying, but she doesn't shed a tear now. She gazes straight ahead at the gathering of veteran firefighters as they fold the flag. No one else from her family is around to accept it.

She takes the folded flag in clasped hands. I put an arm around her as the trumpet plays. Taps. The leaves at the Rhoads Hill Cemetery are tinged orange and yellow, taking their last stand against the encroaching autumn.

John Quirke wasn't someone I knew well. But I know he held a medallion, for far longer than I did, longer even than Frank. In the end, he could still summon its power. It still held wonder for him.

Both men showed me this life is not without end. I won't wield a medallion forever, so I have to make the most of this time. To do so in the service of others, in service of my city and my home, is my duty.

Sean's there with us. He gives Kelly a big hug, and she returns it, adding a peck on the cheek. He blushes but gives a lopsided smile.

Vertigo spins my head around. I put both hands on the back of a chair. I'm instantly nauseated. Two weeks since the final fight, and these spells still hit. Haven't done a thing with the medallion since. Can I ever hope to regain my fighting strength, or my flight control?

Determination quashes those fears. I've read that a man who doubts is like a wave on the sea, driven and tossed by the wind. Unstable, double-minded. I won't be that guy.

I know the way.

We all gather for a seafood dinner and barbecue at Eliana's house. She and her husband, Chad Dachton, have a house out on Cape Ashwin, a big two-story American Federal style house, red brick, gray slate roof. It's located in the crowded, but quiet, older neighborhood of Hamilton Street. It was the home of the Tanzer family for a hundred and fifty years. Even has the widow's peak where Laura Tanzer would supposedly stand, watching to the southeast for her husband's schooner to return from the West Indies. It comes complete with a back porch that looks out to the ocean. There's a dirt path winding through emerald grass and a long, thin stand of oaks, leading to a beach of gray and black sand nestled among rocks.

It's on the porch where we're all gathering, as Chad flips burgers on a stainless-steel grille bigger than Reed's car. He's a big, broad-shouldered guy with a thick brown beard, blue eyes, and a belly laugh that makes you smile. Little Liz sprints past, taking a flying leap down the steps to the yard. A Golden Retriever barks madly, thundering after her. She squeals with delight, flinging a red ball far into the grass for him to fetch.

"Liz, keep out of the mud!" Eliana calls. She carries a bowl of salad to the table. The smells of lobster and blueclaw crab drift from the kitchen, mingled with Old Bay seasoning, and butter, and warm bread.

Reed clinks his bottle of Sam Adams against mine. "Nice night. Bet you'd get a great view up there."

I nod, taking a sip. The western sky's gathering purples and pinks with the setting sun. A pair of stars shine barely visible overhead. "Might take a spin later, when everyone's in bed. But not for the sightseeing."

"Things have been pretty quiet lately."

"That's what happens when two mobs get obliterated." Dennis Marchand limps over. His khakis are immaculately pressed, and his brown polo shirt looks fresh off the hangar. It's the black cane that's new. For a guy whose leg was nearly crushed, he's doing well.

"I heard you had a hand in all that," I say.

Reed winks from behind Dennis.

"Not a big enough one. The department got itself a mouthful from Cezar. Seems all my past business dealings with the wilki and other less reputable scum caught up."

"They going to press charges?"

"No. Being the guy who brought in Cezar and uncovered Mark Vanchev as Domitian was enough for the people who owe me to prevent that. I had Dillard—" He stops, his countenance sagging. I dig through my memories for the answer: Dillard, his partner, slain by Acciai. "I had him put evidence we'd gathered linking Domitian to his crimes into safekeeping, so the minute I got out of the hospital, I dug it out. Presented the whole thing to the DA. But the new captain encouraged me to, quote, 'consider my health' and leave the force."

Reed stares. "They forced you to resign."

Dennis nods. He doesn't seem bitter, or angry. Instead he looks at Reed. "There's a lot I've done, I can't fix. Especially staying with DCPD. By resigning, well, I can get back on the streets in some way. Got an old pal running a private investigation agency. Could always buy him out. That could be fun.

Besides, I owe this city. I owe people like Airfoil."

Reed's without words—which is as surprising for me as I'm sure it is for him. Dennis, though, is standing square in front of him. "Reed. I never said this before, and it's probably way too late, but—thank you. Thanks for taking care of Caroline. I know what you did at the benefit that night. I couldn't be there, and you were. You protected her."

"Yeah. Sure. No problem." Reed's face goes red. "Thanks, Dennis."

The two of them shake hands.

I excuse myself, not wanting to break whatever spell they're under, and find Kelly talking with Caroline just inside the open door to the dining room. Sean's in the kitchen, plucking lobsters out of a pot overflowing with steam. He holds one out, grasped in a pair of tongs, and wags in it front of Reed and Caroline's kids, grinning.

Thomas laughs, makes a goofy face. The girls wrinkle their noses, but poke at the red shell regardless.

"Brandon, come here." Caroline beckons me to the table. "Has Reed shown you these yet? He's so proud of them."

"I know. He's only made me look over the plans eight times." It's a preliminary design for a new Hull Branch, one that will be built by the time next spring rolls around. There are still city crews cleaning up the debris of Domitian's tower, with help from the U.S. Army Corps of Engineers. They've gotten the hole in the ground filled, pretty quickly.

As soon as I get my strength back, I'll make some covert trips late at night to help out. Once it was made public that Mark Vanchev was the one masterminding the whole chain of events—something that only happened when a laptop full of his correspondences showed up on the DCPD's doorstep, miraculously decrypted—the city council reversed their decisions. They authorized the re-opening of Hull Branch Library. Sheehan lost his property. The city councilors who voted in favor of the sale of the library are under threat of recall, and Sheehan got himself indicted on racketeering and weapons charges, to name two of dozens.

As for the budget problem, well, that's still out there. The debates go back and forth. Bottom line, Reed, Kelly and I will have jobs there. We're all working at the main branch for now. The new building will be mostly funded by a memorial bequest from the estate of John Riley Quirke, who left the bulk of his money to the Drake City Free Public Library system.

I smooth a wrinkled portion of the plans. "This will be a great place. A clean slate for us and for the Hull neighborhood."

"I like the idea of starting over." Kelly threads her fingers between mine. "Starting something new. Together."

"Read my mind." I give her a kiss.

My phone buzzes. I check it and instantly recognize the number. "Be right back."

Once out the front door, I answer. "You know, you could just visit like a normal person."

"Please. You know the police consider me a person of interest in this debacle," Frank says. "Never mind that, I'm a known accomplice of Airfoil. Now there's footage of me helping you fight the Polish mob, while driving an armored military scout car that's definitely not street legal."

"You're leaving town for a while, then?"

"Have to. I'm supposed to check in with the Garrison." I can hear the shrug through the phone, a movement of fabrics. There's also the sound of an engine idling. "They were pretty upset when I told them you'd had two instances of someone using a medallion that they didn't inherit. Maybe it's a common ancestry, but farther back in time than anyone anticipated."

John Quirke used my medallion's power. I used both Domitian's and mine. "Did they have any answers regarding the Source? You and Vanchev both accessed it. I touched it, however briefly."

"If they do, they're not telling me. Something else you need to consider about the Source. Domitian was hell-bent on creating an army using it."

My brain freezes at the unspoken implication. "He must have known medallion use wasn't based on bloodline."

"Bingo. Otherwise, what was he going to do? Hope he had dozens of spare relatives who wanted to become ultra-powerful villains?"

"What do we do about it?"

"No idea. Don't worry. It's the Garrison's problem to solve. Anyway, I'll be back around."

"Can't say I like the idea of doing this thing solo, Frank."

"Solo? Brandon, you've already got help. Reed, Sean, Eliana. People you trust, and who care about you. I consider you trained. The Garrison is going to let you keep watch over the city—under the terms you agreed to. You don't need me around. Not for now, anyway."

I wish he'd shown up. I wish for the chance to shake his hand. "Thanks, Frank."

"You're a good man, Brandon. Don't forget that. Remember: whatever's gone between us, Samantha would be proud of you. That's the truth."

"I will." Something still bothers me. "Hey, Frank?"

"Yeah?"

"What happened to your medallion when you could no longer use it?"

The call's silent for so long I assume he's hung up. Abruptly, he says, "They took it and didn't tell me. They think it's better that way, to not know."

"I see."

"Well, they're not right about everything. See you around."

"Good-bye."

He hangs up. Farther up the street, an engine revs. I jog to the sidewalk and catch a glimpse of red taillights heading off as a car does a U-turn. Not just any sedan, but an old Chevelle hardtop, white stripes, deep blue paint job.

I chuckle. That's Frank.

Long after dinner's over, I walk with Kelly and Sean on the beach. We go barefoot, the sand still warm between my toes even as the evening chills. Kelly's cuddled close to me, arm around my waist. Sean talks animatedly to her about watching Airfoil in action, describing our flight with wide eyes and swooping gestures. Every so often he and I share a smile.

"Hey Brando!" Reed's at the path, with a blazing sparkler in hand. Thomas circles him like a maniac, tracing orange streaks in the darkness with two sparklers of his own. "Get your crew up here! We've got enough to go around. On the double, Number One."

I give a fake salute. Frank would hate that. "Roger. We're coming."

"Uncle Reed! Got any marshmallows left?" Sean takes off, kicking up sand.

Kelly laughs. "You want a glass of wine?"

"Yeah." I exhale, watching the stars twinkling, and the lights from distance ships heading into Sculpin Bay. "You go ahead. I'll be along in a few."

She walks off, calling after Reed and Sean. I watch her leave, grateful that I can start a new part of my life with someone, with a partner.

I stand at the water's edge, listening to the waves, feeling the water sting my feet with cold. It's the same prickly, sharp feeling of the medallion.

I remove it from under my T-shirt. Whose was this? Not Samantha's. Supposedly someone's from back in my bloodline. It could be the medallion of Tobias Rankin, used two hundred years ago to bury the very Source I destroyed. Even that supposition could be wrong, if what I did with Vanchev's medallion and what John Quirke did with mine weren't flukes. Still, there could be merit to the distant ancestor theory. How many common genes did we as a species share, back thousands of years?

Questions without answers. Truths proven false. There's much more I need to find out about these medallions. I suspect there's more to the recorded history of Tobias Rankin than one journal. That's where Eliana can be of help.

I wonder at God's hand in all this. The why and the how tug at me.

A flicker of movement catches my eye. There, in the eastern sky, coming from the south. Over the silhouette of the tree line, moving fast, barely a solid shape…

It's a shadow.

The medallion falls against my skin. It jolts with stabbing cold.

No. Oh no.

The cloaked figure flies down to the beach, alighting fifty feet away. It's a darker gray cape and suit than Domitian's, much more form-fitting. I notice because it's a very feminine shape. The first female Ashen I've seen.

She walks toward me, slowly.

I crouch, palms out. My shield is up. The field's positioned into those trusty, imagined rockets that will kick me airborne at a moment's notice. Good to know I can still manage both.

Whomever this is doesn't say a word. She only walks, boots softly padding sand.

My heart's pounding. This danger is bare yards from a house full of my friends. If I move fast enough, I can neutralize her before she strikes.

Yet—she makes no threatening move. I feel like this moment has occurred before, a strong sense of déjà vu permeating the scene.

"We haven't stood on this beach for three years," she says, voice muffled by a flat, gray mask. "Do you remember?"

My hands drop to my sides. My heart thuds deep in my chest. "It can't be."

She's only ten feet away when she removes the mask and smiles at me. I see that smile every morning, on the face in a portrait hanging in my kitchen.

"Brandon. I heard. I knew it was you, even before the Ashen revealed it. I couldn't stay away. I had to see you one more time, to know you were okay."

She walks toward me, that familiar sway in her hips, dark brown hair cascading over her shoulders. In the glow of the porch light, her eyes glitter like sapphires.

I stare, my chest aching.

She places her hand aside my chin and kisses me full on the mouth. Two years since I've felt the same sensation, the familiar taste of those lips. It's as if nothing has changed.

When she parts, that smile is there. "Tell Sean I always loved him."

"You…died." It's all I can manage.

"Yes, I did." Her expression fades to a cold, hard gaze that's utterly new to me. "If you follow me, I'll have to kill you."

My dead wife dons the mask of the Ashen, concealing her beauty behind blank, gray features. She soars up into the night sky.

"Samantha," I whisper. "Why?"

www.steverzasa.com

Made in the USA
Monee, IL
14 March 2025